Shaman Rises

C.E. Murphy

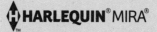

Recycling programs
for this product may
not exist in your area.

ISBN-13: 978-0-7783-1691-6

SHAMAN RISES

For questions and comments about the quality of this book, please contact us at CustomerService@Harlequin.com.

Printed in U.S.A.

First printing: July 2014
10 9 8 7 6 5 4 3 2 1

...honestly, this one's for me.

AUTHOR'S NOTE

Back in Y2K when I wrote *Urban Shaman,* I thought the Walker Papers would be a seven-book series. They grew to nine with the sale of the first "trilogy"—people kept referring to *Urban Shaman, Thunderbird Falls* and *Coyote Dreams* that way—and very quickly I began to see the story structure as three trilogies, with Joanne going through certain steps of growing up in each of those trilogies.

I did not, frankly, ever expect it to span a total of eleven books, if you include *Winter Moon's* "Banshee Cries" as a book (and I do!), or the independent collection of Walker Paper stories, *No Dominion,* as part of the series (and I certainly do!).

Eleven books is a lot, and while I know there are a fair number of dedicated readers who reread the whole series when a new book comes out, I thought I might offer up a quick, rather wildly inaccurate in detail but reasonably spot-on in spirit, recap for you. A jaunt—with all due apologies to a couple of boys—down the road so far:

Urban Shaman: Former police mechanic and now beat cop Joanne Walker is dragged into a world she doesn't want to know exists when a coyote spirit gives her the choice between death or life as a shaman, after she's skewered by Cernunnos, god of the Wild Hunt. She chooses life (look, nobody said it was a good choice, just a choice) and races to save a young woman named Suzanne Quinley from becoming a pawn in a game between Cernunnos and his son Herne.

Winter Moon—"Banshee Cries": Joanne's boss and ~~love inter~~—no, no, no, he's just the boss—pulls Jo on to a case of ritual murders, already trusting her magic more than she does. But Joanne's not the only one on the case—her mother is back from the dead to protect Joanne from the banshee she hunts and from the banshee's master, whose dark magic is more than Joanne is ready to handle.

Thunderbird Falls: Despite two mystical adventures, Joanne's still got her head stuck firmly in the sand—if she ignores her shamanic powers, maybe they'll go away. They don't, of course, but there are ramifications to her ignorance: her beloved cab-driving friend Gary Muldoon is witched into having a heart attack; relative innocent Colin Johannsen and behind-the-scenes manipulator Faye Kirkland die trying to bring Joanne's increasingly dangerous enemy, the Master, onto the earthly physical plane; and Seattle's landscape is re-arranged, creating a new waterfall on Lake Washington. It is not Joanne's finest hour.

Coyote Dreams: No longer able to pretend her shamanic powers haven't changed her life, Joanne finally steps up. But since her spirit guide, Coyote, hasn't been responding since he saved her ass in Thunderbird, Jo's totally on her own when a Navajo maker god begins putting Seattle's police force to sleep. To her humiliation, her suspicions of Morrison's new girlfriend, Barbara Bragg, are (not wrongly) attributed to jealousy. Even when Barbara and her twin brother, Mark, prove to be the god's avatars, Joanne's not so much vindicated as horrified, because god-induced visions make it clear that Coyote wasn't a spirit guide at all, but another shaman, who died to save her. In the end, though, she's accepted that shamanism is her future, and to reader outrage everywhere, she's carefully turned down Morrison's relationship proposal in favor of becoming a detective on the police force.

Walking Dead: The Black Cauldron of legend comes to Seattle, and with it come zombies. Suzanne Quinley makes a reappearance and saves Jo from zombies by calling on her grandfather, Cernunnos, god of the Wild Hunt. Unfortunately, it turns out even gods are susceptible to the Master's cauldron, and Joanne in turn barely saves Cernunnos and his home world of Tir na nOg before she and her police partner, Billy Holliday, manage to destroy the cauldron—through the willing sacrifice of Billy's long-dead sister's soul, which he has carried with him most of his life.

Demon Hunts: A lost human spirit becomes a flesh-eating windigo, and, in seeking Joanne's assistance, leaves a stretch of murders making a beeline toward her. Coyote finally returns, alive, in one piece, and runs straight into Joanne's arms. Morrison has issues with that. Joanne has issues when Sara Buchanan, now the wife of Lucas Isaac, the boy who fathered the twins Joanne never, ever talks about, turns up as the federal investigator on the case as it crosses into national park territory. Gary totally saves the day, and Coyote, after asking Joanne to come with him, returns to Arizona alone.

Spirit Dances: Joanne's partner, Billy Holliday, is nearly killed on a routine investigation. Shooting the perpetrator (not fatally) starts Jo on a slide to the realization she's not going to be able to be both a cop and a shaman. She accidentally transforms Morrison into a wolf during a dance performance known for its healing powers. A werewolf bites Joanne, causing her to go larking off to Ireland for a cure immediately after quitting her job and declaring her love for Morrison. Readers everywhere scream bloody murder at me.

Raven Calls: A romp through time and the Irish Underworld (what Joanne knows as the Lower World, albeit with a different landscape) reveals Joanne's dead mother as the new queen of the banshees and sees Joanne fight off the werewolf bite with Coyote's psychic assistance. Joanne's mother sacrifices everything to buy Jo just a little more time in the fight against the Master.

No Dominion: Gary's history is not at all as he remembers it: he and his wife, Annie, have been fighting the Master longer than he ever knew, and Cernunnos guides him through an attempt to protect Annie from the Master and change their future. Also includes several short stories.

Mountain Echoes: Joanne's dad is missing not just from North Carolina, but from the whole time line. As she tries to find him, the Master finally gets a physical foothold in the Middle World (our world), by way of going through Joanne's twelve-year-old son, Aidan. Morrison arrives with the best entrance in the whole series and saves the day, and our star-crossed lovers finally get their moment together right before Gary calls Joanne to tell him that Annie Muldoon is alive....

Shaman Rises: Is in your hands. Commence reading, ideally with "Wayward Son" wailing on your mental soundtrack!

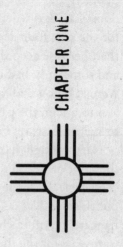

CHAPTER ONE

Friday, March 31, 11:29 p.m.

Annie Marie Muldoon was supposed to be dead.

She had been dead the whole fifteen months I'd known her husband, and she'd been dead the three years previous to that, too. That had been pretty much literally the first thing I'd learned about Gary Muldoon: his wife had died of emphysema on their forty-eighth wedding anniversary, so no, he didn't have a cigarette for me to bum. He'd told me a lot about her in the past year and some: how she'd been a nurse, how she had been the breadwinner in their home for much of their marriage, how they'd traveled the world and how she had been a bright and gentle spirit. Everything he'd said had made me wish I could have met her.

Nothing he'd said had prepared me for the possibility I might. Not even the shamanic magic I'd finally mastered led me to believe it was possible. I did not, as a rule, see ghosts or talk to dead people.

I was, however, perfectly capable of seeing and talking to people lying in hospital beds, which is where Annie Muldoon was, and where, according to her records, she had been for the past four days. The doctors were embarrassed about that, because according to their other records, she was dead, and somebody had clearly made a horrible mistake. Doctors weren't renowned for their apologies, but every time I'd spoken to one in the past couple hours, he or she had apologized to me, and I wasn't even technically a family member.

Gary, though, had made it pretty damned clear to them that they not only could, but should, be talking to me. He'd accepted every strange leap and twist of my life with equanimity, but this one had taken him in the teeth. He sat hunched and haggard at Annie's bedside, looking every one of his seventy-four years for the first time since I'd known him. He'd gotten up to hug me when I'd arrived. Other than that, he'd been sitting with Annie, holding her hand and watching her breathe.

She was a tiny woman, made smaller by sickness. The apologetic doctors had already told me six or eight times that she had emphysema, just like the older records showed, and…and then they faltered into silence. None of them had an explanation for her recorded death. None of them had any idea where she'd been in the intervening four and a half years. None of them were in fact entirely clear on how she'd shown up not just at the hospital, but in a bed, in a private room, and they sure as hell didn't understand how a dead woman's insurance policy was still active. That, of all things, was going to be the most trouble later. I didn't want Gary getting in trouble for insurance fraud.

The rest of it, I could explain.

Friday, March 31, 8:30 a.m.

"Jo," Gary had said on the phone, "I'm in Seattle. It's my wife, Joanie. It's Annie. She's alive." And my appetite vanished.

It should have vanished, of course, because I'd just eaten about eleven metric tons of food at Lenny's, the diner in Cherokee Town, North Carolina, that I'd loved as a teen and still thought highly of as an adult. But this was the bad kind of vanishing appetite. It wasn't sated. It was sick, my stomach suddenly in a hurry to reject every bite I'd just indulged in. I said, "But you were in Ireland," through a rushing sound in my ears, and only half heard Gary saying something about the hospital having called him two days ago and now he was home and Annie was alive.

I got up from the table, leaving my breakfast date, Captain Michael Morrison of the Seattle Police Department, to either pay the bill or skip out on the check. It wasn't that I didn't plan to pay. I just wasn't thinking that clearly as I went out into the cool Appalachian morning. "Gary. Gary, start again. Say that again. Annie—Annie…"

I didn't want to disbelieve him. I didn't want to say the words out loud: *Annie died five years ago, Gary.* My life was too damned weird to brush him off entirely, but coming back from the dead five years later was way beyond my ordinary level of weird.

Gary's voice shook. "Jo, I ain't told you the half of what happened with me when I went riding with Cernunnos."

"…tell me." I got myself across the diner's parking lot and sat on the hood of the Chevy Impala I'd rented to drive around Cherokee in. I pulled my knees up, wrapped an arm around them and put my head against them, like I could protect myself from all hell breaking loose if I curled into a small enough ball. "Okay, Gary, tell me what's going on."

"I went ridin' off with Horns to fight in Brigid's war, and—" My old buddy caught his breath and I could all but hear him editing the story down to the bare bones. "An' I caught the Master's attention, Jo. The rest of it don't matter right now, but he saw me. He looked right inta me, Joanie, an' he promised he was gonna take away everything I loved. He promised he was gonna take Annie away, Jo."

I closed my eyes hard. Gary and I had gone to Ireland together so I could hunt down the source of visions I'd been having, but a funny thing had happened on the way to the forum. My magic had thrown us into Ireland's distant past, where I'd had to prove myself as a shaman by summoning a god. I'd called on Cernunnos, god of the Wild Hunt, who was itching for a fight with our common enemy, a death magic we called the Master. I'd had other things to deal with just then, and Gary had volunteered to join Cernunnos in that battle. I hadn't seen him again until he rode up and stuffed a sword through the banshee queen who was trying to kill me.

I'd thought that was it. He hadn't suggested there was anything else to the story. Of course, in the twelve or fifteen hours immediately after our Irish adventures had ended, I'd been alternating between sleeping, eating and trying to help my cousin Caitríona get her feet under herself as the new Irish Mage. Then a friend had called me from North Carolina and told me my father was missing, and I'd been on the next plane to America. There had not, frankly, been much time for catching up.

Apparently I'd missed a lot. I caught pieces of the story now, stitching Gary's fear and confusion into something coherent only because he repeated bits often enough that I was able to build a time line. He had asked, no, *demanded* that Cernunnos take him into his own past so he could protect Annie from the Master's meddling. But we'd all learned the hard way that time travel didn't work that smoothly. The time line wanted to stay the way it was, without interference. One change in an era meant nothing *else* could be changed. Cernunnos had warned Gary not to make a move until the last possible minute. So he hadn't, and somewhere along the way he'd forgotten things, forgotten about killing the demon in Korea, forgotten about—

"Wait, wait, what? You killed a *demon* in *Korea,* Gary? What the hell, that was fifty years ago and you, dude, Gary, you didn't know anything about magic when I met you."

"That's what I'm tellin' you, Jo, he took it away. This whole damned life I led, this life me an' Annie led. I'm remembering it all now, like somebody's scrubbin' away the fog. He tried killin' her half a dozen times in half a dozen ways, Joanie, an' in the end he got a black magic inside her to eat up her lungs. You remember Hester Jones?"

I sat up straight, blood draining from my face. To my surprise, Morrison was a few feet away, leaning on a different car's hood, arms folded across his chest as he waited to be there when I needed him. My chest filled with gratitude and I managed a wan smile, but I was mostly thinking about Hester Jones.

I'd never known her when she was alive. She was one of half a dozen Seattle shamans who had died a few days before my own power had awakened. She and they had pooled their resources so they could remain in the Dead Zone, a place of transition between life and death, long enough to set me on the path I needed to be on. Hester had had a sour-apples voice and a permanently pinched mouth. I remembered her very clearly, and nodded like Gary could see it.

"She tried helpin' Annie, but it didn't work. Not mostly. She found Annie a couple spirit animals, though—"

I was on my feet again somehow, looking past Morrison toward the blue mountains. "What animals? Morrison, can you go get my dad? Or Aidan? Both? *Now?*"

Morrison, bless him, pushed away from the car he'd been leaning on and headed into the diner without asking any questions. Gary was still saying, "A stag an' a cheetah. She kept sayin' how silly a cheetah was, like that was a young girl's spirit animal, not an old lady's," when Aidan, the son I'd given up for adoption almost thirteen years earlier, came running out of the diner. His mother Ada followed him, and Morrison, now on his phone, came out after them.

Aidan skidded to a stop in front of me, cheeks flushed with excitement. He'd had a hell of a few days. His once-black hair was bone-white and even more shocking in sunlight than it had been in the diner. "What's going on? What do you need? Are you okay?"

"Information on spirit animals. What do cheetahs and stags represent? What gifts do they offer the people they come to?"

"Stags are strength and virility—" He blushed saying the second word and cast a sideways glance back at his mom, who studiously didn't notice. Still blushing, he shoved his hands in his pockets and mumbled, "Um, those are the ones I know about mostly. Cheetahs, I don't know about cheetahs, they're—"

"Time." Morrison's voice sounded unusually deep compared to Aidan's boyish soprano. "Your dad's saying that cheetahs offer gifts of speed and time. Not the way your walking stick spirit animals do, he says, but—" He broke off, tilted the phone away from his head to look at it slightly incredulously, then lifted his eyebrows and went on. "Did you know, he says, that cheetahs are one of a few cat breeds that can't retract their claws, and can't you see how that gives them the grip to pull someone—"

"—past when she died, Jo," Gary was saying in my other ear. "She died at 11:53, seven minutes to midnight, doll, I know that right down in my bones, 'cept she didn't. I'm rememberin' it different now, rememberin' how she held on, Jo. She held on until midnight, an' Cernunnos... I dunno,

Joanie. He came outta the light and she put her hands out to him and…an' that was it. Next thing I knew I was back with the Hunt and I couldn't remember my whole life right, and we were headin' back for you. It all didn't start comin' back to me until the hospital called and said Annie was…there."

"How is she?"

"Dying."

The blunt word hit me like a red dodgeball, smack in the gut. Breath rushed out of me, though I should've known that "dying" was the only really possible answer. "How long does she have?"

"They got her on life support, Jo. She ain't awake. They don't know if she's ever gonna wake up an' they ain't sure she should. Sounds like they think the only thing keepin' her alive is that she's sleepin'."

"I'll be there as soon as I can. Hang in there, Gary. I love you."

There was a startled silence on the other end of the line before Gary's voice came across one more time, gruff with worry and pleasure. "Love you, too, doll."

We both hung up. Aidan peered between me, Morrison and my phone, which was fair enough. Five minutes earlier Morrison and I had been being, in Aidan's assessment, mooshy and gross, and now I was saying "I love you" to men named Gary. I decided to let the kid work that one out on his own, and looked at Morrison.

He handed me his phone. I took it, catching the scent of Old Spice cologne clinging to it, and smiled as I said, "Yeah, Dad, thanks for the help. Um, look, I know I said I was going to hang around, but something's come up. I gotta go back to Seattle, like now."

Aidan said, "But—!" and his mother put her hand on his shoulder, which slumped. I made an apologetic face at him and spoke to him and my dad both. "It's my best friend. His wife is...sick." *Back from the dead* was more than I wanted to try explaining, since I barely comprehended that myself. "I'm not even sure I should waste the time driving home. I think I need to fly."

"Are you willing to leave Petite behind?" Morrison asked.

I snorted, then realized he was serious. "No, what, are you kidding? I thought you'd—I mean, you drove her out here..."

"Walker, do you really think there's any chance I'm letting you go back to Seattle to help Annie Muldoon without me at your side?"

A rush of embarrassed, delighted, teenage-intense emotion rushed through me and turned my face hot. I wasn't used to the idea that somebody, anybody, much less a silvering fox like Morrison, wanted to be at my side. And now that he made me think of it, he was the only other person in the immediate vicinity who understood just how alarming it was that Gary's wife was merely sick. "I guess, I mean, no, when you put it that way...."

"That's what I thought. So either we're both flying or we're both driving."

"I can't...drive fast enough. I mean, the record for driving across the States is about thirty hours, and we've got most of that distance to cover."

Morrison flicked an eyebrow again at the fact I knew what the cross-country driving record was, but he didn't comment on that. He said something far more astonishing instead. "I can call in some favors and get the roads cleared, get us a police escort across the country. How fast can you do it then?"

My jaw dropped. I closed it again, wet my lips, and felt my jaw fall open again. "You have never been as sexy as you are right now." Aidan, hearing that, looked mortified while I kept gazing in stunned lust at Morrison. "You would do that? What excuse would you use?"

"That I had a critical case and couldn't fly, which happens to be true. How fast could you make the drive?"

"About…" I closed my eyes, envisioning the route, the roads, and Petite's top speed before slumping. "Even if I could keep her pegged, which is unlikely, it'd take most of a day, and I haven't slept since…" I didn't know when. Drooping, I tried to rub a hand across my eyes. There was a phone in it, which made me realize I hadn't actually ended the conversation with Dad. I put the phone back to my ear and said, "Did you go get Petite?" and got an affirmative grunt in response. "Okay. I need you to drive her to Seattle."

Morrison's eyebrows shot skyward while I tried not to think too hard about what I was asking. Dad had already driven my beloved 1969 Mustang down the mountain to his house, which under ordinary circumstances would be grounds for kneecapping. I did not let other people drive Petite. Except Morrison had driven her all the way from Seattle to bring her—and himself—to me in a moment of need, and now I was telling Dad to haul her big beautiful wide back end across the country again. I could take it as a sign of maturity and of letting go, but really it was more a sign of desperation.

"You, ah. What?" Dad sounded as shocked as Morrison looked, but possibly for different reasons. "You need me to what?"

"Drive my car to Seattle, Dad. You know the road." A thread of humor washed through that. My father and I had driven all over the country in my childhood. The idea that he might not know the way—which was not at all why he was asking—amused me. Any port in a storm, I guessed.

Dad's silence spoke volumes. Up until about twelve hours ago, we hadn't talked to one another, much less seen each other, in years. My doing, because I'd been on a high horse it had eventually turned out I had no business on. We had only just barely buried the hatchet, though, and it was a big thing to ask. A three-thousand-mile thing to ask, in fact. I was trying to figure out another course of action when Dad cleared his throat. "How soon do you need her there?"

My knees went wobbly with relief. "As soon as possible."

"I'll pack a bag and leave from here."

"Thank you. Thank you, Daddy." I mashed my lips together. I hadn't called my father "Daddy" in well over a decade. It was, in my estimation, kind of a low blow.

A breath rushed out of him loud enough to be heard over the phone, and I decided it wasn't as low a blow as it would have been if I'd *Daddy*'d him in the asking. He said, "See you in Seattle, sweetheart," and hung up.

I folded the phone closed and handed it back to Morrison. "I got the Impala at the Atlanta airport. We can drop it off when we—*crap*. My credit card is maxed out." I shot a guilty glance into the Impala, where lay a gleaming new ankle-length white leather coat. "I have no money for a last-minute plane ticket. Maybe I better drive after all." I reached for Morrison's phone to call my father back, but he put it in his pocket.

"I got this one, Walker."

Part of me wanted to protest. The much smarter part smiled gratefully and whispered, "Thanks."

Morrison nodded while Aidan went to see what it was that had broken my credit card. He dragged the coat out and knocked my drum, which was under it, onto the floor of the car, which made him say a word I imagined his mother liked to pretend he didn't know. After putting the drum back carefully, he held the coat up to me, then made me put it on over my protest of, "You've seen me in it already, Aidan…."

I received a glare worthy of the fiercest fashionista, even if he was a few weeks shy of thirteen years old. Still glaring he studied me, twirled a finger to make me spin and finally gave me a peculiarly familiar smile when I faced him again. "That's an awesome coat. You look like an action hero."

I struck the best heroic pose I could manage, chin up, arms akimbo, gaze bright on the horizon. Aidan laughed, but I'd bought the coat in part because it really did make me feel like a hero, like I was wearing a white hat that proclaimed me as one of the good guys. It was a nice feeling, and I wasn't too concerned with the thought that it also made me a target. I'd done a fine job of becoming a target without the coat's assistance, so I figured I might as well enjoy it if I could.

When I shook off my silly pose, Ada and Morrison had moved away, leaving Aidan still grinning at me without noticing we'd been given some space. I flicked a fingertip at his white hair. "If this stays like that, you won't need a white coat to look like a good guy."

He rolled his eyes scornfully. "You don't watch enough movies. Anybody with totally white hair is always the bad guy."

"Oh. Jeez, you're right. Okay, you're just going to have to buck the trend. Look, Aidan, I'm sorry I've got to go. I really did want to hang around a few days."

His mouth twisted, disappointment not quite strong enough to make him defensive. We weren't that close, which was okay, and besides, he got to the crux of the matter, focusing on what was important. "Is it a shaman thing? Is that why you've gotta go?"

"Yeah. My best friend's wife is sick, really sick, and…" I swallowed, because I didn't at all want to pursue my thoughts to their logical end. "And I have to try to help."

"We can't always." The kid was solemn enough to be five

times his actual age. "You know that, right? Not everything can be healed."

"But sometimes they can be fought," I said quietly. "Sometimes putting up the fight is what matters. But I guess you know that. Especially after the last couple days."

Aidan shifted uncomfortably. "You did most of the fighting. I just...was awful."

"You were possessed, and you didn't give in to it, Aidan. That's what matters. You held out so I *could* fight for you."

"A lot of people still got hurt."

"Yeah, and I know it's not going to be easy for you to accept that none of that was your fault. You and I were both targets, and the thing that came after us loves collateral damage."

"How're we supposed to make that better?"

I looked west, like I could see all the way to Seattle. "That's what I'm going home to do, kiddo. I'm gonna make it better. I'm going to finish it."

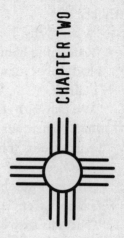

CHAPTER TWO

Morrison spent most of the drive to Atlanta on his cell phone, dealing with airlines and last-minute ticket-changing fees. I listened with half an ear, but concentrated on driving. Food had restored me quite a bit, but I really didn't have any business being behind a wheel. The only reason I was driving was I would've been worse at dealing with airline bureaucracy. It was bad enough listening to Morrison's half of the conversation, full of, "Is that the best you can do?" and, "What about business class?" and, "I'll talk with another airline," which he did—several times—before he finally hung up the phone with a snap. "You're not going to like this."

"Morrison, the list of things I don't like right now starts in Seattle, goes to Ireland, stops by Cherokee County and then swings back to the Pacific Northwest, so you don't really have to try to soften the blow, okay?"

He chuckled, which was probably more than I deserved, given my tone, which I'd been trying to modulate toward rue instead of snarling and had only half succeeded. "All right. Everything direct to Seattle is booked up until the evening flights."

"What? Why?"

"Kids going home from spring break."

I had a brief moment of loathing for spring break. "So we fly indirect."

"Which won't get us there any faster, but will leave us exhausted. When was the last time you slept, Walker?"

I had no idea. "I have no idea. Two days ago? Maybe three."

"You need rest."

"You can't possibly be suggesting I take a nap while Gary's wife is back from the dead and dying."

"That's exactly what I'm suggesting. How much good are you going to be to Muldoon if you're half-conscious and snarling?"

That was as low a blow as *Daddy*-ing my father had been, but it was also very effective. I tightened my hands around the wheel, pressed my lips thin and, after a minute, nodded. "Fine. So, what, we crash out on the airport floor for a couple hours before catching a flight back home?"

"You sound like a college student. No, Walker, we rent a hotel room for a few hours so you can get some actual rest."

"Morrison, I don't know if I'll even be *able* to sleep. There's no point in sitting around a hotel room for hours—"

"Joanne, she's on life support and there are doctors taking care of her. You may have a great gift, but even it's going to burn out if you don't take care of yourself. We'll still be there before midnight. It'll be all right."

I slid a glance at him. He must really mean it, if he was using my first name. Truth was, Morrison looked tired, too. He hadn't had much more sleep than I had. I bit my lower lip and looked back at the road, but nodded. "Okay. All right.

Fine." Right on cue my jaw opened in a yawn big enough to set my eyes watering.

Morrison, manfully, didn't laugh at me. We drove in silence for a minute or two, me yawning repeatedly, before he distracted me from the yawns by bringing up a topic I didn't want to think about. "The Raven Mocker got away, Walker."

My hands tightened involuntarily on the steering wheel. "I know."

There was no way to pretend otherwise. The creature I'd come to North Carolina to hunt, a Cherokee legend called Raven Mocker, had possessed a human body and escaped in the last minutes of our fight. By some accounts Raven Mocker was a fallen angel, but not exactly the Western sense of an angel. More of a sky spirit, a creature from what I knew as the Upper World, a plane of ephemeral beings. In Cherokee legend it wasn't so much a messenger from God as a guide that had itself gotten lost. It didn't matter. Fallen angels were, by anybody's mythology, bad, and this one survived by sucking the life and soul out of living bodies, then taking the bodies as hosts. And we'd lost it. It had disappeared into the woods, fled to the west while we were picking up the pieces of the chaos it had caused.

Under those circumstances, Annie Muldoon's reappearance, alive and more or less well, did not bode well. "I don't know how I'm going to tell Gary."

"We've got until tonight to think about that."

Until tonight wasn't enough. Despite my protests, I slept like the dead in the hotel room and stumbled through airport security like a zombie, which was a phrase I should be careful with, all things considered. I managed to get on the plane with my drum, which I wasn't about to relegate to checked luggage and which didn't technically fit in the carry-on bin above my head, but the flight attendants seemed to be studiously Not Noticing it. I was pretty certain my subconscious was running a "these are not the droids you're looking for" kind of thing on them, and while part of me thought my subconscious probably shouldn't be allowed to do magic without me, the rest of me was just basically glad it was doing so.

I stared out the window the whole flight home, unable to sleep and without much to say. My heart twisted when we flew over the Mississippi, New Orleans a distant smear on the horizon. There had been a brief moment this morning, as we'd talked about driving home, when I'd imagined visiting the bayou with Morrison. For all the traveling Dad and I had done when I was a kid, we'd never hit the Big Easy, and going with Morrison had sounded wonderful. My heart thumped offbeat again and I put my fist over it, trying to breathe.

I closed my fingers on something in my coat's inside chest pocket. I hadn't even known it had an inside chest pocket. I took the thing out, eyebrows elevated. It looked like a sharpened hair stick of pale wood, which I decided for no particular reason must be ash, its end tipped in silver. First I was astonished it had made it through security, and then I wasn't. Ash and silver had enough known magical qualities that even I was aware of them, and I doubted any kind of security could stop magic that really wanted to get on an airplane. I wondered if Caitríona had slipped it into my coat back in Ireland and I'd just never noticed. Except the coat had been balled up repeatedly over the past few days, so I thought I'd have noticed. I squinted down at the distant bayou again, feeling vaguely as though I'd missed something.

Morrison eyed the hair stick, then me, dubiously. "Going to grow your hair out, Walker?"

"Not in this lifetime, but it's pretty, isn't it?" I tucked the stick back in my pocket for safekeeping, and pressed my forehead against the window, watching New Orleans fade in the distance.

When I moved again, a faint circle of sweat and grease was left on the window. I stared at it, then snorted. It seemed like about a million years since I'd last done that, but it had only been fifteen months.

"What?" Morrison sounded concerned.

I slipped my hand into his, not sure which of us I intended to reassure. "This all started flying back home to Seattle. I feel like I'm coming full circle."

"You're better prepared for it now."

"Am I?" I'd been running nonstop for two weeks, ever since a dance performance had caused me to accidentally turn Morrison into a wolf. And that had been the least of it. I'd also quit my job, stopped a sacrifice, gotten bitten by a werewolf, been to Ireland, made amends with my dead mother, defeated an avatar of evil, flown to North Carolina, reconciled with my estranged father, met the son I'd given up for adoption, and released an evil angel into the world. Furthermore, I could count the number of meals and hours of sleep I'd had in that time, which was never a good sign.

Morrison spoke with simple confidence. "You are."

I looked at him, at his clear blue eyes and serious face, at the tiredness in his own expression and the strength of conviction that was such a great part of his appeal. There were deeper lines than usual around his mouth. I suddenly wanted them to go away, so I leaned over and kissed him.

His surprised smile gave me the boost I needed as much as his certainty did. I mashed my face against his shoulder, feeling better. "I need a vacation."

"You can have one when this is over."

"You think we'll be alive to vacate when it's over?"

"I do." Again, his confidence was unwavering.

I smiled into his shoulder again. "Thanks."

"Anytime."

We rented a car at Sea-Tac. Morrison gave me a hairy eyeball for that and suggested the taxi ranks, but I wasn't about to climb into another taxi like I'd done with Gary a year ago. I had visions of dragging some other unsuspecting driver into my unrelentingly weird life, and that would be just too much. Renting the car didn't take long, but it still took longer than I wanted it to. I glanced at the clock as we pulled out into what passed for late-night traffic in Seattle. Dad was probably somewhere around Saint Louis by now, if he was burying Petite's needle. I wished we could do the same, but it took almost an hour to get to Seattle's General Hospital. I took my drum and went into the too-familiar, loathed, sharp-antiseptic-scented building.

For the first time since I could remember, it didn't give me a visceral twist of pain and a seizure of sneezes. I'd been braced against both, and stumbled at not encountering them. Morrison put a hand under my elbow and I gave him a half-surprised smile. Maybe a lot more than I had realized had healed while I was in North Carolina. It was easier to see the scars now, easier to admit my hatred of hospitals came from Aidan's sister dying in one so soon after her birth. Easier, now that I knew she lived on in her own way, in Aidan's powerful two-spirited soul.

"You all right, Walker?"

"Better than I have any right to be." Feeling stronger than I should, I led Morrison up to Annie's room, where every hope I had of telling Gary that his wife was probably a simulacrum embodying evil died on my lips.

Annie Muldoon's aura burned raging, brilliant green around a fist of darkness that throbbed and strained with her every heartbeat. I Saw it without even trying, without triggering the shamanic Sight I would normally use to diagnose a patient with. Gary, ashen and old, got up from Annie's bedside and hugged me until I couldn't breathe. *His* aura wasn't visible: the Sight was registering extraordinary power, like the occasions when my own magic took on a visible component. I hugged him back and mumbled a promise about everything being okay, then stole a glance at Morrison.

His aura wasn't visible, either, but thunderclouds in blue eyes offered an opinion on me promising things were going to be okay. Not for the first time, I wished my cosmic power set came with telepathy, because I wanted to say, "Well, I have to at least *try!*" but I could hardly say it out loud with Gary right there. Besides, I'd said it about every seven minutes on the flight, or it had felt like it, anyway. I did have to try, and I would have even if Annie's aura had been a mire of black pitch and oil slicks.

But it wasn't. The green was vibrant, and I *knew* that color. I knew it down to the depths of my soul. The creature who wore that color within himself had wormed his way in, way deep inside me, and he had no intention of leaving. I would know his mark anywhere. It was Cernunnos's color, blazing green that threatened to burn my eyes, my *mind,* away if I looked at him unguarded for too long. Cernunnos had been there when Annie died, in the memories Gary had recovered.

I set Gary back a few inches, my hands on his shoulders, and met his eyes. "Tell me again, Gary. Tell me *exactly* what happened when she died. All of it. She had two spirit animals with her, a cheetah and a stag—" Embarrassment caught me and I blushed so hard I couldn't speak for a few seconds. *Of course* Cernunnos had been in attendance, if a stag, of all creatures, had come to her. Cernunnos wasn't the horned god for nothing: every year he grew a crown of antlers, becoming more and more of the stag, before shedding them again and regaining something approaching humanity. In the parlance of my teenage years, *d'oh*.

"—toldja, Joanie, at a minute past midnight he came through the damned wall and Annie sat up, reachin' for him, and the whole goddamned world went white and next thing I knew I was back with the Hunt, headin' back to you."

"What did he say?"

Gary shoved a hand through his white hair. He had a headful of it, but it needed washing or brushing or some kind of attention, because it looked thinner than usual. So did he, for that matter. "He said…hell, Jo, I don't know. He said somethin' about the stag and sagebrush—"

I shot a look at Morrison, whose eyebrows were raised. "Call Dad. Find out what sage has to do with anything."

"He's in the car, Walker. He shouldn't talk while driving."

"Call him anyway, please. Go on, Gary."

"And he said somethin' about bending time to come to her when the stag called, an' he said…hell, Jo," Gary said again. It wasn't, I thought, that he didn't remember, so much as, as I had discovered time and again, it was *hard* to talk about magic. People loved stories about it, and liked to imagine maybe it was real, but faced with real magic in their lives, a reticence cropped up even when everybody listening knew the truth. I gripped his shoulders and nodded, encouraging him, and after a minute he went on. "He said we'd been waitin' for the very end so we could make our move, like we'd talked about. An' he said she was beyond my reach, but that she always had been as long as I'd known him. An'…an' he said he'd guide her to her resting place when it was all over."

A tiny thump of hope squeezed the air out of my lungs. It escaped as a laugh, almost without sound. "And she went into the light, is that what you said before? She actually literally went into the light, that was the last you saw of her?"

"Yeah." Gary gave a smile, thin and watery, but a smile. "Yeah, Horns said she'd gone into the light an' he figured that wasn't the fate the Master'd been plannin' for her at all, so it made it kinda bearable. Except..." He looked back at his wife, then at me, all humor gone and his gray eyes hollow. "C'mon, Jo," he said, as quietly as I'd ever heard him speak. "Who're we kiddin, doll? What're the chances that's really Annie lyin' there?"

Morrison glanced up sharply, relief and admiration in his expression. My lungs emptied again, this time with a blow-to-the-gut rush, because although it was what I'd been dreading telling him, I didn't want Gary to have thought of it himself. It was too sad and too cynical, and far too likely, when I wanted like crazy to pull off some kind of fairy-tale ending.

But the fact that he'd thought of it made it a little easier to draw a deep breath and admit "Not good" aloud. "I hope like hell it is, Gary, but..."

He nodded. A nurse came in to check Annie's blood pressure, stopped short at seeing a crowd in the room and said in an excellent, hackle-raising warning tone, "Visiting hours aren't until—"

"This's my granddaughter and her partner," Gary said flatly. "They're family. They stay."

The nurse was old enough to have the authority age brings, but Gary's tone and greater age apparently trumped hers. She stiffened from the core out, then gave one sharp nod and went about her business. Morrison, who wasn't exactly uncomfortable with authority, and I, who often had problems with it, both stood still as hunted mice until she left, pretending if we didn't move she wouldn't notice us again.

Gary's big shoulders rolled down in apology after she was gone. "Sorry 'bout that."

"For preemptively adopting me? I'm okay with it." I hugged

him again and he grunted, casting a look at Morrison. I caught a glimpse of Morrison's smile before he said, "*Partner* works for me. Holliday's going to have to adapt."

To my surprise and pleasure, Gary gave a huff of laughter. "Diff'rent kind of partner. 'Sides, Joanie quit the day job, so Holliday's gonna have to adapt anyway."

He was still calling me Joanie, which meant he was really not okay. Gary had never called me Joanie, always Jo, unless I was undergoing some sort of major emotional meltdown. Unless, as it turned out, *he* was undergoing some sort of major emotional meltdown. I didn't think he even knew he was doing it. I put on my best smile, which was pretty wry, "Yeah. Billy is going to kill me for quitting without even warning him. I'm hoping he'll have cooled down in the two weeks he hasn't seen me."

"Him and Melinda came by yesterday," Gary said. "He's worried, not mad. Worried about a lotta things."

Including, no doubt, Annie Muldoon's reappearance on the scene. I nodded, then lifted my chin a little. "Go on, go sit back down, or go get a drink of water if you want. I'll do everything I can, Gary. You know I w—"

A doctor swept in imperiously and glowered at us all. "Mr. Muldoon, I understand we have some more family visiting. It's already well past visiting hours and we don't normally allow more than one family member at a time—"

"My dead wife turned up again outta nowhere and you're tellin' me my *granddaughter* ain't supposed to be here? I'm an old man, Erickson, and I'm tired. You need to talk to anybody from here on out, you talk to my granddaughter, Joanne Walker. Jo, this's Dr. Pat Erickson. Erickson, this's Jo's partner, Mike. If Jo ain't here, you talk to him." Like a cranky bear just out of hibernation, Gary lumbered back to Annie's bedside and sat.

Dr. Pat Erickson was about forty-five, with expertly dyed

auburn hair and a long nose. She was about six feet tall, just like I was, and I bet she was accustomed to people deferring to her because of her height, if nothing else. So was I, so there was a possibility of an interesting-in-the-Chinese-sense dynamic raising its ugly head, but after a few long seconds of sizing me up, Dr. Erickson sighed. "I'm sorry for the confusion with your grandmother, Ms. Walker. May I speak to you outside for a moment?"

My jaw flapped. Erickson herded me into the hall while I collected my wits and, once we were there, apologized again. "Hospital records get lost," she said unhappily. "People do not. Ms. Walker, can you explain any of this? The only thing that makes sense is that she's been in private care for the past four and a half years, but there are no records of it, and clearly your grandfather has no recollection of that...."

"You're right. She has been in private care." If my suspicions were right, it had been very, very private care, and there would never be any real-world explanations for it. I stared at the bridge of her nose, hoping I was giving the impression of looking sincerely into her eyes as I struggled to pull together a story she might accept. "She, um. We...weren't aware of it. I know that sounds impossible, but it appears that a...humanitarian organization...has been caring for her. They...prefer to remain anonymous, so they can select the people they wish to help without...their doors being beaten down by needy applicants. They specialize in providing long-term life support to patients on the verge of death. Apparently my grandmother...had arranged that if she became very ill, they were to take her away at the point of death. She didn't want us to know, because she felt our lives would better be able to go on, the healing process would be able to proceed, if we believed she was...really dead. It was only when she was returned to the hospital that we were...notified that this had taken place." I was going to give myself an award for fast talking. Maybe Erickson's long nose had inspired me, Pinocchio-like.

Confused relief flashed across the doctor's features. She wanted to believe me, because it gave the medical professionals who had lost Annie Muldoon a way out. Besides, I was almost telling the truth. Or I thought I was, anyway, and that helped sell the story. Erickson's only protest was, "But your grandfather didn't mention any of this…"

"He's had a very hard few days, Doctor. In his position I don't think I'd have tried to explain it, either."

Erickson's shoulders relaxed a fractional amount. "No, I suppose not. Ms. Walker, I understand private organizations wanting to remain anonymous, but it would be enormously helpful if we could receive their medical records for Mrs. Muldoon. If they've released her to standard care they must believe there's some hope or change in her diagnosis. I don't understand why they wouldn't admit her through regular channels, though. I don't understand how they could avoid it. We do not have people simply walk in and claim a bed, Ms. Walker."

"I'll see if I can get answers for you," was probably the most useless promise I'd ever made, but Dr. Erickson seemed grateful for it. She shook my hand and let me go back into Annie's room, where Morrison was standing over Gary like a protective gargoyle.

"Sagebrush is used in shamanic healing to help clear the lungs," Morrison offered as I sat across from them. "Your father says good luck."

"Lungs, of course. Emphysema, or something that presents as it. And the sickness is still right there." I put my hand above her chest, not quite touching her, and added, "Tell him thanks," even though Morrison was obviously no longer on the phone with Dad.

Gary stirred, everything about his actions heavy and hopeless. "Everything okay with the doctor, Jo?"

"Yeah." I told them the story I'd given Erickson, ending with her supposition that the mysterious private carer had concluded something had changed and that was why Annie had been returned to a public hospital. I took her hand as I spoke, letting my consciousness sink more toward investigating her health than the discussion we were having.

It didn't take healing magic to feel her fragility. Paperlike skin lay against knobbly bones, no excess flesh to pad them. Her breathing remained perfectly steady, but a machine was doing most of it for her, so that wasn't surprising. The heart monitor beeped, such a familiar sound from film and television that I hadn't even heard it until I was sitting quietly and listening. An oxygen monitor was taped to one finger, weighting not just her hand, but her whole self: it seemed like she was so light and fragile that without that inconvenient piece of plastic she might float away. She had a strange scent, the hospital's antiseptic cleanliness lying over a deeper, earthier smell. It should probably have been the smell of death and decay, but it brought to mind cool green growing places, and mist beading on leaves. I knew that scent: I'd been to the place that birthed it.

For all that it had only been a moment since I'd stopped speaking, I was still startled when Gary asked, "Is the doc right? Did somethin' change?"

"Yeah. Me. I'm ready now." I pressed my eyes shut and put my forehead against Annie's hand a moment before looking up again, meeting Gary's eyes, glancing at Morrison, basically trying to establish myself as calm, cool and in control. "I wasn't, when she got sick. I didn't know you, and even if I had, I could never have helped. Not back then."

"I nearly called you about a million times, anyway." Gary's

mouth thinned, fair acknowledgment of the twist his life had
evidently taken. At this stage, I was used to my own past not
being quite as I remembered. Weirdly, that didn't make it any
easier to know Gary's wasn't what he remembered, either. "It
ain't normal, Jo, remembering things two ways."

"Sure it is. Cernunnos apparently does it all the time."

That got a laugh out of the old man, which was worth everything to me. I smiled, then spread my fingers beneath Annie's
hand. "Anyway, you didn't need to call me back then, because
you had Cernunnos in your pocket. Gary, I want you to think
about everything he said to you. Did he ever say she was dead?"

"He said she'd gone into the light, doll. He said he was
gonna take her to her resting place. He said…" Gary trailed
off, unwilling to reiterate the list again.

I couldn't blame him, but he hadn't repeated a couple of
the things I thought were important. "And he said he'd bent
time to come to her, and that he couldn't take you where she'd
gone, right? Gary, did you go back to Tir na nOg after that?"

"No, I di—" Gary sat bolt upright, looking like himself
for the first time since we'd arrived. "What're you sayin', Jo?
Did Horns *lie* to me?"

"I think he might've gone a long way to avoid lying to you,
actually. Gary, her aura, it's blazing green, like his. Not as
bright. I can look at it without going blind, but it's the same
color. It's like Suzanne's, not quite human. I don't think she
died, Gary. I think he took her to Tir na nOg to rest until he
could get her to me."

"Jo, give it to me straight. What're you sayin'?"

"I'm saying that if I'm right, this really is Annie. And I can
heal her."

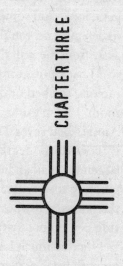

CHAPTER THREE

Morrison's gaze went flat. It took everything I had not to make pleading eyes at him, and instead to keep my attention on Gary. I knew, I *knew* I shouldn't have said that aloud, and if I was wrong I was never going to forgive myself. Morrison wasn't ever going to forgive me, either.

The complete stillness in Gary's face, the utter cessation of expectation, of hope, of fear, of anything, somehow said that he *would* forgive me if I was wrong, and that was almost worse than the alternative. I tried to keep my voice steady. "I could be wrong, Gary. I might be wrong. But Cernunnos wouldn't have brought her to me if he didn't think there was a chance. And that means either…" I swallowed. "Either it's her and I've got a chance, or Cernunnos is corrupt and we're all screwed and have been since the beginning. I choose not to believe that. Gary, with your permission…I'll try."

"No way I could say no, doll. Whaddaya need us to do?"

"Just keep the doctors off my back. I don't know how long

this is going to take. Morrison…" I gave him a pained, apologetic look, and some of his anger faded. "Will you drum me under? And do you think we can move Annie's bed far enough away from the wall that I can build a power circle around her?"

"That's not going to go over well." Whether he meant moving the bed or drumming up a power circle in a hospital room, I wasn't sure, but between the three of us we did edge Annie's bed several inches away from the wall, then rotated it about thirty degrees so it aligned east-west. I squeezed between the wall and the bed, for once not self-conscious about greeting the cardinal directions aloud and asking them to be the points of my power circle. I guessed that meant I was getting better about ritual.

Not that much better, though, because what I really ended up with was a power diamond, with Annie sort of squeezed in the middle. It couldn't be helped: the room wasn't big enough and the medical equipment wasn't mobile enough for anything else, but it emphasized the awareness that my whole shamanic approach seemed to be that rules were made to be broken. I sat beside Annie again and gave Morrison a hopeful look. He got my drum from the corner I'd tucked it in, and he and Gary sat across from me.

Gary did a double-take at the drum, which was fair enough. When he'd first seen it, its broad round surface had been painted with a wolf, a rattlesnake and a raven. Or I'd always assumed it was a wolf, anyway, until the painting had faded and disappeared. Only then did I start to think maybe it had been a coyote, representing my spiritual guide and mentor, whose influence on me had begun to wane. In the past few days I'd found a new spirit animal, a walking stick bug, and a new image had come in strong on the drum, obliterating the coyote: a praying mantis, its sticklike legs folded in its best-known pose. The rest of the drum remained unchanged:

crossbars inside it to hold on to, beads and feathers dangling here and there from the four-inch-deep sides and a drumstick padded with raspberry-red-dyed rabbit fur. Morrison spun the drumstick in his fingers with unexpected grace, then, at my nod, began a steady beat.

Energy burst forth, a visible ripple, like sound waves had been given color so ordinary eyes might see them. Not that my eyes were ordinary: I was using the Sight, calling on magic, but the shock of power seemed so natural I was surprised I couldn't always see it. It leaped from one point of the diamond to the next with each beat of the drum, passing through each of us as it closed the circle. It picked up all our colors—Gary's solid silver, my gunmetal-blue, Morrison's blue and purple— and it came together as a soft white wall of magic. That was what white magic really was: additive, the power of many working together. Black magic was subtractive, sucking life away from one or many in order to feed itself.

And that was what was going on inside of Annie Muldoon. The sickness that had been put inside her was eating away at her life and strength for its own benefit, and to the eventual detriment of the world. *That* wasn't just about Annie. That was simply how the Master worked. Every spark of love and life he was able to extinguish gave him an incrementally larger hold on humanity. Annie was the poster girl for demonstrative purposes today, but it wasn't like the entire battle lived or died with her. There would always be other hills to take. Right now, though, taking this particular hill would be enough. I exhaled quietly and let myself slip out of my body, searching for a way through the darkness to heal Annie Muldoon's body and soul.

An unexpectedly familiar vista came into focus around me as I left my body behind. The first several times I'd spirit-walked, I'd been unable to control it, and had dug my way through to the different metaphysical planes I needed to reach. Literally dug: I'd usually end up in loamy, life-filled earth, my sense of myself turning badger or vole or wormlike as I churned my way through the soil in search of my destination. I was back there again, working through dirt chunked with vast rocks and water-filled drainage points. Back in the day, the impediments probably would have stopped me cold. These days, not so much.

For one thing, back in the day I'd have assumed there was only one path to get to where I was going, and that it lay straight ahead. I smiled faintly at my slightly younger self, then extended my hands upward. I supposed I shouldn't really have been able to: I was packed into dirt and stone, but I'd always been able to move through it while in an astral realm, and at the moment it made me think of swimming. I wasn't the world's strongest swimmer, but I wouldn't drown in a pool, which was enough. For an instant the dirt surrounding me was pool water, and I was on the bottom of the pool. I bent my knees, pushed off all the way through my toes, and burst upward into the heart of Annie Muldoon's inner sanctum, into the garden that represented the state of her soul.

Dirt splashed away from me like water, rolling off my skin and streaming from my clothes. I ran my hand over my hair to get rid of the worst of the "wet," then turned my palm up to watch dirt absorb into the lifeline there, just as water might do. The part of me that would always be six years old wanted to squeak, "So cool!" and do a little dance. Shamanism's basic tenet was change: to heal someone, it was necessary to change their outlook for just an instant, just long enough to get their attention. It worked that way on every level, so if I could make myself believe, even briefly, that dirt was water, well, then, I could move through dirt like I could move through water.

Magic, when I let myself acknowledge it, was really pretty

damned nifty. I shook the last of the dirt away and lifted my eyes, trying to prepare myself for the worst possible visage of Annie's garden.

Unfortunately, I got it. I had just come off a visit to Aidan's war-ravaged garden, a place that had been so damaged it crumbled beneath our feet. Annie's was maybe even worse than that.

What had no doubt once been greenery was infested with black oil. Not just slicked with it, but grayed-out leaves pulsed black ichor through their thin veins like it was sap, and the roots of bleached grass sucked death out of the dry soil. Meadows and scant trees rolled on forever, the size of the place reminding me a little of the jungle that represented Gary's garden. It appeared a life well-led created a tremendous depth of soul that was represented by vast distances. I thought of my own small, tidy garden, and how the walls that penned it in were only just now crumbling. I had a long way to go to catch up to Gary and Annie. Or even Morrison, for that matter. I was getting there, though, and every step I took through my own garden or someone else's helped me become a little more of what I wanted to be.

Feeling a bit braver and more confident, I walked into Annie's meadows, trying not to shiver at the bleak sky above. It twisted in unhealthy purples and blacks, and I had the distinct sense it was pulling at me and at the garden around me. Wonderful. A miniature black hole in the midst of Annie's garden. Just what we all needed. Even more distressingly, it reminded me of the vortex Raven Mocker had come through, back in Carolina. I did *not* want to follow that thought to its obvious conclusion.

Instead, I reached out and touched a branch on one of the sickly, sparse trees as I went by. It crumbled, leaving a tacky substance on my fingertips. My own magic glimmered softly beneath the sticky stuff, shields ensuring that it wouldn't sink into my skin and contaminate me, too.

Which it certainly wanted to do. It smeared across my fingers without help from me, seeking a way in so it could infect this new, healthy territory it had found. I lifted my hand, hoping for a way to get it off my fingers quickly without betraying my cool exterior, then hesitated. There was always a heart to the darkness, and it was just possible I could let the muck guide me there.

Not all that long ago, the very thought would have gotten me in trouble. I was grateful that the stuff didn't instantly slide through my shields and gobble up my soul. Even so, I concluded it probably wouldn't be all that smart to grab another branch and get more of the glop on me. Naturally, that's what I did: coated both hands in the unpleasant crumbly sticky goo, then closed my eyes and did my best to *feel* whether it wanted to tug me in any particular direction. It reminded me of driving on a worn road, where the wheels of the vehicle slid into ruts and rumbled along there whether the driver liked it or not. It meant turning aside was difficult, but I wasn't looking to turn aside just now. I wanted that easy pull, and it seemed like it should work.

Nothing happened.

After standing there long enough to start feeling foolish, I opened my eyes again and swallowed a squeak. Apparently my definition of nothing and the garden's definition of nothing were not the same. I was no longer in a meadow. I was no longer in a garden, for that matter. I stood on the very edge of a black precipice, wind rushing up to rip tears from my eyes. I couldn't see a damned thing below me, but above me was the center of the vortex, screaming silently against the small bones of my ears. Hints of shimmering green quartz ran through the black stone beneath my feet like a source of light, the only real light visible in this place. It gave me an unearthly glow and struck me as just the faintest, tiniest strike against the dark, against evil and misery and dreadfulness as a whole. I said, "Where there's life, there's hope," out loud, and edged one quarter of an inch farther over the cliff, looking down.

The vortex above me was pulling even harder now, straining to haul me upward into it. Straining to pull the very bottom of the world up into it, as far as I could tell, and that made me think there was something at the bottom that it wanted.

Before I let myself think about it, I dived off the cliff.

I had fallen off the side of forever once before, in the Upper World. Then, a thunderbird had caught me. This time I was pretty certain nothing was going to catch me, but I was less afraid than I should have been. I had no idea where the bottom was, though once in a while I got a brighter glimpse of the falling world around me, as the green quartz flared and darkened again in the cliff face. I whispered, *Raven?* inside my head, and though my oldest and best-loved spirit animal didn't actually appear, he offered something he had never shared before: a gift of wings.

I didn't fly. My fall didn't even slow. Not until the bottom of the pit finally came into view, a thin green light that strengthened and brightened as I fell closer. At the critical moment that sense of wings *flared,* slowing me, breaking my fall. I hit the ground in a three-point crouch, feeling like a goddamned superhero, and bounced to my feet crowing, "I'm Batman!"

Bouncing up was nearly my undoing. The vortex's upward pull dragged me up several feet before it lost its grip. I fell again, far less gracefully this time, and stayed down when I hit.

The green light was coming from a crack in the pit's floor, which I could now see clearly because my face was mashed into it. The rock broke away under my weight, which was probably a bad sign, but it didn't collapse entirely while I stared into the light and tried to wrap my mind around what I saw.

Apparently I'd stumbled on the shamanic version of Snow White. An emerald-green stone casket—not really a casket, more a cocoon—was buried beneath the pit, and Annie Muldoon lay within the cocoon. Quiet, soothing power pulsed from it, bringing a soft and unexpected scent of mist and leaves with it. I pushed my right arm into the crack, seeing if I could touch the cocoon.

I couldn't, quite. It had been well buried. I twisted to look toward the vortex, wondering if the cocoon had in fact been *really* well buried and that the vortex was only just now managing to tear its way through the earth to reach it. Assuming the shards of quartz in the cliff were related to the casket, it seemed fairly likely. Which meant—

Well. It meant we'd barely timed this right. If Morrison and I had been half a day later in arriving from North Carolina, the vortex would've gotten to Annie before I did. As it stood, I was afraid to dig her out for fear we'd both go flying up into the great mouth of darkness in the sky. I was going to have to go down to her.

Goose bumps stood on the back of my neck and swept down my arms, sending a chill into my belly, where it churned around a little bit. I had never had a problem with enclosed spaces until two weeks ago, when I'd had to make a mad run out of a collapsing cave system. Since then, I'd discovered a growing tendency toward heebie-jeebies when presented with squeezing myself into tight spaces, which had happened more often than seemed reasonable in a mere two weeks. The upshot was a quick internal lecture about tough luck and the lesson therein, not that I could think of any useful lessons beyond "Stop getting embroiled in mystical altercations that squish you into crevasses and cracks," which seemed like sound, but possibly unfollowable, advice.

I knocked some of the thinning pit floor away with my elbows and knees while ruminating over all of that, and fell five feet onto Annie Muldoon's crypt.

This had all started with a crypt, or darned near, anyway. Me and Gary, we'd gone hunting for a lady I'd seen from an airplane, and we'd shoved the top off a church altar that we'd started thinking of as a crypt as soon as Gary had wondered out loud if maybe a vampire was in it. I had sworn up and down that there was no such thing as vampires, and indeed, there had been no vampire, only a screaming woman who ejected herself from the altar-cum-crypt at a high velocity.

"You can scream," I told Annie through my teeth, "but if you turn out to be a vampire I am going to be *really* pissed off. Vampires don't exist."

Annie, sleepily, murmured, "Of course they do."

CHAPTER FOUR

I screeched and bucked backward. The vortex howled delight and tried to seize me. Swearing, I dug my fingers into Annie's cocoon and hauled myself closer to it. Her lashes untangled, revealing eyes that were vividly green in the cocoon's light. I wondered what color they were supposed to be and muttered, "There are. No. Vampires."

Annie's gaze and voice both grew clearer, as if she was just learning to focus. "What on earth do you imagine the Master *is,* Joanne? Oh! Joanne!" Even caught in the cocoon, she reached for me like a mother might, fingertips trying to graze my cheekbone. "I know you," she whispered in astonishment. "You're my Gary's Joanne. My father painted you."

I gave myself a quick look to see if I'd been war-painted recently without noticing. I hadn't, or at least not on any body parts that were easily visible. A couple seconds later I realized that probably wasn't what she'd meant, and turned red enough that I could see my skin turn a sickly brown in the sarcophagus's green glow.

"Am I dreaming?" Annie asked, then looked pained. "How many patients have I heard say that, but...I remember...I remember...I was dying. The god came. The god." Her eyes widened in a breathless admiration I knew all too well. "The horned god. Did he really come? There was the stag and the cat," and she took a moment out of her admiration to look exasperated at the very idea, which made me absolutely adore her. I was going to bring her home not just for Gary, but for me, because I couldn't help but love anybody whose estimation of a big-cat spirit animal was in league with mine. "The cat," she repeated, "the cat and the light. The white—oh. Oh. I am dead, aren't I. I was a nurse too long, young lady. Don't imagine I haven't heard people talk about the white light."

"You're not dead." My voice cracked. "And I'm going to keep you that way. I've looked into that white light more than once. Usually it's just the sun trying to burn out my retinas."

Perplexity slid across her face, then turned to a smile. Probably she hadn't imagined death to involve people muttering about burned-out eyeballs, which probably gave her some hope that I was telling the truth. "But then what's happened to me? To Gary?"

"Gary's waiting for you, sweetheart. Cernunnos stole you out of time, put you to sleep in Tir na nOg, until I could come help out. You know me." My voice cracked again and tears stung my nose. "And I'm going to. I'm going to save you, Annie."

"No, I wasn't sleeping. I dreamed...I dreamed I was..." She trailed off like the dream had escaped her, as they do, and seriousness rose in Cernunnos-green eyes. "You can't save everyone, Joanne. Sometimes we make sacrifices so others can live. Don't imagine you can't sacrifice me, if you need to."

"Sacrifices are what the bad guys make," I whispered. "Sacrifices are—"

Realizations tumbled together in my mind, pieces crashing into place, making a picture I'd never even known I was supposed to see. Cernunnos and Tir na nOg had come so close to death with the cauldron. All of a sudden I thought it hadn't just been the Master taking advantage of the cauldron's bindings breaking. It had been his move against Cernunnos for stealing Annie from him. Kill Tir na nOg and Annie would die, too. Cernunnos had nearly sacrificed *everything*, betting on me. And he'd won. There had been no sacrifice of his godhood, of his world. I'd thwarted it, even if I hadn't known it at the time. Things kept coming together, circles closing.

Boy, the Master had to hate me right down to the black burned bones of his rotten soul.

That made me happy. More than happy. Absofreakinglutely joyful, and with that joy came a spike of gunmetal magic that shot skyward, spiking through the vortex.

Its pull faltered and a sense of shock washed through me, as if the vortex itself hadn't expected me to fight back at all. As if the thing on its other side hadn't imagined I had it in me. I pressed a finger against Annie's cocoon, near where her own hand had tried to reach for me. "You hang out here a minute. I'm going to go spit in death's eye."

Two minutes earlier I'd have said getting to my feet would be asking to be sucked into the netherworld the Master commanded. Two minutes earlier I might have been right, but things had changed since then. Annie Muldoon was alive and, as far as I could tell, human through and through. A god had bet the rent on me and won. My best friend had traveled through time to save the woman he loved, and the man I loved believed in me.

If I ever needed grounding, those things would always be

there. I stood up, digging my toes into the shimmering green softness that contained Annie. It was cool and earthy, centering me in my world and in Tir na nOg. I thrust my left hand toward the sucking vortex and shouted.

My rapier, the *aos sí*–crafted blade of silver that I'd taken from Cernunnos the first time we met, materialized in my hand. Shamanic power poured into it, healer and warrior no longer at odds with each other. It gathered, strengthened, readied itself, and when I shouted again and thrust the sword skyward, a burst of magic cracked forth like lightning from a bottle. The vortex sucked it in, encouraging it to run faster, until the first splinter of power touched it. Then the vortex shied back, rejecting the shamanic magic. I stabbed upward again, sending another shock upward.

I felt like Conan. I felt like Red Sonja in white leather instead of a chain-mail bikini. I felt like a match for the dark side of the Force, and I was going to take one more toy from the Master right now, because I *could.* "This one's mine, you bleak bastard! The *gods* chose this one, you mean son of a bitch, and you can't do a thing about it. *I* choose this one," I said more softly, "and you're not taking her away."

I knelt, still with power pouring through the sword. The Master wasn't going to let us go easily, once he got over his surprise at my audacity, so I dug my fingers into Annie's cocoon, working my way through its ferociously green threads. Cernunnos's strength was a lover twining around my hand, clinging to my arm, searching for a way into my heart.

I let it in. I had to: I could never shield myself against the horned god. He was too primal and too enticing, and had etched himself in my soul the first time I'd laid eyes on him.

But neither was I his. He'd offered me a place at his side time and again, and three times, I'd taken it. I'd ridden with him and his Wild Hunt, and I knew in my core that if I rode with him again I would lose my humanity, and want nothing but the god. For all my fears and uncertainties, I still wanted my human life. I wanted Morrison. I wanted the future we could share, if we were that lucky. If we survived this. So no matter how deeply Cernunnos's power ran or how eagerly it prodded, I wouldn't let it steal me away. Annie needed his strength more than I did right now, and I intended to leave her everything I could.

Thread by thread, Annie's features came clearer as Cernunnos's magic recognized mine and released its prize to me. Here, under the god's care, in the heart of his magic and at the center of her garden, she was young and lovely, with humor and spark in her face. My fingers touched hers, then wrapped around her hand. I pulled her to her feet, surprised at how tiny she was: nearly a foot shorter than me, and dressed in a full-skirted 1950s dress that made the most of her small waist. She reminded me of Gary in his own garden, a young man in his prime, handsome, fit, confident. They were a beautiful couple, and I was going to see them back together in the Middle World.

The last of Cernunnos's green power unwound, releasing Annie from the cocoon. Some of the unwinding magic swirled around my own, joining the blended silver and blue that raced upward. With that green haze sweeping around my power, the two of us, shaman and god, in it together, it seemed only appropriate to cry, "From hell's heart, I stab at thee," to the cringing vortex above.

That, of course, was a mistake.

The vortex lost cohesion, which sounded like it should be a positive development. Except instead of falling apart, it became a spidery black thing, thin piercing legs breaking apart from the core and slamming downward. Not even at me, not really. At Annie, who was weak on her feet, barely learning to move again after being cocooned for years on end.

Her hand was still in mine. My shields slid around her as snugly as a hug. Her presence within them solidified, as if she took comfort from the metaphysical embrace. I felt the first spark of *her* aura, burnished copper with streaks of red, reasserting itself after the cushion of Cernunnos's magic. The thinnest threads of green still sparkled through it, just as I imagined I felt them in mine: Cernunnos was within us, not quite apart from this battle, but not quite there, either. That was okay. His moral support was enough.

Spider legs tapped against our shields, prickling and prying. The sound settled behind my ears and made hairs rise on my arms. Annie's breath was sharp and rough now that she was out of the cocoon, like the emphysema was coming on full bore.

Like thinking it gave the spidery attack an opening, a chink appeared in our armor. Annie's hand clenched on mine. "It's me. I can't hold it back. It's still in me."

"I can hold it back." Even as I spoke, one of the skinny legs wriggled its way through, making the thinnest stain of black on the inside of my shields. My lip curled and I strengthened them, cutting off the darkness. No more seeped through, but what was there leaped from the shields into Annie, blackening the copper of her spirit and coating her lungs.

My hands were full, one with Annie's grip, the other with my sword, as power continued to roar toward the shattering vortex. I still tried to move to fight the infection, and instead spasmed violently to check myself from my first impulse.

Annie's attention snapped from the emerging spider to me. "What was that?"

"A really bad idea."

She glanced back at the sky, at the killing cloud that had

spent years trying to dig her out of Cernunnos's protective tomb, then gave me an arch look. "Worse than that?"

"Yeah." I looked skyward, too, then drew a sharp breath through my nostrils. "Unless you trust me completely."

"With my life," Annie Muldoon said with such simple clarity that I nearly wept.

Then I drove my sword into her heart.

It was hard to tell who was more surprised, Annie or the evil thing hungering for her soul. Her mouth and eyes turned to enormous circles, but she remained silent. Silent, when somebody had just stuffed a sword into her. Silent, which told me it probably didn't hurt, which was what I'd expected. We were in the much-depleted garden of her soul, but it was her soul. I wasn't attacking her physical body, but the sickness inside it. Still, being stabbed was the sort of thing that might instinctively cause a person to scream, and she didn't.

Nor did the vortex, not yet. I clenched my stomach, wondering why, wondering what I had missed, and it came to me with absurd clarity. *Of course there are vampires,* Annie had just said to me, and everybody knew you didn't kill a vampire just with silver. It took wood, too.

I reached inside my coat and took out the hair stick I'd discovered over New Orleans, clasping it against the hilt of my rapier and infusing the silver with ash.

The vortex became a sound of pain and rage so great I could barely comprehend it. Tornadoes and tearing metal, cats fighting and fingernails on chalkboard, on and on in outrage and fear. A breath escaped me, not quite as triumphant as laughter. Just a breath that acknowledged my stupid-ass idea had some merit, if the howling darkness was so angry at the action.

Because swords—my sword in particular—cut both ways. It was a weapon, by its very nature meant to kill, and there was something here to kill, a creeping illness that ate and tore at Annie's life. I saw that sickness punch downward, gathered by the rapier and stretched, rather than torn, by the complex weave of ash wood inside the silver blade. It came out beside her spine, the rapier driving it through and then out of Annie's body. Mostly out: threads, scraps, still clung inside her, hooked ends catching in the bronchi and alveoli and holding on. Annie shuddered, though she still said nothing, wildfire-green eyes intent on me. Trusting me, which was so brave as to be madness. But her father had dreamed me, Gary loved me, and she had spent years wrapped in Cernunnos's land, protected by a god who knew and coveted me. I was a stranger, but not unknown. I gave her my best smile and a confident nod, and released the sword's other edge within her.

Killing, yes. That was what a blade like this was made for. But scalpels saved lives, too, and my sword, like myself, had accepted its destiny and heritage. A killing thrust to pierce the sickness, but also to drive healing magic through Annie's center. Silver and blue split apart, burning through her veins faster than any heart could send it. It lit her up from within, racing back and forth, up and down, crashing into itself and splashing waves of gunmetal where it merged. Sizzling heat turned to flashes of silver fire where it encountered the Master's invading power. As fast as I saw it, it was gone again, leaving only my magic in its place. My power split again, chasing the sickness and glowing with heat of its own, like molten silver.

Molten silver. I had watched Nuada, the sword's maker, turn his own living silver flesh into this blade, and for the first time I wondered if some part of the elf king was part of this battle, too. If he reached through time in his own way, lending a whisper of elfin immortality to the fight against the Master. It would never make a mortal live forever, but its inexorable age might lend a little more light to the path Annie had to tread.

Because I couldn't get it all. I should be able to, in the heart of Annie's garden, in the lingering warmth of Cernunnos's cocoon. I'd fought so many battles in spirit realms that I'd almost thought it was going to be that easy. That I was going to save Annie Muldoon here in the heart of her garden, and cast the Master out forever.

But from here, watching and feeling the threads of his power burn and hiss, I could tell they reached back into the Middle World. He'd had his fingers dug into Annie's ordinary human life so deeply and for so long in the Middle World that maybe I could *never* have won this fight purely in the spiritual planes. More than that, though, the Master finally had a host in the real world: Raven Mocker was out there somewhere, anchoring him. That meant the Master was more strongly entrenched in the world now than he had ever been in my encounters with him, and I was pretty sure winning a real-world throw-down would tie him to the world far more strongly than any kind of spiritual battle could. After all this time and effort, he wasn't going to settle for second best.

And the truth was, the body he'd taken for Raven Maker was second best. I wasn't kidding myself. Odds of the Master sticking with Raven Mocker's original host body, a guy named Danny whom I'd known as a kid, were vanishingly rare. Annie had called him a vampire, and there were two things I was certain vampires did: kill people, and make more like themselves.

And into that, Annie Muldoon had shown up. Honestly, on every level, I knew the smart thing to do would be to cut the last threads holding Annie to life, and to let her go free. I was pretty certain her soul, if not her body, could escape the Master's claws now. There were shadows inside her, thrown into sharp relief by the sword's brilliance, but they were nothing like the weight of sickness that had brought her to—and beyond—death's door. They were a toehold, a place to start again, not something to forever condemn her soul. I *should*, on any kind of smart bet, let her go now.

I was demonstrably not the type to take a smart bet. Not when faced with the woman Gary and Cernunnos had bent time to bring to me for healing. Not, when I got down to the crux of the matter, when faced with any kind of impossible odds and the slightest chance of setting them right.

"We have to go up," I said quietly. "Right into the maw. It's been chewing its way down through your garden—your soul—to the core of your being. Cernunnos has been protecting you, and that gave me a chance to burn most of the sickness out. But we've got to take it back, Annie. We've got to take your garden back. We have to go through the darkness to come out the other side."

Annie took the shallowest breath possible around the rapier's blade, just enough for a weak question. "How?"

"With this." I nodded at the sword, not wanting to wiggle it and hurt her. Not that it *should* hurt, but wiggling it just seemed cruel. "It'll be just as much of a shock coming out as it was going in, but it's going to be carrying some of your essence, too, when it comes out. Between you, me and it, we're going to punch right through to the Middle World. We're going home, Annie. I'm bringing you back to Gary."

I yanked the sword out before she had time to brace herself.

Power cracked open the sky. My power, Annie's power, Cernunnos's, maybe a touch of Nuada's, too. Cumulative white magic for the second time in a morning, this time born from within. Far above us, far beyond the edge of the cliff I'd dived off—a cliff now illuminated by roaring magic—far up there, the blackened and corrupt roof of Annie's garden suddenly shone, sloughing off the first sheen of dark magic. I wrapped my arm around Annie's waist like I was Errol Flynn and she was Olivia de Havilland, snugging her against my body. The roaring power focused by the sword contracted, swinging us in a cinematic arc toward the breaking sky.

Annie finally did shriek, laughter coming out as a high-pitched shout. That *had* to be a good way to start back on the road home, with laughter and excitement. I focused on it, adding it to the upswelling of magic, and chunks of blackened sky started to fall away. We leaned together, swinging around them, always climbing, scrambling, hurrying upward. There was no vortex left, its spidery legs withdrawn or so quashed within Annie's body and soul that it had no strength to stop us. Part of me thought, *It can't be this easy,* and the rest of me, sounding rather like that little voice that had recently slipped away, said, *What the hell about any of the past year has been* easy?

We ricocheted past the cliff edge I'd leaped off, still careening upward. Above us, not nearly so far above us anymore, the sky split the width of a hair, then broke apart to let a torrent of white magic come pounding in.

It fell around us like rain, bringing Annie's garden back to life where it touched down. It streamed across our bodies, pounding at the wealth of green power that Cernunnos had left around Annie. Her own aura began to emerge, rich with age and deep copper in color. It complemented the remaining green wonderfully, but it complemented something else even more: the silver that began shivering out of the falling magic. Gary's silver, the solid rumbling V8-engine strength of his soul coming to help his wife find her way home again.

Annie's aura went from emergent to radiant in a heartbeat, pouring the warmth of life up and out. It caught in the rain of white magic and spilled back down again, reviving her garden further, until we rushed through the crack in the sky back into the Middle World.

We actually slammed into the hospital room ceiling before

bouncing back to our bodies again. I sat up straight, rubbing my nose. Just within my vision, beyond the shadow of my fingertips, Annie took a sharp, soft breath of her own, not dictated by the ventilator's steady rhythm. Everything else in the room went silent, even the beeping of the monitors. Or maybe not; maybe the next moment happened fast and only seemed to stretch an impossibly long time. It didn't matter.

It didn't matter, because Annie Marie Muldoon opened her eyes and smiled at her husband. "Hello, sweetheart."

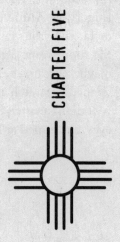

CHAPTER FIVE

Color drained from Gary's face. From his hands, too: I could see them whiten around where they held Annie's, and I bet they were suddenly icy to the touch. Annie squeezed his fingers gently, still smiling. "It's me. I think it's me. I think your Joanne wouldn't have let me come back, if I wasn't me anymore."

Gary shot me a harder look than he'd ever given me before, like for a moment he couldn't forgive me for the idea of not bringing her back. I kind of couldn't blame him, even though his protectiveness came after the fact. He caught up to that realization a moment later and turned his attention back to Annie. His hands were shaking as he lifted her fingers to his mouth, and though he tried a couple of times, he couldn't make it all the way to words.

That was okay, because Annie seemed to have some. Her voice was warm and steady, comforting, even though she was the one newly back from the dead and could be expected to be at loose ends. But then, she'd been a nurse. Maybe that helped. Or maybe it was easier to come back from the dead than to have mourned and moved on, only then to be presented with a bona fide miracle. "It's still there. I can still feel it inside me, making my lungs feel heavy. It wants out. I won't let it," she said with perfect equanimity. "I'll die first. I already did once."

"You won't have to." I sounded just as calm, just as resolved. Annie gave me a brief smile. Gary didn't. I wasn't even certain he was breathing.

"I'm sure you're right, Joanne. Now." Her smile turned stern, though there was a suspicious spark of brightness behind her emerald eyes. She turned all of that stern amusement on her husband, and flicked one eyebrow high up on her forehead. "*Imelda,* Gary? Is there something I should know about Imelda Welch from Kansas?"

Gary's mouth fell open, a blush curdling his face. His jaw flapped a few times and a wheeze emerged. I peered between them, nigh unto bursting with curiosity. Finally his wheeze became a breathless grunt, which he followed up by seizing Annie in his arms and burying his face in her shoulder.

For a woman just back from the dead, she looked to have a hell of a grip as she knotted her own arms around Gary and held on tight. For a while neither of them were coherent, mumbles and breaths of laughter interspersed with caught gasps of sobs. I sat there smiling idiotically, tears running unheeded down my face, until it finally occurred to me that they might want a little privacy. My knees were wobbly when I stood, but Morrison was there, his own face as unabashedly wet as mine. He drew me across the room, then murmured, "Imelda?" so quietly that I wouldn't have understood if I hadn't been wondering the same thing. I shrugged and tugged him a step or two closer to the door. We could hang out in the hall for a while, until Gary was ready to come get us. Morrison glanced back at the Muldoons one more time, a blinding smile appearing on his features. As we stepped out of the room, he took a deep breath. "Did you see them? Walker, I want to ask you—"

His question fell into startled silence as the door closed behind us. I blinked tears away, still smiling at him, then followed his uncertain gaze.

Suzanne Quinley, granddaughter of a god, sat on a bench across the hall.

She glanced up as the door closed behind us, looking lost in a massive gray hoodie and skinny blue jeans. Her long legs were drawn up and her arms wrapped around them, making her all elbows and knees. Ethereal elbows and knees, though, even disguised by the hoodie. She was slim-built with fine bones, and her wheat-pale straight hair still curtained her features.

When she looked up, I thought it was just as well that her hair often hid her face. Her eyes were so green, so vivid and sharp, that they seemed to be the only living, human thing about her. Therein lay the irony, of course, because she'd gotten that stunning gaze from her immortal grandfather, Cernunnos, god of the Wild Hunt.

Cernunnos, whose power I'd just been messing with in the room behind me. My voice broke as I blurted, "Suzy? Is everything okay?"

For a girl who was all elbows and knees, she unwound with surprising grace and flung herself the short distance across the hall into my arms. I grunted and fell back a step. Morrison caught our weight and straightened us up while Suzy clung to my ribs like a hungry leech. "I knew if I came here I'd find you!"

Last time Suzanne Quinley had said something of that sort

to me, she'd been coming to warn me that she'd had visions of my death. Shortly thereafter we'd fought zombies together, a scene which had left me whimpering and sniveling like a child. I did *not* want to reenact any of that, but it was a little hard to say, *Augh! Get off me, kid!* without causing offense. "What's wrong, Suze? What are you doing here? It's the middle of the night."

Suzy pulled out of my arms with an expression not dissimilar to Annie's when she'd mentioned the spirit cheetah. Except I'd had warning about the spirit cat, but had none at all for Suzy's exasperated reply. "It's two in the afternoon. And my best friend, Kiseko, and her boyfriend, Robert Holliday, magicked me here from Olympia last night."

"Rob—" My tongue and brain got all tangled up trying to decide which of those things I should latch on to. Being an honorary aunt of the boy in question, the second bit won. "Robert has a girlfriend?"

Suzy rolled her eyes as only a fifteen-year-old could. "Kiseko says not, but yeah, right. Anyway, they *magicked* me, Detective Walker, isn't that more important?"

"Ah. Um. Not 'Detective' anymore. I'm just plain old Joanne. How did they…magic you? It's two in the afternoon? What?" I had the terrible idea I was so far behind that I'd never catch up, and I was kind of afraid to even try. Even so, I looked to Morrison for confirmation about that last, and he nodded. I held up a palm, silencing Suzanne for a few seconds, and said, "It's *two* in the *afternoon?* It was midnight—!"

"You were under for twelve hours, Walker. More than twelve hours. Muldoon and I were—" Morrison took a sharp, deep breath, then abruptly pulled me into a hug. "I was starting to wonder if you were coming back, Walker."

Muffled by his shoulder, I said, "I did. I always will. I'm sorry. Twelve *hours?*" Now that I knew half a day had passed

I was suddenly incredibly thirsty and a bit woobly of knee.
"I've never been under that long before. It didn't feel that long.
It felt…" It had felt like minutes, just as it always did. But it
had been a hell of a lot of untangling and wrangling in there,
and what I knew about more traditional shamanic healings
didn't generally suggest they happened in the blink of an eye
that I was accustomed to. I'd apparently just about met my
match, which wasn't exactly a shocker. The Master had been
my match—more than my match—all along. "How did you
keep the hospital staff off us?"

Morrison grunted, a sound which may have been intended
as a distant cousin to laughter. "Muldoon went off on a tear
about freedom of religion and infringement of civil rights.
They cited the patient's rights and their own obligations and
threatened to call the police. Finding out my rank took the
wind out of their sails. Aside from checking her vitals they
left us alone after that."

"Jesus," I said, heartfelt, and Morrison tightened his arms
around me.

"Don't do that again, Walker. Try not to do that again."

"I'll try."

"A-*hem.*" Suzy drew our attention back to her, and I
couldn't decide if her tone of offense was for us ignoring her
or for what her friends had done. "They *called* me. Like I was
a magic *dog* or something. And then…" Offense flew out the
window, replaced by a shiftiness that had no business on a face
as young and innocent as Suzanne's. Never mind that she'd
pretty well lost any innocence the day we'd met, when her
adoptive parents had been murdered by her birth father, whom
I had then run through with a sword. "Then some things happened. But that's not important right now!"

Some things happened was not a phrase I wanted to consider
too deeply when discussing two teenage girls and a teenage

boy as participants. Morrison the police captain, however, had no compunction against it at all. "What kinds of things, Suzanne?"

Suzy blinked and turned scarlet from the collar of her shirt up. "Oh. My. God. Not those kinds of things. Omigod. No, it was magic stuff, not—omigod."

The poor kid was fit to die of mortification. Morrison, who could not be embarrassed on such, or perhaps any, topics, studied her momentarily like he was deciding whether she was telling the truth. She kept blushing a flaming blush until he nodded with satisfaction and gave her a brief, reassuring smile. I wasn't nearly that good a person, and merely tried not to laugh. "Okay, so it wasn't that kind of stuff. What kind of magic stuff?"

"It was like stuff with…I don't know, it was kind of creepy. But I've been having visions since then, or I haven't been, and that's the important part, Dete—uh, Ms. Walker."

All my laughter dried up. "Visions of what?"

"I don't know!" The last word was nearly a wail. Suzy collapsed back onto the bench, shoulders slumped, elegant fingers dangling between her legs. "I don't know. Darkness, but not like nighttime. It's alive, it's…it's greedy. It's…it's fighting the green," she said in obvious embarrassment, though I had no idea what she was embarrassed about. "It wants something. It wants something really important, and I can't See what."

I exhaled noisily. "It's the thing that made the cauldron, Suzy. It's the Master. And he probably wants me."

"I don't think so. It more like he wants…me."

My teeth clicked together and a hole opened up in my heart. There were a lot of reasons I could imagine something dark wanting Suzy. "Maybe we better go back to 'what kind of magic stuff?'"

Suzanne sighed deeply enough that I thought I'd better go

sit next to her. That kind of sigh preceded long stories, in my experience. But all she said was, "Kiseko was trying to raise an earth element, and she got me. I guess that kind of makes sense, but whatever. Anyway, when, or once, I came through, so did something else. And it felt…bad. And I fought it, and I won, but it, like, leaked oil inside my head. All I can see is the darkness, futures where everything has gone dark. That, and green. And I'm green, Detec—Ms. Walker. Ms. Walker."

"You can call me Joanne."

Suzy hesitated. "I don't think so. My aunt would *look* at me. But thanks. Anyway, it's like I feel all these dark futures in my head, Ms. Walker, and…and they *want* something. Something that'll help them come true." She swallowed. "I'm afraid it's me."

"Then we won't let that happen." I sat down beside her, put my arm around her shoulders, tugged her closer to me, and did my best to sound like a confident, reassuring grown-up. "It'll be fine, Suzy. I promise."

She sighed again and leaned on me. Morrison, still standing across the hall, got an oddly soft expression, then looked away with a smile. I decided not to read anything into that, because I was pretty sure it crossed into territory I wasn't yet prepared to tread. "How long has this been going on, Suze?"

"Since last night? They only just summoned me."

I closed my eyes, mumbling, "I'm going to have to tell Billy his son is summoning people. That's not going to go over well." Then my eyes popped open again. "Wait, last night? How did you even know I was here?"

"Every paper in Seattle is talking about the woman who came back from the dead. Where else would you be?"

"North Carolina," I said dryly. "That's where I was until…" I paused to adjust my mental time line. "Until last night. Wait, does that mean it's April first? This is all a pretty crappy idea of an April Fools' joke."

Morrison didn't even crack a smile, and Suzy kind of slumped in defeat. Apparently it was a crappy enough April Fools' joke that it wasn't even worth commenting on.

Staring at her toes, Suzy mumbled, "Well, I just, I mean, I thought you'd be here."

"How does anybody even know about Annie? It shouldn't be in the papers. I'd think the hospital would be trying to keep it quiet."

"That Channel Two reporter got hold of it. The pretty one. She was covering some other story at the hospital and heard people talking about this old woman who turned up out of nowhere. So she turned the story into an exposé on the carelessness of the Seattle hospital systems. She was on the national news last night."

I groaned and sat forward to put my face in my hands. "Laurie Corvallis? God, the national news? That's got to thrill her right down to her cold-blooded toes. How much you want to bet she parlays this into an anchor position somehow?"

"That's a bet I wouldn't take," Morrison answered. I smiled in admiration of his wisdom while Suzy peered between us.

"We've met Laurie Corvallis," I explained. "Frankly, we're lucky she's only doing an exposé on the hospital system, not trying to shine light on the magical aspects of the world. Believe me, if she thought there was anything hinky about this, and that she could make a story of it that people would believe, she'd be all over that like white on snow."

"Hinky." Suzy wrinkled her nose dubiously. "Did she really just say *hinky?*"

"I've learned to think of her verbal tics as part of her charm," Morrison said, straight-faced enough that I thought I should be offended. Then he cracked a grin and Suzy let go a relieved little burst of giggles, like she'd desperately needed the pressure release. Morrison was *much* better at kids than I was.

Of course, I was pretty certain giant squid were better at kids than me. That was good. Under the circumstances, somebody needed to be. I drew my tattered dignity around myself and sniffed. "If you're quite finished making fun of me...?"

Suzy giggled again, which pleased me. I squeezed her shoulders. "Okay. First—wait. First, does your aunt know you're here, this time?" Much to my relief, she nodded. "Good. Wait. How? If you got magicked—never mind. You promise she knows?" Suzy nodded again and I struggled past all the hows and whys to focus on the important part. "In that case, I'm basically not letting you out of my sight until this is over, okay? I can keep you safe if we're together."

It occurred to me that I needed to tell Annie Muldoon the same thing, and that I'd just left her all alone with Gary. My stomach turned upside down and I got up awkwardly, limbs no longer responding the way they should. Annie had said vampires were real. And Annie was back from the dead. I wobbled over to the room door and peered through the window.

My knees weakened. I put my hand on the doorknob for support, and my forehead against the window. They were *fine*. Holding hands, foreheads pressed together, looking for all the world like wrinkly teenagers in the throes of puppy love.

"Walker?"

"I just had an ugly thought. Never mind. It's okay." I sounded like I'd swallowed a rasp. Morrison and Suzy—she'd gotten up when I did, though I hadn't really noticed in the moment—came to frown through the window. Morrison's frown cleared a bit as he saw the lovebirds, then deepened again when he looked back at me. I gave him my best sick smile. "You could maybe say I trust her about as far as I could throw her."

"She's pretty little, and you're pretty strong," Suzy said thoughtfully. "I bet you could throw her quite a ways, if you got a good grip. Like the back of her pants and her collar, maybe."

She blinked at us with such innocence in her big green eyes that we both laughed. She brightened, making me realize she'd been trying hard to break the tension, just as Morrison had done for her. Poor kid shouldn't have to be the grown-up. I tugged a lock of her pale hair in thanks, then lifted my eyebrows. "You're probably right, at that. I could probably even chuck you a fair distance."

A spark of teen wickedness sparked in her eyes. "Just try."

I lunged for her and she shrieked, fleeing down the hall. I gave a half-voiced roar and chased her a few yards while Morrison said, *"Walker,"* in despair. I looked back at him with a grin and he presented me with a weak version of the Almighty Morrison glare that used to have me quaking in my shoes. Even that was interrupted by his phone ringing, so he turned away and I went back to chasing Suzy down the hall until a nurse gave us both scathing looks. We scurried back toward Morrison, both of us trying not to giggle.

Morrison's expression shut down my laughter. Suzy put her arms around my ribs like a much younger kid and huddled under my arm, both of us listening to Morrison's grunted responses and a handful of short sentences before he snapped his phone shut and met my eyes.

"There's just been a mass murder at Thunderbird Falls."

CHAPTER SIX

Saturday, April 1, 2:02 p.m.

If Suzy hadn't been holding on, I'd have fallen. As it was, the world didn't gray out: it went black. Not a dizzy sort of black. Dark magic sort of black, swirling up to eat at the auras I was half aware of seeing. Snipping away at Morrison's purples and blues, drinking greedily at Suzy's blaze green. I shouted, a hoarse hurtful sound.

Black spilled away under a rush of my own magic, gunmetal pushing back at the darkness. I swung around, out of Suzy's grip, until I faced Lake Washington. Until I faced Thunderbird Falls, which had been a bastion of white magic in Seattle. I could always See the falls. Power shot upward from it, white magic full of faint rainbow hues that eventually crashed against the clear blue sky or thick gray clouds, and spilled back down over Seattle, bringing a bit more pleasantry and generosity than had been there before. That was a gift of the good-hearted and good-willed New-Agey types in Seattle, by the covens and the other folk who had been drawn to the falls. Their difficult birth had rearranged Seattle's landscape, but it had been turned into a *good* thing.

And now it was dying.

Ichor oozed upward through the column of white magic, its stain growing exponentially. The faint rainbow tints tainted to oil slicks instead, white shading to shades of gray. I could See perfectly well that it still reached for the sky, but it felt heavier, like the darkness was dragging it down. Like it would be happier buried in the earth, though I didn't know if that was true. It seemed to me that if the white magic could rain cheer and contentment down on people, that black magic raining doom and misery would be right up the Master's alley.

On the other hand, the vicious truth was I didn't yet know the Master's endgame. I was good at self-aggrandizing, but I seriously doubted his entire goal was to obliterate me and my friends. It was definitely on his to-do list, because we were a constant pain in his ass, but I didn't think he would call it done and dusted the moment I was a smear on the pavement. In fact, if I thought that, I might've even been willing to become that smear just to offer everybody else a get-out-of-jail-free card. But no, it wasn't going to work that way, and while I was acknowledging that, my feet headed toward the elevators at top speed.

I didn't get twenty feet before I lurched to a halt again. Morrison just about ran me down. "Walker?"

"I can't go without Annie." My legs trembled with indecision. "I mean, I really—if I can only keep Suzy safe by keeping her with me, and Annie's still got the sickness in her—"

"Walker, the hospital is not going to let you walk out of here with a seventy-six-year-old woman who has just awoken from a coma after mysteriously returning from death."

"I could make us invisible."

"You can *do* that?" Suzy's voice popped into the shrill register only attainable by a teenage girl in full-on thrill mode. "Can *I* do that?"

I spared half a second to imagine what I would have done as a teen with the ability to turn invisible and said, "No," without really caring if it was true. Suzy drooped and fell back a couple steps as I twitched, trying to decide which way to go. "I can't go without Annie, Morrison. I can't leave her here without protection. Or if it comes to it, I can't leave Gary here without protection from her. I have to get her. Look, just— just go without me, okay? Go, and I'll try to get the doctors to understand—"

"Walker, I can't go without you!"

That was so preposterous I stopped trembling and gaped at Morrison. He passed a hand through his silver hair. "A mass murder at Thunderbird Falls is your department, Walker. Whatever's happened there, you're going to need to see it. I can't give you what you're going to need in a written report. You have to see it. To *See* it. The sooner, the better, right? Because magic doesn't linger and you can't track it."

I stared at him a long moment or two, wondering when he'd become such an expert on magic. Over the past fifteen months, obviously, but it still jarred me to hear him say such things outright. "Yes. Yeah. You're right. I just—"

A door down the hall behind us banged open. Morrison and I both flinched, reaching for duty weapons neither of us were carrying. A few seconds later, Suzy, now wearing a light blue T-shirt, sailed past, balanced on the back lower frame of a wheelchair occupied by a small figure in a gray hoodie. "Taking Grandma for her walk!" she caroled as they swept past the nurses' station two dozen feet ahead of us. "We'll be back in twenty minutes!"

"Get off that wheelchair, young lady!" somebody bellowed

after her. Suzy jumped off the frame and ushered the wheelchair into an open elevator before anybody had time to stop her. The doors slid closed, leaving me and Morrison goggling down the hall.

Gary, shrugging on a Windbreaker and carrying my drum in one hand, lumbered up to us. "I hear we got places to be, doll." He sounded more like his old self. I stared at him without much comprehension, too, until he swung a finger, lasso-like, and pointed it toward the elevators. "That girl's gonna be out the front door in three minutes, Jo. We goin', or what?"

"Yes! Yeah! We're going. We're…going." I jolted into motion with the first word, and tried not to let my feet slow down as I stuttered toward the end of the sentence. Morrison, marching alongside me, was as apoplectic as he ever had been when facing down the curves my life threw at him. Gary, however, had a grin that looked fit to beat the devil.

Since that was kind of what we had to do, it gave me heart. The three of us got in another elevator and followed Suzy out of the hospital. Nobody gave any of us a second look: there were plenty of other patients in wheelchairs or on crutches, making slow rounds over the hospital grounds. Morrison broke into a jog, gaining ground on us before disappearing into the parking lot. When we were as far away from the hospital front doors as we could get, he appeared in our rented car.

Annie Muldoon clambered inside the car and threw her hood back to reveal a delighted smile. "I always wanted to ride in a getaway car! I apologize, Captain Morrison, for putting you in this awkward position. I'm grateful for your assistance."

Suzy flung herself into the far passenger's side of the car, catching Morrison's look of bewilderment. "I explained everything to Grandma, I mean, Mrs. Muldoon, on the way out."

Morrison breathed, "I sincerely doubt that," and Suzy huffed in exasperation.

"I explained enough. She knows who you are."

"And I appreciate the difficulty of your situation," Annie said. By that time we were all in the car, me riding shotgun after Gary and I had engaged in a silent discussion-slash-argument about whether he or I would take it. In the end he'd pointed ferociously at Annie, indicating he was not moving an inch farther from her side than necessary. I put my drum in the trunk and got in the front passenger seat.

"Mrs. Muldoon, I'm not sure even I appreciate the difficulty of my situation right now." That said, Morrison put the car in Drive and peeled out of the parking lot. "Walker, call Dispatch. Tell them to put out an APB that I am in a rented blue Toyota Avalon, license plate number CTAK3887—"

"You know the car's license plate number?" I asked in admiring astonishment.

Morrison's lifted eyebrow suggested he memorized the plates of every vehicle he ever got in, no matter how little time he expected to spend in it. "And that I am approaching Thunderbird Falls from the southwest, at as high a speed as I can manage. This vehicle is not to be stopped for traffic violations."

Morrison was going to rack up traffic violations on my behalf. I'd never heard anything half so sexy in my life. I put the call in and gasped gladly when I recognized the dispatcher who picked up: my old friend Bruce. "I'll see if I can get any squad cars to clear some streets for you," he offered without missing a beat. "Where are you coming from, exactly?"

I told him, finishing with, "If I could cook I'd make you and Elise the best meal you'd ever had, in thanks."

"I can cook," Annie put in.

I laughed, relaying the offer, although not who it was from. Bruce counter-offered with a cook-off, his wife's tamales against the best Annie could come up with, and then got serious again. "I can get you a police escort starting in about fifteen blocks. I've got other cars moving to clear the road ahead of you, but with the escort you'll have sirens. Be careful, Joanie."

"It's Jo, now. And we will be." I hung up, gave Morrison the down-low and spent the next seven minutes trying not to shriek with speed-demon joy as my staid, steady boss took corners too fast, blew traffic lights, rode the meridian and braked hard from accelerations.

Annie, in the back middle seat, bounced and clapped her hands when the escort, sirens wailing and lights flashing, joined us. I burst out laughing, and Suzy had her knuckles in her mouth, trying to hold back squeals. "Wonder if this is what the president feels like," Gary rumbled.

Morrison shot him one short look in the rearview mirror before bringing his attention back to the road. "The president doesn't usually travel this fast in land vehicles. This better get us there in time, Walker."

That cut the legs right out from under my glee. There was no *in time:* people were already dead. But if I could work a power circle, at least maybe I could contain the black magic swallowing up the falls' power, and if we were incredibly lucky, maybe we could snare the murderer.

Chances were not good that we'd be incredibly lucky.

With the police escort, we got to the falls in record time. I was out of the car before Morrison had finished pulling into a parking space, but somehow he was still only two steps behind me. I half noticed Gary getting out with Annie and Suzy, but he drew them away from the crime scene that Morrison and I ran for. I was grateful for that: Annie might've been a nurse, but Suzy was just a kid, and she didn't need to see the horror smeared across the beach.

I didn't count them. I just saw that there were lots, and

mentally leaped to the number: *thirteen.* A coven. A coven meant they all had at least some tiny flush of magical talent. That had to be the ultimate murder prize for the Master. That had to help him to no end. No wonder the falls' magic was so badly damaged, and no wonder it kept getting worse. I was willing to bet these people had been pouring their hearts and souls into that power right up to the moment of their deaths.

And they weren't just dead. They'd had their hearts ripped out, every single one of them. Their ribs were broken outward like someone had shoved a hand through their backs and emerged clutching the hardest-working muscle in the body. The blood sprays looked like that, too, easily visible because the victims were all flat on their backs in a perfect circle, as if something very startling had leaped from the earth at their center and the surprise had knocked them all over backward. The blood looked like their hearts had been ripped out after that, like the same something had then come up through their spines and taken the hearts skyward. I shuddered, unable to drag my gaze from the red gaping holes in their chests.

Peripherally, I knew mundane things were going on. Morrison had left me standing stock-still a stone's throw from the bodies, and was taking charge of the gathering cops, medical teams and, God forbid, reporters. His calm took some of the edge off rising hysteria, though I Saw glimpses of anger and shock sparking through his aura. Eyewitnesses were babbling stories to anyone who would listen, including others who had been there. Some of them were arguing with one another. Pale-faced cops were trying to take down the comments without looking at the bodies, and I saw my friend Heather Fagan, head of the North Precinct's forensics team, cross under the police tape with her mouth set in a thin grim line. All of this activity was going on around me, and I couldn't move.

Couldn't bring myself to look at the faces I was holding out of focus because I was afraid of what I would see.

Afraid it would be worse than blood and bone and viscera spattered across a sand-addled shore. The horribleness of that made me breathe a sharp laugh, which in turn let me close my eyes. It wasn't much, but it was something. I'd be able to look elsewhere when I opened them again. I did that on purpose, with them still closed: moved my gaze, pointed it in the direction of faces, not bodies. It still took turning my hands into fists to make me open my eyes again.

The first face I saw was a young man. Early twenties, nice-looking, familiar.

"Garth." The name didn't make it past my throat. Didn't even shape my lips as my stomach dropped and left a wake of ice where it had been. Garth Johannsen, Colin's older brother. Colin, who had played host to a dark sorcerer and paid for it with his life in the battle that had birthed Thunderbird Falls. I thought Garth had gotten out of the Magic Seattle scene. It looked like he'd gotten back in.

I knew the other faces, too. Duane, the very decent guy whose blood I'd shared in a rather literally minded ritual. Thomas, their Elder, the male counterpart to the Crone. Roxie, who'd been as cute as her name.

But I'd been wrong. I'd misjudged in my counting. There weren't thirteen bodies. There were twelve.

Marcia Williams, the coven's leader, was missing.

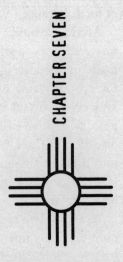

CHAPTER SEVEN

"When?" My question rasped beneath the general babble, not loud enough to gain anyone's attention. I cleared my throat and tried again. "When? When exactly did this happen?"

Two dozen witnesses turned my way with two dozen answers. Well, no, more like with about four answers, the majority of which were 1:53 p.m. I took that as the median and hobbled a few steps away from the bodies. "Morrison? Michael?"

He turned his head half an inch at his surname, indicating he'd heard me, but when I used his first name he came around full circle, eyes dark with concern. "What is it, Walker?"

"What time exactly did Annie wake up?"

"One fifty-three."

Of course. I would trust Morrison to know the precise moment that the world planned to end, so I had no doubt at all he was right. I pressed my fingertips into the corners of my eyes. I wasn't wearing glasses. I hadn't been wearing them for a while, but the world wasn't in soft focus. I wondered, briefly, if all the shape-shifting had fixed my vision, then let it go, because there were far more important things to think about. Like, "Then we have a problem."

If Morrison was the kind of person to give me a *no shit* look, that would have been the time to do it. Instead, a thread of tension knotted his aura and his shoulders, but so subtly I wasn't certain anybody else could see it. "Another problem?"

"One to discuss in private."

A line appeared between his eyebrows. He said, "One moment," to the cop he'd been talking to and gestured for me to lead the way.

I took us several steps away. "Witnesses say this went down at 1:53, Morrison."

"I know. What does tha—" He closed his eyes momentarily before regarding me steadily. "Walker, I want you to tell me there's no connection between Annie's revival and...this."

"I want to tell Annie that."

I knew Morrison could lose control. I'd seen him blow his top any number of times. I was usually the cause, in fact. But when it came down to the job, the man kept his cool better than anyone I'd ever known. Silence stretched for five heartbeats before he said, "Then tell me what happened."

"When I went in for Annie—" I broke off, uncertain if that made sense to anyone but me. Morrison nodded, indicating I should continue. "When I went in, the thing coming for her—for her soul, her life essence—it had a sense of urgency. It felt like the Raven Mocker coming into the world. Like it was being birthed but it—" I faltered, then said it all in a rush. "Like it needed a body to be born into. Like Annie was meant to be its host. And when I rescued her..."

"...it found somewhere else to go. Instantaneously? Is that possible?"

I looked toward the bodies, back at Morrison, and shrugged. "At a guess, I'd say yes. They were using magic right then, so they were primed, and…" I exhaled until my lungs were as empty as I could make them, then inhaled until tears prickled my eyes. "And they were marked, I bet. Somehow. Because this is the coven I worked with last July, Morrison. I knew these people. I worked magic with them, and that…might have made them susceptible. It all comes around." I felt very tired suddenly, a bone weariness that had nothing to do with too little sleep and a lot to do with sorrow and regret.

Morrison's voice gentled. "It isn't your fault, Walker."

I sighed. "Not in so many words, no, but even so. It's coming to an end." I said that for myself as much as him, because I couldn't bear the idea of my associates dying for the folly of having met me.

"Yes." There was a strange note in that word.

My eyebrows furled. "You can't possibly be sorry about that, Morrison. This hasn't exactly been a hayride for you."

"Or for any of us. No, I just wondered, for a moment—" He broke off and shook his head, leaving me scowling at him in perplexity.

"Boss, look, if I've learned anything in the past year, it's that if you've got something to say you should probably get it off your chest, because who knows if you're going to get another chance."

"'Boss?'"

I rolled my eyes. "Old habits. Morrison. *Mike.* Whatever. What's wrong?"

The corner of his mouth quirked. "'Mike.' 'Boss' may be easier to take than that. A maudlin thought, Walker, and not one appropriate to the circumstances. I wondered if you would still need or want me when this is over."

The man's vulnerabilities rose at the weirdest time. There

was absolutely nothing I could say to that, so I stepped forward, slid my fingers into his short silver hair and gave him a knee-weakening kiss right there in front of God and everybody.

Morrison said something like, "Asllfmph," against my mouth, and was scarlet over every inch of visible skin when I finally released him. I put my fingertip against his lips, whispered, "Don't be silly," and kissed my finger away, too. "Now we should get back to business."

Somewhere in that last word the surrounding silence made itself noticed to me. I pursed my lips, practically certain I didn't want to look around, but of course I did, anyway.

The whole crime scene had come to a halt. Everybody—cops, forensics, witnesses—was staring at us. It even felt like the sucking darkness in the falls' power had paused to gape at our inappropriate public display of affection.

"Sorry." My grin and my blush were running even odds as to which would split my head first. I flapped my hand at our observers. "As you were."

Throats cleared, gazes averted, people shuffled, and within a few seconds everybody was back to the duties of the moment. Morrison, still red around the collar, muttered, "You have no sense of decorum, Walker," but didn't sound as put out as I thought he was trying to.

I smiled at him. "I know. It's part of what you find so appealing about me. That totally blew the office betting pool, though. No way we can rig it now. Come on." I took his hand and pulled him a few steps back toward the cop he'd been talking to. "Let's get back to work."

"Wait. Walker, a dozen supernatural deaths in broad daylight. How—?"

"I think that mostly depends on Heather." I squinted toward the lead forensics officer, whose crouched form was silhouetted by sunlight bouncing off the lake. "And whoever is the medical examiner, I guess, because the only logical, real-world way this happened was with some kind of tiny rigged explosives, worn either voluntarily or planted on the coven."

"Explosives of which they will find no physical evidence."

I had to love a man who didn't end sentences with prepositions. "Right. It's a pretty good cover story for the press, though. I mean, I don't like it, because it feeds right into the whole Wiccans as crazy cult types, but most people would accept it."

Morrison sighed, looking out at the lake. "Last time something went down at Thunderbird Falls you gave me a plausible line for it, too. Is that the line you want—" His teeth clenched, and I couldn't blame him one bit.

"I don't want you to give them *any* line, Morrison. I'll go talk to Heather and I'll talk with the M.E. This kind of spin isn't something you should be handling. Let the flack fall on me. I've been a problem employee all along."

"You quit two weeks ago."

I kept forgetting that. My whole face wrinkled up, not at the reminder, but because it meant my only viable excuses to be here were either magic-related, or because I was Morrison's girlfriend. Neither was going to go over spectacularly well with the top brass.

I put that on a mental shelf to worry about later. "So I did, which means any weirdness can be laid squarely at my feet and the emphasis can be on me no longer being a cop."

"The reasons for which are now murky, since half of Seattle just saw us kissing."

"Dammit, Morrison, I was trying to reassure you in a way I thought you'd believe. I wasn't thinking about the consequences." I clearly should have been, but as was usual with me and thinking, I was applying it too little and too late. "The good news is there's so much magic whirling around here right now that everything's going to be a fog for most of these people, so let's not worry about it. I'm going to go talk to Heather. You go...do your thing." As he strode off, I realized his thing, at the moment, was taking the lead on this investigation. Police captains weren't generally supposed to do that, but he was certainly the ranking officer on the scene, and he had a vested interest in getting my mess cleaned up.

Forget whether I was going to want *him* when this was over. He'd be crazy to still want *me*. I sighed—I seemed to be doing that a lot—and worked my way around the bloody circle to approach Heather Fagan.

She stopped me with an upraised palm as I made to step over the police line. "You've already been in here, haven't you?"

"Yeah. Over there, next to Garth. I'll give the guys my shoe information." I lifted a foot and wiggled it a little.

"Garth. You know these people?" Heather put her hands on her thighs and pushed out of her crouch. "Is this going to turn out like the Ravenna Park death?"

"Yes."

"So I'm not going to get any answers I like. And maybe not any at all."

"Right."

Heather gave me a flat look. "What is it with you?"

"...I'm a shaman, and this sort of crap has been following me around for about a year. It's almost over now."

She stared at me a couple of seconds, and I wondered if lying would have been the better tactic after all. Not that she would have believed a lie, either. But she didn't call me on it, only snorted. "Over. Malarkey. Fine. I'll make sure Sandra is the M.E. on this. She'll find whatever is necessary to make this story bearable to the general public. Who's your lead detective?"

I looked over my shoulder toward Morrison, but I knew the answer. "Billy Holliday. He'll be here in a few minutes."

"Holliday. Of course. The one guy weirder than you are. And the one guy you can trust to help cover this up."

"Just like you're about to do." I wanted to be very clear on that. Heather thrust her jaw out, but nodded. I couldn't help asking, "Why?"

"Because I can't do my job if I have tabloid reporters breathing down my neck demanding to know the real story when I can't provide a rational and logical explanation for something like this."

"What if there isn't one?"

Heather pressed her lips together so hard they disappeared into a thin white line before she spoke. "My niece works in a morgue. Last Halloween she dismembered an animated dead body with a scalpel."

"Holy crap! About yay tall," I said, waving my hand at about shoulder height, "wears her hair in a braid? I met her! She's your niece?"

I received another flat look for my enthusiasm. "Cindy wanted to *talk* about it. I wanted to forget everything that had happened that night, but Cindy wouldn't let it go. Two months later, a bunch of frozen bodies shriveled up and turned to dust in the morgue while I was watching."

That wasn't strictly true. *I,* in fact, had been watching at the time. But I was willing to give Heather the poetic license here, since I was certain she felt like it had happened on her watch, if not under her very gaze. "Cindy wouldn't let that go, either, and she wouldn't let *me* let it go. Ever since then I've been seeing things I don't remember noticing, or wanting to think about, before.

"This—" and she jabbed a finger toward the bodies with a certain vicious frustration "—is one of them. I don't *want* to think there's no rational explanation, Detective Walker. I've always believed there is one for everything. But I see you here, and I think about Cindy carving up zombies, and freeze-dried bodies, and facing a dozen dead people with no instantly obvious cause of death—" her lip curled, because burst chests and missing hearts were pretty obviously the cause of death, but I knew what she meant "—and I know the only answer I'm going to get is going to be unsatisfactory, so I would rather provide a rational lie on a police report than leave an entire city of people terrified that if they come down to Lake Washington for an afternoon at the waterfall, their hearts are going to explode out of their bodies!"

"I'm really sorry."

"Be sorry for their families, who are probably going to spend the rest of their lives struggling to understand the lies we tell them."

"If, when this is over, the truth is easier to believe, I'll tell them the truth." It wasn't much, but it was the best I could offer.

Heather's eyes narrowed. "If the truth is easier to believe than the lie?"

"No. If the truth is easier to believe than it is now." Because if we won, I wondered if it might not be. One way or another, there was going to be a lot of magic released into the world. Maybe it would be easier to tell grieving families it had killed their loved ones, instead of letting them believe they had either been forced, or had chosen, to die in an inexplicable cult death at the foot of a newborn waterfall. "I'll cross that bridge when I get to it. Heather, I know this sucks, so…thank you."

"You want to thank me, you…" She hesitated, eyes searching my face. "You go talk to Cindy when this is over. Because if she can't let this thing go, the thing with zombies and…this…" she said with an unhappy look at the bodies, before sharpening her gaze on me again. "If she can't let it go, then I don't want her exploring it by herself. I want her to have a teacher, somebody I know and trust. I don't want to be standing over her body like this someday because she took a wrong turn."

An ache filled my chest. I tried to breathe it away and couldn't catch air at all, only made a small hiccuping sound and nodded. "I will. I promise."

"Good. Thank you." Heather turned away, going back to her job like none of our conversation had happened. Maybe she wished it hadn't. I managed to draw a shuddering breath and stumbled away, confused and touched and frightened by her trust in me. I hoped I could be the guide Cindy needed. I hoped I could be the guide *any* of the kids I'd met needed: Cindy, my cousin Caitríona, Suzanne Quinley…even the Holliday kids, though them to a lesser degree, since they had their parents, who were far more stable than I was.

I was still fumbling with the idea of being a teacher when Marcia Williams rose out of the earth and backhanded me.

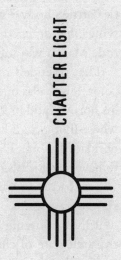

CHAPTER EIGHT

The blow caught me across the cheekbone, picked me up and threw me through the air. Stunned, I flew in a backward arc, already cringing at the idea of Heather's fury at me messing up the crime scene by landing in it.

I missed by about six feet, landing ass-first in sand that sprayed up my shirt and fell into the back of my jeans. My cheek throbbed, right along the scar, and my tailbone, having been violently introduced to the earth, popped loudly. Sand began to itch in unfortunate places while I sat there shaking my head and trying to clear my vision.

Marcia was in her fifties and eight inches shorter than me. No way on this earth could she hit that hard, or throw me that far. It didn't take a genius to know she wasn't the one in charge, even if it was her body doing the dirty work. I shook my head one more time and lurched upward, getting a look at her with the Sight.

Everything about her was the shining opposite of Raven

Mocker. Where it—he, since it had taken over Danny Little Turtle's body—where he was sharp and dark, with angel wings that dragged soot and blackness with them, whatever rode Marcia was soft and shining silver.

That offended me on a visceral level. Silver was Gary's color. Silver was one of *my* colors. Silver was Cernunnos and his horse, liquid metal to dip my fingers in. Silver was Nuada, whose living flesh had made both the rapier I carried and the necklace I wore. The bad guys did not, comma dammit, get to have silver souls.

The bad guys weren't supposed to be *beautiful,* and Marcia's aura was.

It lived, flowing and flexing, so that her wings were in a constant state of change. Misty feathers glimmered, fading and brightening, and sent the shapes of their quills plunging back into her body. Each one struck like an arrow, digging deeper into her flesh like the rider was confirming its hold on her. Marcia's colors had been earthy. There was nothing left of that in her, or if there was, it was buried so deep I couldn't see them without an intimate examination.

I was more than happy to engage in one. I dug my toes into the sand for purchase and launched myself back toward Marcia.

She was gone long before I got there. Under other circumstances I might have admired the rapid grace of her transit, like mercury spilling over the sand. Her toes barely touched as she ran, spiritual wings lifting her, lightening the weight of her body until even without the Sight she seemed inhuman. Angelic.

All around the falls, voices lifted in astonishment and relief as the regulars recognized Marcia. Power swirled in the air, offering her strength, and like a thunderclap I realized what they Saw: one of their fallen returned, graced with an angel's wings. They believed in her. In *her,* and that meant—

Power slammed me in the chest and knocked me back again. I skidded through sand, stopping wrist-deep in cold lake water. Seattle's adepts gathered around me in a half circle at the lake's edge, eyes alight with magic. Marcia had risen from death and attacked me, and by their lights, that made me the bad guy.

There were moments I absolutely hated my life. "Guys, I—" They threw a *net*. Woven of magic, cast by dozens of hands, white at its core and only tainted with gray along individual threads, it spun out and collapsed over me, disturbing the water not a whit. It tightened, squeezing my arms against my sides and flattening me back into the water until I was wet from head to hip, up to ear depth. For a moment, just a moment, I stared up at wisps of cloud in the blue afternoon sky and wondered what I'd done to deserve this.

Then Suzanne screamed. I threw off any pretense of caution and called my physical totems to mind: Cernunnos's sword. The copper bracelet my father had given me more than ten years ago, nestled safely beneath the arm of my coat. My mother's silver necklace, a gift to my maternal line from Nuada himself. The Purple Heart medal Gary had given me that shielded my heart. Purple and copper blended together, becoming a small round bracer shield on my left arm. It was a thing of magic to begin with, but I lent it an edge, filling it with healing magic as I slashed the threads of the net.

None of my captors expected me to be able to do that. The net flew apart, threads untangling and carrying sparks of clean magic back into the users. Or I sure hoped for that last part, because I did *not* need a few dozen thralls on my back while I went to see what was up with Suzy.

The strongest of the adepts adapted before I was on my feet again, throwing a new, darker, stronger net. I lifted the shield and slapped it away, the action as much mental as physical, and muttered, "Knock it off. I'm good at nets," as I stalked through them.

I felt their shock anew as the net rebounded off the shield, then suffered a quick pleased thrill as I realized even the idea of the shield glimmered with my own shields. Coyote would be so proud of me, keeping those things intact without conscious thought.

He'd be prouder if I'd been keeping them over Suzy and Annie without conscious thought. Marcia had gone after them while I was distracted by her posse. Without thinking, I whispered, *Renee?* silently, and took two running steps to get to them.

At the back of my head, a spirit animal shivered to life. A walking stick, my family's namesake, whose gift to me was time travel. I called her Renee because it was alliterative, matching Raven and Rattler, my other two guides.

Time folded, just a little. Only enough to validate the old *time slowed down* cliché, except this time it didn't slow down. It really did fold, letting me cross more distance than I should have been able to in those two steps. I slid between my friends and Marcia in the blink of an eye, and had the gratifying experience of watching astonished rage blacken her face before she slammed into me full force.

My shields should have held me in place. Instead, I went backward into Gary's arms.

Marcia went straight into my chest.

Not literally. Not physically. But spiritually, yeah, she dived right in, and for the first agonizing instant I thought she shouldn't have been able to do that. My shields were going strong, no chinks in the armor. My lungs, filled with raging silver angel, informed me otherwise. I made a desperately quick review of the choices leading up to this moment, concluding it had been either absorb her or let her go through me into Annie or Suzy. Obviously that wasn't going to happen, so I'd chosen Door Number Absorb.

Why the hell I hadn't opted for *bounce her off me* was a question for another time. Or not, since my sardonic inner voice said, *Because now she's trapped,* and I had to agree trapped was better than running around on the beach stirring up chaos. We'd taken the fight to an inner battleground, where she could only damage me.

My shields *were* stronger than they'd ever been. To my eyes, to my sense of the world, we hadn't left the beach. The colors were off, the sky yellower than it should be and the earth redder, but that was just a hint of the Lower World, a place of physical monsters and magic, bleeding through. It was far better that we'd bounced there than straight into my garden, which is where a bad guy would have landed me with a sneak attack not all that long ago. I was so much better than I'd been.

The question was whether I was good enough. I'd lost the Raven Mocker. I couldn't afford to lose the thing that rode Marcia. In this Lower World beach, there was no trace of Marcia at all, only the silver-winged monster that had taken her over. Its face stretched, showing fangs its mouth wasn't big enough to hold, and its clawed fingers tapped together like it was waiting to plunge them into my heart. Its eyes were featureless, no pupil, no iris, just blank shining silver, but I had no doubt it saw me.

Saw me, and saw our surrounds. For the briefest moment it paused, suddenly in serene repose as it took in the yellowed sky and red sand beach. In that moment it was perfectly beautiful, its face flawless, its body—it really was a she—smooth and curved and lovely. If Michelangelo had worked in silver, he might have made such a creature as this one.

Then she snarled a smile and the beauty was gone. She pounced. I dodged. Her wings swept around, beating at me like a swan's, and to my astonishment I went down under the battering. It *hurt,* even if my shields made the damage negligible. I bellowed, *Raven!* inside my skull, on the desperate assumption that one bird knew how to fight another.

Something new happened at the back of my skull. Raven responded as he always did, with a flash of enthusiasm and chattering commentary, but he didn't leap forth the way I expected him to. Instead, he twisted inward, *klok*ing urgently.

My rattlesnake awakened and spun himself around Raven, scales hissing with speed. They turned in opposite directions, becoming more and more one with each other. Sharing the gifts that were theirs: transition between life and death, shapeshifting, speed. They rose up together, slim and strange, Raven's feathers glittering with black-sheened scales, Rattler's scales taking on the soft shining edge of wings. Renee tapped their foreheads with two long sticklike legs, and fire poured from them into me.

There was no pain in a shape-shifting done correctly, nor could there be any at all in the Lower World, where spirit was all. The fire was exultation, pride, power, release, as my spirit guides were able to truly work together for the first time, no longer hampered by my self-doubts and endless denials. They were meant to bring me individual gifts. I'd had no idea that together they could offer even more than that.

I became Raven, but vast. Even in the Middle World, mass didn't displace with shifting: I would be a 165-pound bird, impossibly large. But here in the Lower World, with no constraints except my imagination, I was more than that. Rattler's golden skin shattered across my black feathers, making them shine in the morning light. I gathered Rattler's predatory instincts to me, shedding Raven's scavenging ways. A skree burst from my throat, an ear-rupturing sound of a creature that had once acknowledged me, and whose shape still ran in my blood.

I was the thunderbird, and this, the waterfall, was *my* place.

Claws extended, wings buffeting, I leaped on the silver angel and drove my beak toward its throat. It screamed with Marcia's voice, but Marcia was a mortal concern, a concern that belonged to Joanne Walker, and I was more than that. I opened my beak and hissed, a sound from Rattler that suited this golden eagle very well. My tongue flicked out, forked and tasting the silver thing's fear. I struck again, certain of victory.

It slipped from my claws, narrowing, elongating, taking a new and familiar shape: the shape of my old enemy, the serpent. That was as it should be. We had been locked in this battle, in these shapes, for as long as humanity had existed. For longer, perhaps, but without humans to count time, the aeons before had no meaning.

The snake reared up, still winged, but its wings would never be as powerful as mine. I crashed mine together with the sound of thunder. Dizziness came into its featureless eyes. I cried delight and struck again, but this time it flung itself sideways and rose again, lightning quick in its counterattack. Its fangs scraped my shields, unexpectedly sending blue sparks up: I had already forgotten that the Joanne part of me used magic that color, when Thunderbird-me was as gold as sunrise. We fought, tearing the land around us, waking currents in the water and rending clouds from the sky in our battle. It weakened and I did not. It was only a matter of time, and time was as much my gift as this magnificent shape. Time was Renee, my walking stick, and she was on my side.

A weight smashed into me from nowhere, hitting me between the wings. It flattened me against the earth, impossibly strong. I kicked and scraped the sand, trying to gain purchase and flip myself over, but it pushed harder, crushing my breath and my bird bones. The serpent-angel was beneath me. That was something. I opened my beak and slashed again, determined to kill it before my breath was gone forever.

It sank into the sand as if the thing crushing me was shoving it away, as well, until it was absorbed like silver oil. I screamed, thunderous anger that shook the very grains beneath me, but I couldn't clear the sand away to find the retreating serpent. Rage blinded me, turning my vision molten gold. Under that heat the raven and the rattlesnake began to disentangle, sinking away just as the serpent did. I tried to catch them, too, but they slipped through my feathers-becoming-fingers, leaving me strangely bereft and magicless in the Lower World.

Distantly, very distantly, I heard shouts. That was unusual. Activity in the Middle World didn't generally pass into my attention when I was in the Lower World. Of course, my journeys into the spirit realms, although they seemed to me to take place in real time, often happened inside the space of a breath or the blink of an eye. It was very possible I'd never been in here long enough for things to happen in the real world around me. This made twice in one day, though, and I wasn't sure if that was a good or a bad sign.

The shouts were getting clearer. People were worried about fibbing, which made me laugh. Or I tried, anyway. My chest was hideously heavy, like I'd lost the lottery and was being pressed to death. I forgot about trying to laugh and just tried to breathe. I had magic. I should be able to clear the pain from my chest, but my focus was gone, black and blurry behind closed eyelids. It hurt badly, frighteningly badly.

Defibrillator. That was the word I was hearing, not *fib* at all. That was good. Fibbing would have been silly. Defibrillators, though, that seemed important. Dangerous. Alarming, even, except I couldn't breathe deeply enough to be alarmed about anything except the lack of air in my lungs. A familiar voice said something outrageous in response to the need for a defibrillator. *No*, it said, *let me*. There were arguments, but another voice I knew spoke more strongly. *Get out of the way. Let him help.* I wished they were clearer, wished I could put names to them, but I was choking on a breath, shuddering as I tried to pull it in. My chest weighed so much, like all the anger in the world had built up in it.

Maybe, I thought in horror, maybe that was how the silver-winged serpent burst the hearts out of the coven. I started trying to scrape my healing magic together, appalled at how fragile it felt. My shields were still there, but they seemed to be barely keeping me from being crushed. Fuzzy-minded, I tried to remember if I had directly tangled with Raven Mocker, and if I had, whether it had left me this depleted. I'd been a mess the whole time I was in North Carolina, anyway, so I couldn't say for sure. The wraiths had sure sucked me dry, and it felt like the silver-winged angel had dragged every dribble of magic out of me and sunk it into the sand as it had disappeared.

That was going to be a problem, if it couldn't be stopped. Which was probably the Master's whole plan. He wasn't ever going to face me directly. He was just going to send minions to suck the power out of me.

Power crashed *into* me, as ferocious and shocking as the threatened defibrillator. I arched and gasped, then hit the ground before doing it all again. After the third or fourth time, I squeaked a protest and managed to get my hands up, waving them around. "Okay, okay, I'm fine. I'm fine. What—agh, what is that?" I batted away the tickles attacking my face, twitching my cheeks to try sending them away.

It didn't work. Itchy-nosed and offended by it, I opened my eyes to discover it was Coyote's long black hair falling over his shoulders to curtain us from the world.

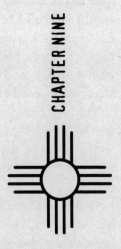

CHAPTER NINE

"Hwaa? Whaa? Kye…wha? *What?*" It was hard to fling one-self into someone's arms from lying down, but I did my best. I only knocked our skulls together a little bit in the effort. Coyote grunted and fell onto his butt, hugging me more gingerly than I did him. He still smelled like sunshine and sand. I dragged a couple breaths of that, holding on tight, then rocked back far enough to gawk at him. "What are you *doing* here?"

"Saving your ass again, it looks like." His smile was genuine, but held reservation, and his gold-filtered gaze was cautious. "Hi, Jo."

"Yes, yes, hi, but what are you *doing* here? How did you know to come? How did—"

"You really think you could just wake me up by shouting through the ether from Ireland and I wouldn't be here when you came home?"

When he put it like that, well, no, I didn't think so. I started to apologize, but before I got that far Coyote looked stiffly at

Morrison, who did not literally hover over us only because hovering was not in his skill set, and admitted, "He called me from the Atlanta airport and told me to get up here as fast as I could. He said you were going to need me. So here I am."

I looked up at Morrison, too. He was leaning over us, face flat with concern. His hands were held in loose fists, as if he was keeping himself from grabbing one or both of us. That stance made me realize there were other people around me, not just my friends, but a handful of bewildered paramedics, one of whom had the defibrillator I'd half heard them talking about. Something had apparently gone very wrong while I was fighting Marcia.

I would follow that thought in a minute. Right now I was too grateful for Coyote's presence, and completely overwhelmed that Morrison, of all people, had called for him. Some of the concern was leaving my captain's expression, but he still hovered. I whispered, "Thank you."

The corner of his mouth curled up. My heart turned into a gooshy mess of goop, then lost whatever hold on cohesion it had when Morrison winked and took a step back, giving us some space. I was still smiling goofily when I looked back at Coyote.

I hadn't known a heart could go gooshy and break at the same time, but the glop of mine shattered. Coyote held himself like he was injured, his shoulders tense and the line of his jaw hard. I'd always been able to read everything in his golden eyes, which let me watch the last vestiges of hope fade away. My own smile disappeared into sorrow, if not regret, and he saw that, too.

Less than a week ago I'd said goodbye to the little girl in me who had loved him, and he'd helped me fight off a corrupting infection, anyway. Today he was here, taking another one for the team, and this time he had to do it while watching me with the man I'd chosen over him. It wasn't fair. He deserved better. And he wasn't going to get it. "Cyrano…"

"It's okay." He cleared his throat, glanced away and looked back. The smile he put on was almost convincing. "You were right, Jo. I couldn't give up the desert for you. It's not fair to ask you to give up the city for me. Even if…" He took a sharp breath, like he could swallow those last two words.

I knew what they led into, though. Even if the student had surpassed the master. Even if I had more power than he could ever dream of. Some part of me thought that if I'd been given that much, maybe I could give a little, too, and go where my less-powerful friend and mentor wanted me to be. The rest of me knew that was a choice, a sacrifice, that had to be made out of unstinting love, untainted by pity, and the truth was, I didn't love him enough. Not now, not after the road I'd been down. He was my childhood and he was magic, and I loved him deeply. But he wasn't the grounded, solid man that I needed, and nothing was going to change that. So I let the *even if* go, because there was nothing I could say.

Well, nothing except, "Thank you for coming. Thank you for being here. Thank you for saving my ass. Again. I'm okay," I said to the paramedics firmly. "You can leave now."

"We…can't," one said, very much like they wanted to and couldn't figure out how.

A little belatedly I realized two of them were kneeling next to Marcia's body, but were staring at me. I pointed at her. "Then help her, not me. I'm fine. You don't have to worry about me. I won't tell anybody."

All of them exchanged glances before the one with the de-fibrillator turned back to Marcia, muttering, "I've met those two before. They're freaks. Forget them. Let's do the job." As a whole, they began to pretend we didn't exist while I, with a jolt, recognized the speaker as a paramedic I'd encountered months ago. Everything was coming around again, and it was only three in the afternoon. I was afraid of who I might see by supper.

That was a bridge to burn when I got there. Once the paramedics were out of immediate earshot, I blurted, "What the hell happened in there? I was doing so well!"

"I got a pretty good look when it was coming at us. I think it was a leanansidhe." The answer came from a totally unexpected source: Suzy, standing a few feet beyond Coyote like some kind of slim teenage goddess. "I've read about them. I've read a lot since this started," she said almost apologetically.

"God, kid, don't be sorry for knowing something. We've all read a lot since this started, but I don't know this one. What's a leanansidhe?"

"An Irish monster. It's this angelic-looking thing that eats hearts as a way of getting at souls."

Hearts for the leanansidhe and livers for Raven Mocker. Just great. I scrunched my face. "Any tips on how to kill it?"

Suzy deflated, which was answer enough. I gave her my best reassuring smile, which probably would have gone over better if I still wasn't plunk on my butt after having had it handed to me, to stretch the metaphor beyond its comfort zone. "Don't worry. We'll figure it out. Still doesn't explain what happened in there. I mean, the wraiths were all about sucking my power out, but this just felt like a meteor landed on me."

Halfway through that I peered at the sky, like a meteor might actually be on the way. One wasn't, but I wondered if I really *had* been doing well against the leanansidhe. Well enough to worry the Master. Maybe he'd put a foot between my shoulder blades and pressed down, giving his creature time to escape. That was a lot more proactive than he'd been in the past, but we were kind of beyond mincing around. Besides, he had at least one and probably two actual avatars running around now, and that had to give him far more physical strength on this plane than I was accustomed to seeing from him.

"Okay," I said, more or less to the sky, "so first we find and destroy or incapacitate the leanansidhe. I'm guessing that'll either bring the Master or Raven Mocker running. We want Raven Mocker first, if we can draw him out, because if we get rid of him, then the Master loses his foothold. Then we take it to the mat with the man himself, and all go out for shawarma."

"How do we take it to the mat if he's lost his foothold?" Coyote asked, but I could see Gary and Annie behind Suzy, and all of them were nodding.

I tapped my temple. "I do it in here. Out there." I waved my hand. "In every realm I can reach into. I'm going to..." I stared at them, all my friends, and suddenly lit up with a grin. "That's what we're going to do. We're going to build a great big power circle to draw their attention, and I'm going to post you all in different planes. We're gonna link up and fight fire with fire. He won't know what hit him."

"Darlin'," Gary said, "ain't all of us magic, you know."

"Says the man who rode with the Wild Hunt for, like, ever."

Suzy spun around, green eyes alight. "You did? You rode with my grandfa— *Oh*."

That, I bet, was the sound of her Looking at Annie, and Seeing the god's green power still swirling around the older woman's aura. "Oh," Suzy whispered again. "Oh, you're very beautiful."

"Thank you, dear." Annie stepped forward and kissed Suzy's cheek. "That's a kind thing to say to an old woman."

Coyote and I took each other's hands, pulling each other to our feet. Annie smiled beyond Suzy at us, her eyebrows lifted with curiosity. "And who is this handsome young man? Introductions were overlooked in the urgency of the moment."

"Your heart was stuttering," Coyote told me quietly. "I didn't think I should take time to say hi."

I put my hand against my chest. Everything in there felt normal, no missed beats or discomfort, no swirl of poison in the blood saying air hadn't been carried well enough. Not even my magic was drained, though I'd certainly felt it sucking out of me as I fought the leanansidhe. "Seriously? I feel fine. I feel great."

Coyote, dryly, said, "You're welcome," and gave me a more honest smile when I knocked into him and mumbled thanks. He turned that smile on Annie, offering his hand, too. "I'm Cyrano Bia, an old friend of Joanne's."

"Annie Muldoon, recently back from the dead."

Coyote froze with his hand in Annie's, trying to look at me without moving his head. "It's okay," I said. "I brought her back. We're, uh…"

"Keeping an eye on me," Annie offered. "Don't worry, young man. I don't fully trust me, either."

"I'm not sure if that makes me feel better," Coyote muttered, but shook Annie's hand, then retrieved his own, managing not to look hurried about it. I introduced him to Suzy, too, and after shaking her hand, he said, "So where do we build your power circle, Jo?"

"An hour ago I would have said here. And it might even still be a good idea, in a kind of take-back-the-night way, except they're going to be cleaning up here for hours. Days." I glanced skyward, letting the Sight wash back over my vision so I could judge the amount of darkness staining the falls' column of light.

It didn't look worse than before. It certainly wasn't better, but maybe my little run-in with Marcia had stopped the taint from spreading.

Marcia. I clutched my chest like I would discover that she'd actually dived into it, physical form and all, though I'd seen her body. "Wait. Wait. Where did that magic go? I mean, I fought it into the ground, but I don't think I defeated it. What…what happened? What did *you* guys see happen?"

"You got between Annie and her, doll," Gary said after a moment. "She tackled you like a pro linebacker. You hit the ground and she…exploded?" He looked at the others for confirmation. Suzy nodded uncertainly, glancing between me and the sky like maybe she'd seen something a little different. I raised a finger to suggest she hold that thought, and she held her breath instead. Or maybe the thought was in her mouth and she was holding her breath so it couldn't escape. Either way, there was holding going on.

"You weren't breathin' by the time you hit the ground," Gary went on. "You were cold and goin' gray. We yelled for help. The paramedics came, checked your pulse, started talkin' about CPR and defibrillators, an' then Coyote here showed up outta nowhere and woke you up again. You been here for the rest."

So things had happened more quickly in the Lower World than in the Middle, as usual. I hadn't missed much, not really. I pointed my still-uplifted finger at Suzy and made questions of my eyebrows.

"She went up," Suzy whispered. "I think she went up. I saw the wings—*Saw* them, I mean?" I nodded my understanding and she continued with more confidence. "I Saw them flare when you smashed into each other, and I got a…a blur, I guess? Just a glimpse, like she was running away."

"Or running to," I said grimly. I'd have been happier if she'd squished into the ground and disappeared, since that was where the pressure in the Lower World had forced her. On the other hand, if she'd squished into the ground I would no doubt find ways to read that as returning to the hellish place from whence she came, so maybe it just didn't matter. "Screw it," I said aloud. "Seattle's my town, and Thunderbird Falls is my damned territory. We'll do it here. Morrison?"

He stepped up like he'd never been out of the conversation. Strangely, very few of the professionals were paying attention to us, even though Morrison kept slipping in and out of the actual investigation going on around us. People usually forgot about magic as fast as they could, but I'd never seen them forgetting it while things were still going on under their noses. That wasn't me. I wondered if it was the Master, or if it was just pragmatic desperation on the part of humanity. Hear no magic, see no magic, speak no magic. Just get on with life, even if life meant picking up the pieces of the violently dead in preference to noticing a gathering of magic-users in its midst.

A *large* gathering, because even if the cops weren't paying attention, the murder witnesses were. They were drawn to the falls *because* it was magic, and enough of them had some trace of talent that Marcia's and my little throw-down hadn't gone unnoticed. They were gathering around us in a loose circle, far enough back to be unobtrusive, but definitely interested. "We're going to need to get them out of here," I said to Morrison, then lifted my voice.

"Look, everybody. Magic Seattle people everybody, I mean."

A ripple went through the onlookers, surprise mixed with the first hint of humor they'd felt since the murders. Nobody talked about Magic Seattle in an out-loud voice, not even at the falls. Some of them glanced toward the cops and investigators, who paid us no attention at all. I wondered if I was holding a "don't look here" shield in place, but I didn't seem to be. It was just easier not to see us.

I bet that wasn't going to last, once I got started. "Listen to me. You all just witnessed something horrible, and once the shock wears off you're probably going to want to do something about it. I have something for you to do: go home."

Morrison's warning tone came over quietly: "Walker..."

"I know. I know they need to be interviewed and all of it, Morrison, but listen to me." I addressed everybody else, too. "There is something *bad* coming down the pipeline. The power here is already tainted. It's going to start swilling around Seattle pretty soon, and I can't be everywhere at once. You guys need to become Seattle's first line of defense. I want you to go home, or go to your community centers or your churches, wherever you think you can do the most good, and I want you to shield it. Physically, with magic, if you can, or with prayers if you're a believer, or good thoughts if you're not. I want you to call your friends, especially the Magic Seattle ones, and ask them to do the same. Call in sick to work, or do it from work, I don't care. Protect the schools. Put everything you can between this city and the thing that did *that*." I pointed beyond them at the bodies. "Because Seattle's going to need your help."

Somebody said, "Who are you?" and somebody else asked, "What's coming for us?" at the same time.

I wished I had a name that would inspire confidence in the hearts of the listeners, but I wasn't a superhero. "I'm what woke up to watch over Seattle after Hester Jones and the other shamans died two Christmases ago. My mother was the Irish Mage, and my father serves the land with healing hands. I'm Joanne Walker, and Death is coming down the line."

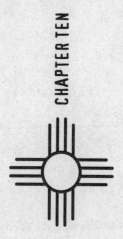

CHAPTER TEN

Saturday, April 1, 3:25 p.m.

Not in a million years did I think that would be enough, but to my bewilderment, people nodded and broke into smaller groups or away. I couldn't help remembering the bonfire the now-dead coven and I had set in Ravenna Park, which no one had noticed, either. Magic had a way, consciously or not, of going unseen. Shields shone here and there, some as sturdy-looking as my own, encompassing one or two or five people. They merged and strengthened as they passed by one another, then faded back to normalcy when people parted again. Men and women stopped to talk to the cops, leaving their contact information, and after Morrison spoke to them, the cops let the witnesses go, furrows creased between their eyebrows.

A few of the adepts put their hands to their hearts as they met my gaze on their way past. I nodded, trying to look confident instead of confused, and when the bulk of them had left, I breathed, "I cannot believe that worked."

"I can." Suzy's eyes were bright. "You were like the president or something. You sounded like a, a, like a king. Like my grandfather. And you're *glowing*."

I glanced at myself, then at my other friends. Gary nodded, a smile twitching his mouth. "Even I can see it, doll. You could lead armies, General."

"I told you I don't want to be a general, Gary. I don't want to be sending those people into battle."

"An' I told you sometimes we gotta do things we don't like. They're gonna keep the city safer, ain't they?"

"And maybe make themselves incredibly vulnerable in the effort."

"Then we better get this thing finished before too many folks get hurt. Tell us where you want us, sweetheart."

I looked at the falls' tainted power again and pressed my lips together. "What I really want is for us to surround the falls and reclaim it, but that means…healing its magic. Twelve or thirteen people died to contaminate it. That's a lot of black magic, and I'm not sure…" My gaze skittered to Annie.

She bowed her head. "I won't participate, of course."

"That's the thing. I'm not sure you shouldn't. I can't keep an eye on you if you don't. And the touch of power they've left in you means you might be exactly the key I need to call Raven Mocker or even the Master straight to me. Or you might be the fracture point." That wasn't exactly the most delicate way I could have put it.

Gary's face went bleak. "Listen here, doll, that's my *wife* you're talkin' to. You watch your tongue."

Annie put her hand on his arm. She looked far less fragile than she had in the hospital. I couldn't decide if that was good or bad. "It's all right, Gary. We know this is difficult."

"I don't know that," the big man growled. "You're my Annie, sweetheart. I *know* that."

"I could keep an eye on her," Coyote offered, but I shook my head.

"No, I need you in the circle, 'yote. You're my left hand, man. I wouldn't know what to do without you. And I can't do without Suzy, either, because you're kind of fiery green power wrapped in girl skin," I finished to her.

"Which means I might be the vulnerable point, too," she reminded me. "My visions are still black, Ms. Walker."

"I know, but…" This wasn't going to work. It hit me hard enough that I rolled back on my heels, frowning faintly around my group of friends. The concept was solid, but Annie and Suzy represented too much vulnerability, and I had nobody that I could set to watch over them that I couldn't use *more* inside the circle. "But it's such a good idea!"

That came perilously close to a whine. I stared at the gathering again. Morrison, with the magical aptitude of a turnip. Gary, about that magical himself, but invested with a certain long view, after his adventures with Cernunnos. Suzy, bursting with magic and maybe already in danger. Annie, back from the dead and unquestionably tainted, but maybe a useful tool. And Coyote, the only one of us who knew more about magic than I did. I wished Billy was here. I knew he'd be here soon, but I needed him now.

"Shit." I stomped in a circle, then pointed a finger at Coyote. "Okay. You're going to have to keep all of them safe, 'yote. I'm going to have to do the power circle by myself."

Five jaws dropped in perfect synchronization, and after a heartbeat, five voices all started talking at once. "Are you crazy, doll—? You're going to try healing the falls alone—? Are you nuts—? You're going to call the Master or the Raven Mocker down on you all by *yourself*—? What're you thinking—? Don't you remember what happened when you faced Raven Mocker in North Carolina, Walker—? You can't be serious—"

"Jo," Coyote said under all of it, quietly enough to be heard clearly, "I can't shield like you do. If I falter—"

"You won't. You can't." It was very simple, as far as I was concerned, and I put the fact that reality didn't work that way firmly out of my head. Sometimes reality *did* work that way, and right now I needed it to. "They need you, and Cyrano, in all the time I've known you, you have never failed to come through for me when I needed you."

"No pressure, then."

I smiled lopsidedly. "None at all. Look, Annie may be tainted, Suzy may be tempting, but I'm the big shiny red target. If he or they can take me out, everybody else becomes much easier, so I think if I lay down some bucket loads of power here, anybody coming for us is going to gun for me. Just keep things on the down-low while I do the showy stuff."

Somewhere in there I concluded that was probably the wrong approach. I didn't *know* that Coyote was envious of my supersize power set, but it couldn't be easy to watch me surpass him. On the other hand, surpassing him meant I was, in fact, the shiny red target, which really ought to be some kind of comfort. Nobody in their right mind would want to be in my position right now.

Which position was already beginning to sketch a power circle around the falls. It was going to be a pain in the ass, with bluffs to climb and probably a corner of parking lot to encompass, but I wanted to make it as round as I could. I clapped Coyote on the shoulder as I stepped away. He gave me one last unhappy look, then gathered the others closer with his desert-sky-and-dunes aura extending.

Morrison's voice was the last thing to break Coyote's protective circle. "Walker." I looked back. "Watch yourself, Joanne."

I flicked a lighthearted salute that I meant all the way to my bones. "Aye, aye, Captain."

I couldn't get over the idea that nobody was trying to stop me. Police officers and forensics teams and an increasingly large gathering of busybodies were in the area, with the latter being fended off by some impatient-looking cops, but nobody seemed to take any notice of me climbing bluffs and muttering greetings in each of the cardinal directions. There had to be some kind of low-key "look away" vibe emanating from me, even if I wasn't aware of putting it off. Most of the time I wasn't aware of keeping my shields up anymore, either, so maybe the two things were going part and parcel. I was grateful, but I also felt a niggling sense that it would be important to figure out at some point soon.

Not right now, though. I had bigger fish to fry. A handful of stepping stones got me across the head of the falls themselves, but I had to go into the lake to keep the circle from being lopsided. I figured the lake, like the parking lot, had been part of what was affected by the falls' birth, so it seemed appropriate even if it meant finishing the circle with wet feet.

When it was done, since my feet were wet anyway, I went back up to the top of the falls and stood in them. They were about calf-deep, rushing water more powerful than I expected. I spent a moment or two looking up the stream that fed them, wondering where all that water came from. We'd screwed up the water table mightily when we'd created the falls. All the local neighborhoods had been without water for weeks while the city got it fixed. I still felt bad about that. Maybe later I would go around, knock on everybody's door and apologize. Right now, though, I tipped my chin up to take one more look at the contaminated column of power.

It was, frankly, huge. Vast. Enormous. Very large. Troublesomely large, really. It had been made clear to me over the past fifteen months that I had unusually deep reserves of magic. I came from two magical bloodlines. I was a new soul, mixed up fresh for this fight. New souls apparently came with boundless energy. No common sense, but lots of energy. Put it together and I was something special, and I had repeatedly pushed the limits of that specialty. Often, admittedly, because I didn't know where they were.

I didn't have to know where they were to be daunted by a pillar of magic broad enough that three of me couldn't have put our arms around it, particularly when that pillar was stained and dripping gray. If I wanted to cleanse it, I was going to have to empty my reservoirs. That was a scary prospect, given what else I had to do today. But cleansing it was the only way to be sure it didn't rain down poison on Seattle, and that it didn't keep feeding the Master through his avatars. And I needed him as weak as I could get him, because I wasn't fooling myself. Cosmically speaking, he was a very large fish, and I was a wiggly little tadpole.

"But I've got *spirit,* by gum," I muttered, then snorted laughter at myself. Well, it worked in the movies. Human ingenuity and spirit overcame the worst odds. I'd take my inspirations where I could find them. Stomach clenched, eyes still on the column of magic, I finally triggered the power circle, awakening it.

A roar deafened me. Shook me right to the bone, leaving me trembling in the waterfall's current. I wasn't used to magic having *sound,* but the rise of my power circle did, like a shout against the darkness.

Darkness answered, slamming out of the column to smash against the walls of my circle.

I knew instantly that I was never going to win.

Panic surged in my belly. I clamped down on it, certain I wouldn't get out of there alive if I let myself panic. It still sent cold thrills through me, yellow-orange spider legs of fear shooting through my power. The taint swarmed toward those spikes of fear, hungry for them. That didn't exactly make it easier to tamp down on them, which was all too obviously a feedback loop I didn't want to be part of. I wrapped my arms around myself, feeling the cold pressure of my hands even through my coat and clothes. But it helped: hugs always helped, and this one was invested with reinforcing my personal shields. Terror didn't so much disappear as get tucked deep into the blankets like a hard-to-find cat.

The tainted magic of a dozen slaughtered witches scraped and scrabbled at the walls of my power circle even after I'd gotten my fear under control. Tendrils held them to the column, white magic leaking out like so much lifeblood, black magic surging back in as it passed through the corrupted souls. The falls' magic darkened further with every passing moment. I might have phenomenal cosmic power, but I couldn't hold back a year's worth of magic being corrupted. Not all in one go. My mother had done it in Ireland over the course of her lifetime, and in the end it had taken a goddess to ignite the power Mom had laid down. I was not in a position to repeat that feat, not today.

But if I couldn't heal it, I could at least use it to draw the leanansidhe's attention, and through her, the Master. Raven Mocker was out there somewhere, too, probably heading for Seattle, but I was going to have to deal with that later.

I seemed to be putting a lot of faith in there being a later. Some part of me was therefore confident. That was a relief. Unless it was just raging stupidity, not confidence, which wasn't so much of a relief. I decided not to think about it, and to distract myself, went ahead and let that clamped-down fear back out again.

Screams of glee shattered through the power circle as the corruption swept down on the freshly offered emotion. Food. Dark emotion and blood were food to the Master. I wasn't about to offer up any blood, but I had no problem with letting anger follow fear. I pushed it out of me, unloading myself into the column of rising power, and after a while realized I was bellowing. "You want it, buddy? Come and get it. Right here, a delicious Joanne sandwich full of how much I hate you. You have fucked up my life, asshole, and I am in the mood to give a little back. Come on, eat up, because you and me, we've got a reckoning today!"

I felt something ripple the edges of the power circle. A *purr,* vibrating and tickling, like I'd pleased a giant cat. The darkness gathered, taking a shape: Marcia, massive, winged, deadly and strangely beautiful. Her mouth opened in something that looked like a razor-sharp laugh, and the purr ripped through the circle again.

My fear and anger disappeared like a tap had been turned off, replaced by satisfaction. It surprised both of us—Marcialeanansidhe because she'd been feeding off the fury, strengthened by it, and me because I'd kinda figured blind rage was all that was gonna get me through this. But a deeper and smarter part of me knew I'd been pouring out all that emotion as a gauntlet, and now somebody had picked it up. I had every reason to be satisfied.

Marcia's silver wings pounded hard enough to disturb the power column itself, then closed around her. She contracted, making a weird little inverse hiccup sound, then did it again. She seemed more solid after the second one, less of a shining ghost. It happened again, then again, faster each time. I gathered magic, preparing for the inevitable attack, but not certain what would happen if I struck first.

In less than thirty seconds she'd reduced from giant-size to human-size. Her wings unfurled and she lifted her eyes, full of a dark sparkle.

Then she blew me a kiss and walked out of the circle.

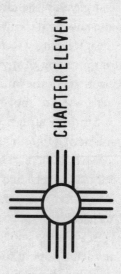

CHAPTER ELEVEN

I stood there stunned for an embarrassingly long time, gaping at where she'd walked away. She shouldn't have been able to. The circle was a keep-things-in circle, meant to contain the power of the falls.

It came clear to me in slow, agonizing heartbeats.

I'd had her. God damn it, I'd had her. When she'd hit me and I'd pulled her into the Lower World, it had disembodied her. Now with this stupid-ass stunt, I'd poured enough anger and fear into the circle to reincorporate her. And she'd taken all that emotion, *my* emotion, and walked out of *my* circle because she tasted of *me*.

I'd walked right into the Master's trap. Forget rage. I bordered on despair, my power circle faltering as the magic sustaining it shriveled with horror. I had made everything worse. Again. I mean, *maybe* Morrison was just outside the circle, had noticed Marcia walking away and had shot her dead, but I couldn't hear the echoes of a gunshot and I doubted a bullet would take her down anyway.

I gave up the circle, letting it go with no ceremony at all, and collapsed to my knees in the waterfall. That was a terrible idea: freezing water splashed to my armpits as it rushed by, no more caring of my presence than of the rocks it also passed over. Hypothermia would not help matters, but I couldn't get myself to move. I was probably less danger to the world as a frozen lump in a stream than fighting this battle, if my method of fighting was to give the bad guys a leg up in getting a foothold here. The Sight had slid off when I dropped, and I looked over Lake Washington as if I'd never seen it before. The water was hard and blue, with white light bouncing off to half blind me. Sunlight warmed my hair enough to contrast with the iciness of my skin. I lifted one hand to put it in my hair, hoping to warm my fingers, but instead cold water drizzled down my neck and made me even colder. Things were not going as I'd planned. I sat there awhile, trying to figure out what to do next.

"You fell." Coyote and Morrison were both there, gazes concerned and hands extended. I looked at them dully, then put my hands in theirs.

It was about as much as my water-laden, half-frozen muscles could manage. They had to pull me to my feet, and even so, I fell, soaking Morrison almost as badly as I was drenched when he caught me. We got out of the waterfall's stream and Coyote slung his leather coat over my shoulders. Its warmth made me start shivering violently. He said, "Jo," in a perfect blend of exasperation and worry.

Desert heat rolled over me, a light touch of his healing power sinking into my bones and driving the chill from my body. It did squat-all to dry me off, but after several seconds I regained enough motor control to squirm out of my coat and start wringing it. It hadn't gotten wet when I'd fallen in a river in North Carolina. Apparently I'd spilled enough magic just now that my subconscious couldn't cope with details like that. Coyote took the coat and began wringing it himself so I could rub my chest instead. "Th-thanks."

Morrison stepped up to wrap his arms around me. His body temperature felt like it was about five hundred degrees, compared to mine. I expected to see steam rise where we touched as I huddled against him gratefully. "You fell," he repeated. "What happened?"

"Everybody's okay?" I whispered. "The shields held, Coyote? Nobody attacked?"

"Attacked? No. You did it." Coyote was hushed with awe. "You did it, Jo. I didn't think you could."

"I did what? I let Marcia walk right out? Yeah. Yay. Good job me."

They both stared at me, blue eyes and gold equally befuddled. Coyote nodded toward the falls. "No, you *did* it. You cleansed the magic here."

I stared back at them, uncomprehending. It took a while to think to use the Sight, to look beyond them at the column of magic rising from Thunderbird Falls.

It was white again, the taint entirely vanished. Morrison must have seen recognition of the fact in my face, because he gave a sudden grin and clapped my shoulder. "I knew you could do it, Walker."

"No." I sounded faint. "No, I mean, maybe I did, but I didn't. If the dark magic is gone it's because she needed it to reincorporate. Like the wraiths feeding Raven Mocker's arrival, Morrison. Oh, we struck a blow, maybe," I said bitterly. "Two of them. We took Annie back first and then we knocked the leanansidhe out of Marcia, probably because it wasn't as firmly embedded in Marcia as it would've been in Annie. But then I built it a nice big circle to suck power from and filled it up with my own hate and now she's out there again and it's all my fault."

I was proud of myself. I'd come a long way in the past fifteen months. When this started, those last three words would have been pure snivel. Now they were grim acceptance. I felt Coyote and Morrison exchanging glances, and by some arcane male signaling, it was apparently decided that Morrison should speak. "Walker, Marcia Williams's body is down there by the falls. The paramedics have been working on her since you and she crashed together. Remember? They declared her while you were up here."

"…the leanansidhe didn't take the body back?"

Morrison shook his head. Hope lit and fizzled in me all at once and I had to repeat myself to even start believing it. "You mean she didn't reincorporate?"

Carefully, like he thought I had perhaps dropped forty or so IQ points along the way, Morrison echoed, "She didn't reincorporate, Walker."

I swayed, running through the implications of that, half-aloud. "So that's good, then. Because it means she's just a malevolent spirit right now. And it's bad, because it means that she needs a body. Oh, God." I straightened up, all malaise burning away. "Malevolent spirits. Any of the mediums in Seattle could be vulnerable, Morrison. *Billy*. Have you heard anything from Billy since this started?"

"He's on his way down here now."

"No. Not here. Not—agh! You left Suzy and Annie alone!" I shook the men off and ran for the bluff, which was another of those things I didn't think through so well. Lucky for me, I didn't have enough momentum to really fly off the fifteen-foot-high cliff face, and mostly only slid and crashed my way down its rough slope. I looked like a mud bunny when I hit the bottom, water and soft dirt caking most of my body. I wiped my face clean as I ran for the Muldoons and Suzy, and concluded from Suzy's sudden burst of laughter upon my arrival that I hadn't done a very good job. She clapped her hands over her mouth apologetically. I smeared more muck around, sighed and gave up. "Are you all right?"

"She came at us." Suzy's humor fell away like it had never existed. She tapped her temple. "I Saw her, silver against the black, and I got between her and Annie. She wanted me. It was like I felt her tasting the green inside me, but I braced myself and she hit the black first and…it was like it scared her, Ms. Walker. She ran. Away," she added as my gaze went to Annie. "That way." She pointed west, which brought my attention back to her.

"Can you track magic?"

Suzy's eyebrows turned quizzical. "Track it?"

"See where it's going, or gone. Like it's left a trail?"

Her eyebrows dropped, and beneath them her expression became nonplussed. "Sure. Can't you?"

"…no. No, I can't."

She brightened up like I'd given her a pony. "Really? I can do something you can't? That's cool! I wonder why!"

Gary cleared his throat with a rumble. "I'm guessing it's 'cause it's your grandpa who's the god of the Wild Hunt, sweetheart. Wouldn't be much of a hunter if he couldn't track something. Maybe it came down through the genes."

That made such perfect sense I wanted to kick myself for not dragging Suzy in on a couple of cases where tracking magic would have been really, really handy. Like with the windigo. Or the werewolf. Then I reminded myself she was fifteen and hauling her out on police-turned-magic cases would probably be illegal, never mind the obvious dangers. On the other hand, she was here now and I already had to keep her in sight so I could keep her safe, so I might as well take advantage. "Can you See where she's *going?* Or if she's stopped anywhere, or—"

Suzy's scleras blazed green as she ignited her power. "A park. A baseball par—oh!" The fire in her eyes shut down, fear replacing brilliant color. "I felt it, Ms. Walker. The black. It…" She shuddered and wrapped her arms around herself, looking exactly like the lost little girl she'd been when we first met. "It surged when I used my magic. It was trying to get deeper in. I don't want to use it again."

"You don't have to." I put my arm around her shoulders and squeezed, forgetting I was covered in wet mud. She made an excellent "Blee!" face and tried to cringe away politely. I said, "Oh, God, sorry," and tried brushing muck off her, only to compound the problem. I knew I was making it worse, but I still couldn't stop myself until I took a deep breath and physically stepped back. It didn't take a genius to interpret my frantic attempts to tidy Suzy as apology for messing up with the leanansidhe. Once I was far enough away that I couldn't spontaneously begin my grooming efforts again, I said, "Woodland Park. It's got to be. It's still a black mark on Seattle's psyscape."

Morrison and Coyote, the latter carrying my trench, joined us again just in time to hear me say the last few words. Morrison gave me exactly the look I deserved for coining a word like *psyscape,* but it got across what I needed it to. "If I'd known that was going to be an issue I'd have asked Melinda to wash it. All right. I guess that's where we're going, then."

"You might want a shower first, Walker."

For a moment I worked on twisting that around until it sounded like an invitation, but Morrison's tone kind of forbade that. I made a face. "I'm pretty sure the Master isn't going to care if I'm fresh and lemon-scented, Morrison."

"Probably not, but you rolled through something unfortunate on your way down, and if you want the rest of us to put up with you all day, you need a shower."

Oh. And I'd smeared it on Suzy, too. I pulled a wan smile together. "At least the car's a rental?"

"I knew it!" A triumphant voice pierced not only our discussion, but the general background noise of cops doing their job at a crime scene.

My spine went rigid as an iron bar. The voice approached, exultation increasing as it got closer. "I *knew* you had to be involved. First a woman returns from the dead at Seattle General, then a mass murder at Thunderbird Falls? Joanne Walker *had* to be here. I knew it!" The voice stopped behind me, then said, "What have you been rolling in, Detective Walker?" with distinct distaste.

I sighed. "I'm trying not to think about that, Ms. Corvallis. And it's just Joanne now. I left the department a couple of weeks ago." I turned to face Laurie Corvallis, Channel Two news reporter, as I spoke.

She looked like she'd been put on this earth as a compare-and-contrast to Joanne Walker. Like me, Laurie was of mixed ethnic background, only she was petite and striking, light blue eyes emphasized by warm brown skin tones and long black hair. She was also possessed of an impeccable dress sense, a sleek trench coat open to reveal a blouse just red enough to be stunning without seeming aggressive, and a genuinely terrific knee-length black wiggle skirt. I supposed I'd want to be dressed to the nines, too, if I was likely to be broadcast on national news at any moment.

Speaking of which, her cameraman, whose name I'd never learned, was a few steps behind her. He tilted his head out from behind the camera in greeting, then went back to looking through the lens. I wondered if he became detached from the world, watching it through a camera lens all the time, but it didn't seem like the time to ask. "I hear you're coming up in the world, Laurie. Congratulations. But there's no story here for you."

"Oh, there's a story, all right. I'll just never be able to tell it." Her appraising gaze swept everybody with me, lingering on Annie.

"Then why bother? You gave me the windigo footage."

Laurie glanced back at me, almost surprised. "Because it's my job to find out what's going on, Dete—you quit?"

"Being a shaman and being a cop were becoming mutually incompatible."

Sounding not at all professional or predatory, Laurie said, "Wow. Sorry to hear that. Ray said you were turning into a good cop. I wonder why he didn't mention you leaving."

"You're still dating Ray?"

"None of your business." The response was snappy, but she smiled, so I figured they were still dating. That was kinda cool. Ray was one of my coworkers, a fireplug of a man who seemed way below Laurie's league. On the other hand, he was obviously discreet, if he hadn't mentioned that particular bit of office gossip to his girlfriend the reporter, and a reporter would probably appreciate discretion in a partner. I hoped they lived happily ever after.

Laurie, sharing none of my sentiment, picked up where she'd interrupted herself. "It's my job to find out the heart of the story, Joanne. It's not about telling it, or not always. It's about knowing."

"You should've been a spy."

"I said *not always*." Laurie Corvallis actually sparkled, nearly winking, as she said that, and then her sparkles turned diamond-hard. "So I'll be coming with you."

"...okay."

Identical squawks of protest rose from several throats. I focused on Morrison, who had the most real-world authority of our gathering. "Look, we can spend a lot of time and energy arguing with her, and have her follow us anyway, or we can take her along, keep an eye on her, and let her help us keep an eye on each other."

"It's dangerous."

"I'm an investigative reporter, Captain. I do danger with lunch."

"She was awesome with the wendi..." I had no idea why I was trying to convince Morrison. It wasn't his decision. It wasn't even my decision. I knew Laurie well enough to understand it was hers alone. "Well, anyway, I'm going home to take the world's fastest shower. Maybe we should all get into Laurie's news van. There's probably something metal I can sit on and not stink up, in there."

The cameraman emerged from behind the camera again, this time with an expression of dismay, but Laurie's satisfaction trumped it. "Great idea. I'll start my interviews while he drives. Mrs. Muldoon, I'd like to start with you. What's it like coming back from the dead?"

Annie Muldoon gave Laurie a penetrating look, then put her hand on Gary's arm and let him escort her away from the crime scene. Laurie, undeterred, chased after them. Morrison touched my shoulder, stopping me as I started in that direction, too. "You have too many people to watch over already, Walker."

"She's like a Komodo dragon, boss. Once she gets hold of something she keeps her teeth in it until it rots and falls apart. Or something like that."

"I know. I'm just worried about you, Jo." He emphasized my name a little, bringing us closer when I'd used the distancing *boss* nickname. "How are you going to keep an eye on all of us?"

I watched the others trailing along behind the Muldoons and Laurie, and sighed. "You and Laurie are probably the least vulnerable to magical attack, and Coyote can protect himself and some of the others. Gary. I'll pair Coyote with Gary, because they know each other, they've worked together before. Annie and Suzy I've got to keep with me. Annie, Laurie, Suzy, jeez, if we had any more ee-sounding names we'd be a girl band."

Morrison laughed. "Joanie."

I twitched and he laughed again. "We'll put Suzy on the bass," he decided. "The long pale hair, the haunted green eyes. It'd be her style. Corvallis is clearly percussion. That makes Mrs. Muldoon lead guitar, which leaves you as the vocals. Can you sing, Walker?"

"Tell me your favorite song, then ask me that question again in a few weeks."

Morrison, straight-faced, said, "'Corvette Sally.'"

Laughter burst out of me so loudly Gary and Annie glanced back to see what was so funny. Beaming, I said, "I'd kiss you if I wasn't filthy. 'Corvette Sally.'" I laughed again, and Morrison let his stern demeanor crack until a grin shone through. Still giggling, I shoved my hands in my pockets so I wouldn't hug him, and tilted my head toward Laurie's van. "C'mon. Let's go get a shower and go hunting bad guys."

CHAPTER TWELVE

I didn't live all that far from Thunderbird Falls. A couple of miles, maybe three.

Laurie Corvallis asked a truly amazing number of questions in three miles. It didn't seem to bother her at all that nobody was answering, or that when she turned her attention on Suzy—the most vulnerable of us to interrogation—that I interrupted before her first question was out. "Leave her alone, Laurie, or I'm going to come lean on you."

Contempt pulled her pretty face into a shark's deadly sneer. "You think a little pressure from a former police officer is going to stop me from getting the story?"

"No, Laurie." I waved one filthy arm. Gary, who had manfully chosen to sit next to me—because Morrison had to drive the rental car to my house, and therefore wasn't available to draw the short straw—shrank back. "I mean lean. Literally. I will get you all dirty, and you won't look nice for your national news stories."

"I'm not afraid of a little dirt, Joanne." She didn't, however, try asking Suzy any more questions. Suzy looked like she couldn't decide whether she was relieved or disappointed. Probably both. I'd have been, at her age.

Somewhat to my dismay, the cameraman drove us straight to my apartment building without asking where it was. I eyed Laurie, who shrugged and offered one of her barracuda smiles. I decided not to push it and we all fell out the back of the van like clowns being disgorged from a Volkswagen Beetle. Morrison pulled up and gave us an amused look as we got straightened out and headed inside. Gary and Annie called for the super-slow elevator in the building's lobby and the rest of us took the stairs up five flights, me in the lead. I was unlocking the door when it occurred to me I'd left for Ireland without stopping at home first, and that in the ensuing two weeks everything in the fridge had probably taken on a life of its own. I muttered, "You might want to hold your breath," to my little army of followers, and pushed the door open.

Not only did it not stink, but the whole place looked unusually clean. I wasn't the world's worst housekeeper, but I wasn't the best, either. I stopped inside the door and peered around dubiously. Everything was in its place, living room sofa, comfy chairs, computer desk in the far corner. I was pretty sure there had been random articles of clothing lying around when I'd left. I was *certain* the kitchen, off to my left, had not been sparkling. Everybody barged in behind me, pushing me farther into the apartment, but once there I turned and gave Morrison a suspicious look.

"I had to drop by to get your drum, Walker. I thought I'd leave the place tidier than I found it."

"If I wasn't filthy..." I repeated, and he smiled in a way that warmed the cockles of my heart, even if I didn't know what cockles were. "Someone order food," I suggested. "There should be a menu for Mrs. Liu's Chinese delivery by the fridge."

"Food, Walker?"

"If we're stopping for a shower, Annie hasn't eaten anything in, like, five years, and I haven't had much since yesterday morning."

"You ate half the food in North Carolina yesterday morning," Morrison pointed out, but he headed for the kitchen with both Suzy and Laurie's notoriously food-bribable cameraman on his heels. Coyote threw himself into my couch and Laurie sat across from him in one of the chairs, clearly intending to pepper him with more questions. I'd never had so many people in my apartment at the same time before. It was almost like a party, except I wasn't sure if people would have end-of-the-world parties. Probably. I excused myself as Gary and Annie came in, and went to shower.

After a very swift mental debate, I took my boots off and got into the shower fully clothed. At least that way the jeans and sweater would be rinsed and not lying around stinking up my apartment. Skimming out of soaked denim was not my favorite thing to do, but I struggled free, rinsed everything again once I was out of it, and threw it in the end of the tub, where I hoped I would remember it before it grew mold. Then I stood there, eyes closed, short hair plastering to my head, as I breathed steam.

For more than a year I'd been lurching from one crisis to another, rarely stopping to think in the midst of them. In North Carolina I'd started to realize I was never going to have time to unwind—to eat, to shower, to tell somebody I loved him—unless I *made* time for it. A year ago I'd have run around Seattle smelling of dog poop, too, in my frantic attempts to keep all the balls in the air before something even worse went wrong. In retrospect, I probably could have stopped to eat a few more times than I had, without anything going significantly more awry than it already had. I might have even avoided a few conks on the head, in fact.

Which didn't mean I could stay in the shower all day long. I sighed and opened my eyes, glancing at the pile of wet clothes at the end of the tub. I kind of wished I might see Coyote there, cock-eared and grinning around a lolling tongue, the way I'd seen him the first times we'd met after my shamanic gifts had reawakened. Odds were I would never see him like that again, which, given that I was naked and in a relationship with somebody else, was as it should be. It still gave me a sad twinge, a heart flutter for something that I'd left behind. Regret was probably part of growing up, but if so, it sucked. I dragged myself out of the hot water and into a fuzzy towel, and attacked my hair with a blow-dryer. It needed trimming. My hair, not the blow-dryer. The short-cropped bangs were inclined to brush my eyelids now, and the pixie cut was hiding the tops of my ears. A shower and food were within reason, but probably stopping to get a haircut was a little more blasé about crises than I should be. Some gel lifted the spiky bangs far enough out of my eyes for government work, and I went to find clothes.

I didn't own anything besides the new leather trench that seemed really appropriate for endgame battles, so I put on clean jeans and a warm sweater over a tank top, found another pair of stompy boots and returned to my guests as laughter erupted in the living room. It silenced abruptly with my arrival, which went a long way toward making me feel awkward and self-conscious. I stopped in the bedroom doorway, hands twisting together like a nervous ingénue.

Morrison got up and came to give me a kiss. "I was telling Mrs. Muldoon how we met."

"Oh." My ears hurt from turning so red. "I didn't think it was that funny a story."

"Maybe 'cause you ain't heard Mike tell it." Gary got up as the doorbell rang, letting a scraggly-bearded kid bearing about forty bags of Chinese food into the apartment. I edged past Morrison in search of my wallet, and was obliged to accept the cash everybody handed over, because I had about enough money to cover my share of what appeared to be one of everything on Mrs. Liu's menu. Judging from how we tore into it, it looked like one of everything might be almost enough for eight hungry people. Annie, who was by far the smallest of us, put enough away for three men Morrison's size, and slender teenage Suzy ate as steadily as a metronome. I actually looked like a piker in comparison to everyone but Corvallis, who said, "Evidently unlike the rest of you, I ate lunch today," after a modest snack of spring rolls and barbecue pork.

Her cameraman, obviously offended, said, "So did I," then looked faintly guilty at four or five empty boxes spread around him.

Corvallis laughed. "I've never seen you turn food down, Paul."

"If you were the one lugging that camera up and down mountains in your wake…" he said with the cadence of a familiar and unmeant complaint.

I said, "Paul," under that, just audibly enough to be heard. He raised his eyebrows and I made a face. "I didn't know your name. Sorry."

"Nobody does. She's the talent. I just make her look good."

"It's true," Laurie said with a degree of fondness I'd never have attributed to her. It disappeared instantly into a piercing look at me. "So what's the plan, Joanne?"

"I filled her in while you were showering," Coyote said. "It didn't seem like there was any reason not to."

That was an unassailable argument, even if I had the vague, uncomfortable feeling that one shouldn't go around confessing all the complications of the magical life to a reporter. I said, "The plan," like saying the words would make one leap fully formed into my mind, then blew out a breath that verged on being a raspberry. "We're going to Woodland Park. Suzy tracked the leanansidhe's retreat to there, and it makes sense. We—" My cell phone rang, startling me into silence. Practically everybody I knew who might call me was in this room. "Um. I have the horrible feeling that might be important. 'Scuze me." I left a half-finished plate of Mongolian beef balanced on the arm of the couch and went to dig the phone out of my trench pocket.

An unfamiliar male voice said, "Joanne Walker?"

I frowned and retreated to the kitchen, not that a doorway and pass-through wall provided much in the way of silence or privacy. The gathering in the living room quieted down, which was polite, but also meant they could hear every word of my conversation. "Yes?"

An explosive sigh came down the line. "This is Lieutenant Dennis Gilmore. We met in North Carolina, if you remember?"

"Yes. Yes." I put one hand on the counter, clutching it for balance. "Yes, of course I remember you." Lieutenant Gilmore had been his unit's only survivor of Raven Mocker's attack. "What's wrong?"

"Nothing. Nothing, exactly. I just wanted to let you know we've found Daniel Little Turtle's body in Arizona."

My stomach twisted so hard it cut the strength from my knees as I ran through every worst-case scenario I could. I knew people in Arizona. *Coyote* was from Arizona. I looked at him, reassuring myself he was really here. "Arizona? Where in Arizona? What was he doing there?"

Coyote straightened, flicking black hair down his spine in an action strangely reminiscent of his coyote-form's ears twitching with concern. He got up and came to the other side of the counter, leaning on it like he, too, needed bracing. "Phoenix, ma'am."

I crouched, fingers of one hand wrapped around the counter's edge and my forehead pressed against it beside them. My question came out as a thready whisper. "Mark Bragg?"

The beat of silence was worse than any confirmation could have been. Gilmore said, "Missing, ma'am," in cautious tones.

"It's not fair." I was hardly aware of having spoken aloud. I *was* aware that I had begun gently hitting my forehead against the counter's edge, but I couldn't seem to stop myself. Mark Bragg had been a researcher at the University of Phoenix. He'd gotten tangled up in one of my messes, and his twin sister had died of it. He was supposed to be *safe* in Arizona. Far away from me and the trouble that walked with me.

"I'm sorry, ma'am. We're looking for him. His image has been forwarded to the airports and he'll be detained if he tries to fly."

My forehead was starting to hurt, but it didn't stop me from calculating the hours it took to drive from Arizona to Seattle. Lieutenant Gilmore continued speaking as white sparks began showing in my vision, the maybe not-so-gentle impacts starting to have effect. "It appears Daniel Little Turtle did fly, although we'd flagged him, too, ma'am. We just weren't fast enough."

"Why'd he go to Arizona?" I whispered. "Why not come straight here?"

Gilmore cleared his throat. "It may have occurred to him that we'd be looking for him coming off a flight to Seattle, ma'am. You did warn me."

A broken laugh caught in the roof of my mouth. "Lieutenant, what are you telling your superiors about this?"

"The official story remains that there was a disease outbreak in Qualla Boundary, ma'am. My superiors are concerned with finding Patient Zero, that's all. We're still working with the CDC to make certain the incident remains contained. We will continue to do so until Mark Bragg is located and it's determined whether he's infected and contagious." Gilmore hesitated. "Ma'am, why didn't the infection spread among the air travelers on the plane with Little Turtle?"

"You want the official line or the answer?" I stopped hitting my head because it interfered with thinking, and Gilmore deserved me to be firing on all cylinders for this.

"I'll take both."

"Officially, it's spread through touch, and if no one else is infected, we're lucky. The real answer is that first off, you can't make wraiths from people who are still alive. But more importantly, Raven Mocker is trying to find a host strong enough to contain him, and I think spreading himself out right now would do him more harm than good."

"Is Mark Bragg strong enough?"

"No. But if Danny got Raven Mocker halfway across the country, Mark can probably get it up to Seattle."

"And what happens there, ma'am?"

"I take care of it."

Another silence followed my response. Then Gilmore said, carefully, "Ma'am, would it be…better…if we were unable to apprehend Mark Bragg?"

"Yeah."

I could just about hear his next promotion going down the drain in the crispness of his voice: "Thank you, ma'am. I'll keep that in mind. And if I may say so…"

"Say away. God knows you've earned the right."

"Thank you, ma'am. Good luck, ma'am."

"Thank you, Lieutenant." I thumbed the phone off and pressed my forehead against the counter again, then hit it a few more times for good measure.

Coyote eventually said, "Jo?" which made me look up.

The whole gang was gathered on the far side of the counter and in the kitchen doorway, peering at me with nervous concern. "You should all go away from me," I said flatly. "Go away and stay away, because I'm a bad luck magnet like nothing I've ever dreamed."

"And who will protect us from your enemy if we go?" Annie asked with a hint of humor.

I wished I had any to share. Instead I said, "Danny Little Turtle was found dead in Mark Bragg's house," to Morrison, the only one I was sure knew all the players right now.

His face fell, though he recovered quickly. "Where's Bragg?"

"Missing. Presumably on his way here."

"*Who* is Mark Bragg?" Corvallis cut to the heart of the matter, and I let Morrison make the brief explanation about Mark and his sister's involvement in the previous summer's Blue Flu. Laurie glanced between us, her mouth pursed. "Sounds like being a thousand miles away isn't any protection anyway, Joanne."

"Thank you. Thank you, Laurie, that makes me feel a lot better."

"It makes me feel better," Suzy mumbled. "I'd rather be here where I can maybe do something to help instead of hiding out a jillion miles away knowing the bad guy could come for me anyway."

"Kid's got a point," Gary said. "C'mon, Jo. This don't change anything, except maybe giving this Raven Mocker a face. An' that's good, ain't it? 'Cause at least we know who we're lookin' out for."

"Yeah," I said, knowing exactly how petty and nasty I sounded, "but I liked Mark. I didn't like Danny."

Morrison was the only one who looked disapproving. "You're better than that, Walker. Now get up and let's get down to business."

I got up, although I wasn't the least bit sure I was better than that. I didn't want anybody to be dead because of me, but Danny's own anger and hurt had made him a great temporary host for Raven Mocker. It was bad enough that had killed him. Mark Bragg hadn't invited any of this onto himself. He'd just gotten caught up in my world. If I had to pick and choose, at least I could see some kind of cruel cosmic justice in Danny's fate. Mark flat-out didn't deserve any of it. "I hate this."

"None of us love it. Maybe you can save him," Coyote said quietly. "It's what you do, Jo. Don't give up faith yet."

"Okay." I nodded once, then rubbed my fingers over the tender spot on my forehead. "Woodland Park. The leanansidhe's probably going to be sucking as much residual power as she can out of the half-finished power diamond the banshees left there. She needs a host. I'm sure she needs a host. So if she finishes that circle she might be able to draw one there. Someone vulnerable." My stomach curdled again. "Morrison, have you heard from Billy?"

Morrison shook his head and walked away, cell phone already in his hand. Gary snorted. "Holliday ain't the vulnerable type, sweetheart."

"Gary, everybody who's close to me is the vulnerable type right now. I wish to hell I had—"

My mother. For the first and only time in my life, I wanted my mother. My father would have been handy, too, but Mom had brought the fight to the Master in a way Dad clearly never had. She was a mage, a fighter, and I wanted somebody I knew could fill those shoes. Somebody who could protect my friends while I took myself into battle.

"Joanne," Laurie said into my silence, "everybody in this room has decided being at your side is the safer, smarter or more interesting place to be right now. I understand that you feel like you need to protect all of us, but with the exception of Suzy Q there, we're all competent, capable adults. You need to stop thinking about how to protect us and start thinking about how to use us."

I stared at Laurie, vaguely offended. Suzy Q was *my* nickname for Suzanne, although I imagined anybody who'd ever heard of the song or the snack cake probably used it, too. It was no doubt completely in character for Laurie to use it.

I was offended anyway, and took it out on her in snappy tones. "And how am I supposed to use you, Laurie? You're almost completely on the outside of this. You don't have any skills I can use here. You've seen a few things most people would dismiss. Why won't you be *smart,* and get out of here?"

"You're wrong. I don't have any magic, but I have something you can use."

"What?"

A faint cold smile curved Laurie's mouth. "Nerves of steel."

I started to protest, then thought about her lying in the snow, my spear so close to piercing her heart that I'd drawn blood. She hadn't flinched. I said, "Shit," under my breath, and triumph flared through her smile.

"Tell you what." She turned and whirled a finger at the cameraman like she was gathering him up and pointing him toward the door. "You get out of here, Paul. I know your nerves are as good as mine, but we can't use the footage, anyway, and it'll make our urban shaman here feel better."

I said, "Your *what?*" in quiet dismay, barely able to hear myself under Paul's protests and threats that he would bill the station for a full day's work anyway. He stole three more spring rolls on the way out the door, though, so I thought most of the protesting was pro forma. At least it meant being rid of one of them. Nerves of steel or not, I was considering whacking Laurie over the head and leaving her tied up in the bedroom to keep her safe when Morrison returned with his mouth set in a thin straight line.

"Holliday's not answering his phone. I called down to the crime scene and nobody's seen him. I think we'd better get down to that park."

CHAPTER THIRTEEN

Suddenly the forty-five minutes for a shower and food seemed like an unnecessary luxury. I tried stuffing that thought back into my brain and ran for the door. Five adults and a mostly grown teen followed, and for a minute we were a latter-day Keystone Cops struggling into the hall. I popped free and the rest of the knot loosened, though Morrison, from the middle of it, muttered, "We're not all going to fit in the rental. Where's your cab, Muldoon?"

"Back at Seattle General. I didn't think of driving it, what with pullin' off the great escape."

Laurie perked up. "Escape?"

I gave her a quelling glare that did nothing to quell her as we thumped down five flights of stairs. I was used to going on adventures with one or two compadres. Having half a dozen of us was starting to feel silly, but I needed Coyote's expertise, had to keep Annie and Suzy close, and could hardly ditch Morrison or Gary at this late stage of the game. I sent another glare Laurie's way, just in case she might take the hint and depart for greener pastures, but I was wasting my time.

"Call Keith," I suggested to Gary. "Have him drop a spare cab off at Woodland Park. We're going to need it eventually."

"You call him, doll. Pretty young things get told yes a lot more than old dogs do."

"Yeah, but I'll have to buy him flowers." I pulled my phone out and made the call, anyway, while Suzy volunteered, "I can sit on somebody's lap," with the casual air of someone young enough to still do that sort of thing frequently.

Laurie sized herself up compared to everybody else and sighed. "So can I."

"I can't drive a rented vehicle rated for five with seven people in it!"

I lifted my eyebrows at Morrison. "You're the captain of this precinct's police department. Who's going to ticket you?"

His upper lip worked in a way I recognized of old as preceding a top-blowing explosion. It made his mouth look very kissable, which came as something of a relief. I hadn't been losing my mind all those times I'd thought that, back in the day. But he pulled the rant back under control and, with the expression of a man who knew when to give up a fight, gestured for us to all pile into the car. I finished asking Keith at Tripoli Cabs to send a spare car and joined the muddle.

Annie, by dint of being the most fragile in our collective perception, got to ride shotgun, while Laurie, to her obvious delight, sat on Coyote's lap. Coyote didn't look too upset about it, either, and I told myself firmly that it was no longer my business. Shaking my head at unpredictable jealousy, I squished into the center seat while Suzy sat on Gary's lap, put an arm around his shoulder and kissed his cheek, charming him completely. Once we were buckled and settled to the best of our ability, I grunted, "To the park, James."

Morrison shot a startled look at me over his shoulder and I let out a laugh that was too big for the space I was squeezed into. "Sorry. I wasn't being funny. I actually forgot about that. To the park, Morrison, and be quick about it. Or I'm going to asphyxiate."

Gary and Coyote both tried scootching away at that complaint, and for an eighth of a second I could breathe again. Then they relaxed and I got smooshed, but I was a big girl. I could handle a little not-breathing for a while. I kept telling myself that the whole drive over, while Laurie persisted in asking Morrison what I'd meant by *I forgot about that*. Morrison, exasperated, finally said, "You're a reporter, Corvallis. Look it up online if you're so curious."

Laurie looked sullen but subsided as we once more poured out of the vehicle, this time at Woodland Park. I broke away from the crowd, my feet determined to run even if my mind thought I should be hanging back to be the newly appointed superhero Protection Girl.

I didn't get far anyway. We'd come in from the parking lot nearest to the baseball diamond that had been a murder site last winter. My greatest fear was finding the Marcia-shaped leanansidhe laying down new bodies on the old sites, and closing the circle to gain power of her own.

My imagination clearly did not reach far enough.

Ashen-faced people stood along the baseball diamond's lines, just far enough apart that their extended arms didn't quite touch their neighbors' fingertips. Dozens of them, more than I could count at a glance. They all faced inward, and all trembled as if a great force was pulling them ever closer together. Their auras stretched from their bodies, glimmering faintly between each other but mostly dragged toward the pitcher's mound, where the Marcia-shaped leanansidhe stood with her head thrown back and her arms spread. She was translucent, the people on the far side of her wobblingly visible through her semi-solid body.

Billy Holliday stood alone with the creature's shape, his arms wrapped around it as though he could contain all the hatred in the world within the compass of his embrace.

His shields were like nothing I'd ever seen from Billy, so bright, so fierce, that I had to Look twice. It was his colors, orange and fuchsia, but there was something else supporting them. Not Melinda, who was sunshine-yellow and orange, but something more than just Billy allowed him to hold the struggling leanansidhe in place.

It wasn't enough. Threads of the life force she dragged from the gathered adepts slipped through the shields, strengthening her with every passing moment. I couldn't for the life of me understand why she hadn't already taken him, with his gift of seeing and speaking with spirits, but I was grateful for the small favor. His grip shifted, changing to try to contain her as she fought, and I thought he didn't have much more time.

I said, "Coyote," dimly, and reached for his hand. It found its way into mine and I squeezed. "Keep them safe." Then I released him, and poured my soul into trying to break the feed between the leanansidhe and the gathered adepts.

I had built so many shields in recent months, shields that kept a group together and safe. But we'd always *been* together, with the bad guy on the outside, and this time the bad guy was right smack in the middle of us. One shield wasn't going to work. I needed dozens, small, individual, unassailable. Thirty-nine of them, the back of my head informed me as I reached out my magic. Thirty-nine spirits that needed explicit protection, thirty-nine souls that needed to be untangled from the leanansidhe's hunger and returned to their rightful bodies.

I had one of those increasingly rare moments of wondering just how exactly my life had come to this, but for once it was tinged with wry humor. That helped, as if a thread of faint amusement in my seeking magics was a touch of humanity that the leanansidhe couldn't compete with. It dashed along the power I extended, separating one blur of colors from another. Given half a breath to do so, the gathered mediums clawed their auras back into them, too, helping me help them. Unaccustomed to trying to assist people who *could* help me or themselves, I couldn't stop from sending a wash of surprised gratitude down the line, too. Evidently gratitude was also a more human emotion than the leanansidhe could strive for, because it gave the adepts a little more to work with.

Their auras untangled from one another in a sudden rush, the right string pulled to loosen the Gordian knot. The leanansidhe keened, not unlike a banshee, though her sob lacked the soul-shattering edge of banshee cries. She still had hold of the mediums' life forces, but more weakly now. Her physical struggle with Billy heightened. I ground my teeth and sent a tendril of power toward Billy, offering support.

It rebounded like a slap in the face, Billy's aura flaring red-edged with panic. Bewildered, I withdrew with injured feelings. Irrationally injured, because if Billy rebuffed me he had some reason to do so, but I'd only been trying to help. Petulant, I returned all my attention to shielding the mediums.

I had to do it one at a time, which felt like it took forever. It was like laying down layers of paint on a car body: each color had to be selected, marked off, laid down, dried and the tape removed before I could go on to the next. I unthreaded one dazzling aura of yellow and red: Sonata Smith, the one person here I knew well enough to individualize her aura. It was a place to start, which was more than I'd thought I would have. I tucked her aura up against her body before wrapping her, aura and all, in gunmetal shielding that could withstand the worst a leanansidhe could throw at it. I hoped. Again and again, until I felt like a mother hen sitting on thirty-nine glowing eggs that could not be allowed to hatch.

The leanansidhe grew more frantic, but not stronger. She became increasingly translucent, wings spreading and battering the ground and Billy. Even all the power she'd taken on at the falls wasn't enough to keep her borderline corporeal. She really needed a body. Maybe if I could just keep her distracted long enough she'd burn out.

I didn't believe it for a minute. I didn't think the Master would make his final play on grounds that shaky. Still, the leanansidhe clearly went through magic like a penguin went through water, so even if I couldn't burn her out I might be able to keep her weak until I figured out how to kill her.

Like she'd heard the thought, she shrieked again and for half a moment became dust. Billy's arms collapsed around the space she'd been in. He staggered with surprise, looked around, saw me, wheezed, said, "Took you long enough," and dropped to press his forehead to the earth as he caught his breath. The leanansidhe ignored him entirely, coming together with wings solid enough to make sound as she flew at the circle of mediums.

She bounced off.

For an instant I thought she was as surprised as I was. Then I laughed, partly because I could feel her fury at being thwarted, but more, really, because I was so prone to doing that kind of thing myself. I'd never imagined the bad guys might fumble that way, too. But the leanansidhe hadn't thought it through, assuming she could think at all.

They were linked, all the mediums, through the shields I'd built around them. It wasn't exactly a power circle, but it wasn't exactly not, either. The leanansidhe ran at them, slamming from one shielded body to another in an attempt to break through. The tries became more frantic, more directed at individual bodies, until I realized she wasn't trying to break *through*. She was trying to break *in*. Trying to take one of the bodies as a host. I didn't know why she hadn't the moment a medium showed up, though my gaze dropped to the baseball diamond lines.

Every medium was just on the outside of those lines. Just on the outside of the bloody lines written on the earth through the sacrifices of three women. By hook or by crook, they had managed not to cross into territory the Master had marked as his own. I'd seen the glimmer of power shared between them before I brought my own magic into the fray, but only now realized they had managed to create a link between themselves that prevented the leanansidhe from escaping once they were in place. I had sent Seattle's adepts home from Thunderbird Falls, telling them to warn the others and to be wary. I wondered if forewarned had been forearmed, for those gathered here.

Forearmed, I thought irreverently, was half an octopus. What should have been a laugh felt more like a tremor in my chest. The leanansidhe might burn through magic like it was kindling, but she was strong, and I was trying to keep forty people safe. I could keep us here indefinitely—maybe—but I had no idea how to move forward. That was going to become a problem sooner rather than later.

"Stop." Annie Muldoon joined me, her chin set in a way that I recognized as implacable, even though I'd never seen the expression on her face before. "Stop," she said again. "Joanne, this is foolishness. You cannot protect us all."

"I'm not. Coyote's got, what, five of you? Haha." The laugh sounded pathetically like I was actually saying the words in an attempt to inject humor into the situation. Not at all convincing. I would have to work on that, but since it had failed anyway, I gritted out, "I can't stop trying, either."

Nor was I going to, even though I had to speak through clenched teeth. Sweat beaded on my forehead, which was new and unusual. Holding magic wasn't normally a physical effort like this. Of course, I wasn't usually trying to keep three dozen mediums, people whose natural magical talent encouraged them to host other spirits in their bodies, from being possessed, either. My shields glittered around them, swirling and sparking when the leanansidhe renewed her efforts to batter her way into a human body.

"Joanne." Annie sounded worryingly calm. "I want you to look at this gathering. What do you see?"

I sent a fast glance around the baseball diamond, wondering what I should be looking for. Strained faces blanched with fear looked back at me, but I didn't think that was what Annie wanted me to see.

"They're all women, Walker." Morrison's voice was low, distorted with concern and uncertainty. "Why are they all women?"

"They're *not*—" But he was right. Excepting Billy—who was more in touch with his feminine side than any other guy I'd ever known—every other person who'd been called to the field was female.

"He needs a woman." Annie still spoke with great clarity. "I can nearly feel it in my soul, Joanne. I can feel it in the places where his stain still colors my body. He needs a woman of great strength or complete corruption."

Nobody here was completely corrupted. That was kind of the point of holding the line. I opened my mouth to say so and halfway through the first breath realized we *did* have somebody of great strength.

Me.

It all became very clear suddenly. I took half a step toward the hungering leanansidhe, wondering how to prepare myself for possession.

Turned out it didn't matter, because delicate little Annie Marie Muldoon popped me one in the nose.

CHAPTER FOURTEEN

Shocking white pain blinded me for just an instant. I howled like—well, like a banshee, but under the circumstances I wished I could have thought of a different howling thing. At any rate, I howled and clapped my hands to my nose, astonished at the power of Annie's punch, and sent magic sizzling through my own face to clear the pain away.

By that time Annie had put on a burst of speed that somebody recently off her deathbed shouldn't have been able to manage. My shriek of horror sounded high-pitched and girlish above Gary's heart-wrenching bellow. He and Morrison were in motion already, too, but the linebacker and the cop were never going to catch the small woman running pell-mell toward her doom. I gathered every spare wisp of magic in me, knitted it together and threw a net.

Violently green magic, a fire-green blaze, burned my net away before it came near Annie. I whirled on Suzy, whose colorless face vindicated my suspicions. "It wasn't me," she protested, voice rising. "It wasn't me?"

A string of invective tore from my throat. "Coyote! Laurie! Do—do *something* about her!" I spun away from the girl again, launching myself into a flat-out run that had no more chance of catching Annie than Gary or Morrison did.

The leanansidhe, unconstrained by middling details of physicality, whipped around, closing the distance between herself and Annie at a literally inhuman speed. Way too late I remembered I had that trick in my own repertoire, and shrieked *Renee!* inside my skull.

Rattler, not Renee, answered with a burst of snake-speed that drove me forward so fast I felt like my mind was being left behind. Back there, trying to catch up, it remembered that a cheetah had come to Annie when she'd done her spirit quest. That made her astonishing quickness comprehensible, at least to somebody moving with a snake's striking speed.

Unfortunately, the cheetah had a head start, and Renee didn't slip me between seconds this time. Maybe a dreadful, ungrateful part of me would rather Annie took on the leanansidhe than myself, although I really hoped I was a better person than that. Maybe too much of my magic was already tangled up in trying to shield the dozens of mediums. If so, I was starting to hate discovering I had limitations, even if they lay in a range that most adepts would consider stupendous.

I passed Gary and Morrison and was barely ten steps from Annie when the leanansidhe took her.

It hit her in the spine, smashing her to the ground. Furrows kicked up where her hands hit, old grass and dark earth startled at the disruption. Her back arched in the shape of a scream, though no sound escaped her. Blackness erupted in her lungs, the same darkness we'd fought so hard to eliminate. It flowed through her like blood, coloring her skin where thin veins lay near the surface. I hoped like hell it was just the Sight showing me that, that Gary couldn't see it, too. Another convulsion rocked her and she did scream, a tired and weak sound, like she'd been fighting a battle too long already.

Gary fell to his knees, roaring with rage and grief. The Annie-thing twisted to show black, black eyes, and with a terrible smile stretching her mouth. "The body is weak, sure and so. Not the host my master wished for me. Not what he'd prepared, no, but oh, his taste is inside her, and she will grow strong again with my spirit."

Then the horror of her mouth contorted, a visible struggle beneath her very skin. Her eyes filtered from black to fiery green and back again, before the green dominated a few desperate seconds. "Weak so she has to *concentrate* to keep me alive, Joanne. Weak because if she lets me die her master can't come through. Corruption or strength, and I have neither. Kill me now, Joanne. Kill me while I can give you the chance."

She was right. I knew she was right, and, knowing it, I stalked forward. Gary screamed, coming to his feet in a run. Morrison slammed into him, tackling him to the ground. Dirt and grass flew as they fought. Annie allowed herself one anguished glance, then returned her gaze to me. "I've been dead all this time anyway, Joanne. I'm not afraid. Promise me—"

I nodded, took my final step in to her, spun and delivered a roundhouse kick to the side of her head. She didn't even have time to look surprised as she collapsed. Panting like I'd run a sprint, I stood over her unconscious body and whispered, "Absolutely *not*."

Gary bashed into my side like a SCUD, and as I hit the ground I felt a pained ghost of amusement. My head bounced off the earth, less agonizing than smashing into a diner wall, but the whole thing had a familiar ring to it. A ring that was currently in my ears, and only barely quieter than Gary's grunt of angry confusion. I pushed, trying to dislodge him, and he half sat up, bushy eyebrows beetled over storm-dark eyes. When I had enough breath to speak, I said, "You didn't really think I was going to kill your wife, did you, Gary?"

He sat back on his heels, hands pressed fingers-inward on his thighs, and lowered his white-haired head. I admired the old guy's flexibility: he was wearing jeans, which were never the easiest thing to kneel in, but he didn't seem to be suffering the instant lack of circulation to the legs that I always got in that position. After a few seconds he looked up, face bleak. "Thing was, I wasn't sure you shouldn't, doll. But didja have to *kick* her?"

Speaking of which, I crawled the foot and a half to Annie and turned her head carefully. A rather horrible bruise was forming, but my healer's magic didn't warn of any real damage. My own head dropped and I sighed. "Yeah, I kinda did. Not just because turnabout is fair play, either. Back in the Qualla everything I threw at the wraiths and Raven Mocker just made them stronger. They kept drinking up my power like I'd turned on a soda fountain. This thing—"

Gary growled, which I thought was patently unfair, since two seconds ago even he'd confessed to not quite trusting Annie. "The thing in Annie," I corrected myself as patiently as I could. "It appears to be of the same nature. It's trying like hell to swallow as much power as it can, so I was afraid to try knocking her out with magic."

"Sorry." Morrison appeared with the incongruous word. I blinked at him and he rubbed his jaw, eyeing Gary. "He got away. Sorry."

Apparently I'd missed a fine bout of fisticuffs in the seven seconds I'd been beating up Annie. "It's okay. He hits like a pile driver."

"Yes, but—" Morrison shut his mouth on the protest, which I suspected had something to do with masculine pride and thirty-plus years of age difference between himself and the man who'd just taken him in a fistfight.

"The point," I said, raising my voice as if I could make sense of the world if only I was loud enough, "the point is that if we can keep Annie unconscious until we figure out how to disinfect her, we might have a fighting chance. She says the Master needs a fema…" I stared down at Annie's unconscious self with dismay. The Master had taken Danny and then Mark for Raven Mocker, and needed a woman to host the leanansidhe. There was an obvious conclusion there, but this, I felt, was not an Occam's razor moment. He would not have groomed an old lady if he intended to get himself a host the old-fashioned way, and besides, I couldn't really see him patiently waiting nine months to be born into this world.

On the other hand, a baby couldn't fight him off, and that might offer him a truly staggering amount of power. "Billy?" My voice was low enough to scratch, and I was half surprised that Billy responded.

He wasn't even all that far away, it turned out. A lot had been going on in the few seconds I'd been dealing with Annie. He'd gotten up from his breather and come to join us, though from the way his attention kept scattering back to the shielded mediums, I could see his concerns were divided. That was good, because I didn't feel like I had enough spoons to be keeping tabs on everyone. "Billy, go home and get into Melinda's sanctuary. Raise the walls, ask her goddess for every damned bit of help she'll give, and keep your children *safe*."

That took his attention off the mediums. Well, sort of. He said, "I think you can let them go now. I think you've trapped the malevolent spirit," in a peculiarly gentle tone.

To my complete embarrassment, my eyes filled with tears. It had been two hard weeks since I'd seen Billy, and practically the last thing that had happened when I'd last seen him was he'd been attacked by somebody I subsequently shot. I hadn't killed the shooter, but right then, with Billy's gentle voice offering me a moment to relax, the raging conviction that I *would* have killed her, that I'd do it again a hundred times to keep my friend and partner alive, was totally overwhelming. I actually did what he told me to and released the shields that— as it turned out—weren't just protecting the mediums, but at this point were holding them physically in place.

The sense of relief from them, and the rush of power back into me, was palpable. I staggered the few steps to Billy and wrapped him in a hug. "Hi."

Billy Holliday, like Gary, was taller than I was. With my face ducked against his shoulder, it wasn't hard for him to put his chin on top of my head as he squeezed me. "Hi. I can't believe you left me in the lurch, Walker. I can't believe you quit the day after I almost got killed."

"I'm sorry."

"Okay." Billy set me back, hands on my shoulders as he examined me. "You okay? You look…"

Behind us, Morrison muttered, "After the rants he's been unleashing on the Homicide department the past couple weeks, I thought he'd blister her skin off," to Gary.

Billy ignored him while I waited for the verdict on how I looked. "Tired," he said after a minute, "but whole. You look good, Walker. Are you good?"

"I'm good." It was true. "A lot's happened. I don't have time to tell you about any of it. How did you know to come here, Billy? Morrison said you were heading for the falls."

"Sonny called." He tipped his head toward the mediums, who were gathering together in tears and hugs, supporting one another. I saw Sonata Smith's head among them, and wondered if everyone who'd ever met me would end up eyeball-deep in this mess. "She said she couldn't stop herself from coming here. When I got here there were a couple dozen of them already, struggling not to cross into the diamond. When I realized they were all women I bet on being safe myself and came in to hold the line for them."

"You could have gotten yourself killed, Billy."

"All in the line of duty, ma'am." His humor fell flat and he shrugged. "The important thing is that I didn't. You got here in time. I knew you would." He looked me up and down again, then lifted his eyebrows. "Nice coat."

A laugh barked out and despite everything I took a step back and twirled so the split skirt flared. "Isn't it? I'm a hero." I stopped spinning before I got dizzy, and frowned at Billy. "I meant it. Go home, gather the family and get into Mel's sanctuary. Keep the kids safe. He's going to be looking for a host, and your children are…"

"Talented," Billy offered, and half smiled. "They're already there, Joanie. Mel woke us all up hours ago and brought us downstairs. I only left when the call came in about the murders."

"That was exactly the dumb thing to do."

"Maybe, but would you expect me to do anything else?"

"No." I folded my fingers over my lips, wanting to ask how Mel had known, but Melinda Holliday wasn't like anybody else I'd met on my spiritual journey. She said she wasn't a witch, only a wise woman like her grandmother, but whatever she was, I was damned glad for her wisdom. "Okay. I need you to go hunting, then. I need you to find Raven Mocker for me." Slightly too late I remembered Billy hadn't been there for the mess in the Qualla, and tried again. "Mark Bragg. We're looking for Mark Bragg. I expect he's on his way into Seattle, maybe on a chartered flight or by car or train."

"Mark Bra—" I watched Billy swallow a dozen questions and change them all to, "I can't track magic, Walker."

"Neither can I, but Suzanne can, and Laurie Corvallis—"
The penny finally dropped. I'd been wrong. Laurie *could* be
of help. I smacked my forehead and shouted, "Laurie! C'mere,
I need you to be a famous news reporter for me!"

"Jo…" Coyote's voice broke on the one syllable.

Stomach cold with dread, I turned my attention on the
three I'd left behind. Coyote's back was to me as he crouched
across from Suzy, whose knotted and bloody hands were
pressed against her mouth.

Between them, Laurie Corvallis lay dead.

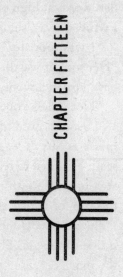

CHAPTER FIFTEEN

It was not the kind of dead one could mistake for anything else. Her right side had been ripped out, red blood darker than her crimson shirt, dying it a dreadful shade. Viscera stained the ground beneath her, and as I tore my gaze away, I saw her wide-open staring eyes instead. Her color was already fading, waxy tones setting in, and makeup I hadn't even noticed before looked garish against her skin.

It had been less than five minutes since I'd left them behind. I was sure it had not yet been five minutes, and in that time my worst fears had come to fruition. I stood and stared, unable to think beyond that flat fact: I had failed. At the very least I'd failed Laurie, and it was fast becoming clear I'd failed somebody else, too.

"I looked to see if I could help you," Coyote whispered. "When I looked back—"

"No! No! *No,* I didn't, I couldn't, I didn't, Joanne, I didn't, I swear I didn't, I couldn't—!" Suzy's hysteria came on in sudden words at high pitch. Her green aura burned so brilliantly I winced away, shutting the Sight off out of self-preservation.

"I was too late." Coyote sounded as bewildered as I felt. "Her soul, it was already…gone. I don't even know if I could have healed a wound this bad, but I couldn't even try…."

"Not unless you can create a liver wholesale."

Coyote bowed his head and put his hands—as bloody and messy as Suzy's—against the earth, his head lowered in despair. I wanted to reassure him. I wasn't sure even *I* could create organs from thin air, and even if I could, it had still been too late for Laurie the moment I'd turned my back on them.

Suzy had *told* me. She'd *warned* me. Black magic getting inside her magic. The leanansidhe backing off. I'd trusted her too much because I knew her so well. Or I thought I did, anyway. I'd trusted her, when instead I should have isolated her and made working the darkness out of her my first priority.

"How did you get here so fast?" I asked her dully. Not her. Raven Mocker, the thing inside her. And then I had the answer, as quickly as I'd asked.

Her friends had summoned her. Summoned an earth magic, and gotten Suzy for their efforts. But a dark thing had come along, too. Suzy had told me she'd fought it, but that it had gotten inside her magic. The Master would be a fool to not take advantage of that kind of magic working, and while I didn't think of him as an earth magic, death, whether I liked it or not, was part of this earth.

I whispered, "Power and corruption," and looked at Annie, huddled on the ground. "Billy, Morrison? Gary? Take Annie away from here. Take her to Mel, I guess, if Melinda's goddess will help hold a circle to keep her in. Call and ask her to ask her first, because I don't want less than god-level power between Annie and your children. Right now, don't let her touch Suzanne. Suzy's got the power, Annie's corrupted. We can't let them come in contact."

Morrison, despite being the smallest of the three men, crouched to lift Annie. "What happens if they do?"

"I don't know. Bad things."

Coyote, suddenly even more strained, called, "Joanne?" and pointed east. I turned, saw nothing, remembered I'd let the Sight slip off, and triggered it again.

The column of power rising from Thunderbird Falls was black as pitch, and raining midnight over midday Seattle.

"Jesus wept." I'd only encountered that phrase recently, while in Ireland, but I felt it had the appropriate grim depth to it.

"Walker?"

I loved how Morrison could put entire volumes of questions into one word. It was an amazing talent. It might have been nicer if the word wasn't usually my name, but it was amazing anyway. I followed that thought all the way to the end, because it was stupid and pointless and not thinking about Laurie, whose death was going to hit me hard any minute now. If I kept talking and thinking with deliberate calm, I might get through it. "I cannot catch an even break. The leanansidhe let the power she'd taken from the murders go. It's back at Thunderbird Falls, and it's turning the city into an oil slick. People are going to start dying. God forbid it should get into the weather front. The whole coast will turn to chaos."

"Can that happen? Why would she do that? Why would they go back?"

Billy beat me to the answer, at least for part of it. "It wouldn't be their decision, Captain. Ghosts are usually tied to the place they died, especially murder victims. It's why I've always needed to go to a crime scene to talk to them. It takes a lot of strength to call them away from their deathbeds."

"She has a body now," I said to the other part of the question. "Annie's body. She's finally where she was aiming for. So in terms of wreaking havoc, letting the coven's spirits return to where they died and continue to poison the system is worth more than amalgamating power for herself. None of this is about power for her, remember. The Master has always needed someone to feed him. He's going to get more strength from this rain than she could give him by herself. She can't get to everybody in the city. The state. This can."

"It's not raining, Walker."

"But it is." I turned my palms up, watching black dust gather. "We're breathing it in right now. I don't know what it's going to do, but for God's sake, if you start to feel aggressive or angry, try really hard to stop and think about what's driving it."

"Can you keep it out of us?"

I started to say yes, then looked at Annie, a boneless lump in his arms, and then at Suzy, whose single burst of petrified terror had been silenced behind her bloody hands. "No. Not... not and fight, Morrison. And I have to fight."

"Walker."

I heard a hundred things in my name again, and tried to close myself off to them. Morrison wouldn't—couldn't—let that happen. "She's only a kid, Walker."

"I know."

Suzy's eyes were huge with fear, but she hadn't run. I thought Raven Mocker would be smart enough to run, but then, if Raven Mocker and the leanansidhe had some kind of ritual they needed to do, of course she wasn't going to run while Annie was still here. She. I'd been so certain they needed a male and female, after seeing Raven Mocker take Danny.

Briefly, tiredly, I wondered what had happened to Mark Bragg, and then the earth tore apart under my feet.

Flight was not on my list of awesome powers. My coat flared up behind my head like a cape, but only because I, like everybody else, was falling. Falling a long way: the ground kept tearing apart beneath us, loam and stone and roots ripping to pieces. The earth howled in the small bones of my ears, the shimmering blue life that ran through it under attack. I shouted and blasted downward with healing magic, trying to stop the wrenching quake. An instant later I hit bottom, first among a rain of men. Morrison, somehow, still held Annie in his arms, though he wasn't on his feet when he landed.

The black dust fell past us and squirmed into the earth, digging deeper in a bizarrely familiar way. It came to me after a few breathless seconds. I turned and drove my fist into the soft surrounding ground, bellowing with frustration. "It's just like the stuff that fell at Halloween! God *damn* it, if zombies start rising again—" There was nowhere to go with that. If zombies started rising again, I'd have to find some way to deal with them, even if they creeped me the hell out.

"All the stops," I said in an almost normal tone, although I lost the handle on that again almost immediately. "He's pulling out all the stops at once. I mean, of course he is, but Jesus *Christ,* I barely handled most of this crap the first time around when it was coming at me one at a time. I might be more cohesive, no, amalgamated, uh, consolidated—" God, I hated it when a rant got derailed by my mental thesaurus coming up short on the word I wanted. "I might have my shit together now," I finally shouted in frustration, "but I'm *sorry,* that just does not equip me for every single damned thing getting in my face at once!"

"Look at it this way, doll," Gary said into my shouts. "At least there probably aren't gonna be any werewolves this time. Now are you gonna get us out of here, or what?"

I bared my teeth at him, but he'd taken the wind from my

sails. The five of us—me, him, Morrison, Annie and Billy—
were separated from Suzy, Coyote and Laurie's body by a
heave of earth. For a few sick seconds I contemplated what
danger Coyote might be in, but the truth was, he was a lot
better equipped to face Raven Mocker than Laurie had been.
I was going to have to trust him to hold on for a few minutes.
Hopeful, I knelt and put a palm on the ground, imagining
I could lift it back up to ball field height where it belonged.

My brain fritzed out at the idea. It *shouldn't* have: I had
done far more unlikely things. But somewhere in it, a spark
went, *You're a healer, not an earth-shaper,* and the all-important
belief that I *could* guttered out and left us at the bottom of a
twenty-foot pit.

Worse, though, I felt the black dust working its way deeper
into the soil. Not just here, but all across Seattle, where rents
had opened in the earth, leaving it vulnerable. I could See it
starting to happen: black magic reaching for cracks and fissures
in the bedrock. The coven and I had opened caves beneath
Seattle, caves I'd only recently re-sealed. The Master's magic
was looking for something much deeper than that, looking for
a way to work its way down into the fault line that ran from
Alaska to California.

A chill numbed me as the potential ramifications of that
raced ahead of me. A normal earthquake lasted seconds or
minutes. One backed by black magic could last hours. The
San Andreas Fault was one side of the Pacific Ring of Fire. If
the Master dug deep enough, he could sink, shatter or burn
half the world away.

That sounded *exactly* like something a death power would
thrive on.

All of a sudden the conviction that we were utterly fucked
if I didn't get us out of this hole overwhelmed any lack of confidence I might have had. Magic surged through me, throw-

ing us upward again. I held on to it as long as I could, trying desperately to reach out to other damage in the area. I sent healing magic chasing the black dust, and all too quickly realized I *might* be able to burn it out, but that I'd exhaust myself in the effort. The big bad needed to be dealt with before fixing the damage became practical.

"Go," I ordered as we regained our feet. "Get Annie out of here. Billy—"

He shook his head, cell phone in hand. "No reception."

"We're in the middle of a damned ball field! I can practically see satellites from here—!" I yanked my phone out, too, determined Billy was right, not that I'd really doubted him, and in a fit of rage flung my phone halfway across the field. "Magic is not supposed to screw up technology!"

Morrison, accepting Gary's hand on his elbow to help him up—he still had Annie cradled safely in his arms—muttered, "Magic seems exactly like something that would make technology stop working. Walker—"

"I know. You don't want to leave me. But—"

An explosion of power threw us all to the ground. Earth splattered everywhere, carried on shards of green magic sharp and particular enough to linger where they struck the earth. One slammed past my right cheek, so close I felt a sting. When I touched it, blood came away. I sat up, head pounding, and was knocked onto my back again as another explosion rocked the air. Dune and blue this time, which made no sense at all. Coyote couldn't fight with his magic. It would turn on him, as mine used to do to me.

Green shattered against his multivariegated shields and I decided to put my prejudices aside for the moment. Maybe too much exposure to me had changed his abilities, or maybe even healer's magic was willing to play hardball if the only other choice was dying.

Suzy's next strike was so bright I shut the Sight off to save my eyesight. I still saw it, and a quick look around at Gary and Morrison said they did, too. Huge magic tended to have a visual component, but at least it wasn't eye-bleedingly brilliant through normal vision. I got up for the third time and, once on my feet, finally got a sense of what my friends must see when they watched *me* in battle.

Coyote and Suzanne went at it like hyenas fighting over Laurie's body, magic boiling in their cores. Coyote's shields were a desert sandstorm, so full of speed and danger they blocked out the light. Within them, he crouched and hunched and slunk like his animal namesake, seeking a place to strike from. When he *did* strike, it was with clear blue magic, the shade I thought of as healing color. It became a weapon, though it shouldn't have been able to, and all I could wonder was how pure the intent had to be, for him to turn healing magic into a throwing star.

Into a thousand of them, spinning and sparking through the air. Most hit Suzy's ferociously green shields and exploded, another air-smashing blowout that rocked me on my feet. A few got through, maybe hitting places where the blue magic's impact had weakened the shields. One or two of *those* survived long enough to plunge into Suzy's skin, and those were absorbed with no obvious effect. Well, no, there was one effect: she smiled, the same wild, sharp smile that Cernunnos owned, and then she drew a sword.

My sword was a real thing. A magic thing, but real: it was forged of silver and I had taken it from a god's hand. Suzy's blade was pure power, green godling magic given edges. I recognized the shape of it, too: short and elegantly crude, like the blade her grandfather had carried since I took the rapier from him. Suzy was a modern teen, not, I imagined, trained in weapons at all, never mind swords. But she held the thing like she knew what to do with it, and when she ran at Coyote to swing the blade, she never exposed her body to attack. She moved sideways, she slithered, she slipped and she struck so hard the conflicting magics rang like bells.

As the reverberations washed over us, Coyote changed. One moment he was a man, the next, a golden-eyed coyote. He darted in, foregoing a man's fighting technique for a canine's. Suzy's sword disappeared barely in time to reform as shields: Coyote's teeth scraped so close to her hamstring that her jeans tore. I saw green pressed against her skin, protecting her from his bite. She flung herself away, onto the ground. Coyote pounced, and in the moment he was airborne, Suzy flipped onto her back. She caught him in the ribs with her long legs and threw him over her head, powering the thrust with magic. He flew, yelping, and Suzy came to her feet with her hair flying and eyes blazing. *"Joanne! Do something!"*

I startled all the way to my bones, so rapt in the fight it hadn't occurred to me that I should interfere.

Before I could, Annie awakened with a surge and raked clawed fingers across Morrison's face.

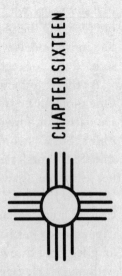

CHAPTER SIXTEEN

Morrison shouted and nearly dropped the woman. Nearly. I would have, but he was far too much the cop to let her go. He did try to grab her clawing fingers. Given the tears streaming from his eyes, I doubted he could see well enough to catch them, and leaped to help.

Annie wrapped one arm around Morrison's neck like a long-lost lover, then hefted herself up and bashed her forehead against the bridge of his nose. He shouted again and, to my never-ending admiration, tightened his grip instead of letting her go. Annie raked his face again before I caught her arm. She flung herself in my direction, trying to unbalance Morrison. He staggered but kept his feet and I got my arm around Annie's upper arms, pinning them down. She thrashed like a wildcat, black eyes open wide, head thrown back and almost visible rage pouring from her throat as she screamed.

Gary shoved himself between me and Morrison and slid his arm around Annie's throat. In slightly less than ten seconds, she collapsed again, limp and fragile-looking. Gary threw himself away from us like he'd murdered somebody and covered his face with his hands. I said his name helplessly, but he just shook his head, despair rolling off him.

"Joanne!" That was Suzy again, panic turning her voice thready. I spun around in time to watch Coyote come back from his tumble in a long low leap that brought Suzy to the ground. Her magic flared, green and then midnight-black. As the blackness took over, the much-abused earth opened around her and swallowed her down, leaving Coyote snapping sharp teeth on torn grass instead of her throat. He snarled, shook himself all over and stood on his hind legs, which looked very strange.

It looked even stranger when between one step and the next he became human again, his long black hair disarrayed. "I can't go through the earth like she's doing, Jo. You have to go after her."

"I can't—" Well, yes, I could. I'd just done it. I shook my head anyway. "She's got to surface again, and she's going to do it where Annie is. Billy—" I couldn't possibly send Annie to his house knowing Suzy would be looking for Annie. "Dammit. Change of plans." I wheeled, looking over the landscape like it would give me answers. Mostly to myself, I said, "The smart thing would be to take it out of the city, somewhere remote where there aren't many people to get hurt, but this damned *rain*—"

As if I'd conjured it, real rain began to fall, massive cold drops that came from clouds I hadn't noticed gathering. Once I looked up I didn't know how I'd *missed* them; they looked like Armageddon rolling in, almost black as they narrowed the horizons to touchable distances. Reluctantly, I brought the Sight to the fore again, unsurprised to see stains of corruption swelling the clouds. Every raindrop drove black dust into the ground or tried to force it into our skin. I pulled shields over us all, making a little dome of dryness in the heart of a building storm.

Sonata and the other mediums who'd been drawn to the site were gone. So, I realized, was Laurie's body. I hoped the mediums had fled, rather than been buried, which is what I imagined had happened to Laurie. I stared at where her body had been, at where black raindrops crashed violently against the soil, and I thought again of zombies. I was not up for another bout with the walking dead, especially if the walker was someone I knew.

Billy cleared his throat. I glanced at him and discovered everybody was waiting on me. I'd forgotten I'd even been talking, so it took a moment to gather myself again. When I did, it wasn't to speak. Instead I lifted my hand to Morrison's face, soothing away the scratches and welts from Annie's attack. His eyes stopped watering and a faint look of amazement ran over his features. I'd never healed him before. Turned him into a wolf a few times, yes, but never used the base component of my magic. My voice cracked. "Better?"

He nodded and I smiled. It didn't last, but at least it happened. Then I looked back to the close horizons, still searching for answers there. "I haven't done the things I should. I'm sure I should have made a…a sacred place for myself. Somewhere I could go now, knowing it had power built up that might help us. The falls were as close to that as I had, and the Master got to them already. Everywhere else is so…populated. The troll, my apartment building, Pike Place Market…"

"Seattle's your sacred space, doll." Gary sounded exhausted. "I been watchin' you run hell-bent for leather all over this city for the past year. You don't got any one place because you belong everywhere. That said, there's only one image that matters in the skyline, sweetheart."

"The Space Needle." I'd been trying not to think of it at all, because Gary was right. I hadn't just started this ride there in a lot of ways. I'd come to use it as a place to center myself and get a look at what was going down in my city. "But do you know how many tourists are there every day, Gary?"

"We'll take care of that." Morrison, still holding Annie as if she was weightless, turned to Billy. "You drove your squad car over?" At Billy's nod, he continued, "Go see if the radios are working. Talk to the West Precinct. Tell them we have to shut the Seattle Center down." He glanced at me. "If Walker's right about this rain, there might be enough trouble on the streets already to justify it, but if she's not...talk to the captain. Say we've heard from a local resource, a geologist, that these tremors are running so deep he's concerned about the Needle's stability."

He turned toward me. "You know a geologist, right? Crowder, the guy who found you when the falls were born. Can you get him to back us up on this story?"

"We're not exactly close personal friends, Morrison. He might back us up, but how am I supposed to call him?" I went to take my cell phone out and wave its lack of functionality at him in a demonstrative manner, and remembered I'd thrown it into the field somewhere. "Shit."

Morrison actually looked relieved at the reminder. "Good. Then nobody's likely to be able to contradict us until it's too late."

"I find it more comforting when you're not devious," I informed him, but I had to agree it was a story we might be able to sell. I was still trying to come up with a better one when Billy shrugged his shoulder holster off and offered it to Morrison, whose eyebrows bent inward.

"I've got a backup weapon in the car," Billy said. "You're in a rental and haven't been home since you got back from

North Carolina, have you? I didn't think so. Take the gun. You might need it." Morrison nodded and Billy helped him slide the holster on without dropping Annie.

I admired both of them for their practical streaks, and addressed Billy. "I don't suppose you'll go home and hide after you radio this in, will you?"

"Do you really have to ask?"

I sighed. "All right. Let's go."

"What about…?" Coyote gestured to where Suzy and presumably Laurie were buried.

"We have Annie. She'll follow us."

"What if she hunts along the way?"

"Then people are going to die, so it would probably be good if we got our asses in gear and move to territory we choose for the big fight. So far we've been running like hell in the wake of the Master's messes. I'm ready to take a stand. Can we go now?"

"I just don't like leaving this place unprotected."

"Then stay here, Cyrano. I've got no other resources right now." Frustrated and hurting, I stomped past him, bringing my dome shield with me. Everybody but Coyote scurried along. When I looked back, he had knelt to put his hands on the ground, and was already drenched from the downpour. His expression was precisely that of a wet dog's. An angry wet dog's, as another tremor rattled the earth. I waved as Billy split off to go to his squad car, and the rest of us ran for Morrison's rental. I was taking the keys out of Morrison's front pocket, something that under different circumstances could have been quite entertaining, when Coyote called, "Wait up, I'm coming with you."

My shoulders dropped with relief. I did not want to do this without Coyote at my side. He jogged up, took a look at me squirming around in Morrison's pockets, and volunteered, "I'll hold her," with a nod at Annie.

Morrison shook his head. "I've got her, thanks. Walker, you drive."

"Words you will live by for the rest of your days," I told him, and got a faint smile for my efforts as we got into the car. Coyote took shotgun while Gary and Morrison tucked Annie into the backseat and buckled in on either side of her. As I backed out of the parking lot, Billy pointed at his squad car's radio and gave me a thumbs-up. "Radio's working," I reported. "Let's hope the West Precinct captain is feeling obliging."

We weren't a quarter mile out of the park when it became clear he probably would be. A Tripoli cab was halfway into a ditch that hadn't been there when we drove in. I pulled over and jumped out to find a soaking-wet man in his late thirties crouched on the vehicle's far side, examining the damage. I said, "Oh, God," by way of introduction. "Did Keith send you? I'm Joanne."

His eyebrows, well-groomed if wet, went up and he stood to offer me a hand to shake. "I am Keith. Nice to finally meet you in person. Thanks for all the flowers."

I grinned weakly. "Looks like I'm going to owe you some more. Are you okay?"

"Sure, fine, for a guy who was driving when the road opened up under him. Don't think I'm going to be much help ferrying your crew around, though."

"It's okay. There…aren't as many of us as there were."

Dismay darted across his face, creasing lines that were deep enough to make me revise his age up a decade or more. "Earthquakes get somebody?"

"Yeah." It was easier than explaining the truth. "Look,

Keith, get in the cab and stay there until somebody radios you, okay? This rain isn't good to be out in."

He cleared his throat. "We're not getting rained on right now."

I looked up, discovering I'd brought the dome shield up automatically when I got out of the car. "Ah. Yes. So we're not. All the better, then. Turn the heat on so you don't die of exposure, and stay safe."

Keith leaned past me to look into the rental. I glanced back to see Gary wave a greeting, then caught Keith's questioning expression that clearly sought Gary's guidance on whether he should listen to me or not. Gary nodded. Keith made a surprised sound. "All right. Be careful on the roads. They're a mess. People are abandoning their cars to get indoors." He got back into the cab, saying, "Don't forget those flowers," as he closed the door.

I breathed, "I won't," as I got back in my own vehicle. Another tremor hit as I did, asphalt groaning beneath us. I gunned the car, hoping I wasn't gunning us straight into a pit. I wasn't, nor did one open behind us, but my heartbeat stayed uncomfortably elevated for the next several minutes.

Keith hadn't been kidding. There were cars everywhere, lots of them in potholes and ditches or driven up over meridians and sidewalks that had suddenly lurched into the road before them. Some people were sticking it out with their cars, but far more of them were abandoned. It looked like a post-collapse apocalypse scene from a movie, and the bad stuff had hardly gotten started.

It got much, much worse as we approached downtown. So bad that none of us wanted to speak, just stared out the window with haunted gazes. Seattle was a hilly city. There were pileups at the bottoms of many of those hills, like the earth had shrugged all the cars off and sent them flying to land as they pleased. It reminded me of the slick snow days we'd seen more and more of recently. Every time one came along, it was like nobody had ever driven on snow before and had to make all the same mistakes over again before they could stop sliding around, rear-ending and piling up. The streets looked like that now, but worse. Sirens were clearly audible, louder than usual because so many engines were stilled. Even the emergency vehicles, though, were having a bad time of it: we passed one fire engine winching another one out of a crevasse while paramedics double-timed it away from the trucks to approach a particularly bad pileup down the block.

Police began appearing in greater numbers as we crept along. I saw acts of violence between cops and citizens that made me hiss and made Morrison swear. People climbed through shattered store windows, carrying loot, which seemed remarkably opportunistic. It hadn't been *that* long since the massacre at the falls. I glanced at the car's clock to be sure of that, and was right: it was barely 5:00 p.m. Only three hours had passed.

The last hour of that, though, a contaminated rain had been beating the city with black magic conjured by death on wings, and it had never taken all that much to turn a crowd into a mob anyway. "Screw it," I said abruptly. "It'll be faster to walk from here."

"It's another two miles to the Seattle Center, Walker. Are you going to carry Annie?"

"Do you want me to?" I killed the engine and got out. Rain slapped my shields as I extended them over the car. "Come on. We should move as fast as we can."

"Through these crowds?" Coyote asked dubiously as he climbed out. "They'll hold us back, especially since—" He glanced at Morrison.

"Since he looks like a cop? Well, they can't hold us if they can't see us. Where's Billy?"

"I lost track of his squad car a while back," Morrison reported. "There was a bad wreck. It looked like he pulled off to help."

Maybe he'd be smart and go home after that. If not, well, he knew where we were going. I put my arms out to Morrison, offering to take Annie. He gave me a dirty look and hefted her himself, though in a fireman's carry rather than the more graceful bride's carry he'd been using. Gary protested and subsided in almost the same breath, making my heart ache, and collected my drum from the rental's trunk instead. I fell into step with him and put my hand in his. "Hey. How're you holding up?"

"Tell you what, doll, if you hadn't healed up my heart last year, no way I'd be survivin' this." He put both of our hands over his heart. "And I ain't talkin' about just the magic, Jo. What about you?"

"The same. On all counts, Gary. I couldn't have made it this far without you. I'm so sorry. This isn't what I hoped would happen when I got to the hospital last night."

"Darlin', it ain't nothin' any of us hoped for, but we all knew it was coming down the line."

"It wasn't supposed to involve your wife."

"It was never not gonna. We just didn't know it."

"You realize that sounds like something I would say."

To my surprise, a broad grin flashed across Gary's face. "Yeah, doll. I thought about that more than once, riding with Horns. I get it better now," he said more solemnly. "Why it's so damn hard for you to talk about the magic, even when you're talkin' to folks who know and trust you. It don't matter how real you know it is. It sounds crazy comin' out of your mouth. And it gets worse when you're talkin' about the time line changing, about things you remember one way when they happened another."

"Think there's a support group? Time Travelers Anonymous?" I focused on the street ahead of us for a moment, watching people brush to the sides of my shields without realizing they were doing it. We were alone, a little army of magic in the heart of a mundane world. It was liberating and alienating all at once. "Time travel sounds so freaking cool. 'Go anywhere, see anything, change the world!' But the world doesn't like being changed."

"And I did change it, doll." Gary took a deep, uncertain breath. "Can't help wonderin' if that means I brought this down on us. If I hadn't fought for Annie—"

"Then you wouldn't be the man she and I both adore," I interrupted. "I mean, damn, Gary, you challenged death and time itself for love. That's…that's amazing. That's everything. That's love conquering all."

"Hah. Horns said the same thing. Guess he'd know," Gary said more softly. "Guess he's been around long enough to know what endures."

"So listen to the god," I suggested, then sighed. "Besides, you said it yourself. Annie was always going to be involved. Lives don't go along without touching each other, do they? So if your life and mine were ever going to get involved, maybe the rest of it was going to happen, too. And you said it was like a fog lifting from the real memories. I don't think you changed most of the time line, Gary. I think the Master clouded the truth in hopes that you not knowing what had happened would weaken you enough that he could get to Annie one last time without interference. I don't think even he can yank one time line out of place and replace it with another that thoroughly."

"Why doncha think so?"

"Because he'd have done it with me and made sure I never survived to be born, if he could've."

Gary went quiet a minute. "Pretty good argument, doll."

I took a bow as we walked. "Thank you. I do my best."

Gary started to smile, but before he got anywhere near done with it, a building fell down in front of us.

CHAPTER SEVENTEEN

Dust rose like a wall, black-spattered and vindictive. It swept around us, my shields thoroughly in place even as screams filled the air. Glass rained, dull and ugly in the dust and downpour. Metal twisted and shrieked as more of the building came down, and as I watched, bricks imploded under the strain of falling struts. The ground continued to shake, great rolling waves that could have been further earthquakes or could have simply been impact upon impact as twenty stories came down on the street.

I could not imagine how many people had just died. Dozens, maybe hundreds: the street had been busy with looters, refugees, families trying to work their way out of the shock-ridden city center. A second rush of filler, dust, brick, things I didn't know the name of, came rumbling down. I threw shields as widely as I could, trying to protect those who were still unharmed, then fell back as far as I dared, trying to assess the damage.

I couldn't, not from where I stood. I put my hand on Gary's arm. "Don't let me fall down."

"Eh?" He slid his arm around my waist, though, and I tried something I'd never really done deliberately: I shot out of my body, not in search of an astral plane, but just to have a look at this one, to see what we were facing.

From a vantage of a couple hundred feet, seen with the Sight, it looked far worse than my piddly imagination had envisioned. Buildings by their nature glowed with green intent, protective, comforting; they knew their duty in shielding men and beasts from nature's crueler elements.

The building just in front of us, and half a dozen more all the way down the street, were ripped and torn apart not just physically, but spiritually. Their steadfast green bled red and orange with pain and tinted toward black despair. They had failed their people: they had fallen, and in falling, taken lives. That was not their *purpose,* and for all that they weren't sentient, their spirits still felt the pain of failure.

Below those shards of pain lay the living heartbeats of people trapped within broken bits of building. Some flickered and went out as I watched, and more flared with fear when another quake rattled more debris down. Half a block lay beneath the fallen buildings, and more people than I could count.

I snapped back to my body with tears running down my face. "I can See them, Gary. If I could only change this stuff, if I was strong enough—" I remembered my father walking through a blood rain that turned to rose petals under the force of his will, and extended my hands.

Coyote caught my wrist. "Jo, you can't."

"I have to try!"

"It's hundreds of tons of building material, Jo. If you try, if you succeed, you're going to have to hold it in place, never faltering, never doubting, until every single person has crawled free. You can't do it. Nobody can."

"Then help me!" He was right. He was horribly, horribly right. I had to change it all at once, and keep it that way. If I lost confidence for even a heartbeat, it would all change back again. It might collapse, might kill people, when at least right now they were tucked into nooks and crannies that existed and might continue to exist until they were freed. I dropped my hands, then lowered the dome and fell to my knees. My hands came up again as my head lowered, wrists crossing like I could gain just that much more support by resting one against the other.

"Jo, what are you doing?"

"I'm going to keep them alive." Tears streamed down my dusty cheeks and my voice sounded throttled even to me. "I am not going to let anybody else die in there. If I can't get them out, at least I can heal them and keep them alive until somebody else can get them out. Now shut up or help me."

"Joanne, if Annie wakes up—"

"Don't let her! Gary! Morrison! Just—*don't let her.*"

Coyote protested again, but I shut it out. I shut everything out, crushing my eyes closed and turning my focus inward.

The magic was there, as it had been for so long now. Not tied in a knot under my breastbone, but coursing through me, as natural and life-giving as blood or breath. "I need so much of you now," I said to it, or to myself. To my spirit animals, who sat together within my mind, quiet and focused. "I need so much of anyone who can give it right now, anyone who can spare a thought or a hope for the people trapped in there."

And there were *so many* people whose thoughts and fears and hopes were directed that way. So much energy, coiling uselessly through the air: prayers and positive thoughts offered up, unable to affect anything without guidance.

"Thank you," I whispered to every single soul whose best wishes I could turn into magic, and did.

I had once asked Seattle to hit me with its best shot. I'd put the city's lights out that time. This felt almost like that, except I was only taking what I was given, and it was so much more powerful for being offered. Emotion slammed through me, converting to magic, and I became faintly aware that I could barely breathe through the tears and snot running down my face. But my own magic wasn't about to let me asphyxiate, so I didn't worry. I just let the healing power flow.

There were people trapped beneath the rubble who were barely scratched, and there were those who were dying. The scratches and bruises were nothing, a quick rub with a bit of polish on a rag as my power swept over them. I couldn't afford to linger over each of the more badly injured bodies, or I would lose some of them. "Be well," I said again and again, "be well." I believed I could make them well, and most of them—most of them—were in no condition to disbelieve. They became well, broken bones healing, torn flesh knitting, opened veins closing. I didn't let myself think about how many of them there were, or wonder what would happen if the goodwill of the gathered crowd faded. That shared strength came in from all over Seattle now, waves of hope and desperation as word spread of the latest disaster. For a few shining seconds, prayers even beat back the black dust, setting it on fire, turning it white with compassion. The weight of the buildings seemed lesser after that, as if spiritual offerings could lighten physical loads. It helped. It all helped.

But the impossible ones weren't just broken, but crushed. Legs, arms, chests, pressed between pillars and girders, lungs or guts pierced by shards of glass and metal. I could heal them around those injuries, but it wouldn't do much good to be healed all except for the pane of glass cutting through one leg.

Dad had turned blood rain to roses. It had changed back again when he'd stopped concentrating, but there had still been rose petals on the ground. They hadn't reverted. Only the new stuff had been unchanged. One. I would try it with one man, someone close to me whose leg *was* half-severed by a huge sheet of glass. Aside from that piece, the space he was in was clear and safe: I could feel it trying to be a protective place, and feel its anguish at failing, just as clearly as I could feel the man's harsh breath and shocking pain. Nothing balanced on the glass. There was nothing that could fall or shift with its removal. "Air," I whispered. "Just be...*air.*"

Air. I almost felt the glass consider that idea like it was new and interesting. It was meant to be seen through, as air was. It had that in common with air. It hesitated, vibrating, and I felt—almost heard—the man swallow another cry of pain. Then the glass acquiesced to my strange request, accepted the tenet of shamanism that was change, and it became as I imagined it: air, clean, clear, breathable.

Blood went everywhere, horrible spurts from a sliced artery. I clamped down on it like it was a fuel line, and felt the man's astonishment, astonishment so great that for a critical moment he believed anything was possible. In that moment, it was, and he was healed.

A sob of relief shook me. This was my magic as it should be used, and I thought my heart would tear apart from the joy of succeeding. I went on, finding others who were terribly damaged, hoping to save more lives that could not reasonably expect to be saved.

There were people I didn't dare try it with. Removing fallen girders was an engineer's job, checking to see what was balanced where, what else would come down if it was moved. I hesitated over those people, heart tearing all over again, then chose to dull their agony. Maybe it was wrong. Maybe they would have preferred to be aware of their pain, knowing it told them they were alive, but I couldn't do nothing.

Then they were all healed or helped as much as I could do, and I snapped back into myself, shaking and still sobbing. I had no will to keep using the Sight; it would show me things I couldn't help, right now. "Get paramedics. Get fire engineers. I can tell them where everyone is, if they can just *get* to them."

"You've done enough, Jo." Coyote's voice sounded strange, and his eyes were shadowed when I looked at him. "I wouldn't have thought it was possible. I tried to stop you. It was like throwing myself at a steel wall."

I stared at him in befuddlement. I'd had no sensation at all of his attempts at interfering. "Why would you do that?"

"I was afraid you were going to kill yourself. I was—Joanne, you can't do what you did. No one can. You were… unassailable."

I had never heard the note in his voice before. It wasn't respect, not exactly, nor was it precisely shock. It encompassed those things, but there was more to it, and I hoped the rest wasn't anger or envy. If it was, I tried heading it off with the truth. "I had a good teacher."

Coyote made a short sound bordering on amusement. "You did. Jo—"

"She's waking up again, Walker." Morrison's warning made me twist toward the other two men, who sat together with Annie Muldoon stretched across their laps. Gary stroked her temple very lightly, avoiding the purpling bruise where I'd kicked her. He looked old again, old and heartbroken. They were all coated in dust that kept rolling from the falling buildings.

"She's getting weaker," Morrison said. "We can't keep knocking her out."

I pulled the dome-shaped shield back in place and crawled

to them, Coyote dogging my heels. The air in my shield was still thick with dust, making Gary cough when he drew a deeper breath. I shoved the idea of a filter through the dome, catching all contaminants in the air and pushing them out the side of the shield, so we were in a peculiarly clean little circle at the heart of devastation. Annie took a deeper breath, too, eyelids flickering. I touched her cheek, sending the faintest whisper of healing power to fade the bruise on her cheek. I sent a tiny suggestion of *sleep* to her, too, afraid to do more. Afraid I might feed the leanansidhe within her if I made absolutely certain that Annie slept. But the bruise looked better, at least, and Gary's gaze lifted to mine, gray eyes wet with tears and with thanks. I reached past Annie to take his hand and squeeze it. "I should've done that earlier. Sorry."

He grated, "You been busy," and we left it at that.

Coyote, standing behind me, said, "I can See you're still filled with power, Jo. Maybe if we worked together with her…?" and knelt, reaching for Annie's shoulder.

"No." Gary gathered his wife closer, as much to my surprise as Coyote's. "Nah, kid, we can't risk it. Not right now. If she wakes up and can call Suzy to her here, where we ain't ready to face the two of 'em…" Reluctance and pain filled every word, but he was adamant. "I gotta get my Annie back, Jo. We gotta be certain, when we act. No dominion," he whispered to Annie, like it was a promise that I couldn't understand.

I knelt up and leaned forward, putting my hand behind Gary's neck to pull his forehead against mine. "You're the bravest man I've ever known, Garrison Matthew Muldoon. I love you, you know that, right?"

"Yeah, doll. I know. I love you, too."

Morrison, deliberately, said, "Hnf," and everybody, even Coyote, laughed. I sat back again, looking between the three men, and wondered how I'd been so lucky as to end up with all of them in my life. In fact, it seemed like a good time to say just that. "You three are my rocks. I don't know what I would do without you. Thank you all for everything. For everything. I love all of you."

Coyote looked down, his smile shadowed, but I couldn't give him more than what I already had. When he glanced up again, his expression said that he knew that, and that he'd accepted it. "We love you, too, Jo."

Morrison didn't join in the declarations of love. Not aloud, anyway. He only smiled when I met his eyes, and that was enough. More than enough. My hard-as-flint police captain's eyes were soft and fond, and I didn't need more than that.

"Arright. Enough with the love-in, doll. What're we gonna do about Annie?"

"We're gonna—"

Stone scraped behind me. I was on my feet, facing the rubble, my sword in hand and brilliant with magic before I'd even known I'd drawn it. We'd had too long a reprieve. Suzy would be coming for us, and we hadn't made it to the damned Seattle Center. This was not where I wanted to make my last stand, but I'd spent too much time here, and would pay the consequences.

A fistful of detritus spilled from the collapsed building in front of us, and then a greater scrape sounded. It struck me that Suzy would not be digging her way out of the ruins. She would blow her way out, destroying half of downtown in her arrival. Somebody was in there, trying to get out. I ran forward, half intending to use my sword as a lever to clear rubble away, when one last chunk of brick shifted and a man emerged blinking into the light.

I knew him. Even without the Sight, I knew he was the man I'd first risked healing, the one closest to me. The one whose leg had been half-severed by glass. His jeans were a red, sticky, dusty, matted mess, and brown spatters marked where the artery had sprayed blood over the rest of him and mixed with dust. His thigh was scarred, a thin line where the glass had cut through him. I stared at that scar, vaguely offended by it. I didn't leave scars when I healed people. On the other hand, I didn't usually heal hundreds at once, or dozens of life-threatening wounds. A scar was much less distressing than being dead.

The man lifted his eyes, brown in a dusty face, and gaped at me. *"Bruja?"*

For a few seconds I wondered why anybody would think a woman with a shiny blue sword standing in the ruins of downtown Seattle would think I was a witch rather than a crazy lady, and then memory hit me with the force of a sledgehammer. A sledgehammer, because that was this man's tool of trade. I'd met him once, less than a day after my powers had awakened. *"Manny?"*

"You blessed me, *bruja*. You blessed me. You saved me." The faint Hispanic accent I remembered was much stronger just now, and his voice shook.

I threw my sword away and staggered forward to hug him. I didn't think of myself as a really huggy person, but there were tears streaming down my face again and all I wanted to do was really reassure myself he was alive. Reassure myself that just this once, encountering me hadn't been a death sentence. Manny smelled like smoke and dust and, very faintly under all that, of baby oil. It made me remember everything I'd learned about him in the few minutes we'd shared space while I was trying to use my new powers to accomplish something useful.

He closed his arms around me slowly, then tightened them like we were long-lost lovers and he would never let go. The breath squeezed right out of me and my sobs turned to a squished little laugh. I squirmed out of the embrace, saying,

"I saved you. Oh, thank you, Manny. Thank you. Go home. Go home to your pretty wife and the twin girls and the little boy and the new baby, and keep them inside until the storm passes."

Something like awe struck his dusty features. "You know all that? About me?"

"I guessed about the new baby." I sniffled and wiped my nose on my arm. "Go on, go home. Stay out of the rain."

Manny nodded, touched his heart, then—unlike any of my closer friends—actually did what he was told, breaking into a run as he left the wreckage.

I watched him go, then turned back to my friends with a smile blinded by tears. "It's going to take hours for the paramedics to get here, with all the chaos. This will all be over by then, one way or another. We can come back to help then. Come on. Come on. Right now I think we can actually win this thing."

CHAPTER EIGHTEEN

Saturday, April 1, 6:44 p.m.

It took almost two hours to get the two miles to the Seattle Center, but the traffic—both vehicle and human—had cleared out by the time we arrived. The only people around were cops. Morrison handed Annie to Gary—they'd been trading off with her and my drum, after a brief argument about Coyote being perfectly able-bodied. "Able-bodied," Gary had growled as he took his wife, "an' one of two of us who can see somethin' magic coming down the line. You and Jo gotta keep your hands free."

I didn't like that, after the flutter of consciousness, Annie had gone back under again. I kept stealing glimpses at her with the Sight, wondering if it would tell me that she was awake and faking it until the moment was right to strike. Her aura was mostly flat and black, with only the occasional spark of Cernunnos-green in it. After a while I began to suspect it was *Annie* keeping herself unconscious while the leanansidhe struggled to waken their shared body. I became convinced she wasn't faking it, anyway, because it was really hard for a conscious person to maintain the boneless floppy-bodyness of unconsciousness.

I also didn't like that Suzy hadn't reappeared. Every step of the way I expected her to explode out of the pavement. By the time we got to the Seattle Center and Morrison was ordering wet, grumpy cops to set up a perimeter, I was paranoid enough to shatter if somebody touched me.

That was probably a good mental space for me to be in, as far as the Master was concerned. With that thought in mind, I tried hard to shake the paranoia while we assessed the damage and tried to figure out where best to set up for our anticipated fight.

The buildings had taken a fair amount of damage from the still-rolling earthquakes. The Needle hadn't yet begun to cant, but the Science Center had huge cracks in its walls, one large enough to step through. The International Fountain, off to the east, had broken in half, leaving water to rush wildly upward before falling to flood the grounds. Lawn and concrete were broken into chunks, surrounded by ankle-deep mud. My leather coat dragged through the muck without getting dirty. My feet didn't fare so well.

Wind came from every which way, bringing the scent of burning buildings from the city. The downpour, which I'd largely kept off us with my shields, seemed like it should be enough to put fires out. I had the uncomfortable feeling it was instead encouraging them. I did not, at the moment, feel the laws of physics could be trusted. Seattle was under magical attack, and I had on occasion defied those laws myself with magic.

Part of me wanted to climb the Needle and have a look at the city. The rest of me thought if I did that I'd either go into a conniption or lose the will to fight, neither of which would be helpful right now.

Morrison came back from talking to a thin-shouldered cop whose poncho did nothing to increase the width of his shoulders. The cop sneered after Morrison, whose face was set when he returned to me. "The only thing keeping these officers from taking their anger out on civilians is that the civilians have been moved off-site. I know that man, Lieutenant Hardy. I asked what was driving his anger and he couldn't answer. Hardy's a good man, Walker. He works with troubled teens. You can't do that successfully if you don't know exactly what triggers your own high emotions and how to defuse them before it gets that far. Would we be in the same condition if you weren't shielding us from this...fallout?"

"Probably."

Morrison folded his fist in front of his mouth, then released it. It looked for all the world like he was capturing a question and releasing it unspoken. I lifted an eyebrow and he shook his head. "I want to ask you to shield everyone. Protect the city. But you can't, and I know it. Are we going to lose Seattle, Walker?"

"No. There are bastions of sanity, where the adepts we sent home have set up circles. Schools, churches, community centers. They're fighting back, and they'll be there to pick up the pieces when it's over." I sounded more certain than I felt. The truth was that the pervasive rain and low dark clouds blocked even my Sight after a few blocks, so I could really only hope I was right. This, however, seemed like an excellent time for some reassuring lies. I needed them as much as Morrison did. But then a bout of honesty took me and I admitted, "It's gotten worse a lot faster than I thought it would. And this is only what we can see. I don't know how bad it's getting outside of Seattle. This is the epicenter."

"The eye of the storm." Morrison waited for my nod. "The eye is where the calm is, Walker."

"I know. But since all we've got to communicate with is shortwave radio, all we can *know* about is what's right here. The rest of it we're going to have to fix later."

"What if we can't?"

"I choose not to accept that as a possibility."

To my surprise, Morrison chuckled. "You're pathological, Walker." Then he drew me into his arms and we held on to each other for a minute, taking comfort where we could.

I pulled away reluctantly. "All right, this won't get it done. Let's set up a power circle and..." I trailed off, looking up at the Needle. "I think I have a really bad idea. Do you think we could use that thing as a lightning rod?"

Morrison followed my gaze, then eyed me. "Walker, are you suggesting we try to draw all this dark power to Seattle's most recognizable landmark?"

"Yep." It was an awful idea. I didn't know if it would work. I didn't know *how* it could work. For one thing, drawing a power circle around the Space Needle would be a work of art, because there were different levels, parking lots, exhibition centers, amusement parks, museums and conference halls in the way. Furthermore, most of those had been knocked around in some fashion, making them considerably more difficult to navigate than usual.

"Wouldn't that be—" Morrison was clearly searching for a word that could convey the exceedingly high levels of doom inherent in the idea. "Wouldn't that be very bad for the Needle?" he finally asked, with the air of a man accepting that language strong enough to encompass the potential disaster would only sound hyperbolic.

"I expect so. On the other hand, it might be a great deal

better for, say, the entire Pacific Rim than the current situation."

"Can you be sure of that?"

"Of course not."

Morrison pursed his lips, looking at the Needle again. "So that's the plan, then."

I smiled. "Yes. Yes, it is. Okay. Gary? Coyote?" I shouted their names and Gary got up from the broken fountain where he cradled Annie. Morrison went to get my drum and Coyote came around a corner a minute or two later, looking less rattled than he had in a while. "What were you doing," I demanded of him, "eating your Wheaties?"

"Something like that. Checking out the grounds. They're a mess."

"I know. And we have to build a power circle around them, anyway." I explained the plan, trying to ignore the dubious looks Gary and Coyote exchanged. "There are four of us, one for each cardinal point, so we—"

Gary's bushy eyebrows went up and he hefted Annie a few inches, like she was a question.

"I'll keep her with me. I'm best equipped for that. Morrison, I want you opposite me in the north. Coyote and Gary can take east and west. I don't know how we're going to manage to line up exactly, with this big of a circle and with us not being able to see each other, but we're going to have to make do. Morrison, I want you and Gary to walk around together. Coyote can go the other way. Crap, how are we going to signal that we're in the right places? You can send up a spark of aura," I said to Coyote. "You two—well, you do your best to think about being ready. Maybe I'll be able to see your auras."

Coyote squinted. "Jo, separating us like that is just asking for trouble. Why don't we go up and use the restaurant as our circle? It's the right shape, and we'll be close enough to one another to provide some backup."

"Because I kind of thought being *in* the lightning rod might be a bad idea, you know? Also, do you really want to be five hundred feet off the ground if the Needle fries and goes to pieces?" My vehemence was born of the fear he was right, that the Center grounds were just too big to build a power circle around.

"I really don't," he admitted, "but are you saying you couldn't keep us safe if the Needle came down? I told you, Jo, you were unassailable back there when the buildings fell. After all that nagging, your shields are finally flawless."

I said, "Nothing's flawless," but I returned the rueful smile he offered. "Fine, then, but if we survive I expect you to take full credit because you *did* nag me endlessly about the shields."

Coyote lifted his voice slightly, not that there was anybody beyond the five of us within hearing range. "I'd like everyone to note that Joanne has just given me permission to take credit for saving the world if we get out of this alive."

"I'm practically sure that's not what I said...."

Laughter drowned out my objection, and I didn't mind at all. We traipsed into the building, Coyote pushing the elevator button without much hope. A small cheer went up when the doors actually opened, though Morrison said, "Do not take an elevator in case of emergency," under his breath.

I patted his shoulder as the elevator began to rise. "Don't worry. I'm practically certain we won't be coming down in it."

"That doesn't make me feel at all better, Walker."

Since the elevator was working, I was less astonished that the restaurant on top was still rotating. In fact, it looked bizarrely normal. Empty, but normal: nothing had been destroyed or even shaken out of place. Silverware and glasses still remained on the tables, which sat neatly in place. If I kept my focus very near, on items in the restaurant itself, I could almost ignore the black clouds hanging so low outside that it seemed we were actually within them. I could almost ignore that—despite the clouds—it was easier to see farther from here than anywhere else in Seattle. I could almost ignore the signs of destruction in my city.

Almost, but not quite. We all stood in the elevator door for a long moment, trying not to see what lay beyond the windows, but then I shook myself and stalked forward. I had to see, as if it would remind me what I was fighting for. As if I needed the reminder.

The Alaskan Way Viaduct and everything along and under it had disappeared, leaving smoke and rubble in its place. No more Pike Place Market, no more Pioneer Square. I swayed, staring at the reminder of how much of Seattle was built up. It had only been a couple of weeks since I'd been crawling through Seattle Underground. My stomach twisted at the thought of the homeless men and women who lived down there, people who had had probably no chance at all to get out. I wondered what had happened to Rita.

I let the Sight filter on bit by bit, afraid I would be overwhelmed if I turned it on all at once. The rain turned black, increasingly laced with dark magic, and it wasn't just rising from Thunderbird Falls anymore. The whole city was feeding it, death and fear and bleak opportunism giving the Master's proxies strength.

There *were* pinpoints of light, and sometimes whole bubbles of it, where Seattle's adepts—whatever sort of magic-users they might be—had gathered to offer sanctuary. There were other places that glowed with a different light, and I thought those might be spiritual centers, fighting against the dark with prayer. They were heroes, choosing to stand against evil. I admired them.

And I feared for them. They were surrounded by a sea of anger, fear, despair, loss, all the dark things that not only drove humanity, but fed my ancient enemy. "The Devourer," Gary said all of a sudden, and I flinched. "S'what Horns called him. The Devourer. S'what he's doing, too, isn't it? He's eating Seattle."

"He's feeding himself with Seattle." The difference in phrasing seemed important, but I nodded either way, then forced myself to step away from the windows. Watching wasn't going to help.

"Okay." I wasn't really talking to my gang, but they all came to attention anyway. "I'm going to do two circles. A big one around the perimeter and a smaller widdershins one inside that. Not right in the center, but I think that won't matter. It's not like I can line up the points to the compass anyway, with the restaurant turning in circles. Sit tight. I'll be back in a minute."

"You want us to take points?" Gary looked like he needed something to do, but I shook my head.

"Not yet. In the smaller circle, yeah." I went around the restaurant anti-rotation so I wouldn't get confused when I did the smaller circle in reverse. It didn't really move that fast, something like one rotation an hour, so I could and did pause and acknowledge the cardinal points when I reached them. Maybe doing that would hold them in place even if our location changed relative to them. When I got back to the boys they'd taken up a back-to-back, shoulder-to-shoulder stance, keeping eyes out in all directions. My drum was on a table and Morrison was holding Annie again, though Coyote kept glancing at them like he was ready to swoop in and save the damsel if necessary. I nodded at the floor. "You can put her down now. I'll build the circle around her."

"Is that wise?"

"I guess we'll find out. No, it is. I've got to protect her as much as anything else. I want her inside both circles. If I do this right, the smaller one will keep things out while the big one keeps them in. It'll be a ring trap. I hope."

Morrison knelt without further argument. I pointed Coyote and Gary to opposite sides of the circle. Gary took up his position with the confidence of long familiarity and the need to do something. Coyote bounced on his toes like an impatient five-year-old, watching me for his cue. Morrison stood and backed away from Annie a few steps, and I backed up with my arms outstretched, gesturing for the others to do the same. When we stood with touching fingertips, I nodded and dropped my arms.

Other shamans could probably do the next part without feeling silly. I still couldn't. I had to clear my throat and shuffle in place a little bit to get myself started. "Raven. Rattler. Renee." The alliteration had seemed a lot cooler when I didn't have to say it out loud in front of people, but my spirit animals didn't seem to mind that a blush climbed my cheeks and made the little scratch on the right one itch. I felt them come to me—Raven perched on one shoulder, Renee on the other, and Rattler winding around my waist like a living belt. Even Raven's usual humor was subdued: he felt as serious and focused as I've ever known him to be. Rattler, who tended toward sarcasm rather than silliness, held his forked tongue on this occasion and poor beleaguered Renee, my newly acquired walking stick who had no evident sense of humor, sat and waited with the patience of a creature for whom forever was a quantifiable and considered window of time.

"Coyote."

Coyote startled like I'd pulled his hair. I gave him a lopsided grin. "No, not you. *Coyote.*"

He mouthed, "Oh," and nodded. I didn't really know if

Coyote was one of his spirit animals, but it seemed unlikely he'd carry the moniker without a direct connection to the big guy. I held Gary's gaze a moment. "Tortoise."

To my complete surprise he inclined his head, but said, "Don't forget Raven, doll," as a snow-white corvid appeared on his shoulder.

My jaw fell open. My *mother* had been friends with a white raven I'd called Wings, but he had been a truly ancient spirit friend, his whiteness earned through age. The bird on Gary's shoulder seemed younger somehow, and wore his brilliant color like it was a battle scar. My raven offered one quiet and dignified *klok!* to his compatriot, who spread his wings a little in acknowledgment. Then he hopped carefully to Gary's other shoulder, and as he did, I saw a familiar hint of the tortoise shell that had protected Gary in the past.

I was dying to know when Gary had picked up a raven companion, but it was obviously going to have to wait. I cranked my mouth shut again, scrambled for dignity and said, "Right. Raven, too," before squinching my face apologetically at Morrison. "Wolf."

Morrison looked dour but didn't object. I grinned, then looked down at Annie. I didn't want to leave any stone unturned. We needed every bit of help we could get, even if the subject was compromised. "Stag," I whispered, "and cheetah. Help me, please. All of you, help me if you can. A thing is coming to kill this world, and we're all that stands between it and success. Anything you can give me, I'll accept. I awaken the outer circle."

Power lanced from me, setting silver-blue fire to the restaurant's perimeter. "Keep it in," I whispered. "All the power we bring here, all the darkness, please, I ask you to keep it within this circle."

Half a dozen spirit animals, creatures of light and line and magic, leaped away, racing to keep the border I'd ignited. Cheetah chased Stag, who jumped straight upward in the middle of the race. Cheetah rushed beneath him, unable to stop in time, and when Stag landed, it was to chase Cheetah instead. A white raven flapped above them, cawing hilarity that matched a wolf's long amused howl. A tortoise crept along steadily, ignoring the others' antics, his solid slow presence anchoring their activity.

No. Not half a dozen. Only five. Coyote had kept his spirit animal close. Five without, four within. One for each of the rotating compass's points. I didn't have time to smile at him for the thought. "I awaken the inner circle. Keep it out. This is our sanctuary, our safe place in the storm. Darkness cannot cross here; nothing can that I do not allow. Recognize those I do allow: my heart." Now I smiled at Morrison, then at Gary. "My soul." Finally, to Coyote, I said, "My guide," and sent power into our small circle, enclosing us in white-hot magic.

Coyote said, "At last," and pummeled me with Raven Mocker wings.

CHAPTER NINETEEN

I wished I could say I rallied. That I'd anticipated it all along and was prepared.

I didn't. I hadn't. I wasn't. Black wings smashed into me and I fell, too stunned to think, much less act. The floor hit me vindictively, knocking what breath remained out of my lungs. I couldn't inhale again, nor was I even sure I wanted to. My world meant very little, maybe nothing, if Coyote was one of the bad guys. It might be better to never breathe again. To never think beyond staticky white shock rushing through my mind, drowning out the sound of blood in my ears.

Someone was screaming. Not outside my head: inside it. Probably me, then. Screaming bewilderment, fear, loss, horror. Screaming at the vast black wings battering our little keep-it-in circle. Screaming as Gary fell beneath the beating wings. Screaming as Morrison fumbled for the gun he'd borrowed from Billy, then fell, too, all of us huddled lumps of confusion and pain.

Coyote stepped over us and knelt beside Annie, his terrible wings encircling her as he crooned, "Forgive me, my love. They would not let me hold you. Wake now and join me at long last. Let us call our master together. Let us—"

Gary, bless him, roared, "That's my *wife!*" and bashed into Coyote from the far side. They both slammed across the little circle, crashed into its wall directly above me and slid down in a writhing, wrestling four-hundred-plus-pound mass that landed more or less on my rib cage.

I hadn't had any breath to lose anyway, but the impact shook off the shocked paralysis holding me in place. I shoved upward, aware that while I was pretty strong, there had to be magic helping me throw that much weight off in one go. That was fine. Better than fine, since it was nice to know the magic chose wisely even if I felt like I was flatlining. But Coyote rose much higher than even a magic-assisted boost could account for, massive wings slamming the circle's walls as he lifted himself out of our reach. There was far too little space for him to fly, but men with wings held no more account-ability to physics than rain-born fire. His face contorted with hatred as he searched for room to maneuver, a way to reach Annie without exposing himself to the rest of us. I put a hand out to Gary, making sure he was all right.

He grunted. I took that as man-speak for "I'm fine," and folded myself into a crouch. *Raven!*

Raven couldn't give me wings, not here in the Middle World. Not unless I was willing to shape-shift, and I wasn't at all sure I could shift into an angel anyway. Natural creatures, yeah, but nobody had—*Coyote* hadn't—given me a primer on shifting into supernatural beings. Of which werewolves didn't count, since a wolf was technically a normal animal.

But I didn't need wings. I just needed to jump high enough to catch Coyote and bring him down to fighting level. I thrust out of my crouch and gained far more height than I should have, a sensation of wings crazy around my spine.

Coyote backhanded me the moment I came in reach, then battered me down to the floor again with his wings. I lay there wheezing and wincing for a couple seconds, trying to come up with a better plan. *Renee?*

It would not be safe to slip through time, she responded, which made me cross my eyes like I could see her inside my head. "Seriously? Because it's not so safe out here, either."

You spoke of your enemy unraveling you from time. Now you lie cheek by cheek with two of his most powerful creatures. This is not the time to take that risk.

Ah. The voice of sense and practicality that I'd needed for the past fifteen months had finally arrived. Her timing was not, I thought, spectacularly good. *Rattler?*

Sssssomeday, my sibilant spirit companion said, *you will learn to think first of me when we mussst fight, Joanne Walker. My friend,* he said to Raven in a much less scolding tone than he'd used with me. My brain was still wondering what messages to send to my muscles when I leaped upward again, snake-strike fast, and body-checked Coyote against the power circle's wall.

Rather to my petty satisfaction, the circle went *BZOT!* like a magically powered electric fence, and for a heartbeat Coyote went slack-jawed and vacant-eyed, his wings turning to black mist.

I took the chance I was given, and rudely invited myself into his garden.

It was not the place I remembered. Oh, the parts were all still there: the hard desert sky, the endless reshaping dunes, the rock garden that held hidden cool spaces for a coyote to wait out the heat of day. But it was subtly wrong: the sky was the wrong color of hard blue, the dunes ever-changing but showing black dust with each shift of wind. The rocks weren't just cool, but cold, the cold of dead things and dank places. I stood alone in that unpleasantry for a moment, fingers steepled against my lips, before daring to whisper, "Coyote?"

For a long time I thought he wouldn't come at all. When he finally did, it was over the rocks, which clicked and knocked together as he climbed them. He had always been silent in his approach before.

He had also always been brick-red with golden eyes before, or a coyote. Now he was neither: the rich color of his skin was cracked and blackened, burned at the edges. He had always been beautiful, but that beauty was ruined now, pain leaking through to corrode the surface.

Wings, black and sooty, trailed across the rocks behind him.

"Coyote." My voice was as broken as his beauty. "Coyote, what happened?"

"Do you really need to ask?"

I did. I thought I did. But I waited before asking again, waited for the answer to come to me. It made no sense. He'd been with me since the beginning. Since long *before* the beginning. Since my childhood, and his youth. Since I was a little girl standing under the desert sun, all unknowing as I showed him the path that lay before him. Since I dreamed coyote dreams as a young teen, learning magic in my sleep. Since I had walked away from those dreams, only to waken to them again with Coyote as my guide. He had helped me, protected me, saved me—

—and the final time he had saved me, I had broken his heart. He had fought the werewolf infection with me, for me, and we had taken me all the way down to the bones to do it. Bones that didn't lie; bones that said my choice was Morrison.

Coyote had retreated in that moment, leaving me alone. He'd come back, but I knew now he had come back broken. He hadn't saved me, when we fought the werewolf infection together. He had sacrificed himself. He'd taken that infection into himself—

His laughter broke over my understanding, shattering it. "You think I'm that noble, Jo? Even now, you think I'm that good?"

"You've always been good. The best," I whispered.

"No. Second best." The whole of his garden flickered with those snarled words, dark images dancing across the sky. Me, surpassing him. Morrison, being chosen over him. Other faces and places I didn't know, though one old man appeared repeatedly. I bet on it being Coyote's grandfather, though I'd never met him. From what little I knew of him, it seemed impossible that he might have belittled Coyote in any way, but imagined slights could be more poisonous than real ones. I, of all people, knew about *that*.

"I didn't *take* the infection," he spat. "I'm not that good a person. I *broke,* Joanne, and it got in. I broke, and it left an opening. My master took it—"

"The Master." I interrupted him in a soft, dangerous voice. "The Master, Coyote. Not your master."

"My master."

"I do not accept that. I don't accept *this,* Cyrano—"

"And what did you expect of a man called Cyrano?" he demanded, which made me stare and then made me laugh, though not happily.

"I don't buy that, either. Cyrano. Coyote. 'Yote." I went through the names deliberately, from the one I called him when I was mad or serious, to the name I used all the time, and finally to the nickname I'd settled on, the one that made me feel closest to him. "We aren't defined by our names. I should know."

"Siobhán." He snarled that, too, like its weigh could curse me.

"Siobhán Grainne MacNamarra Walkingstick. God, what

a mouthful, right? Or just plain old Joanne Walker. I'm both of them. Siobhán's got all this legacy to it and Joanne is who I choose to be. Cyrano has legacy. Who do you choose to be?"

In hindsight, that was a stupid thing to ask just then.

The force of his attack took me off my feet. I went ass over teakettle, bouncing across the dark-laced sand, and skidded to a stop with my feet pointing up a sand dune. "…Ow."

The second attack was just as startling as the first. The earth exploded beneath me, dropping me a dozen feet into Coyote's garden, and I realized if I didn't get my act together he could very easily tear me apart. This was a place where his will ruled supreme, and the only reason I wasn't dead yet was—

Well, probably because hardly anybody could resist their *No, Mr. Bond* confession moment. And I had every intention of drawing that moment out until I got through to Coyote, my Coyote, because no way in hell was I leaving him like this, possessed, infected and one of the bad guys. "Coyote…"

This time when the blow came, I blocked it. It reverberated off my shields hard enough to make sand slip and fall into the pit he'd dug for me. I tapped my snake-speed and jumped, feeling the sensation of wings as I leaped farther out of the pit than even I expected. I landed a dozen feet from him in a perfect three-point superhero crouch. The coat, which knew its duty, settled around me like it had been choreographed.

Coyote also knew its duty, and rolled his eyes with a level of disdain usually only attainable by six-year-olds exasperated with their parents. "The *coat,* Joanne. Really?"

"Really. Maybe you should borrow it, 'yote. It makes me feel heroic, and I'd say you could use a little of that right now." I didn't want to try a full-on assault. Not here, in Coyote's garden. Instead I sank tendrils of healing magic, pure blue, into the sand. If I could burn away some of the infection—

because I refused to accept it was anything *but* an infection—then maybe I could get through to him.

Dune-colored magic rose up, seized my threads and yanked downward. I slammed face-first into the sand. It filled my mouth, my nose, my eyes, and tasted worse than grit. It tasted of bitter oil and dry decay, and it clawed its way down my throat, trying to gain purchase.

Vomiting sand was not high on a list of things I wanted to try again. I spat out mouthfuls, shuddering before clean healing magic washed the flavors away. Coyote snarled as I got to my feet and lobbed fresh magic at me. It hit me square in the chest, but I braced and only skidded backward, rucking up sand, instead of getting knocked halfway across creation. "Coyote, I don't want to fight you."

"Oh, but do. Your defeat will be so much more satisfying to my master if you struggle before it ends." Stone burst from the sand and slammed shut around me. Blind panic turned my vision red for a few seconds. I *hated* being enclosed, and the knowledge that it was a new fear and where it had come from did nothing at all to alleviate babbling terror.

It is only stone, Renee said, *and stone wears away with time.*

Before I could remind her that she'd just warned me not to mess with time, my encasement dissolved into fine blue-tinged particles. They felt old, as if they'd aged thousands of years, and they settled into a pool under my feet. A surge of confidence rushed me. The shining sand beneath my feet was *my* territory, even here in the heart of Coyote's garden. I'd made it my own, and maybe even reclaimed a little something of my friend.

His black-laced golden eyes narrowed. "How did you do that?"

I couldn't help it. I grinned brilliantly and said, "Magic!" in the perkiest tone I could.

A gigantic earthen hand rose up, seized my ankle and slammed me all over the landscape. I wasn't exactly *hurt;* my shields and the shimmering pool of space I'd claimed for myself saved me from that, but nor was I exactly functional when he finally lost interest in bashing me around. I lay on my back, whimpering at the dark sky, and tried to remember when I'd last gotten my ass kicked this thoroughly. Less than a week ago, probably, because it had been a bad couple of weeks, but even then I'd known I was facing the Master, and now—

Now I wasn't able to accept that, because the Master was working through my friend. And I really didn't want to fight my friend, even if the smart part of me recognized that I kinda needed to.

Dimly, it occurred to me that this was the reason he'd been able to fight Suzy. He wasn't using healer's magic. He was using Raven Mocker magic, and Raven Mocker was—

Raven Mocker was the reason I'd lost Marcia Williams in the Lower World. Coyote hadn't been there to save me. He'd been there to save *her.* But he *had* saved me. He'd used healing magic on me, even though that couldn't have been part of the Master's game plan.

Which meant Coyote still had to be in there. He *had* to be, because I wasn't going to take any other answer. My confidence surged, then plummeted again as cold horror made me dig my fingers into the sand. "Oh, God. Oh, God, Coyote. You killed Laurie. You murdered Laurie Corvallis."

"I was so hungry." The confession was a sigh. "You were so busy trying to save your ridiculous Annie, and the reporter was so vulnerable. So delicious, with her will to fight and her fearlessness. The girl saw me, of course, but it was easy to steal her tongue for a little while. To siphon her mind, and taste *her* magic. I didn't dare drink it all, of course. Not with my master's touch on her already, but the taste was enough to numb her thoughts long enough to mislead you."

"How—?" I could move now, and did, rolling over to hands and knees while my chest filled with pain and sorrow. "How did you...numb her mind?"

"What is Raven Mocker but a vampire, Jo? Not the silly things they tell modern stories about, with hearts and passions, but a thing that lives on the blood and viscera of others. A thing that hypnotizes so it can feed more easily. All I had to do was fog her mind for a little while. This power is..." He closed his eyes, spreading arms and wings alike. "It's all I've ever imagined. All I've wanted to be."

"No. My teacher is a good man. He's never craved power for its own sake."

"How would you know?"

"Because a man who wanted power for its own sake would never have let me find my own path." I raised my gaze to his. "He would have kept me far closer than you did. He would have kept me dependent on him. You let me make far too many mistakes for somebody who wanted power for its own sake. I cursed you for it about a million times, but right now I'm glad you did, because it means I'm sure about this."

"Maybe I'm smarter than you think, Joanne."

"I think you're pretty smart, Coyote. Even if I'm wrong, hero worship does tend to make a girl think that way, and I worshiped you for a long time. Let me help you, 'yote." That came out a lot more softly. "Let me help, because I don't want to have to take you down."

"You think you *can?*"

"Let's find out."

I slammed back to the Middle World.

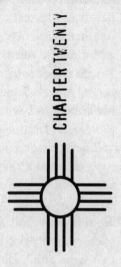

CHAPTER TWENTY

We hit the floor as we came back, having barely finished slithering down the power circle's wall. I had a fistful of Coyote's shirt, anyway, so I took advantage of being that close and took my attack to a purely physical level: a fast elbow swing to the jaw made his eyes cross and bought me four or five seconds of time. "Morrison, he killed Laurie—!"

"Figured that one out on my own, Walker." Morrison was helping Gary to his feet, hauling him bodily toward Annie. "Take care of Bia. We've got this."

If only I knew how. For a split second I considered seizing the gun Morrison carried, but even if I was sure it would work against Raven Mocker, I wasn't willing to use it on Coyote. I forgot about the weapon and turned full attention back to Coyote just in time for him to shake off my hit and seize my lapels in both hands. He spun and slammed me into the power circle's wall, then stretched black wings backward and smashed Gary and Morrison aside. In the same movement, he released me and flipped backward, swear to God, flipped backward from a standing position, and landed over Annie. He crouched above her, hands spread wide, and I Saw the power pour from him into her: black magic, all the gathered power of the wraiths, of a continent's worth of genocides, of the rituals that had brought Raven Mocker to the Middle World at full strength. Annie surged to wakefulness, leanansidhe-silver burning bright. Coyote leaped back with a raw-voiced howl of delight as she came to her feet, leonine grace at odds with her visible age.

There wasn't enough room in the circle for them to stalk each other, but they did. Power poured off them, weighing the rest of us down, pinning us in place. I had felt like that when the Master had come to Tara. I fervently hoped this would not be followed by what that had, which was to say, excruciating pain, but honestly I didn't think the chances of that were good. But I didn't move, and I wasn't sure if it was because I couldn't or just didn't.

Gary was less conflicted, roaring again with rage. I struggled to lift a hand, staying him. "Wait." My voice shook. "Wait. Let them."

"Are you crazy, doll?"

"Yeah." I looked past Annie and Coyote, who circled each other like dancers waiting for the music to bring them together. Looked past them to the storm-cloud-ridden city, to the fires and the aural flares that spoke of pain and fear. "Yeah, I'm crazy, but this was our idea, wasn't it? To gather the power here, so it would give Seattle a break. A chance. But we're fighting this like crazy, and the city is still getting thrashed. We have to do something. Maybe in this case, something is nothing."

"You sure about this, Jo?"

"Yeah." I wasn't, but I could hardly say that to Gary, who was trusting me with something a lot more important to him than his own life. He looked at me a long minute, then nodded.

They *were* dancing. Ritualized steps, at least, and using

identical motions of arms, heads, bodies. They never touched, though their dance became more frenetic and drew them closer to one another. I saw echoes of storytelling in their movements, thrusts and steps that reminded me of the things I'd done over the past year.

No. They didn't just remind me of them. They *were* the fights and mistakes and fears I'd had. They danced genuine spirit dances, telling the story of the Master's coming, and in this time and place, it was my story, too.

It would be absolutely stupid of me to join in, so that's what I did.

I didn't *exactly* mean to. It was just that I saw—Saw—the failures and the sorrows, but nothing of the successes. I had lost Colin Johannsen, it was true. I'd lost Faye Kirkland. But that same day I'd saved Melinda. They weren't dancing that part, so I did. They danced the serpent; I danced the thunderbird, remembering its strength from a year ago and from just that afternoon.

They danced Barbara Bragg's possession. Aching with regret, I danced my refusal to fight the Navajo god Begochidi, and felt their anger grow. They danced the walking dead and I threw the cauldron's shattering back at them. On and on we went, and with every step I felt power coalescing above us, around us. I didn't dare look out the windows, afraid to take my concentration from Annie and Coyote, but I thought—I hoped—we were bringing the bad magic clouding Seattle to us. And if we were, I would not let it be all bad, because the past year had been hell, but it had offered the best moments of my life, too.

A shocking, familiar sound bounced into my bones: my drum coming to life, heartbeat thump waking a wild joy in me. I caught a glimpse of Morrison playing it, and for the space of one breath, Coyote and Annie's dance faltered. Breathless with hope, I took the lead.

I danced meeting Gary, all his gruff generosity and the difference it had made in my life, and they were pulled along with me as much as I'd been pulled along with them. They countered me: they danced the danger he'd faced because of me, the sword strike, the heart attack. I threw the tortoise at them, and they danced Gary's sorrows no more. Before they could take point again, I danced my long story with Morrison, and that, they could barely touch at all. I danced our animosity and our attraction, because they were one and the same, and there was almost nothing they could do about it.

Then they seized a moment of his true anger, a moment when my mistakes had outweighed any fondness. I had endangered a civilian, and Morrison's fury had been well deserved. They took that, strengthened it and regained their place in the dance. Not as leaders, but as competitors: I fought to hold the line, and they struggled to take it.

Without Morrison playing my drum, without Gary's half-heard echo of the beat, I could not have stayed the course. I had been granted tremendous power, but Coyote and Annie were lackeys to a creature older than night. My gifts were the gifts of life, and life, regardless of how brightly it burned, was ephemeral. I would eventually lose, but by *God* I was not going to let them walk away with the win.

It got more difficult the closer we came to now. They became the werewolves, and fear sang in my bloodstream, memory of the shift, of the wild cruelty and hunting hunger coming awake. But I had been saved twice in a handful of moments there, and so I threw Cernunnos's threat into their teeth: I was better off dead than the Master's minion, and he was remorseless in his willingness to be the cause of that death.

Annie responded to that. Not the leanansidhe, but Annie herself, some part of her remembering Cernunnos's embrace. She threw me a lifeline, a single thread of green magic that said *continue,* and after that the Hunt itself couldn't have dragged me from the dance. She was in there, and if she was, so was Coyote. I could get them back, if I fought hard enough. I danced the banshee queen's destruction at Gary's hand; they mocked me with my own mother's taking up of that mantle.

When we came to the battle at Tara, black lightning struck the Space Needle.

It wasn't as though the Needle wasn't designed to take lightning strikes. Any ridiculously tall building was. But there was lightning, and then there was this stuff. Darkness flashed over the restaurant just as electric-blue light might. A sizzle signaled the electronics burning out, begetting the acrid scent of burned wiring. The floor shuddered as the mechanics that kept it turning ground to a halt, and the air outside our smaller power circle turned smoky.

The second strike set something on fire, but I didn't dare stop dancing. I was sweating now, but so were Annie and Coyote. My chest heaved and I tasted the stink of burning plastic as all three of us danced my mother's final death, the one that ensured her spirit would never return to the cycle of reincarnation. It was a blow for both sides: great wisdom and power lost to the good guys, but she had shattered the Master's hold on his banshees, and hurt him in the shattering. She had saved my life—again—and in so doing, left me to face him now. Neither Coyote and Annie nor I could gain the upper hand in that particular telling of my story, but in the last seconds I thrust a spear into the air, shaking it and heralding the awakening of the *new* Irish Mage. I felt impotent fury sluice through the dance, and counted that one in my column.

Lightning fell around the Space Needle in sheets of blackness, throwing us all into ultraviolet relief. Gary's, Morrison's and Annie's hair glowed blue; Coyote's shone with highlights so deep I thought I could dip my hands in them. The whole building rocked and shook in time with our steps, in time with the drumbeat. In a way it was magnificent.

We moved faster than sense could accept as we reached the crescendo. The Master had very nearly won in the Qualla; my only real triumph there was in saving Aidan. But he was my son, and his survival meant more to me than my own. And I had reconciled with my father, an unexpected gift, so while their dance was strong and sure, mine at least brought a counterpoint of joy in the memory of mountain echoes.

When we reached the moment I'd walked into Annie's hospital room and laid hands on her, the earth ripped and the Space Needle listed sharply, throwing us all against the side of the power circle.

Throwing Annie and Coyote together for the first time, their hands finding each other's unerringly.

The sky tore open, and a miasma plummeted into our circle. It brought silence as it fell. The lightning stopped; the creak of the tilting building stopped; the groans of the earth stopped. Even the drum's beat stopped. All that remained was harsh breathing: me, Coyote, Annie. Moonlight, dazzling bright, crashed through the newly washed air outside as if its only purpose was to burn away the black dust that rain had brought.

Except all that dust was inside the restaurant now, making dark living shadows out of tables and chairs and broken chunks of wall. It leaned on our smaller power circle, trying to break in. I caught a faint glimpse of my spirit animals holding their ground, fiery white against the darkness. I was going to have to do something really nice for them if we got out of this alive. And if we didn't, at least I wouldn't have to figure out what qualified as a really nice gift for spirit creatures.

Coyote began to speak what I assumed was Navajo. Annie backed him up in Irish, though I was pretty sure Annie herself didn't speak a word of Irish. Their voices rose and fell in opposites, one strengthening when the other faltered. I scrambled my brain, trying to think of something I could throw into the mix, and landed on Chief Seattle's prayer. It wasn't exactly in keeping with my heritage, but on the other hand, it did belong to Seattle in a very real and particular way, so I lifted my voice and chanted all the ideas in it that I could remember. "'Every part of the earth is sacred, the beasts and the people, we all belong to the same family. The earth is our mother and the rivers our brothers. The wind is our breath, and this we know: the earth does not belong to us. We belong to it.'"

I heard Gary's and Morrison's breath rush out when I started to speak, like I'd given them permission to come alive again. Then they looked at me like I was bonkers, but since I had no credible evidence to the contrary, I didn't mind that so much. Gary, though, apparently kind of figured out what I was doing after a few seconds, and joined in. Not with Chief Seattle's prayer, but with Shakespeare. Because he was Gary, and only Gary was awesome enough to know the whole of the best speech ever written to throw in the teeth of overwhelming odds. "'Once more unto the breach, dear friends, once more!'"

On and on he went, wonderful words that had been spoken millions of times over the years, lending them even more power than they had on their own. Hairs rose on my arms and I gave him a brief, dippy grin as his deep voice echoed against the power circle's walls and drowned Coyote's tenor out.

Morrison stared between us, then straightened and spoke, as well, a speech I should have guessed would resonate with him. "'Four score and seven years ago…'"

A prayer for the land, a preparation for a fight and a plea for equality. It seemed like a fine trio of speeches to meet the Master with. Gary and Morrison came around the circle to flank me, and together we shouted our defiance back at Annie and Coyote.

Even if it was haphazard, it seemed to help. They were struggling already, their bodies trembling and their heartbeats staggering with the strain of calling their master through to the Middle World. Coyote's golden skin had paled, and Annie's was graying, the effort clearly too great for a woman just off her deathbed.

The miasma swirled and flexed, coming together and falling apart again. Coyote's grip on Annie's hand looked hard enough to crush her bones. Sweat rolled off both of them, turning Coyote's hair lank and wetting Annie's until it lay flat against her head. Two people, a man and a woman, striving to bring a third into the world. A new one, born of their efforts.

Born of their lives. Even Annie's god-strengthened green aura was flickering as her strength failed; Coyote's was already nearly depleted, and their heartbeats were becoming increasingly erratic. They were going to die birthing the Master, and there wasn't a goddamn thing I could do about it.

"No." I heard myself under the roar of the storm, under the pounding rain and the howling wind that had taken up life within the Needle itself. *Everyone* heard me, for all that I spoke very quietly. Maybe they heard me *because* I was so quiet: it made them lean in and pay attention. "No. Gary didn't fight so hard for Annie to have it end this way. I am not giving up on Coyote. I am not letting anyone else die because they crossed paths with me."

"Walker—"

"I'm sorry, Morrison. Remember that I love you." Before I had time to think about it further, I ran forward, reaching for Coyote's and Annie's outstretched hands. Offering them what they needed: a body, a new soul, to pour the Master into.

Gary got there first.

CHAPTER TWENTY—ONE

Saturday, April 1, 7:17 p.m.

After the year I'd had, I would have thought I was beyond being surprised by much of anything. I would have been wrong, because I just had not seen that coming. I should have. In the instant that his big linebacker self lumbered between me and birthing Master, I knew I *should* have seen that coming, and I just flat-out hadn't. I crashed against Gary's broad back and *felt* the shock of the Master slamming into him. Every hair on my body stood out, every nerve went to pin-prickles, and Gary howled from the bottom of his gut.

So did I. Horror, disbelief and anger all ripped out of me in a single word: *"GARY!"*

He turned, awkward with the burden he now carried, and casually backhanded me.

I flew across the little power circle, blinded by tears that were only half brought on by pain. The circle caught me and dumped me on the floor. I landed on my feet somehow, the stupid coat flaring and settling gracefully around my legs.

About two seconds had passed. Coyote and Annie still didn't know what had happened, their faces drawn with exhaustion and bodies trembling. They leaned on each other, ghosts of their former selves. Annie looked near to death's door, and Coyote like he could vomit.

Morrison *did* know what had happened. His blue eyes widened with shock, face as pale as his silvering hair as he launched himself into motion and arrested that motion just as quickly. He didn't know where to *go,* gaze torn between Gary and me.

And Gary. My beloved Gary stood nearly in the center of the circle, bending light in toward himself. *Everything* bent in toward him: the circle, the light; even the floor dipped with his weight, tilting it so Morrison and the others started sliding toward him. I clenched my gut and spread my toes inside their boots, like I could keep myself from being pulled toward him, too. He shone with blackness that sucked the color away, leaving the world dim and dull and thin-looking. I didn't need the Sight to see any of that, and I didn't want the Sight for what I *did* need to see.

It came to the fore anyway, and I looked into Gary's tarnished soul.

All the rumbling V8 silver that I knew so well was corroded and black. It crumbled, flaking into pieces that didn't disappear, but collected around Gary's feet, deepening the floor's downward tilt. There was no garden left, just a wasteland streaked by blood so dark I could hardly tell it from the burned earth. My heartbeat was erratic, pulling out of my chest, like it was trying to go smear itself across the landscape. It made an aching empty place beneath my sternum, one that spread deeper and made my stomach feel sick and hollow, just the opposite of how the shamanic magic within me had felt when it came back to life. That had been a fluttering, pushing thing, trying to live. This was trying to kill me. I tried hard not to think that letting it might be okay, and tried even harder to pull myself out of looking into that endless deathscape.

I wasn't sure I'd have been able to, if Gary hadn't moved. His knuckles, where he'd hit me, were rough and bruised. He lifted that hand and rubbed them, then raised gleaming black eyes to mine. I jolted, seeing the real, Middle, world again, and then almost wishing I wasn't. Even if his eyes had been the right color, I'd have known that what was within Gary's shape was not my friend. The thing inside him knew nothing of gentleness or kindness, much less love. Only death and hunger saw me. Assessed me, sizing me up as a curiosity, as a danger and as a meal.

The corner of his lip curled back in a false smile, and the voice that spoke was all the worse for being Gary's own: "Hello, doll."

Somehow that was worse than his eyes, worse than the bleak wreck of his soul. Air rushed out of me like I'd been hit in the gut, and on the breath I said, "Oh, no. No, you don't get to—"

"Ain't this how you always saw me, sweetheart? An old man." Gary smiled again, and even though I knew his teeth were false, I was still surprised they hadn't gotten vampire-sharp and pointed. "Looks to me like this is about perfect. You an' me, doll, together again for the first time. Ain't that how you say it?"

Ice shot up my spine and over my arms in an uncontrollable shudder. "You don't want him. You want me."

"Reckon that's right." He started to move, the first steps as if he was testing out the body. The floor shifted under him, like his presence was a black hole, dragging everything down into it, but it recovered—mostly—when his weight shifted to a new place. "On the other hand, this fella's given me a lot of trouble, and I figure I can make him last awhile." Gary's gaze snapped from me to Annie. The smile happened again, bare teeth with no emotional content behind it, and his voice dropped about an octave. "And *you*. Sweetheart."

Annie didn't look good in the first place, her bones sharp beneath thin papery skin, but she looked worse after those three words. Like all her hope had been sucked away, just like that. Like a lifetime of fighting had turned out useless in the end, and like that was more than she could bear.

Coyote put a hand on her shoulder and—both stupidly and admirably—called healing magic, weary dune and soft sky blue shoring Annie up enough that an unnatural stillness overtook Gary before he pulled his lips back from his teeth again. "Raven Mocker."

"No." Coyote's voice shook. I had to admire him for being able to use that word in the Master's presence. I wasn't sure *I* could have.

Gary guffawed, which should have been a comforting, familiar sound. Instead, it was loud and empty, echoing around the restaurant in search of something to give it meaning. It found nothing and faded. Gary's face had never shown a hint of real humor. "No? It's kinda late to say no now, Raven Mocker. You brought me through. After so long, someone brought me through." His *s*'s got a little sibilant there, like Rattler when he was excited about something. Gary had never done that.

Not that I was under any illusions that Gary was in control, or maybe even alive. I couldn't See *anything* of him in the black desert that had once been his garden. Even from outside, the Master's *weight* was incredible, still pulling all of us toward him. It was hard to imagine Gary hadn't just been crushed beneath it. It was hard to imagine there was any point in trying to fight something that distorted gravity in its immediate area. I was used to being overwhelmed. I had been pretty much since the moment Cernunnos and his incredible, vibrant presence had ridden into my life. The Master was that overpowering, only much, much darker.

"I reject you," Coyote whispered. He didn't sound very convincing. "I was so, so stupid—"

"That's enough, kid." Gary closed a big fist loosely and Coyote's voice cut off. More than his voice: a short choking sound emerged and his face went red, then pale. Coyote's hands went to his throat, scrabbling to find something there that he could pull away, but there wasn't anything, just Gary's—the Master's—will, strangling him.

My own voice broke thin and high. "What're you using, the Force?"

For just a heartbeat, less than a heartbeat, startlement crossed Gary's face. That'd been one of the first things I'd ever said to him, when he'd driven out of the Sea-Tac parking lot while turned around in his seat to have a conversation with me. Whether the Master remembered it or Gary did, it broke through, and in that instant he lost interest in Coyote again. Coyote dropped, hands splaying against the dipped floor while he tried to drag in deep breaths of air quietly.

Gary cocked his head at an unnatural, or at least unnatural to Gary, angle as he turned back to me. Then he moved it to another angle, the motion between looking weirdly snakelike. "The Force. Reckon I am, darlin'. I reckon I am."

My mouth went dry. "I've got a hell of a lot more Force than Gary does."

"Really want me outta here, doncha, sweetheart? Mmm-mmm." Gary shook his head, the same serpentine motion. I guessed that made sense. The Master had an affinity for snakes. I thought nervously of Rattler, and told that part of my brain to shut up. Then I reconsidered, because I already felt like I was thinking too slowly. Way, way too slowly. I had to get the Master out of Gary before something awful happened, and given that Coyote was still struggling to breathe, awful was already on the line. I needed all the parts of my brain that were willing to think at all, even if they were thinking stupid things. Rattler was my spirit guide, not the Master's back door into my skull.

That, I realized with a mixture of hope and alarm, might even be a useful thought. *Rattler?*

My rattlesnake spirit animal was not a creature prone to saying, *You have* got *to be kidding me,* but as he came to life at the back of my skull, I had the distinct impression that was what he was thinking.

Well, can we? Can we trick him that way? I demanded. *Can you be that sneaky?*

I, he hissed, *can be far sneakier than you, ssssilly sssshhaaaman. But this is foolishnessss.*

I had absolutely no doubt he was right, but I didn't have any better ideas, either. *Bide time,* Rattler ordered, and with the word *time,* my walking stick spirit awakened, as well. I felt her there, not speaking, only waiting. Well, if anybody knew when the time was right to strike, it was a snake guided by a time traveler. I bided. Bode. Whatever. I waited, trusting my guides, and aloud, croaked, "You bet your ass I want you out of there. I don't even know how you can *fit* in Gary. He's only human."

Gary laughed again, that sharp blank sound. "Aw, c'mon, sweetheart, doncha think better of the old man than that? Maybe he ain't magic-born, but he's been steeped in the stuff his whole life. And more, he has stood against me, thrown time in my teeth, *stolen* from me—" He didn't sound like Gary anymore. His voice had lightened, resonating instead of rumbling, and the words were different from the ones Gary would choose. I wondered if it was easiest for the Master to use the familiar cadences of the host body's usual speaking patterns, and if he only saved his own vocal idiosyncrasies for the really important moments. Like now, as he spat the last of his words and jabbed a finger toward Annie. *"Thou. Art. Mine."*

"Never." Annie lifted her chin, her rejection far more confident than Coyote's. "Not in all the years of my life, and not in the hereafter." She got to her feet as she spoke, slim and defiant. "You think we ordinary humans can't stand against you, but that's all most of us ever do. You can kill me, but you can't break me, and you're too late to make me yours. I belong to Cernunnos now, if I belong to anyone besides my husband. You lost."

Gary's lips peeled back to reveal the awful smile again. I knew people conveyed a lot of subtext with their mouths, but I didn't usually *notice* it so much. I wished I didn't have to notice now. "I have him," he said to Annie. "Would you like to feel his heartbeat? How it races? How it pounds? How long can it continue this way without giving up? Without bursting?"

Way back in the back of my throat, where I was sure it wouldn't come out, I made the shape of the word *forever.* Because the Master was right: Gary *was* steeped in magic. He'd ridden with Cernunnos. He'd fought with me and with Brigid. He'd chased down a demon or two in his time, and perhaps most importantly, he had two spirit animals, one of whom had come to him after a heart attack, to offer him strength and longevity. Buried in there somewhere was the staid, steady tortoise, its protective shell still holding in place. As long as that creature was with Gary in some way, I had no doubt at all that his *body* could take what the Master meted out.

The very brave part of me thought maybe the same was true of his soul, but that part apparently hadn't taken a good look at the pitted ruin of his garden.

"I may lose, too," Annie said quietly, "but humans do. We live and we love and we die. If Gary dies, I'll be devastated. Of course I will. But you will still have lost *me,* and I think you probably take that as a far greater insult than bowing to the inevitability of death is to me. I was a nurse," she reminded him. "I've seen this happen hundreds of times. You, on the other hand..." Somehow she managed a smile. A real one, faint but gentle, an agonizing comparison to the emotionless thing Gary kept spreading across his face. "I think you're not used to losing at all, but right now you're standing between the only four people on earth who have defeated you in living memory. And you think *we* should be afraid?"

When he tried to seize the breath from her body, I was ready. Shields leaped to life, clinging to Annie like an ethereal wedding gown. The Master's black power hit so hard *I* swayed with it, but Annie stood straight and tall and not just a little arrogant. I wished she'd been around for all of our adventures, because I could've used her kind of positive thinking plenty of times over the past year.

Gary whirled toward me again, big hands curled like claws. The Master was getting better at using the body: everything about the action was sinuous and easy and horrible. I tried to match Annie's expression of fearless arrogance, but he hadn't let up on the pressure he was bearing down on Annie, and it was starting to feel like a tidal wave. I thought keeping my feet was doing pretty well.

Actually, I thought it was way more than just doing pretty well. I thought it was enormously unlikely. The Master had flayed me from the inside out a number of times back in Ireland, and all he was doing here was trying to deflate a few lungs. I dragged in a breath like the idea made it hard to breathe, and forced words out under the weight of his presence. "What do you *want?*"

"You really gotta ask?"

I really didn't like him sounding like Gary again. Trying to fight something that looked like Gary was going to be bad enough. At least if he sounded different it was easier to remember that my friend wasn't the one in control. Not that I was going to forget, but it didn't damned well help. Maybe getting him to talk more would bring out the other voice, the one he had to think about to use, so I managed a sick curve of my lips. "I've never been all that good at figuring things out."

"Ain't that the truth." He prowled forward, never lessening the crush of power directed at Annie. She held her ground like it was nothing, but my head was starting to hurt. I didn't know how long I could protect her. Something was going to have to change, and fast, or he'd just obliterate me. And then everybody I loved. He stalked around me and I tried not to watch, pretending a cold chill didn't skitter over my whole body at having him behind me. Gary could be graceful, but he didn't move like that. I wished he'd stop.

He did stop, right behind me. Close enough that I felt his breath against my neck when he spoke. "Blood. Fear. Pain. Death."

I shivered like the stereotypical leaf in the wind, but also found a snort of derision brave enough to make itself heard. "Yeah, I know *that*. That's what you feed on. Death magic, woo woo." Ah yes, sarcasm, my old friend. The only thing to get me through a lot of stupid, dangerous situations. It never helped, except in making me feel just a tiny bit better. "No, seriously, for a big scary death magic you're also kind of lame, aren't you? All these avatars and servants. You don't *do* anything yourself. They just feed you from afar, because you can't even manifest a body. But c'mon, guy like you, what do you even *need* a body for? They break easily, and it's not like you can't get people to do your bidding."

I carefully didn't look at Coyote during that last bit, but in not looking at him, out of the corner of my eye, I saw Morrison's face twitch like he couldn't believe I was baiting the Master, and also like he couldn't believe that he couldn't believe it. It was Schrödinger's twitch, neither believing nor disbelieving until we got out of here alive. I was glad to provide him with some thread of humor in the midst of this mess, but I also really wished he would just grab Coyote and Annie and run away.

"Gotta have a body to fill up, doll. Can't get sated if you got no stomach. 'Sides." Gary came around to face me, eyes glinting black. "You got one thing right. It ain't this body I want."

"Then take this one!"

A collective sound of dismay emanated from Morrison, Coyote and Annie. Gary's attention strayed to them, which was exactly where I didn't want it, so I shoved him. Put a hand on his shoulder and shoved, which *did* get his attention, but also shot black pain through my palm and up my arm. It actually had color, that agony: despite my shields it slid right up through my veins, discoloring them. I gasped and knotted my other hand around my forearm, cutting off the sluicing black magic.

When I looked up, Gary's vicious grin was three inches from my face. "Sweet, darlin'. You're a better fit, no doubt, but you're not thinking things through." He moved that grin even closer, as if he'd kiss me with it, and for a wild moment I wondered if he'd been harboring some secret truth under all the teasing we'd undergone about being a couple. From right there, half an inch from my mouth, he whispered, "I live on pain, babe. You think I'm gonna take you first, when everybody you love is standin' right here? Don't be stupid, Jo. We're just gettin' started."

CHAPTER TWENTY-TWO

A lot of things happened at once, or close enough to count. I snapped, *"Go!"* to Morrison and the others, then seized Gary's face and kissed him.

The good news was the only expression of surprise I had to deal with was his, as I couldn't see Morrison or Annie. The bad news was Gary actually kissed me back, which I really hadn't been expecting.

And the worst news was that in some awful, hideous way, it was a *terrific* kiss. Not so much the brain-spiking agony that came along with it as black power flowed from the Master into me, trying to take my magic, to feed on it like he fed on everything else. That wasn't great. But this was Gary's body, and it had been pretty clear from the get-go that if he'd been thirty years younger I'd have been following him around with puppy-dog eyes. *That* part of him knew how to kiss a girl. The guy with the roguish grin and the twinkle in his eye, the guy who quoted Shakespeare at the drop of a hat and called it like he saw it, well, when he called a kiss like he saw it, it turned out to be toe-curlingly, knee-weakeningly, butterfly-inducingly good. It reminded me of the moments when I'd been allowed to glimpse his garden or see the world he'd once known through his garden self's eyes, and it told me, all over again, how in almost every way that counted, he'd shown me how to grow up and how to love people. It was a kiss that rushed us through the bad times—heart attacks and demon hunts—and lingered on the good, on the friendship and laughter and adventure.

When, shocked, I let him go, he dropped a wink that was pure Gary, and my heart turned to a cold stone in my chest. If Gary was still in there somewhere, and he had to be, if the Master could kiss me like that, then it made what was almost certainly going to happen much, much harder.

On the plus side, we weren't in the Space Needle anymore.

Unfortunately, we weren't in the Lower World, either, and that's where I'd hoped to bring us. The whole point of kissing him had been a distraction, to haul him into another plane. I wanted this fight to be out of sight and out of reach, especially out of Annie's sight and reach. Morrison could cope and Coyote wasn't really in a position to object, but if it came to it, Annie did not need to see me destroy the thing that her husband had become.

But instead of the Lower World's yellow sky and red earth, we were shrouded in mist and green-gray silence. A sense of eternity and expansion flowed through the soft air, as if our immediate surrounds were solid only out of an obligation to our mortal forms. I had the feeling that if I could only run fast enough I would burst through the physical world here and find myself in a lost expanse of space, looking down at the stars. I pulled a startled breath, tasting the rich rot of dying earth and the cleansing dampness of wet air.

The breath burst out of me in a *"Wuh?"* and for a moment or two I let myself forget about the problem at hand as I stared around. I knew this place. I'd been here three times: once to see the land Cernunnos called home, once to steal a sleeping half god's body back from its resting place, and once to heal the dying land. I was pretty certain a fourth visit meant I was going to be stuck here forever, although that was possibly only if I came with Cernunnos.

Which was the only way I knew to *get* here. Tir na nOg was more than a different plane. It wasn't like the Lower and Upper Worlds, crooked reflections of the Middle World, the earth I knew. It was a world of its own, somewhere only reachable through the stars. Time travel was appalling enough. I actually turned an eye inward to stare in horror at Renee. *You don't* tesseract, *too, do you?*

She shook her head no, but I wasn't really listening, because I didn't really think she was responsible for our arrival in Cernunnos's home world. "What, I can't—how did we get *here?* Cernunnos? Where—what the hell?" I was sure I should be able to do better than that, but my mental faculties were too busy slamming up against walls of impossibility for me to get beyond half sentences and stupid questions. *"Gary?* Did you—I mean, how could you, you can't, you're—but you did ride with him for, like, ever, so did you—?"

A little belatedly, I realized he wasn't, like, trying to kill me dead, or take over my body, or do any of the other things I might expect the Master to be doing while I stood there flapping my jaw like an idiot, and I finally tore my attention from our bewildering surrounds to look at him.

He wasn't my Gary anymore. I mean, he was, but he was the Gary of forty years ago, young, strong, in his absolute prime. He was beautiful, broad-shouldered and smiling, wearing the soldier's uniform I'd seen him wear in his garden. His arms were spread, face uplifted, and every breath he took shifted the mist, pulling it deep into him. It sank into his skin, too, lending it a glow that was more than health: power flowed through him like blood in his veins, strengthening him with every moment.

A penny dropped at the back of my head. A cold penny, dripping all the way down my spine and sending goose bumps over my arms. Mist clung to the lifted hairs while I worked to get a word out. I knew the look on Gary's face. I'd seen it on Cernunnos's; I'd felt it on my own. It was a relaxation and relief and gladness and acceptance of familiar problems. It was an expression almost anybody could recognize. It said one thing: it said—

"Home," breathed the Master, and my vision went white with panic.

Trying for the Lower World had been dangerous enough. It was powerful, full of inherent magic, because even if the power Gary had been infused with tapped out, it was entirely possible the Master could take sustenance from the Lower World itself. I'd figured it was a risk worth taking, because I *knew* he could plug into the Middle World, full as it was of pain and fear and loss, especially in Seattle right now. If I'd been braver, I might've tried taking him to the Upper World, which was purely a place of spirits, and somehow seemed less vulnerable, but I wasn't all that confident of my own skill set there.

Tir na nOg was a freaking *disaster* for me, if the Master knew it as home. I mean, it knew me, we'd had some good, world-saving times together, but I wasn't *of* Tir na nOg, and it was starting to look like the Master was. He was speaking again, not at all to me, although I was his only audience. "Home. Oh, I knew not how fortunate I was when this body came to me. It knows this world in its old bones, when I have not known it in the flesh at all. I had thought myself thwarted in the pursuit of the old woman, but I see now that it was necessary. This is as it was meant to be, only I could not see clearly enough to know it. For this—" and it suddenly sounded like he was talking to himself "—for this I shall save her for last, that you might eke every moment out of your possible time together. Such is my magnanimity."

"Wait." My voice came out as a rasp, hardly a sound to disturb the roaming mist. "Wait, how can it be your home? How can... What? How? I mean... Who are you?" Of all the stupid questions that it had never really occurred to me to ask before, but then, I'd never been given the sense that the Master *had* a home, not until this very moment, and it suddenly seemed that if he had a home, then maybe he had a name and motivation beyond *kill all the things*.

"I have no name." The answer came like poison through the mist, staining it and corroding the breath in my lungs. "My brother took form and name and would share neither with me, consigning me to endless hunger and emptiness. I have strained and I have struggled to survive. I have eaten the very body of this world and the flesh of men, and I have struck at him time and time again, starved for sustenance, and *finally I am made*. I will not be unmade. This body you so love will be my strength until its inborn power fades. Then I will have each of those you love, until there is nothing left for you but despair, and then you will be mine for eternity. Within you, I will make your world *mine*."

"Hah!" The sound blurted through my lips, surprising me. "I've already been made that offer by somebody a whole lot more appealing than you, and I turned him down."

Black eyes or not, Gary gave me a very sly, very Gary look, and dropped his Master cadences for Gary's. "Yeah? Didja kiss him that way, too, sweetheart?"

Heat erupted around my collarbones and swept upward. I had, in fact, kissed—or been kissed by—Cernunnos in a very similar fashion. Gary let go a bark of laughter that, unlike the others before it, sounded real, like he was starting to understand humor. It went flat, though, flat with rage and hate, and though he retained Gary's manner of speaking, nothing about him was Gary-like. "You're talkin' about my brother, doll. You shoulda taken him up on that offer, 'cause on your own, you can't stand against me. Never could. Never will."

"Your bro…" The sensation of draining blood, the wash of sudden cold, was so abrupt and real I looked at my feet, expecting to see a seeping red puddle expanding around them. There wasn't one, but no warmth returned to my body as I wrenched my gaze back to the Master's. "Cernunn… Oh, my god. Oh, my God. You're… No, shut up, shut *up!*" I pinched my fingers together as Gary drew breath to speak again, like I could squish his lips shut with the gesture.

Surprise shot his bushy eyebrows upward and he said nothing, which astonished the part of my brain given over to thinking about details like that. Most of me, though, was trying to scramble through the jigsaw pieces and put them together at top speed. "You're two-spirited," I said in pure bogglement. "Like Billy and Caroline, or Aidan and Ayita. I mean, aren't you? Pretty much? Except what, what, you're—"

I was actually pacing, talking faster and faster, while my mortal enemy stood there watching me and looking increasingly amused. I didn't think this was any kind of reprieve. I was pretty certain he wanted very much for me to put all the pieces together so I could understand just how badly I was screwed before he got busy with obliterating me. It would be more fun that way. More *painful* that way, and he thrived on pain.

It came together with an audible click in my ears, stopping

me in my tracks. I wasn't even looking at him, only staring blankly at the whispering mist as I spelled it out. "He's an agent of order. I always knew that. He rides to collect souls, to bring them back into the circle of reincarnation and birth and death. Nobody's ever going to convince me death is a good thing, but I get what he does and how he fits in. And you're the other side of it. You're the chaos aspect. You're the reveling in pain and killing for the sake of it, no order or sense, just agony. And the thing is that you're inseparable, aren't you. I never thought about it, but you don't just get one without the other, no matter how hard we might try. But, what?"

I turned to him, to Gary, to the Master, whose face was contorted with the hatred of comprehension. "Two spirits, one body. I know what that does in a human, I've seen the kind of power, the depth of magic, the resonance and the understanding it creates. Only, what, when you're god-level magic, there's only enough room in a body for one spirit? And he won it, back at the beginning of time?"

The question woke a battle in the mist, two vast amorphous creatures locked in a struggle that had the sense of eternity to it. Life sprang into being in Tir na nOg while they fought, and the idea of physical presence drifted into their awareness. They sought form from the world itself, and the world would only give up a certain amount of itself to them. Moons, oceans, continents, living things and dying bodies: they were shaped and shaved and made smaller, the intensity of eternal existence binding itself into a comprehensible form over an impossible amount of time. Pieces were shorn off, aspects that one or the other desired or rejected as they strove to fit into a body too small to contain all of eternity. In the end Cernunnos rose from the battle, so massive that his footsteps left lakes, kicked up mountains, felled species. But each step he took reduced him, not in power but in size, until his form bled with it, until he was more than an archetype. Until he was a god, a thing that could walk among men and awe them with his presence. He was all of the things that he had chosen in his making, all of the things that his other half had rejected: he was an acceptance of life's circle, a thing that prided itself on smoothing that circle, on offering a kind of raw comfort in the face of oblivion.

He left the Master behind, nameless, formless, enraged and not, in the end, without power. The Master faded into the mist, becoming part of it, carrying hatred and pain into it until those things were invasive, easy to breathe in, impossible to separate from the body when inhaled, able to influence but never able to possess. For time immemorial he had struggled to *become* in the way that Cernunnos had, and for as long he had been denied.

Until now. Until today, when my best friends and I had brought him into the world.

"Oh, my god," I said again, much more softly this time, and for the second time I was speaking to someone specific when I said the words. "When we first met, Cernunnos wanted me to ride with him. He almost said it in as many words, that he wanted me to be the other half of his soul. We'd be unstoppable, he'd said. Because if we were one, he'd be complete. There'd be no room left for you. All of this might have been averted. So many people might still be alive." Frustrated rage suddenly spun me away from the Master, erupting in a useless bellow at the mist, as if Cernunnos would hear it: "You could have fucking *mentioned* some of this!"

"Have you no pity for me?"

Had he spoken in Gary's voice, it might have worked. It almost did anyway. I turned back from my flash of fury to gape at the youthful lie that was my friend. He was not only strong and handsome, then. He was alone, hideously alone, a thing that had been abandoned in its making and had never found a place of safety in the world. Shaped into human form, in that moment he looked nearly broken, shoulders sagged and face averted. Anyone could pity something that pathetic.

But then like a misbehaving child, he glanced at me to see if the pose was working. To see if I was buying it. Any pity I had evaporated. "No. I don't. Death, maybe death is inevitable, but you're strife. You're conflict and pain and hatred and cruelty, and you've pretty well chosen to be that, so no."

"He took everything else from me!"

"I *saw* it, buddy. I watched your fight with Cernunnos. I just saw you both shed everything you didn't like and keep what you thought would make you strongest. Trouble is, he was right, you were wrong. And now it's over."

Gary's mouth peeled back in a vicious smile. "It ain't over until your heart's broken and your body's mine, sweetheart. Let's dance."

He came at me, and the world shattered around us.

CHAPTER TWENTY-THREE

We were *supposed* to snap back to the Middle World. I could feel it in Gary's intent, in his hunger for Coyote and Annie, and especially for Morrison, who was my heart. I assumed he had some kind of plan for me during the time that he was torturing and eating them, since it wasn't like I would hang out and applaud his efforts without interfering, but that wasn't foremost in his mind just then. He wanted to get us back to the Middle World.

Thwarting that was, for the moment, sufficient for me. I held the image of the Lower World in my mind as hard as I could, envisioning the yellow road that Coyote often walked along to get there. But it was mist-shrouded, just like Tir na nOg, too airy and breezy to hold on to. Gary's nasty grin split again, and since I was right there, face-to-face with him, both of us tumbling through the ether, I took a page from a long-ago fight with Cernunnos and kneed the Master in the crotch.

It worked just as well on him as it had on Cernunnos. Outraged shock and pain wiped every other expression from his

face and for a heartbeat I was able to take control of our headlong tumble through the ethereal planes. I was definitely putting that one in the handbook of fighting gods: groin shots
were totally fair. I didn't even feel guilty about it technically
being Gary's body, because if there was any chance of getting
him back, it would be worth tenderized *huevos*.

I tore apart the mist, wrenching us toward the Lower
World. The dispersing mist cooled, turning whiter, and the
sky lightened until it finally tinted toward pale blue. The air
chilled until I saw my breath on it, none of which was right
for the Lower World. Despair shot through me and, like I'd
offered him delicacies on a silver platter, the pain washed out
of Gary's face and turned to triumphant glee. My stomach
clenched and I held on to him harder, desperate to reach the
Lower World instead of crashing back into Seattle. We fell,
picking up speed, until I was pretty certain terminal velocity
would smear us both across the restaurant floor when we hit.

Mist became clouds and we broke through their bottom,
falling past the edge of the world.

For a little while we were both too surprised to kill each
other. The edge of the world zipped by, waterfalls cascading
off it into fog and clouds. Stubborn greenery clung to the sides
here and there, softening the wall of rock. Clouds receded,
and after not very long at all, the bottom of the world, as flat
and sharp-sided as the top, flew past. I looked for elephants
carrying the whole disk on their backs.

There weren't any, but below us there was a whole lot of
nothing. Blue and clouds went on pretty nearly forever, and
where they faded, they did so into the glimmer of stars. The
only real sound was the wind screaming past our ears.

"Hah." The sound tore away like the soft breath it was. I'd
missed hitting the Lower World, but the Master hadn't gotten us to the Middle World, either. We were in the Upper

World, and I thought that might be just a smidge more in my favor than his. Either way, Morrison and the others weren't here, which made it a place I was happy to be.

I didn't, of course, have any particular idea how to conduct a fight while falling at top speed through an endless world of sky, but I still felt this was a better situation than I'd been in a few minutes ago.

Now, Renee said, and my body burst apart.

It came together again in a heartbeat, taking on a shape that was becoming familiar: the thunderbird. Rattler's golden color cast itself over Raven's vast wings; speed became second nature, a breathless, comfortable part of my being. Dangerous claws flexed and clenched: I had Gary's body in their grip. My eyesight was agonizingly sharp, showing me all the stars into which we fell, but I had no more fear. I had wings, and with them flew, pulsing higher into the endless sky. Sooner or later I would reach the top of the world, and from there I could dash my prey against the ground and destroy it.

Gary twisted in my claws. I clenched them tighter, but he slithered and wiggled, more than just the shape of a man struggling to escape. I dropped him and dove after him, taking the moment of freedom to see what he fought to do.

Wings erupted from his body as easily as they'd been born from mine, but his were white in their moment of creation, and stained black in the endless sun an instant later. I remembered too late that he now had a raven spirit animal as well as the tortoise.

They came together as Raven and Rattler had, making a creature greater than the sum of its parts. Black feathers shellacked with thin tortoiseshell, their patterns perfectly reminiscent of Native Alaskan paintings. The bird's neck extended, vulturelike, beak sharper and more deadly than a tortoise's and stronger in its snap than a raven's. Its legs shriveled, becoming thinner and more birdlike than a tortoise's, but still four of them remained on its sleek long birdlike belly. Its tail elongated, thinning, whipping the sky with audible cracks, and the very, very human part of me buried in the thunderbird's brain said, *That's a motherfucking* dragon, *guys.* I got no dissent from the varied parts of me that were the spirit animals, even though I really, really wanted them to disagree. Still in the back of my brain, I said, *Fuck,* and slammed into the thing at hundreds of miles an hour.

It should have been broken into a thousand pieces beneath my force. Instead its tortoiseshell absorbed the impact, ripples of power shuddering through the broad wings and long spine. Or ripples of pain that it converted into power: this was a place of spirits, and where the flesh was weak, the spirit, in this case, was more than willing to work with that. We broke apart in a thunder of sound, its wings clattering like wooden wind chimes. It didn't fly as easily as I did: it was weightier, clumsier, either with lack of practice or because tortoises were not known for their aerial skills. Neither, of course, were rattlesnakes, but at least snakes were lithe and quick, whereas tortoises tended to be more ponderous. Still, it flew, and until I could capture it and tear it back into its component parts, I wouldn't be able to smash it against the earth and end it.

A spike of distress rolled through me, more poignant than the panic of naming my opponent a dragon. The thunderbird was murderously practical; it had no objection to destroying Gary's body in order to kill the Master. I knew it was right, and that I shouldn't, either, but it was an archetype, an idea of cold passions and no humanity. I was still very much human, and Gary was my best friend. Part of me knew what I might have to do, but I wasn't yet ready to take it as writ.

The truth was, I would never be ready, even if that meant the end of the world.

I didn't even have time to roll with that, to try to figure out what it meant for this whole fight, before the reshaped Master slammed into me with claws as deadly as my own. More deadly, maybe: heat blossomed where they struck me. A *skree!* broke loose from my throat and I tucked my wings, spinning in the air to dislodge the monster on my back. It shook free and I flung my wings wide again, stopping myself just long enough to get him below me. Healing magic spilled through me, cooling the fire within as I dived, plummeting at top speed to bash into him again.

His beak slashed me, making another line of fire across my shoulder. I bit into him as hard, coming back with a mouthful of flame, and spat it at him. It clung to his shell-covered feathers, but didn't burn through. Of course not. Pain was his weapon. Mine was healing. I poured gunmetal-blue magic into his wound and he screamed.

He also healed, which was not at all what I'd hoped would happen. Swearing under my breath—it turned out a bird did that kind of muttered angry sound very well—I released him and backwinged to gain space to dive again, hoping to break him apart if I couldn't rip him without damaging myself. When I hit again, he rolled and seized me with his claws. We bashed each other with our wings, slashing and clawing, never fearing to hit the world below as we fought like earthbound creatures tumbling through the sky.

Trouble was, hitting the earth was starting to sound necessary. The heat pouring through me from his attacks was incredible, my healing magic barely mitigating it. That had happened once before, too, back on the day we'd created Thunderbird Falls. The fire of *wrongness* that I'd experienced then had stunted my ability to heal. This felt like that, only vastly increased. His taint was heat, stronger than me, but then, he was a *god,* and I, for all my power, was only human. A very impressive human, with a newborn soul and all the attendant power boost that came with it, but in the end, I was human, and he was a disembodied god.

Well, now he was an embodied god, actually, which didn't help at all. Gary's spirit animals were strong enough to take a lot of abuse, and that was exactly what the Master wanted to mete out. I had to figure out how to separate them, to get the Master out of Gary without killing Gary. Thinking rationally while spinning through the air was not my strong suit.

Especially with the fire sluicing through me. Forget separating Gary from the Master: I was burning up, heat from the dragon's strikes killing my guides and me. The fire felt like it came from the core of me, and pretty soon nothing I could do would hold the Raven-Rattler-Joanne compound together. I folded my wings, becoming a dead weight on the dragon, and after a few seconds it released me to escape and achieve a better angle of attack. I crashed my wings open, gaining height and trying to think of an escape route.

Rattler and Raven tightened their grip on each other, intensifying their presence as the thunderbird. I slipped, even though that was impossible. *I* was the body. They were the spirits. There was no way they could retain physicality without me in the mix.

Renee whispered, *Wrong,* and the thunderbird broke away from me.

Together, still bound as one, a creature of pure spirit, Raven and Rattler struck the dragon with claw and beak, and tore from it Gary's spirit tortoise.

For an instant, a heartbeat, an eyeblink, I thought it was going to work. That they would rip the tortoise away, weaken the Master and come back to me. The tortoise pulled away, its link to Gary stretching and weakening and finally snapping. Gary fell, his raven wings faded to nothing: one spirit animal was not enough to hold the spirit-shaped dragon form. Inside that heartbeat, triumph spiked through me so strongly I felt faint from it. We were going to *win*.

The next heartbeat lasted forever, a gut-wrenching contraction as I realized that coming back to me had never been Raven and Rattler's plan. They kept flying, tortoise spirit in their thunderbird talons. Kept climbing higher, receding fast as the Master and I fell away at speed. I saw, or maybe just imagined, my entwined spirit animals looking back at me once, and felt a whisper of a touch inside my mind: *Goodbye, ssshaman.*

Far, far away, in the distant reaches of the Upper World's endless sky, thunderbird became phoenix, and immolated with the tortoise in its claws.

Gary hit the floor of the spire restaurant so hard it reverberated. I didn't. I *sank,* slipping through like I was a ghost. A spirit. Like I was nothing, like I no longer existed, and I couldn't stop myself from falling.

I am sorry, said Renee, and time unwound itself just a little.

A moment later, I hit the floor, too, my bones bending with the force of impact. I snapped upward, returning to my body from where my spirit had been sinking through the floor. My head bounced off rubble, and in the stars I saw Renee knitting *then* and *now* together.

Then was a heartbeat ago in the Upper World, two of my spirit animals given physical form by the third, who stole it from *now* to lend to *then*. She had taken my body away from the moment of impact and lent it to Rattler and Raven, giving them the ability to rip Gary's tortoise away while releasing Gary and me back to the Middle World. He'd come all at once, part and parcel, but I'd been split spirit from body, and my spirit had landed first, falling through the floor. My body had come after, catching up after its physical presence was no longer needed in the Upper World.

Then and *now* became one, a time-slip of only a few seconds smoothing itself out without effort, but I lay where I'd hit, unable to even blink. I knew what would happen if I did, and I couldn't let tears fall.

Instead I spoke. Whispered: speaking aloud was far beyond my capabilities. "You...killed them. You let them die? You..." *Raven? Rattler?* Their names inside my head were desperate and empty, echoes their only response. I felt naked, naked *inside,* somehow, as if everything that had shored me up for the past fifteen months had been stripped away. "No. No, no, no, no you can't, you can't be gone, you can't, Rattler, Raven, *Raven,* Ravenravenravenraven please come back, no, no, no, don't do this don't *do* this—"

But it was too late. They'd done it already, all three of them, made a decision I hadn't gotten to take part in. I searched helplessly, hopelessly, for some kind of answer from within my mind, and got nothing. No snarky hissing rattlesnake, no enthusiastically bouncing raven. It was just me.

Me and Renee, and sensing her, I went cold. So cold I could hardly feel my own body. *She'd* survived, when my sweet, crazy Raven hadn't, and I was never going to forgive that.

I am sorry, Renee said again.

"Go away." They weren't words. They were a growl, a snarl, a threat of such violence I couldn't comprehend how to carry it out. Renee winked out of my consciousness and I screamed, the sound bloodying my throat. I rolled onto my forearms and shins, head ducking between my arms, and the worst of it was I wasn't even allowed to scream again, or to mourn at all, because in rolling I ran into Gary's gray, still body, and a whole new panic rose to sandwich the pain of loss.

My magic was still there. Horribly, impossibly, it wasn't even diminished without Raven's and Rattler's presence. It was still there, and it leaped into Gary, searching for lingering life within him.

It was there, barely. His heartbeat stuttered, no longer shored up by the tortoise's strength. More than that: pulled out of rhythm by the tortoise's loss, as much as my own gut and heart were torn and abused by Raven and Rattler's. My hands were nothing but cramps, my body in throes of agony that I couldn't soothe. I'd been hurt so many times over the past year, but the only thing I'd ever felt as unforgiving as this was Ayita's death. Ayita, Rattler and Raven. I was still screaming as I healed Gary, a thin high wrenching scream that hurt my throat as badly as the first one had. I couldn't stop. I could hardly breathe around the sound, but I couldn't stop, and the magic did nothing to ease it.

It didn't do enough to ease Gary, either. It wasn't the magic: I felt it in me as strongly as ever. It was me, so angry, so hurt, that I didn't know how to get beyond it. Someday I would be able to stop screaming. Maybe then. Until then, Gary was not dying: his heartbeat was steady, his breathing was regular, and that was as much as I could do. The rest, the spark of life, the healthy color, all the things the Master had drained from him, those weren't things I could fix. Not right now. Maybe never.

"Call. My. Brother." The grated voice was half-familiar. I dragged my gaze from Gary's barely breathing form to find Morrison standing above us. His eyes were black as death and his skin a terrible pallor, almost as bad as Gary's. He had no magic in him, nothing to feed the Master except his own life source, and that would burn out in no time at all.

There was no way. No way the Master would choose Morrison over Coyote, even if he was desperate for a host. I stared at him without comprehension, trying to understand why of all people here, the Master would choose *Morrison,* until his face contorted and he snarled, *"Call my brother,"* again.

When I still didn't move, Morrison drew the duty weapon

he had borrowed from Billy and pressed it against his own temple. This time his voice was soft, even calm. "Call my brother, Walker, or this body dies."

CHAPTER TWENTY-FOUR

"Get out of him." The scream was gone from my voice, but what was left sounded like the ruin of my heart. It probably was. "Get out of him and I'll do it."

"C'mon, Walker. If I get out of him, what's to make you keep your end of the bargain?"

"If you kill him, I will sure as *fuck* not do what you want. Get out of him. Go..." There was only one place he could possibly go in this scenario, even assuming Coyote or Annie were still around and hadn't run away like sensible people would. None of my friends were sensible, but I wouldn't let myself look for them as I got to my feet, raggedly, and spread my arms. "Come to me."

"And spoil the fun of watching you watch your friends die?"

"You lack imagination," I said bitterly. "Wouldn't it be so much more fun to feel my horror when you force my own hand to kill them? I bet that alone could feed you for years."

The black eyes in Morrison's so-familiar face couldn't

brighten, but they glittered with interest. "You might be right. Come here, Walker."

"Is this really necessary?" It was, of course. It was all showmanship. I had never hated showmanship so much in my life. I'd never hated anything so much in my life. Hate ran so deep it left me cold, but not numb. I stepped over Gary's exhausted form, and finally realized that Coyote and Annie were in fact still there, standing behind Morrison at the heart of the double power circle.

The circle wasn't going to do anybody any good. It was mine, after all, and in a few seconds I'd be taking the Master on and would no doubt reduce it to rubble. I took it down myself, feeling a distant surge of power as its magic poured back into me. I automatically made it into personal shields, strengthening them like it would do any good, and spoke to Coyote as I reached Morrison. "No matter what happens next, get them out of here, 'yote. Get them all the hell away from here. Promise me."

"I promise." His voice sounded as awful as mine, as if his tears were made of glass, and he'd drunk them all away. I nodded, then met Morrison's black eyes.

The gun was still at his temple. I folded my hand around the barrel and moved it away. The Master didn't resist, but he did direct where it went: to my own temple. No chance for a double-cross.

"Works for me," I said in a low voice, and pressed my mouth to his.

The weight of the Master's presence was incredible. Inside a breath I had a raging headache, and before I opened my eyes I could tell that the world was darker than it should be, like the darkness of his eyes bled into the way he saw the world. I did open my eyes to see Morrison's horrified blue gaze before mine. He yanked the gun away from my temple, and I struggled for a smile.

It worked. It took almost everything I had, but it worked. I was still in control, my shields holding the Master apart from my own mind. Just barely, but that was all I needed.

"Morrison." It hurt to say the word. Everything hurt, but talking when the Master was battering at the inside of my skull was almost impossible. He was already *winning:* just within my range of vision I saw my coat bleed to pitch-black, marking me as one of the bad guys. My shields were turning to blasted crystal, scored by his relentless power, bursting at seams that hadn't been there a moment ago. They would be beautiful when they fell, I thought: a crystalline spray, like ocean surf turned to razors. The razors were already cutting up my mind in waves of pain I could barely see through. "Morrison," I said. "I love you. Go with Coyote. I've got something to do."

"Walker, you can't—you can't!"

"Watch me."

I turned away from him and, stiffly, walked out of one of the shattered windows at the top of the Space Needle.

I didn't know what I thought might happen. I supposed if I was really lucky I might kill myself and take the Master with me, but I didn't have much faith in that succeeding.

It didn't. Black magic clouded around me, thickening the air and slowing our descent. After tangling with the Morrígan, I'd suspected he could do things like that, but it had been worth a shot. And he didn't push through my shields, even though I was pretty certain he could. But I was also pretty certain he was afraid Cernunnos would know somehow that it wasn't me calling him, if he broke down my shields and took me over completely. I'd be a great host for a long time, but Cernunnos was his real goal, his forever home, and he didn't want to blow that. So I risked doing stupid shit like walking out a fifty-story window, and it didn't kill either of us.

In fact, we landed with flawless grace that didn't even dent the already-broken concrete at the foot of the Needle. I stood up, feeling the Master's anticipation, his urgency, and his great difficulty in restraining himself from shattering my mind as I pulled together the magic I wanted. And he *was* restraining himself, too, despite the constant barrage of tiny explosions I felt within my skull. They made bright colors, silver-blue and white against the black background of his own power, and I could hardly think through each eruption inside my head.

It had been a binding spell, in the beginning. I held on to that thought, struggling to follow it through. Gary and I had found it and he'd made me uncomfortable by reading it aloud. Later on I'd reversed it and used it to free Cernunnos's son, the Boy Rider, from the sleep his half brother, Herne, had laid on him. I had evidence that what I wanted to do worked. The only trick was making it work as well as I needed it to without the Master cluing in, but since I'd just walked out a window without him stopping me, I thought I could probably hang on a few more seconds. The truth was my head and heart hurt so badly right now that after those few seconds, I almost didn't care what happened next.

I wanted to do more than just call Cernunnos here. I wanted to unleash him on the earth, just as we had unleashed the Master. It was an alarming prospect, really. He was a god, a collector of souls, a master hunter, and while I was drawn to him, even liked him, I hadn't forgotten that he was all but impossible to contain, or the dangers an unconstrained god represented.

On the other hand, a constrained god had no chance at all against the Master, and a god was about the only chance I figured we had.

"I call on the stars to guide thee to me. I call on the green things to welcome thee." Starlight in his ashy hair. Fiery green in his gaze, burning as hot as the stars themselves. "I call on this earth to know thee again." It had known him once, all the year around, until the world and the gods had changed so much as to diminish him. No more. Despite my rage toward her, I reached for Renee, asking for her delicate touch through time. Asking her to carry the love of wild things and the awe of the hunt from time immemorial into today, awakening something I hoped was only sleeping, and not forever dead, in the heart of humanity. "I call on things to be known now, that were only known then.

"I call on the god who has so often heeded me." An ache began to build in my chest, hope and love and regret, though it was nothing to the pain hammering my skull. I lifted my hands to the sky, welcoming, and wondered if he would see or notice or care about the tears burning hot lines down my cheeks. Maybe not. He was there, just on the other side of the sky, waiting, straining, anticipating. I knew it. I felt it, and no matter what else happened, knew that after this, nothing in my world would ever be the same. He was magic. He was the Hunt. He was a god, and gods did not walk this earth lightly. He would change us, as we had once changed him.

"By my will and by these words," I whispered, "Cernunnos, I free thee to eternity."

I emptied of all power.

The unmaking of a god was not a small thing. It took centuries, millennia, to unmake one, to whittle away its believers and thus its power. Even now in our own world, the old gods lingered: Zeus and Odin, Sekhmet and Kali. We might not worship them, but we knew their names, and so long as those names remained some spark of their power would, too.

They were bound now, much lesser than they had once been, but still they remained.

It was much faster to make a god. First, maybe there was the struggle, like what I'd seen between Cernunnos and the Master. Maybe that didn't always happen, though. Maybe most gods weren't archetypes given physical form. Maybe most of them were passion and zealotry that spread quickly, miracles buoying hopes, promises of a new world under benevolent rule to earn a young god strength commensurate with its predecessor's withering. To begin anew was a great gift. I should know.

But for all the energy of a new beginning, there was something to be said for old ties, too. And my god, my lord of the Wild Hunt, my Cernunnos, had not been wholly diminished.

The earth heaved. The sky heaved; the stars themselves heaved, ringing with exultation as a thing changed within the universe. As a fettered god was given freedom, and as a choice was made for a world. My choice, my world: Cernunnos was the devil I knew, and if unleashing him would save my friends, then it was a choice I could live with. If it meant humanity had to face the magic they had so long denied, so be it. I did not for an instant imagine it would be an easy choice or that the path that lay ahead would be smooth.

All that mattered was that there would *be* a path, a path of light and life, a cycle of death and rebirth, rather than an endless drain into bitter darkness. Left unchallenged, the Master would take each of us by the soul and have us destroy that which we most loved, as he was trying to do with me. I was rich pickings, but he would burn me out eventually, and move on to the next, and the next and the next, until nothing was left to this world but a blackened cinder. His stolen lives would extinguish, and he would start his unliving existence anew, hungrier than ever for a taste of the life he had known.

I would never be able to stop him, not by myself, and a bound god wasn't enough to help me.

Cernunnos rode free.

The sky itself couldn't hold him: it filled with storm clouds that raced like baying dogs, the howling wind their cry. Where shadows lay within the clouds, black birds burst forth, flapping wings and raw cries heralding the return of their master. Pain and loss twisted through me, turning my vision hot as I thought of how pleased Raven would have been to see the rooks that were his smaller, gray-beaked cousins. As the shadows parted from the clouds, the clouds themselves became the white-bodied, red-eared hounds of the Hunt. Behind them, thunder rolled in the rhythm of horses' hooves, beating broken earth into place again.

They led him for once: a dozen riders I knew by sight, and then more, more, more, riders on bays and blacks, on grays and on browns. Some seemed to nod to me as they rode the horizon: the bearded king, the slim-faced archer. The child, the Boy Rider, upon whom I had laid a spell not unlike the one I had just called Cernunnos with, but also not the same. He, of all of them, was the one I was certain greeted me: he pulled his golden mare around and galloped past me twice, emerald eyes locking with mine. I saluted, but even he couldn't hold my attention, because even he wasn't *him,* the lord of the Hunt. The boy turned from me and rode hard again, leading the others. They swept across the sky, laying claim to it, and the moonlight cast off its natural milky tones and instead burned green.

Finally came the god. From the stars, from the night, from the quiet gray-greenery of Tir na nOg, he came to this world where he had once been known, and would now be known again in his full and deadly glory. He rode down sunset paths, and he rode straight for me, his gaze hot on mine, as if I was the only thing that mattered in this or any world.

I had never seen such joy before: wild, raw, untamed joy, so huge it seemed even a god must burst with it. Cernunnos reined in his silver steed before me, and the image seared into my vision just as his first appearance was forever burned there.

He had been everything then, and he was so much more now. The stallion was no longer liquid silver: he was molten, heat pouring off him, though his color remained unchanged. The god upon his back was one and the same with the beast, an animal creature himself, with eyes that trailed green fire and a whipcord body that bespoke such strength that I both feared and desired a touch of his hand.

His crown, thick and heavy antlers, wound around his head and contained his starlight hair. He was perfect, complete, free, and his smile was all the emancipator of a god could hope for.

I blurted, "I'm sorry," and then my mind was no longer my own.

CHAPTER TWENTY-FIVE

It had been so easy. So easy to manipulate the host into giving up her body and calling my brother to her like he was a lost dog.

The shape of the thought gave me momentary pause, its form so different from how the old man had spoken. Such was the price of a mortal shell, that their small minds wore thoughts and words into familiar patterns, like a river cutting through soft soil. I could reshape them if I wished.

But some of the sweetness of agony came from letting whatever spark of the host's mind remained hear and see and think in the way she was accustomed to, forcing her to feel my actions as if they were her own. In desperation, she wanted to think of me as *the Master,* a thing separate from herself, but it was my delight to make us one, and leave her unable to protest. So: it had been *easy,* and I reveled in the way she thought it, because it hurt her all the more for me to think that way, too.

My brother came as if this host were the star around which

he spun. He burned more brightly than he had in our last encounter, strengthened, perhaps, by her affection, and that pleased me.

He knew in the moment of change that he had been tricked. Some outward seeming of this body's demeanor: the blackness of my eyes, or an uncanny sight that showed him my domination of the small shamanic spirit. His pleasure turned to pain, then to fury, almost as furious as the captured soul inside me. She screamed within my mind, puny fists pummeling me, louder by far than either the old man or her lover, but even so, too small to be so much as an irritation. Strange that she could also be large enough to feed my hunger for rage and despair. She had capitulated so easily, her companions such easy marks, and now before me stood an angry green god.

Hungering, I reached for him.

An emptiness swallowed me, startling and brief. It was this body's nature to use its own power, and there was none to be had.

In that instant, the green god struck at me instead.

He showed no regard for the host's fragile body, driving a silver blade deep through its chest. Pain, more intimate and immediate than any I had ever known, lived in me, though the buried voice of my host laughed in agonizing familiarity. Guided by her, I lifted my gaze, struggling for breath to make the words. "Really, my lord god of the Hunt? Again? We keep doing this dance. You stab me, I stab you…"

I wrapped my hand around the blade itself and withdrew it from my own body. My heart stuttered, knees weakening. Blood spilled, coating my chest, my clothes, making red streaks on my black coat. I tried again to breathe and couldn't: there was a hole in me where there shouldn't be.

Two holes. A physical one, piercing the body, and an emptiness where her magic had been. I scrabbled for it, hands making useless claws that closed on nothing. My weakened knees failed and I fell to them, broken stone sending lesser shards of pain through my legs.

Foggily, faintly, it came to me that I had perhaps been tricked. That this host had known what magic it would take to call a god from beyond his time, and had done it more willingly than I'd known. It had used all the magic she had inside her, and all that was left for me to feed on was her pain and rage.

And even that was diminished. Worse than diminished: gone. Fallen into exhaustion, unsustainable. She hadn't even left me with so much as despair. She was still *there*, still present, a hint of life within my mind, but it was as if she slept, and intended to sleep forevermore. There was no anger, no hate, nothing but weary calm.

With astonishing clarity and for the first time in my impossibly long existence, I thought, *I will die here,* and believed it. I would die here, because a snot-nosed mortal and my brother had conspired together without speech, and I had let it happen.

No. If this body couldn't be healed by its own magic, then the lives of this world would feed me as I bled, until I forced my brother from the shape he knew and took it for myself. With bared teeth and my own rage to feed me, I shoved to my feet again, searching for the nearest dregs of humanity to feast upon.

To my delight, it came in the form of the old man and his wife, in the form of the Raven Mocker, and in the form of the one Joanne Walker loved. Their fear for my host was rich, powerful and, if not healing, at least sufficient. Still bleeding, I gathered their anger, their hatred, their worry, and coiled those weighted emotions in my hands like whips. I cracked them once, and even I rocked at the sound: thunderclaps in our very presence, knocking the mortals aside.

I lashed again, bringing the whips of my power together to catch a god.

A young goddess rose from the earth and caught the strike.

For half a heartbeat, had I a heartbeat left, I stood stunned, gaping, as taken aback as any of the mortals. Not so much, perhaps, as my brother, whose despair was suddenly piquant.

I *knew* this girl. Not just through my host, whose horror was sharp enough to waken her from silence within me, but in my own right. She was new to me, a recent taste; a recent taint. I saw it within her, black roots spidering through a green that blazed nearly so bright as the god himself. They were tied together, child-goddess and ancient god, blood calling to blood. Power calling to power, and all power, from the start of the universe until its end, had a choice to make.

I would make her choose me, and through her I would have Cernunnos, my brother, her grandfather. Through her I would bleed my brother dry forever, and never again fear hungering for pain.

I pulled the whips and she stumbled forward, unable to release them. Never able, had I my way: the spidering blackness inside her was already reaching to connect with the magic I bound her with. But the goddess only stumbled, then stopped. Held her ground, leaned back against the pain of my whips, and spoke with a shaking, determined voice. "Leave my grandfather alone, you son of a bitch."

"Is this what you've come to?" I crowed to Cernunnos. "Hiding behind children? Letting them die for you? This is better than I ever imagined, my lord god of the Hunt. This is *rich*."

"He's not hiding," the girl whispered. "I'm protecting him. There's a difference."

"There is," I said gleefully. "Okay, kiddo. If you can stand against me, I'll give him to you." I hadn't imagined, when I began to take human hosts, how their own words would affect mine, but the cringe of discomfort on the girl's face as I spoke with her friend's voice was well worth it. My host had reacted the same way when I had used the others, and used their voices. I'd known having a body would be superior. I hadn't realized it would be *fun*.

The girl paled, then lifted her chin. Her eyes were those of her grandfather, emerald-green and startling in a so-human face. "I'm strong," she said. "You don't scare me."

I smiled. It was easier now, having practiced with the old man. "No. I *terrorize* you, Suzy." That was the name the host knew for this girl, and she blanched again when I used it. "But I don't have to. Join me, and let me show you what you might be."

It had always been easy to pluck dreams of greatness from the minds of mortals; it was how my creatures had come to me, time and again. They had a need they imagined I could fill, and this child was no different. She had strength and knew it. She had undone a life in her time, a dangerous and terrible thing, but to her, worse than that, was the thought of how she might *make* one, if she could so easily undo one.

She had lost her parents, I saw. Mortal parents, no blood of her blood, but those who had raised and nurtured her, given her the link to humanity that she still clung to. Their deaths were a still-raw wound, and she had dreamed of salving that pain.

"Like this?" I gestured and they stood beside me, Rachel and David Quinley, startled and joyful.

The girl gasped, and the darkness in her grew. She lurched a step forward, but I waggled a scolding finger at her. "Not yet, Suzy. They can't live again until you're mine. That's how this works."

"Suzy." The old man's voice grumbled over my winning

ploy. "Suzy, you were there, doll. You remember Archie Redding. You remember what he did to bring his family back, and you gotta remember it wasn't ever really them. That ain't Jo in there and you know it. It's the Master, and he's about death and pain, not about giving you your loved ones back."

"You got your wife back!" The girl's voice cracked in accusation and agony. Laughter bled in me just like the wound in my chest, but I held it back, knowing Suzy was fragile and that laughing now would lose her.

"Only 'cause she never really died. Your own gran'pa there took her and kept her safe for me, Suzy."

The girl whirled on the green god, her pale hair a living thing. "Then why didn't you save my parents?"

His gaze went to the old man and woman, then returned to the girl. "I had meddled too close to that time already. Time would not allow another change."

"Why did you choose her?" Misery rang in the girl's voice.

I sighed contentedly, tasting her betrayal, tasting her sadness and fears. Tasting her loneliness, and offering a salve for it: her mother's simulacrum stepped forward with outstretched arms. "Suzy, sweetheart. Come to us. We miss you so much, baby. I'm so sorry we left you."

"You didn't leave. You were taken." The girl had more strength in her than I imagined: she didn't turn, although she trembled with the effort. Instead she looked on my brother, still seeking answers he wouldn't give, while she spoke to the images of her parents. "It wasn't your fault, but I still hate that you're gone. Sometimes I hate you for being gone."

Tears scalded her voice, tears of fire, tears so sweet I could feel their fire and revel in them. I was healing, the body knitting itself back together with the meal of her rage and sorrow. I'd be ready to strike soon, and tried to hold myself still with the anticipation of it.

"Why?" The girl threw the question at the god again. "Why did you choose her, and not my parents?"

"Because I too see all the possible paths, and their deaths led to this moment, where their survival did not. Because *her* survival led to this moment, and her death did not. If it could have been otherwise and led here, I might have chosen differently."

"Why? What's so important about here?"

"You." My brother took a step forward, just as her false parents had done. I didn't like that, didn't like that they continued to speak, but I was so nearly healed, and her pain was so great, that I knew I could be whole again before she had made her choice. Then I would have her whether she wanted it or not, and then I would have them all.

"You," the god said again. "Even more than my corrupt little shaman, in this moment you are important, granddaughter. Your parents died so you would awaken to your heritage. Annie Muldoon lived so this moment could come, with you aware and able to choose."

The girl half turned, her gaze glassy between myself and the green god. "Are you telling me the fate of the world rides on what I choose?"

My brother almost laughed. "No. Only my fate. You know that our fates are not fixed, granddaughter, but you also know that they...trend."

"But I can't see the trends anymore. It's just all black." Despair rose in her, blackened and strengthened by the false faces of her parents turned hopefully on her. "If it's all black, then the paths are chosen, aren't they? There's no point in even trying."

I had her. In that moment, I had her, and triumph rose in my chest. The wounds sealed, my strength burgeoning as I drew darkness from girl. It was startling, how weak these bodies were, but in a minute or two it would no longer matter. Now it was just the joy of waiting, the stretching out of anticipation. I coiled a little, ready to pounce.

The green god spoke as though I wasn't even there, much less of any importance. "Being unable to see the path does not mean it has disappeared. It means only that you must trust yourself, and if you cannot trust yourself, then trust me. I still see the paths, and I tell you that neither your fate nor mine is yet written on them. Find a light, Suzanne. Cling to it."

Impossibly, her power in me weakened, fading away as her strength to resist grew. Seeing that, I risked all. To the hissing, spitting rage of the host mind, I gave the mother-simulacrum palpable form, and with it touched the girl's face.

Suzanne's resistance crumbled.

For one instant I wrenched control back from the Master and screamed, "Suzy, no!"

It came too suddenly to stop. I'd never imagined that a mortal mind could wrest control from me, and in my surprise, I lost the simulacrums. The mother-thing vanished and the girl's face changed profoundly: horror, sorrow, resolution.

"Joanne's good," she said in a clear light voice. "Joanne's awesome. But I'm a quarter god, and that trumps good. Come on, you son of a bitch. Catch me if you can."

She fled, and I left Joanne Walker behind to pursue her.

I hit the ground like a sack of rocks, every muscle spasming from the Master's sudden release. I fumbled for healing power, trying to calm the convulsions that wracked me, and wasn't exactly surprised when the magic didn't answer. I'd emptied it breaking all the laws of how gods worked when I brought Cernunnos into this world, and whatever hideous stitching-back-together the Master had done after Cernunnos had impaled him did not exactly lend itself to healing magic thinking everything was all systems go.

The warmth of a low desert sun relaxed my twisting body, and the heat of desert sand washed upward, taking the pain away. I melted against the ground, immediately aware that it wasn't soft giving sand, but actually concrete, and smiled up at Coyote. "Hey. Thanks." I sounded like I'd been drinking glass.

His return smile was sad. "You're welcome. Better power up, Jo. Things are going to hell." He offered a hand and pulled me to my feet.

It felt weird to be fully back in control of my own body. I leaned on Coyote, taking quick assessment. The headache had vanished, for which I was eternally grateful. Morrison and the Muldoons no longer looked like they were under any kind of attack, but their distress hadn't lessened one bit at all. I followed their attention, wondering what had gone wrong in the five or six seconds since the Master had abandoned me.

Well, nothing new had gone wrong, exactly, except the Master was now a roaring dark cloud chasing Suzy all over hell and breakfast. A miasma, as he'd been before. But now he rushed around with a sense of urgency, as if he was uncomfortable unbodied among mortals. This, despite pretty clearly having it all over all of us in terms of raw power. Nice to know even world-ending cosmic powers had their insecurities.

Suzy was doing something impossible. Something I thought I could do: blurring from one step to another, like she was bending time itself to stay ahead of the Master. I tapped Renee, and she swung gently, her whole body moving in a negative. *No. She does not share your gift.*

"Then what…?" Cautiously, I triggered the Sight. Apparently it didn't need a lot of power, because it slipped on.

The world turned to fire-green pathways. One after another, they flared, burning so brilliantly they hurt my eyes. Suzy leaped from one to another, sometimes crossing dozens of yards with a single step. Every jump lurched the air, and each path she left behind burned out, becoming a black hiss against the concrete before it faded entirely. The Master howled with impotent outrage, leaping on the fading black paths like a cat not quite fast enough to catch a string. The landscape changed beneath them, broken concrete to smooth lawn to forest floor back to concrete, and a dozen things in between as they leaped from…not from place to place, but from time to time.

"Oh, my God." I breathed the words, watching as the girl left green fire trails behind while she ran from one time line to another, time lines that she could see and anticipate. Time lines where the Master wasn't there, time lines where this moment played out a little differently, so that she avoided his attacks by stepping into an alternate world where his attention was directed elsewhere. I wondered if, to her eyes, there were dozens, maybe hundreds, of copies of her, all leaping frantically from one time line to another, or if she was the only variant who had thought of this ploy. "My God. Can she even do that?"

My god, which was a phrase I would have to reconsider using from here on out, stood at my side, his own blaze-green eyes burning as he watched his granddaughter lead the Master in a merry chase. "It seems she can."

"Can you?"

"Not with such alacrity. I lack the…flexibility. Watch thyself, my Siobhán." He stepped away.

I blinked after him, wondering what that was about, then blinked back at Suzy's helter-skelter chase. "Morrison, are you see—"

Suzy appeared immediately in front of me, arms already thrust straight out. She caught me in the chest, knocking my breath away and knocking me a few hard steps backward. "Wha—!"

The world burned green.

Time twisted. Not like I was accustomed to it doing. I slid back and forth through this time line, when I moved through time at all. This was a wrench, a twist that told me the very world around me was not the same as it had been. The place hadn't changed: I was still in the Seattle Center, but this one hadn't been ravaged. Tourists were everywhere, breathing air that tasted wrong in my lungs, pointing at exhibitions that had never been displayed there in my world, watching televisions that showed news anchors I didn't know. All except one. Laurie Corvallis was on CNN, chatting up the president of the United States.

I stumbled, and Joanne Walker caught my arm to help me up.

For a couple seconds we gaped at each other, nose to nose and shock for shock. She looked very like me, except her hair had been trimmed more recently. She also brimmed with power where I was empty, and all of a sudden I knew what Suzy had done. "Wild, stupid, amazing, crazy kid," I said to Suzy, even if she wasn't there, and to the other Joanne I said, "I am so sorry about this."

I put my hand on her chest and recharged my batteries. Power zinged from her to me and an image of Petite and jumper cables leaped to my mind. I hadn't thought that. My doppelgänger lifted her eyebrows, then broke the cable connection and said, "Woo," all dizzily.

I said, "Sorry," again, and then Suzy grabbed me by the collar and dragged me back to our world.

The moment had cost her. She'd taken me somewhere to

recharge, but she hadn't been able to plot out her next jump while she was doing that. The Master was on her heels, and scrambling to escape, Suzy tripped. She fell away, across another time line, and caught a few seconds of freedom in it, but she was not on her feet when it spat her back out, and the Master was only a few steps behind. She pitched herself forward, fear keening from her throat. The Master rose to take her, a black boiling mass of hunger.

Herne, first-born mortal son of Cernunnos, father to Suzanne Quinley, broke free of the earth between them.

The impact took Herne's very soul out of him, miasma suddenly contaminated with the roaring green power of an earthborn demigod. The green disappeared in waves and twists, fading into blackness. In less than a breath Herne's soul had been consumed, and the Master stood in a new, living body that had once been the flesh of a half god.

CHAPTER TWENTY-SIX

For a moment the silence was thunderous, the shocked quiet of an audience after an unexpectedly brilliant performance. It was broken not by applause, but by two voices screaming loss: "Father!" cried one, and, "My son!" cried the other.

I took about half a second to wonder just how Suzy and Herne's reconciliation had gone, that she called him father, but under the strain of these circumstances, maybe a little poetic license was advisable. "You murdering bastard who killed my adoptive parents and tried to sacrifice me," just didn't have the same ring to it.

Beneath the snark, though, cold and calm satisfaction rose. The Master had made his first real mistake.

He was half a god now, but he was all of this earth, his bitter, black aura bound to it. Herne had been born to a human mother, and I had brought Cernunnos back to this world in full. The god *belonged* here, belonged in a way he never had before, and Herne had been his son. The power of those things was tremendous, so great it came off the Master in waves, making it clear to me what had been done. Herne had given up his soul to save his daughter and—perhaps intentionally— to offer the temptation of flesh sculpted to the Master's prefer- ence. Flesh that he couldn't easily discard, as he'd done with me. Flesh and form, body and bone.

I finally had something I could *fight*.

A shudder ran over me from scalp to soles. The power I'd borrowed from my counterpart came to full life inside me, and was deepened by the focused will of my friends, my bro- ken city, my god and his granddaughter, who still remained free. I took it and armored myself in it, bracer shield on my left arm and Cernunnos's silver rapier in the opposite hand. My mother's necklace, which had never offered more than moral support before, warmed and changed, became the liv- ing silver it had been made of, and slipped down my torso as—

I took a quick look to be sure and exhaled in relief. As a silver breastplate and greaves, not a chain-mail bikini. Thank goodness.

My coat, gratifyingly, turned white again.

For some reason that in particular brought a grin to my face. A vicious, sharp berserker's grin, to be sure, but a grin. I lifted my gaze and found the Master watching me. Not waiting; he wasn't gentleman enough to wait. I thought maybe he was adjusting. It had, after all, taken him a minute or three to get fine motor control going when he'd jumped into Gary, and a demigod's systems might work differently from a human's.

And it was new. It wasn't Herne, with his stooped shoul- ders and long sad face. It was a face I knew better than that. Young. Hot. Multiethnic.

My own face, looking back at me with black eyes, black coat, black blade in hand. My blade, but made of obsidian.

"Please," I said softly. "I've battled my demons. You're not going to get anywhere with that guise."

"I'll get far enough," he said in my voice, and fifteen months of pent-up anticipation burst free in a headlong rush.

In the first minute or two neither of us had anything even vaguely resembling strategy. We got in too close to even use our swords, which both disappeared when it became clear fists were the choice weapon of the moment. We each had one of the other's lapels and pounded each other's faces with the free fist, all schoolyard brawl and no finesse at all. Every hit that landed on me was of skull-splitting agony, but every one I landed on the Master carried a fistful of healing magic, and hurt him just as badly. I healed: he didn't, not exactly, but he was full up of godling power, and it let him repair himself without reaching beyond the two of us to suck the lives out of the people around us.

I had to cut his ability to do that. If I could keep him from draining lives to repower himself, eventually even Herne's life force would run out and I'd find myself pounding on a sack of meat.

That sounded extremely satisfying. Not easy, but satisfying. A hit cracked my cheekbone and the pain blinded me. I loosened my grip on his coat and he slammed his arms up, freeing himself. I healed as we backed away from one another, and then, like prizefighters with the thirst for first contact satisfied, began to circle each other. He looked wary, which was a lot more than I expected. I tried not to look like I'd already had the crap beaten out of me, in hopes of striking fear into the heart of my enemy.

Then I thought about the time I'd just spent with him in my head, and concluded I didn't actually want him to fear me. Fear strengthened him. I wanted him to think I was easy pickings, that I didn't stand a chance of defeating a creature like him. Only then I got scared, which didn't help, either. I said, "Oh, fuck it," under my breath, called my sword to life again and charged him.

His black blade reappeared as well, singing with the blow, but not breaking. Not obsidian, then. Obsidian would have shattered under the weight of that blow. I had no idea what kind of metal came in pure and glittering black. The dark heart of a meteor, maybe, which was a lovely image and did nothing for my confidence. My sword was only silver, which wasn't exactly as hard as meteor iron.

Of course, my sword was also magic, which probably evened the odds. I swung my shield, using it as a weapon, as well. Black lightning smashed into it, absorbed by purple and copper. Nothing more than a faint sting came through to my arm, and even that swelled and altered, purifying and changing from his death power into my shamanic warrior's magic.

I'd never seen him falter before. It gave me hope, and I pressed the advantage, yelling as healing power roared into my sword. It cut him deeply, magic crackling and shriveling his flesh. He screamed and fell back, but when the sword left his body, the wound remained. Healing fire danced in it, flat lightning snaps as ruthless as his own magic. I had no idea what it thought it was healing, but it hurt the Master, and not in a way he seemed to gain strength from, so I was all for it.

It occurred to me, as we came together again, that this was likely to be a very long fight. It would do me good to not think about every play, every strike, because I would exhaust myself mentally long before the job was done. I fell back myself, looking around. Reminding myself of who and what I was fighting for.

They stood as far back as they could: Gary and Annie holding hands hard, Morrison standing alone with clenched fists, like he was preventing himself from throwing himself into

the fray. Coyote's hands were steepled in front of his mouth.
Suzy stood over her grandfather, who knelt with empty, open
arms, as if he cradled the ruined soul of his son. The half-
wrecked shambles of the Seattle Center stood as their back-
drop, a testimony to defeat.

It wasn't exactly the tally-ho I might have hoped for, but in
a way, the ruins and the wrecks of hope bolstered me. What
destruction I saw now, what loss and anguish, what fears and
worries I saw among my friends, would only be magnified
across the world if we failed here.

If *I* failed here.

I looked back at the Master, whose attention had followed
mine. Not for the attack, but out of what—had it actually
been on my face, rather than a reflection of me—I would have
called perplexity. As if he wondered why I would stop fighting
and look to my friends, when the pause could easily kill me.

The fact that it hadn't made me wonder if function followed
form, and if in taking on my guise, he'd made a greater mistake than he'd known. It had been one thing sharing headspace
with him. That had been of necessity, in both our opinions.
Making himself in my image—

Well. That was what men did with gods.

I chuckled and swept my blade up, nearly touching it to
my nose in a salute that would have done my fencing teacher
proud. I wondered how Phoebe was doing, anyway, and
whether she'd yet been affected by the tremors and troubles
rolling through Seattle. I wondered—assuming we all survived this—if she would forgive me for being a magic-user,
for being something that didn't fit comfortably into her view
of the world.

If we survived this, of course, there were a lot of people
who were going to have to face things that didn't fit comfortably into their view of the world.

I completed my salute, sweeping the sword out to the side, then lost myself in battle.

A rhythm came into the fight, flow and ebb. I hurt, I healed, I fell back and I struck again. The Master, time and again, took a wound he could not heal, blue fire sparking inside his body. Each time, he reached beyond himself for the power he'd once known, but I had the way of it now. He was of the earth, and I could shield and block things of the earth. His power reached out; mine knocked it aside, placed a wall before it, threw a net around it and hauled it back. Exhaustion burned in my body, muscles laden with lactic acid that, as the moon climbed higher in the sky, even healing magic couldn't numb. We were matched, better matched, than I had ever imagined, and I thought again of function following form. Had he kept Herne's shape, or given himself a god's face, maybe I couldn't have met him stroke for stroke and magic for magic.

Maybe I could have. Herne and I had danced once, too, and I'd changed him then. Maybe function would have followed that form, too—maybe, maybe, maybe. I moved across broken concrete, scaled shattered glass that should never have held my weight, and I fought on. The Master's rage followed me, always burning red and black to my silver-blue. Moonlight reflected off water from the broken fountain until the light we struggled in was bright as day, and I became uncertain as to whether we fought in daytime or night. At times I caught glimpses of the watchers. There seemed to be more of them than there had been, but I hardly trusted my vision. I hardly trusted anything, not even the rise and fall of my sword arm, which ached until I didn't know how I could lift it again. Magic rolled out of me so steadily I wasn't certain I had anything left to keep my heart beating. The best I could hope for was that the Master was equally weakened, but I saw none of that in the attacks he constantly pressed, or in the defenses he rallied with when I gathered myself to go on the attack myself.

None of it felt real.

Ghosts began to visit me, and I didn't see ghosts. That was Billy's department. But ghosts they were: my mother, of whom there wasn't enough left for a ghost. When I tripped and fell, it was the sight of her that brought me to my feet again. She stood as Morrison had in my last glimpse of him: leaning forward, intent, hands fisted as though she could fight this battle for me. I smiled at her, then thought maybe she was another of the Master's false copies, here to taunt me.

Caroline Holliday came when Mother faded, a sweet-faced little girl whose love for life was written across her face. That was hard: tears flooded my eyes, making the battle impossible to see. It turned out I didn't entirely need to: I Saw the Master even if my ordinary vision was blurred, and my sword or shield moved again and again to block him, even when my thoughts were turned to offering an apology to Caroline. She shook her head and smiled again, and then she, too, was gone, leaving the sound of a baby's cries echoing in my ears. The newest Holliday, baby Caroline, who was her dead aunt's namesake. Little Caro couldn't possibly be here, but the memory of her cries helped ease the elder Caroline's passing.

They came faster after that. Jason Chan, whose little sisters would never love Halloween again. Lugh, the *aos sí* whom the Irish remembered as a sun god. Barbara Bragg, who still looked angry, even after death. Mark Bragg didn't appear. I hoped that meant he wasn't dead. On and on, even up to Nakaytah, luckless girlfriend of a power-hungry sorcerer and dead three thousand years before I ever might have met her. More and more of them, coming more frantically, throwing themselves at me as the faces and names of people I had lost or who had died because of me.

They were the Master's feint. I was certain of that now, but he had made another mistake. Maybe he thought they would weaken me, but instead they gave me more, always more, to fight for. He could give them form, but for too many of them I knew the thoughts that had really lain behind their visages, and I had made my heartbroken peace with almost all of them. It was exhausting, though, seeing each of them, and in the end, they were my undoing.

I knew they didn't exist, but as they crowded me I became less and less willing to strike through them. Their faces were too real, and there were so many that I lost sight—even lost Sight—of the Master, of my other face. Only for a moment, but that was all it took. He slipped between the ghosts and seized my sword arm, sending black pain deep into the nerves. My hand spasmed and I lost the blade. Triumph blared over my own face, through the black eyes of the other me, and my own smile looked sharp enough to rip my throat out.

I couldn't rally. I was too damned tired, too worn down with losses and failures. I braced my shields, fumbled for the sword that would not come to my hand when called, and chose my last word on this earth: "Morrison."

The strike came as black lightning, faster than the eye could see. It hit me in the side, knocking me to the ground. An impressive weight pressed me down. Concrete scraped my cheekbone. I wondered that I could feel enough to care just before the scent of burning flesh filled my nose. But there was no pain, or none besides my banged-up face.

It took a terribly long time to understand that the weight on me was not the weight of crushed bones, but was instead Coyote's body.

CHAPTER TWENTY-SEVEN

I fell. I wrapped my arms and legs around him, and I fell. I didn't think. I just fell, fell right out of the Middle World and into Coyote's garden. It was so hot there, desert sky almost white with heat, and when we landed—gently—on rolling sand, it all but burned me through my jeans.

Coyote was torn to pieces, blackened and burned. His beautiful hair was half gone, even here, in his garden, where he should be as complete as possible. Sobbing, I called for healing power, only to have it turn to dust in my hands. I screamed for Raven, for his ability to slip between life and death, and he didn't answer. There was only emptiness where he was supposed to be, and terror turning my voice shrill as I clutched Coyote against me. "No, Coyote, no, please don't, please… please don't. Oh, god, Coyote…"

The Master had struck so fast. Nobody could have beaten him to the punch. Well, maybe I could have, when I had Rattler's speed to boost me, or in extreme circumstances, Renee's gift of bending time. I begged for her help now, needing more than the difference in Middle and garden-world time to save my friend. I felt her inside me, folded in on herself, alone and sorrowful, but she didn't respond. Rage cracked through me like lightning and I shoved the thought of her away, not wanting her help anymore even if she would give it. I could do it *myself:* I had since the beginning, and didn't need a goddamned spirit animal to ease the way. Not unless it was Raven, and he was gone. Trembling and afraid, I called healing power a second time. Coyote rebuffed it again, sending it pooling into the golden desert sad.

"Stop that, Jo. There's no time. You know there isn't. Too much damage." He was right. He was so badly hurt, his body burned and broken. I could hardly bear to look, could hardly stand to see the terrible damage of a mindfully cruel lightning strike. I tried again to call magic, and again it sluiced away, running over the hard desert sand and disappearing like water into thirsty earth. "Don't worry. Doesn't hurt. Burned out the pain receptors, I think."

The air was impossibly hot around us, as if maybe it drew the pain from his poor tormented body. Whatever the reason, I was grateful, but my trembling hands called for power again and once more Coyote denied it. "Stop. Just glad I was fast enough. You aren't the only one with a rattlesnake companion." Coyote closed his eyes and smiled faintly. "Well, you weren't. Guess you will be now. Had to use it all up, saving you."

I couldn't breathe. I wasn't sure I ever wanted to again. But I tried to laugh, because I thought he wanted me to, and his smile grew a little when I managed a choked sound that might have been construed as laughter. "There's my Jo. Laughter in the face of adversity. S'what I like about you."

"Coyote, why...*why?*"

"Had to do something, Jo. Couldn't let you die. Be bad… for the world. Sorry." He fumbled for my hand and I wrapped both of mine around his, holding his knuckles to my lips.

"Don't. Don't be sorry. Just let me heal you."

"No. No. Wanna say it. I blew it out there. Just got so jealous. We were so well matched, Jo." He opened his eyes again, pure coyote gold in the fading color of his face. "Back when we started? We were a perfect match. The raven, the coyote, the snake. We were a holy triumvirate, twice. Two-spirited. I thought we were two-spirited. Only your spirit wasn't shared with mine after all. Not in the end."

"I'm sorry, Coyote. 'Yote. I'm sorry. You shouldn't have… you shouldn't have…" I bowed over his chest, hands helpless above him. "Won't you let me heal you?"

The desert beneath me changed from dune waves to hard flat whiteness, and the heat became unbearable. I sucked in a shallow breath and looked up into Big Coyote's starry eyes. He was solemn, even sad, his precious-metal fur dull for once. "Won't you let me save him?"

"You shouldn't even be here, Jo." Coyote, Little Coyote, my 'yote, spoke so weakly I almost couldn't hear him. "The fight's out there. Save me, lose the world. Don't do that. It would kinda…" He coughed, a fragile sound. "Kinda defeat the point."

I bent over him, kissing his forehead and smoothing his hair back. "Hang on, okay, 'yote? Hang on. Just hold on and I'll come back for you as fast as I can. I'll beat this bastard and I'll come back and bring you home. Just hold on. Don't let him die," I said desperately to Big Coyote. "Just don't let him die, okay? Just don't let him die."

Big Coyote smashed his forehead against mine and sent me back to the real world.

So little time had passed that the Master was still standing above me figuring out what had gone wrong. Hardly even knowing something had gone wrong, until with a howl of hurt and fury I pushed my poor Coyote's body off me and surged to my feet. Fire burned in me, so much fire I thought I would be consumed with it. My rage knew no bounds: the universe itself couldn't contain the size of my loss. I came to my feet with my blade blazing blue in one hand and my shield a shining mass of silver on the other arm.

For the first time, I looked into the Master's black eyes and I saw fear. Not enjoyment of it, not feeding on it, not thriving with it, but the same bone-deep, gut-level fear that drove humans to build fires against the night and stand watch against the creatures that hunted them.

I was a hunter, a warrior, a shaman, and I could not let this stand. Not this time. Not Coyote. Not my beloved friend, my teacher, my guide. He was not, in the end, my everything, but he had been my beginning, and I would not lose him. The very core of the earth was not so hot with power as I was; the moon itself was faint in the light of my magic.

The Master's face contorted and he leaped at me, a desperate measure of a desperate creature. His meteoric blade rose and fell in a death blow.

I caught it on my shield. Power blazed. Iron fragmented, and I stood eye to eye with an unarmed monster.

Fear split his face again, then defiance so transparent that on another day it might have made me laugh. He had not spoken since the fight began, but now, with lifted chin, spat words: "Kill me if you can."

"Oh, no." I shook with rage, with hurt, and with determination. "Oh, no."

I threw the sword away, released the shield. They became a part of me again, grew into the breastplate my mother's necklace had become, until I was armored all over with a blaze of light. Copper bracers and arm guards. Gloves of flexible ash wood, fingertips glittering with silver. Purple laced the joints of armor so fluid it moved with my every breath. All the gifts I had ever been offered from family, from friends, from the inhuman to the unusual came together and made me into a thing of power, a thing as endless as the Master himself. I was what he had never understood, what he had struggled for and fought to attain for an existence longer than eternity.

I was love, honed to a blade by loss, and I thrust myself into the very heart of the Master himself.

We had danced it all together, me and Coyote and Annie. I took that dance with me into the Master's garden, a place of cold and dark beyond comprehension. Even in the darkness, I could see the light of those things that had been born around him, and if those were two impossible things lying cheek by jowl, then in the depths and darkness of his garden it was not a conflict. There could be no shadow without light, and I did not deny that shadow must exist. But I would bring the light to the shadow if it was the last thing I did. He would know what he had taken: that would be his punishment for killing my friend. Not death. Death was too good for him. Death was an ending, death meant there was no more pain, and this was a pain upon which the Master could not thrive. He would feel it, feel it until the end of time, because now I would not let him die.

I danced in the darkness, pouring out the story of my life and the story of my love.

My mother's love, misguided or brilliant as it had been, giving me up to my father to keep me safe. Such love there, and it had taken me so long, too long, to understand it. It was love, honed to a blade by loss, and I thrust it into the Master's garden. Forced it to take root there with each step of my dance, driving it into barren earth that had only dreamed of life.

My father's love, awkward and misguided, too, trying to protect me from the fate my mother had sent me away from. So many mistakes, muddying the path that I was always bound to walk, but done with such good intent. Not a road to hell at all, but love, laid down across the countryside to heal and strengthen it. I took that love and danced it into the garden, demanding that the garden accept it and become fruitful.

Gary's love, running so deep. It became the soil, ready to grow. Morrison's love, patient as only the earth could be. Coyote's love, so bright it had burned him; it became the sunlight to warm the fields. Annie's love, soft and unending, the rain to water the land. Billy, Melinda, their passel of amazing kids: I danced that love of family, of standing together, into this place. My crazy cousin with her fire-engine-red hair and her excitement over the magery burgeoning in her, I danced that, too, letting the idea of magic take root. I danced for my son, and for his sister, and the love I felt for them was something I threw into the Master's teeth, making it a strong part of this new land so that he could never look on his garden without remembering the blade of loss. I danced and I built on everything my story had ever been, making it part of the Master's story, too.

This was not what he wanted, a pain that lived inside him. The pain of love, much sharper than he could have imagined, the pain of loss when love failed—no. He had used that before, made slaves of those whose broken hearts made them vulnerable, and he feared that fate for himself. He did not want this, tried to throw it off, and I pulled him close to snarl in his ear: *"I don't care what you want."*

Love would grow here, the price of a life.

I left his garden.

The Master, my other self, fell with my soul-sword still piercing his body. Exhaustion swept me, but the battle wasn't over yet. There was so much to do, too much to do, and I was so terribly tired. All I could do was ask as I'd asked once before, ask everything of everyone, and take what I was offered. I knelt over the shuddering, screaming, stolen body of the Master, and whispered, "Help me, help me, help me."

I opened my soul to the world around me.

There was so much magic gathered in this place, in these moments before dawn. I had known there were others here now, more than those who had watched our battle begin, but I felt them now, bright and vivid marks on my soul as they came into a circle around me.

Fuchsia and orange: Billy, whose power gave the dead a voice. Across from him his wife, Melinda, in orange and yellow, blooming with the wise woman's knowledge of life. Paired, a perfect complement. They were the west and the east, dying day and dawning sun.

Green and silver, fire without secondary attributes. Gary and Suzy, age and youth, standing north and south. The four of them, the four of them alone brought such strength to the circle that I cried out with it, hurting in my hands, my stomach, behind my eyes. Too much power already, and more were coming into place.

My *father*, what was my father doing here, his forest green and earthy browns stepping up to meet my own silver and blue, earth and sky together to make the world. I hadn't even known I was part of the circle, had thought it was coming into place *around* me, not *with* me, until he placed himself opposite me. Tradition and madcap methods, tied together by blood.

Annie, no longer burning green, but wholly and fully mortal again, her colors copper and flame. There were seven of us, almost the strongest circle I had ever known, and then came the god.

How fair, I thought, *how perfect.* How perfect that the god he had sought to unmake would instead be part of the un-making of the Master, that the brother of spirit he had tried to conquer would instead conquer him. Cernunnos was each of the things we brought to the circle, all in one. He was a voice to the dead, who served the living. He was eternal, age and youth encompassed in him. He was tradition, born of long cold nights and ancient needs, and he was fresh and newly made, given to the modern world. He was mortal, bound to this world by his son, the Boy Rider, and he was immortal, an undying god.

Morrison. I looked up, eyes blind to the world around me, only seeing the power that flowed and burned in everything. Morrison had not joined the circle.

"I'm here, Walker." He stepped through, a blaze of purple and blue, and in his hands was a round thing of white magic. My drum. Scalding tears rolled down my cheeks and I nodded once. He knelt across from me, on the Master's far side, and began to beat the drum.

Power ignited.

I had been fighting the wrong fight all along. Up until these past few moments, I had been making a terrible, fundamental mistake. I had seen the Master as the villain, and he was. Unquestionably. But he was also broken. He'd fought to be embodied, to be a thing that could walk the earth, and had lost that fight an impossibly long time ago. Now he finally had the body he'd always craved, and with it, he might take its inherent magic and climb it until he rivaled Cernunnos. Until the lord of the Hunt, the new god of my world, was as endangered as he had ever been.

I could kill the Master. I could end it that way. But that would never satisfy *me,* and my vengeance could run as deep as any god's.

I didn't want to kill him. I wanted to heal him.

To help his spirit not to die, but to finally be born. To take on the physical aspect of life without being more than that. I had blunted him already, by setting life in his dead garden. By sowing love there, a punishment I would never regret. But there was more to be done. I had to give him some kind of real life, something that could hold him in place.

I didn't want to. I didn't want to give him peace of any kind. I was not that good a person. Unfortunately for me, I also wasn't—quite—that stupid a person. If I didn't finish the job, it would come back to bite me on the ass. It might anyway, but it was sure to if I didn't finish.

The garden inside him was beginning to bloom. It was white fire, burning away the darkness that had bound him for so awfully long. Some part of it shook loose, a small part that modeled consciousness, and met my eyes.

It was dead, it said. It had never really lived. It could not be born now just because I insisted it would be.

"Don't bet on it, buddy." It was right, of course. Under normal circumstances, it certainly couldn't. But I'd left normal behind months ago, and today I had the help of a free god. There had, I thought, never been a person on this earth as stupidly, painfully full of magic as I was right now, and all I wanted to do was get rid of it. I put one hand on the thrashing body's forehead and the other over its heart, and whispered, "Live."

Once. Twice. A third time, because three was a lucky number. Then the fire within, the garden I had sown, leaped for the life magic, the healing power, that I now offered it. Love was an unconquerable power, and life called to life. I answered, pouring the borrowed strength of the human heart and the endless power of a god into the birthing of a thing that had gone long unknown, unborn, unloved. It would be known, it would be born, it would know love every day until the day it died, and I hoped it would hurt for every single one of those days.

I had no sense at all of the time it took. It could have been mere seconds or it could have been all of forever, and I wasn't at all certain it wasn't both. Whenever it happened, it began slowly and picked up speed, until one of my beloved vehicle metaphors turned the entire process into speeding down a highway, Petite's windows rolled down, wind in my hair and the needle buried. It was the very fastest thing of all, and yet so slow. Making life, refusing death, was complicated like that.

Slender, delicate hands settled themselves over mine, and the life I had been trying to give this broken form leaped upward, sinking into pale skin. I yelled, clawing at it, but Suzanne Quinley pressed my hands harder against the collapsing body, and challenged me with a gaze of unearthly green.

"He's my father."

"He's not—!"

She curled her hands, taking the Master's shattered miasma into them. "No. He's not. But he is, or was, and you need something that can contain him."

"Suzy, this is what he *wanted,* he *wanted* your body—"

"He wanted," she said, and her emphasis was so slight as to make mine seem hyperbolic, "to destroy the world. I can See what you're doing, Joanne. You've made life inside a thing that feeds on death. You've put love there, and now he loves the world, and that hurts him more than anything else. But if you just let him have this body and then let him go, he'll go crazy just like Herne did, and then you'll have a crazy half god to hunt down, just like Herne.

"But right now he's just a spirit, Jo. He's not bound to the body yet, not with love. Not the way you want him to be. So if *I* take him, he's going to suffer exactly what you want him to. He's going to understand love and loss and all of it, and he's never going to be able to break away. I'm the granddaughter of a god, Joanne. I'm pretty sure I'm going to live forever, or close enough to count. You want him to be punished? Let me take him. He killed my parents. He killed my father. He's tried to kill everybody I know and love. He's going to have to live with all that human pain, *forever*. And it's never going to make him stronger." Power streamed off her so brilliantly my eyes watered. "You told me everybody who has power has a choice to make. This is my choice. I'm going to be his jailer, and you're not going to stop me."

I looked away once, through tears, at Cernunnos. His face was as terrible as Suzy's, as stern and as still, but he dropped his head in a single nod.

"Okay." I hardly heard my own whisper as I turned my palms up beneath Suzy's, releasing the magic I'd built into her.

It coalesced and resolved, becoming smaller and denser and full of light. Darkness streaked through it, making shadows that tried and failed to dominate. In Suzanne's palms, it looked like a diamond that had come to life, glittering and surging.

It was beautiful, and frankly, I hated it. I leaned in, speaking to it. "Go away from here. Go with Suzanne, and don't imagine for a moment that this is a gift. You'll live. You'll survive. You'll feel all the pain you ever wanted, and it will *hurt you,* the way you've hurt us. Your only chance of not going mad is learning to live with it, just like we do, and you've got this girl here whose heart is a lot bigger—" and a lot crueler, I didn't say "—than mine. She may be your prison, but she's your savior, too. You should understand this: stay quiet. Stay very, very quiet. I never. Want. To see you. Again. If you cross my path, if you show your face, I will tear you apart. I will end you. I will…"

I was reaching the "tear up the bits of you and jump on them" stage of threats, and since I had even less chance against a god within a god than I'd had against, well, the Master, it seemed foolish to continue. I lifted my eyes to Suzanne and whispered, "Be careful, Suzy. That thing is dangerous. You be careful, you be smart, and if you ever even *think* you need my help with it, you come running. You hear me?"

She nodded, pale hair cascading over her shoulders as she folded the spark of godhood to her chest. "I promise."

"Good girl." I closed my eyes. "Just take it away."

I didn't wait to see if she did. I just went inside, went back to the hard white desert with its impossible heat and the flat blue sky pressing down on me.

There was no one else there, just me and the hanging tree.

CHAPTER TWENTY-EIGHT

I waited. I waited a long time, hoping against hope that Coyote, Big or Little, would come back to me. I knew neither of them would, but I still couldn't bring myself to leave the painfully hot desert. Breathing hurt, but fighting for sips of scalding air made it almost impossible to think about Raven or Rattler, or about Gary's tortoise, or about Coyote himself. Every inhalation was an agonizing little hiccup, and I was grateful to face that pain, and hide from the rest of it. Sunlight beat through my clothes, bronzing my skin so fast it stung, but that was okay, too. I wanted to stay. I wanted to stay forever, because here it was hot and awful, but it was also silent and a barrier to the ramifications of the past hours.

I didn't know how long it was until I felt Morrison's hand on my shoulder in the Middle World, and heard his quiet, concerned voice. "C'mon, Walker. Come back to me. C'mon, Joanie."

My eyes opened reluctantly. I wasn't at all certain I'd be

able to see, but the obliterating Sight that had burned my vision earlier was now gone. The world was made up of Morrison's worried smile, and the relief in his blue eyes when mine opened. "There you are. There you are, Jo. You came back to me."

I leaned forward—the Master's body that had lain in front of me was gone—and put my arms around Morrison's neck. Buried my face in his shoulder, and held on. I would have been happy to stay there forever, not letting the world intrude at all, but eventually he mumbled, "I'm sorry, Walker, but there's a rock digging into my patella. If I don't move we're going to have to amputate my knee."

To my surprise, I laughed. A muffled little sound, but a laugh. I hugged him tighter for one more instant, then let go enough that we could both shift and start to get up.

Finding the Muldoons, the Hollidays, two gods and my father looking down on us was something of a shock. I'd known they were there, but I hadn't really *seen* all of them, and I stared from one face to another uncertainly. Finally I focused on my father. "Dad?"

"Jo. Anne. Joanne." Dad paused, then whispered, "Joanie," and, despite the broken glass and concrete-riddled ground, dropped to his knees to pull me into a hug.

"Dad. Daddy, what are you… How did you even get here? It's only been, like, a day…a day?" I took my face from his shoulder and looked in bewilderment to the pinkening eastern horizon. "Was it only a day?"

"Shamans can go quite a while without sleep. And that invisibility trick of yours turned out to be pretty helpful on long stretches of speed-trapped highway in the badlands."

I stared at him. I'd never thought of that. Invisible driving. It would be awesome, except if a semi came out of nowhere. I started to say something like that, wanting to scold him, but it was a little hard to scold a man who'd just driven twenty-four hours straight to be at my side in the nick of time. "Thank you."

"You're welcome. Petite's in the parking garage. She's fine," Dad said as my spine straightened.

I was sure she was. I just had the irrational desire to see her. Everything had been turned upside down in the past day, all changed utterly. Seeing Petite would reassure me that *something* hadn't changed. "Where's Coyote?"

Morrison's face went bleak in preparation for giving me the dreadful news. I shook my head, stopping him. "No. I know. I just… I want to see him. I need to see him."

"Over here, doll." Gary's voice was solemn. More than solemn. I let Dad and Morrison help me to my feet. I felt oddly light as they did, like some heavy weight had burned out of me. Everyone, even the gods, stood aside as I walked slowly past them to where Coyote lay on a bier of concrete.

He wasn't burned or blackened anymore. A small favor, a gift to me, though from whom I didn't know. His beautiful hair lay quietly, no wind to disturb it, and someone had folded his hands neatly over his breast.

His eyes were closed, but he didn't look like he was sleeping. His color was wrong, his face too still. I knelt beside him and unfolded one of his hands, hating that it was already cool to the touch, and pressed my forehead against the back of it. After a minute or so, I heard the others slowly move away, for which I was grateful. I heard them shifting, taking seats, speaking quietly among one another as the light gradually changed, but they stayed away, giving me space for things I couldn't even name. I wasn't at mourning yet. My rage was burned out, poured into the Master's punishment and release. I was too tired for anything else, too emptied of emotion. Sooner or later it would come back, but right now, later sounded okay.

I had been sitting there maybe half an hour when a scream like the thunderbird's tore the air far above me. I flinched out of my solitude and threw shields around my friends, wondering if shields would even protect from a thunderbird's claws and wondering what a thunderbird was doing hunting us at this late stage of the game anyway, and if the thunderbird even existed anymore, after the fight in the Upper World. We all looked up, hands cupped around our eyes to block out an incongruously brilliant sunrise.

The Space Needle's restaurant, already at a dramatic cant that tilted opposite of the direction the Needle itself listed, let go of another few yards of height with another metal-rending scream. It jolted to a stop just long enough to notice, then dropped again, and again, glass and concrete and metal shattering with each collapse.

After the fourth, it gave up all hope of retaining integrity and slammed, crashed and bashed its way down the Needle's slender spire in deafening roars. Dust and debris flew, clouding the clean air. Chunks of metal bounced off my shields repeatedly, and we all shrieked with each impact, so our screams made shrill counterpoints to the impossible noise of the restaurant's collapse.

The fall itself lasted only a few seconds. The debris took longer to settle. All nine of us, even Cernunnos, just sat there, staring upward through the shimmer of my shield, like Moses on the mountain waiting for the commandments. Bit by bit the ruins came clear as wind swept the dust away to reveal the restaurant caught about halfway down the spire, where it began to flare toward the earth. It looked like somebody had been playing horseshoes with a UFO.

"Well, shit," I finally croaked. "Somebody's gonna have to clean that up."

Then I put my face in my hands and began to cry.

CHAPTER TWENTY-NINE

Sunday, April 2, 6:59 a.m.

Cernunnos, unexpectedly, was the one who came to me. He put one hand on my shoulder, turning my sobs to a gasp, then crouched beside me, long and elegant fingers dangling just above the earth. I drew a shuddering breath and dashed tears from my eyes, though they rolled down my cheeks again without a moment's hesitation. Still, I could see him. Or See him, more accurately.

As somber as he'd ever been, he was also glorious in the rising sun. His fire, the power that so easily blinded me, had new depth to it. It was still green, but it had always been emerald wildfire, a color so rich it had edges. Now there were shades to it, from that pure hard emerald into new leaves and from there into fading grass, with all the subtle differences in between reaching deep into the earth. That was it: when he moved now, it was with a sense of belonging. Like the green of this earth had claimed him. Not that he'd lost the green of Tir na nOg, but looking at him now, I felt like I'd always been seeing only half of what he was supposed to be. Now he was whole.

Whole, but at huge cost. I closed my eyes against his beauty, wondering what had happened to Herne's body. I wondered what the hell he'd been doing here at all. He had not been part of my plan. Not that I'd had much of a plan, but insofar as I had, it hadn't included gods dying.

My stomach clenched, ice sheeting over my skin as hot tears scalded my cheeks. I'd been wrong. It hadn't taken a god to defeat the Master.

It had taken three. One freed, one dead, and one…changed. The truth was, I didn't know what had happened to, or with, Suzy yet. I was a little afraid to find out. So there were a lot of things behind my apology when I whispered, "I'm sorry, Cernunnos."

"Thou'rt difficult, little shaman."

I opened my eyes again to stare at him, waited until it was clear I had to speak next, then said, "I thought we'd settled that 'little shaman' thing a while back."

"We had, and yet in the light of this new day, I find I do not wish to speak thy name quite yet, my shaman. Thou hast done…much, this day."

"Yes." We'd also settled the thee-ing and thou-ing thing, but for once I thought maybe the god's formality—sensual and shivery as it was—might be more appropriate than the more common language I'd become accustomed to from him. My shoulder was against Coyote's bier, a cold hard reminder of what had changed. As if I needed one. "Sorry for the sum-moning."

"No." Cernunnos barely whispered the word, then took my hand in his. His touch was gossamer, so light that if I didn't see our fingers intertwining I wouldn't be certain it was happening. My heart missed a beat and heat rose in my cheeks. I tried hard not to look at Morrison, who was studiously looking the other way.

"Be thou not sorry, my shaman. I might have refused thy call had thy casting not made so clear thy intentions." A note of doubt lingered deep in the claim: he wasn't certain he *could* have refused it, but I wasn't about to call him on that. He shifted a few inches, turning himself toward me. Toward Coyote, to whom he lifted his gaze before he spoke. "It is I, mayhap, who should offer an apology to thee."

"You sure as fuck should." I wasn't talking about Coyote. I wasn't ready to talk about Coyote. "The *Master,* Cernunnos. The frigging *Master.* You could have *told* me."

"The Devourer." Cernunnos had the grace to look away from Coyote and pay full attention to me. "For that, too, yes. What would I have told thee, *gwyld?* That the thing you feared and hated most was half of me? Wouldst thou have trusted me e'er again? No," he said very softly, "and without trust between us we could never have wrought this day."

"The *cauldron,*" I said in despair. "You almost dying in Tir na nOg. You bet everything on me and *lied* to me about it."

"I did not lie." Cernunnos sounded very slightly affronted. "I withheld truth, but I did not lie."

"To*may*to, to*mah*to. And you would have killed me back in Ireland, rather than let me become a werewolf. One of his monsters. Only because then *your brother* might have ended up on equal footing with you."

The silence was very long indeed, before the green god breathed, "Not only."

He couldn't have hit me harder if he'd shoved an iron sword through my gut. All my breath went away and left a hollow in my stomach that felt echoed in my gaze. I couldn't look away from him. Two little words, two words of promise and regret, and every part of me except my vocal cords wanted to demand that he explain himself, that he make that hint absolutely, undeniably clear.

My vocal cords, though, were in rebellion, too tight to speak, and in the end it was Cernunnos who looked away. Looked back toward Coyote's body, and murmured, once more, "I am sorry. I could not save him."

"Neither could I." There it was, raw and broken. The tears started again, wrenching through me in a shudder I felt to the bone. Cernunnos drew me up with his touch. I followed blindly, tears too thick to see through, until he stopped and I bumped into the solid shoulder of a silver stallion.

The beast bent his neck around and shoved his forehead against my arm. I stumbled and he caught me, hooking his big head beneath my arm so I leaned on him. Then he shook me off and pressed his face against my torso. All of my torso: his head went from my collarbones to my thighs, a reminder of how preposterously massive the god's horse was. I supposed he had to be, to carry Cernunnos in his fully fleshed, broad-shouldered and antlered form.

Mostly when I'd been this close to the stallion, he'd been trying to kill me. This was nicer. I put my forehead between his ears and mumbled something idiotic. He snorted down my pants, then pushed me away and tossed his head. I blinked away tears in time to catch an expressive eye roll before he looked pointedly at his own back.

"We would offer thee a gift," Cernunnos said quietly, "and ask a boon of thee all at once. Ride with us a final time, my shaman. Not to the stars and not between worlds, but here in this place, through this city. Thou hast made thy people mine, and I thine. I would not leave them broken and ravaged where I can help. The earth is mine as it was my son's, and it will be soothed by my presence. But the gift of healing is thine, and so I ask thee: ride with me, and help me heal this land."

"Cernunnos…" I wanted to. I always wanted to, when he asked me, and on this occasion he was asking something different. Usually he was asking for something that would bind me to him irrevocably, and that wasn't a ride I was willing to take. Not yet. This, though, wasn't a ride through the stars or time or space. It was a sharing of a world that had become ours, instead of belonging to one of us or the other. I wanted to, and just this once, I thought I might be able to get away with it.

But my father was here. Billy and Melinda were here. Gary and Annie were here, and Suzy, who should not be left alone with strangers right now, was here.

Morrison was here. And we all had a hell of a lot to work through, and I had finally grown up enough not to walk out on a difficult moment like this. I couldn't abandon them, much as I might want to go with the horned god.

I was still struggling to find a way to explain that when Morrison said, "Go on, Walker. We'll manage here. We'll…" He didn't quite look at Coyote's body. "I'll call someone."

"Cindy. Heather Fagan's niece. She works for the coroner and she…understands." I wasn't sure how understanding would help explain the death of an apparently healthy and undamaged young man, but it wouldn't hurt.

"All right. I'll call you when we're settled somewhere."

I lifted my eyebrows, but closed my eyes as I said, "My cell phone is lying somewhere in the middle of Woodland baseball field," because I didn't want to see Morrison's expression at the reminder.

I didn't need to. The volume of his silence expressed it just fine. "Then we'll be at your apartment," he said after a while, then came over to wrap his arms around me.

I startled a little, then buried my face in his shoulder for a minute before mumbling, "Gary's got a key. Wait. You have my keys." Of course he did. That was how he'd gotten in to clean up. Either that or he was an expert at breaking and entering, which was too strange a thought to contemplate.

"I have your keys," he agreed. "Go on, Walker." He kissed me, then nudged me on my way. I turned back to find Cernunnos watching both of us thoughtfully, and for once was grateful that my powers didn't include telepathy. I really didn't want to know what he thought of my relationship with Captain Michael Morrison of the Seattle Police Department.

Lucky for me, he didn't volunteer his opinion. He merely leaped onto the stallion's back with absurd and impossible grace, as if the earth itself had shrugged a little and thrown him skyward.

Or not. I'd watched the earth shrug and throw a lot of people around today, and it wasn't nearly as pretty as Cernunnos getting on his horse. He offered me a hand. I took it and he pulled me up like I weighed nothing at all, settling me behind him on the stallion's broad back. The big animal pranced a time or two before looking at Cernunnos, obviously waiting for his cue.

Cernunnos, though, waited on me, his head lowered and turned in profile so I could see the sweep of his bone crown through the tangle of his ashy hair. It swirled and spiked from his temples, protruding horns dangerously sharp. They came together at the back of his head, then spilled downward to strengthen his neck and broaden his shoulders. His scent was musky, more animal than I remembered it being, and I couldn't help thinking of the first time I'd ridden with him. He'd offered to take away my pain, then. Right now, with my arm around his waist and the line of my body against his, the world I'd just stepped away from, the world the horse still stood on, seemed very far away, and very full of pain. All I had to do was not get off this ride.

I made myself look away from Cernunnos. Made myself look at Morrison, and despite the sudden distance from the world that I felt, I smiled when I saw him. He smiled in return, sad, relaxed, tired, and as abruptly as I'd considered staying with Cernunnos, I considered throwing myself off the horse and back into Morrison's arms. I didn't, but it was good to know he had every bit as much pull as the horned god. I gave him a little nod, said, "Okay," to Cernunnos, and glanced over the rest of my friends as the stallion stretched his legs to take us away. "Wait!"

Cernunnos sat deeper into the stallion's back, stopping him, and I got the impression both of them, god and beast, verged on snapping, "What *now?*"

"Dad." I cleared my throat and tried again. "I need Dad. I can heal people. I can heal a lot of people. But Dad can... He does this magic thing," I said lamely. "He turns blood into roses."

Cernunnos's silence briefly matched one of Morrison's better ones for thunderous. I tried again. "There are people out there, people who are trapped and too badly hurt for me to try healing them. Or there were last night. Yesterday. Whenever that was." I honestly had no idea how much time had passed. It had been at least a day since I got back to Seattle, but if somebody'd told me it'd been a year and a day, I wouldn't have doubted them. "If Dad can convert the buildings into... roses...I can heal them."

"Joanne, I can't. I don't have...I don't have that kind of raw power. Your kind of power." Dad came up to me, Cernunnos and the horse, and managed not to look too awed by the latter two. Possibly hanging out all night while I threw down with an elemental had taken the edge off, or—more likely, judging from the haggard lines across his face and shadows under his eyes—he was just too damned tired to be awed right now. We all were.

"This once," Cernunnos said, more than a little dryly, "I think power will not be a problem..." He cast a sideways glance at me and finished with, "Master Walkingstick," rather than whatever variant of *little shaman* or *puny mortal* had first crossed his mind. He flicked his fingers and the Boy Rider joined us, golden mare dazzling in the rising sunlight. The Boy had always been especially ethereal, even among the Hunt, but today—now, after all of this—he looked somehow as though he'd come into his own. There was new power in the slim lines of his body, and a presence that felt more rooted in this world than he ever had before.

Dad, staring at him, paled visibly. I snorted. "What, afraid of a horse, Injun?"

"Hey," Gary rumbled. "Perpetuating stereotypes through joking isn't funny, doll."

I laughed, even if it was a little watery. "Long time since I said that to you."

"Long time. Good times."

"You're crazy, Gary."

Dad looked between us like he'd glare if he could get up the energy, and instead took the Boy Rider's hand, allowing himself to be pulled onto the mare's back. "I'm not afraid of horses," he muttered at me as they passed by us. "Riding with gods, though..."

"That one's only a half god," I offered helpfully, and got a withering look in response. It lifted my spirits a little and I mashed my face against Cernunnos's shoulder, rather like he might be a more godly version of Morrison, as I mumbled, "Okay, we can go now."

He said nothing, because I suspected he wanted to say,

"Hnf," and regarded that as being insufficiently godly, so I was smiling as I turned my head again and waved goodbye to Morrison and the others.

I'd ridden with the Hunt before, but it had always *been* a hunt. It had always been fast, busy, breathless. This time we walked, long-legged horses picking their way carefully over broken ground. Cernunnos didn't speak, but I felt vast power rolling from and through him: green power. Earth magic. The land didn't exactly stitch itself back together as we passed over it, but it didn't exactly *not,* either. Dirt and stone shivered and settled, sometimes swallowing shattered concrete and ruined buildings, sometimes just smoothing them until they were passable.

Time and again we paused when I could feel lives struggling to hang on inside the walls of fallen structures. I wasn't exactly tired anymore, or empty. I still felt remote, but that was a blessing, something I owed Cernunnos for. Viewing Seattle's wreckage from within the Hunt was just within the limits of bearable. I would have fallen apart on my own, on foot, and this was exactly the wrong time for me to do that.

The first crushed buildings lay not that far from the Seattle Center. Cernunnos settled the stallion there without me asking, and I sent threads of magic into the twisted girders and torn concrete, searching for lives to save. Some were easy; others, like Manny, were complicated. I'd never felt spread so thin as I concentrated on one, then another, of the broken bodies, preparing for the moment to unleash full healing magic. Only when I was absolutely certain I held every thread in hand did I whisper, "Okay, Dad."

I got a wild-eyed stare in return, though it took me a full minute or so to look his way when it became apparent he wasn't doing anything. "Just…turn it all to roses, Dad. Or air. Air would be better. I don't want rose petals inside of wounds."

"Joanne, it's half a city block. I can't change half a block of anything into anything."

I expected Cernunnos to answer. Instead, it was the Boy Rider, who shared his mount with my father, who turned and touched a fingertip to Dad's forehead.

Most of the adepts I knew went gold-eyed when they used magic. Dad had, back on the Qualla. But beneath the Boy's touch, his eyes turned fiery white, power visibly curling away from the corners like a thing with life of its own. He gave a raw gasp like he'd sipped flame, and without warning a block's worth of rubble became air.

It had a sound, which I didn't expect. Soft, surprised, not unlike the gasp Dad had just uttered. Buildings did not, it seemed, expect to become something else. But a thrill of power rushed through the change, too, as all the broken windows and walls gave up their sorrow at having failed in their duty, and became something other. Something freed.

In the same moment, under the white power of Dad's make-it-vanish act, I poured magic through the threads I'd built, healing those who had survived this long. The threads flexed, reaching for one another and becoming a net that briefly united the survivors. Maybe more than briefly: I heard voices cry out in astonishment and relieved pain, in confusion and hope, and then people who seconds earlier had been trapped began scrambling toward one another, tears of joy and disbelief and loss streaking their faces.

My head went wobbly, but Cernunnos touched my knee and the world straightened out again. He nudged the stallion into a walk, and we went on to the next stretch of devastated city. Over and over we stopped and changed and healed, and left believers behind when we rode on. They were tied together now, all of the survivors, the strands of my healing magic touching them and reminding them we were all in the same boat together. They were tied together because they stood as one, watching a new-old god walk the earth, and watching magic happen in his wake. Their awe and hope and love—and their fear and hatred and despair—built a massive wave of power throughout the city, helping to replenish me and my father long after we should have collapsed.

We rode all day, never going very fast and never stopping for more than a few minutes. I was distantly aware that sooner or later I was going to become the Joanne Who Ate Seattle, since the Chinese food of the day before was a distant memory, but for the nonce I seemed to be existing on universal love and magic. Occasionally universal love and magic announced I really needed to pee, but the need kept fading into inconsequentiality. I bet I would regret that a lot, later on, unless some hind brain part of my magic was keeping everything in working order.

By the end of the day all I could really remember was that a lot of people had died, a lot had been saved, and that Seattle was going to have to be rebuilt from the ground up. The worst of it was clearly the downtown area, but I had no idea how far the damage ranged. Even hopped up on god-power, I couldn't fix it all. We'd smoothed a lot of streets and vanished a lot of buildings, which meant the more mundane emergency services could do their jobs. I would come back out and help tomorrow.

I must've said the last word aloud, because Cernunnos turned his head, then slipped his hand over mine at his waist. "At last you weaken? I wondered if we might ride together forever after all, from this day onward. Thou hast done far more than any might expect of you, and then gave more still. For my part, I thank you. For theirs, they lack the words."

"S'okay." I hadn't noticed that I was leaning against him, my cheek against his shoulder and my eyes so heavy they pressed my jaw into slackness. "Can you bring me home?"

"We are there."

I pried my eyes open and stared, befuddled, at my apartment. Not my apartment building, but my apartment. The inside of it. I knew Cernunnos could walk through walls, but I still couldn't wrap my exhausted mind around being inside the apartment. The stallion stood very, very still, as if fully aware one misstep would break my furniture to bits and tangle him in a most undignified way.

Cernunnos slid from the beast's back and caught me as I, no longer supported by him, fell. I curled into his arms, too tired to even be surprised that he carried me into my bedroom and settled me on the bed as if he'd done it a thousand times. My eyes were already closed again as he drew the covers up, and his whisper was a benediction. "Fare thee well, Siobhán Walkingstick. I'll see thee anon."

I felt a silver kiss press against my forehead, and slept.

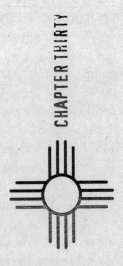

CHAPTER THIRTY

Monday, April 3, 11:22 a.m.

I awoke to the smell of pancakes and maple syrup.

It was so incongruous I just lay there for a while in the warm dark, wondering if I'd lost my mind. A lost mind that provided heavenly olfactory illusions didn't sound half bad. My covers weighed a ton, preventing me from throwing them off and getting up. In fact, it was a struggle to not allow them to just sink me back into sleep, but I heard the occasional clank and bang in the kitchen, suggesting someone else was here. I probably hadn't lost my mind, then. That was probably good.

I still didn't get up, because as long as there was clanking, someone was presumably still cooking, which meant breakfast wasn't quite ready yet. Voices roses and fell, quietly, but enough to suggest there was more than one person out there. Mostly men, but Annie's soprano was easy to distinguish, even if I couldn't understand the words. Morrison. Gary.

But not Coyote. My eyes got hot and I pressed them closed

even harder, trying not to cry. Trying not to think, honestly, because I was too tired and, I suspected, still far too overwhelmed to think about what had happened over the past couple of days.

The scent of bacon, and then after a bit, eggs fried in bacon grease, joined the pancakes and syrup. My stomach growled, but I wasn't really all that sure I could move. The covers were heavy and I felt weak as water, like I'd used up every last bit of energy within me and then wrung myself out for more.

Which was more or less what had happened, even if I'd been given a great deal of power that wasn't my own to work with. *Raven,* I said inside my head, tiredly. *Rattler. Renee?*

Raven didn't respond. Rattler didn't respond. Renee, very quietly, appeared at the back of my mind, but she had nothing to say. That was okay. I didn't really have any goddamned words for her, either. Maybe she could take the long view. Maybe she could see a necessity in their deaths that I couldn't, because I sure as hell couldn't. I would have found a way. I always found a way.

I could not, at the moment, even begin to consider that asking Rattler and Raven to die was the way I might have *had* to find. I shut Renee away from me and lay in the semi-quiet warm darkness with tears leaking down my temples and into my ears.

An exceedingly loud and unpleasant mechanical sound finally drove me out of bed. I was still wearing yesterday's clothes, including my coat. I shrugged the coat off, noticing that at some point during the night I'd attained enough consciousness to remove my boots, although I had no memory of that at all. Still, they were under the covers, trapped at the foot of my bed by the sheets, so I had to deduce I'd taken them off without Cernunnos's assistance. For a minute I sat on the edge of the bed, staring at my socks and wondering if I should just head out to the kitchen or if I should shower first. I couldn't remember the last time I'd showered, even if I was sure of what day it was, which I wasn't.

The bacon and eggs could wait another few minutes. I threw the rest of my clothes on the floor and wobbled to the bathroom.

Coyote did not visit me in the shower. I sat on the bottom of the tub and cried for a long time, steam helping keep my snotty nose clear. My head hurt and my eyes were raw before sobs finally turned to shudders and then to exhausted leaning against the side of the tub. Only the eventual cooling of the water was enough to get me on my feet again. I hoped breakfast would still be there. I dried off without looking at myself in the mirror, got dressed and walked tiredly out to the kitchen.

Morrison, in a T-shirt, jeans and sneakers, the latter of which I'd never even suspected he owned, looked up from a truly impressive table of food and smiled at me. "There you are." There was more relief in his voice than I bet he cared to cop to. He stood, came around the table and *oof*ed slightly as I stepped into him and put my arms around his waist. "Welcome back," he said quietly. "How're you doing?"

That wasn't a question I was yet prepared to answer, so I only nodded. He nodded, too, then held on while I peered over his shoulder at the food-laden kitchen table.

He obviously remembered the sheer volume of food I'd put away post-adventure in the Qualla. There were pancakes, eggs, bacon, toast, milk, cereal, oatmeal, fruit—some of which I couldn't even put a name to—and an assortment of store-bought muffins, croissants and doughnuts. At least, I assumed they were store-bought. If Morrison was capable of making fresh croissants in my wreck of a kitchen, I was luckier than humanly possible. And he was in the wrong business.

"What was that awful noise?" I sounded like I'd been on a three-night bender. Clearing my throat didn't help.

Morrison offered me a very tall glass of very orange juice that, when I brought it to my lips, smelled unbelievably good. "The juicer."

I drained the entirety of what was obviously fresh orange juice and handed the glass back to him. "I don't own a juicer."

"You do now."

"Ah." Of course I did. I wondered if I actually owned a brand-new juicer or if he'd brought one over from his house or what. He handed me another equally tall glass of juice and I decided it didn't matter. I drank the juice and sat down to eat.

The maple syrup was in a small ceramic jug, not a bottle. I poured some over my pancakes, took a huge bite, then stopped with the next mouthful already at my lips, even if my mouth was still full. "Thaff nah nurml srrp."

"Old family recipe," Morrison said. "Cup of water, two cups of sugar, teaspoon of mapleine. Boil the first two, add the last."

I swallowed incredulously. "You make your own maple syrup?"

"In lieu of growing maple trees, yes."

I was going to marry this man. The thought popped into my head and I turned crimson. Morrison's eyebrows rose. I stuffed most of three pancakes into my mouth so I didn't have to say anything, and after a moment he went back to cooking. After about fifteen minutes of steady, silent eating, I dared another comment. "I didn't know you could cook."

He flashed a startlingly bright grin over his shoulder. "Good thing one of us can."

Yes. Yes, it was. I smiled back a little idiotically and returned to eating without surcease. Another fifteen minutes took the edge off, and I ventured, "Didn't I hear Gary and Annie?"

"You did. They went for a walk when they heard you getting out of the shower. Annie thought you might want some alone time." His mouth twisted and he made a deprecating gesture at himself that either meant "Don't mind me, I'm only chopped liver," or "Presumably she thought present company would be excluded."

"That was nice of her. Of them. I mean, it would've been fine if they'd stayed, but..." My appetite faded and I pushed the plate a few inches away. "What did I miss yesterday? Yesterday?"

"Yesterday. It's Monday morning now. Suzanne's staying with her friend Kiseko Petterson until her aunt can get up here to pick her up. She's all right. Shaken up, but all right. Annie's..." Morrison poured himself a cup of coffee. Not, I thought, out of thirst, but out of needing something to do. "Physically she's fine. She regained a lot of strength during your..."

I offered, "Healing spate?" and Morrison chuckled.

"I'd been thinking more along the lines of 'miracle of loaves and fishes,' but I thought you might not like that. Yes, your healing spate."

He was right. Miracles were not my department. Except after yesterday, even with only a foggy sense of what we'd really accomplished in our journey through Seattle, I was fairly certain it at least *looked* like miracles were, in fact, my department. "How's Gary?"

"Acting like a struck ox. Not that I blame him, but I think this is harder on him than on Annie. He's had years to become accustomed to her absence. He won't let go of her hand, like he's afraid she'll disappear if he does."

I nodded. "I wonder if we know any good paranormal psychologists. I can't believe I just used that phrase straight-faced, but they're going to need to talk to somebody."

"Neither can I." Morrison sat down kitty-corner from me and tangled our legs together under the table. "Your father's still sleeping it off at my place. He called around one in the morning from the parking lot where he'd left Petite. Said he'd woken up there, and that he didn't know where you were or where you lived. He drove Petite over—she's fine," he assured me. I was pretty sure the quirk of his lips said volumes about how my expression had gone all worried over Petite, but not over my own father. Well, I'd dealt myself those cards a long time ago. It would take some practice to prioritize family over the car. "He drove her over and I gave him the spare room. I left a note in case he wakes up before I get back."

Of course he had. Morrison was more responsible than any other three people I knew put together. "Thank you. Is Petite still at your place?"

"I drove her here."

I shot out of my chair and was halfway to the door before I'd even conveyed a proper expression of gratitude in Morrison's direction. When I glanced back, he was smiling and collecting a croissant and orange juice before ambling after me. I let him amble, and ran down five flights of stairs to burst into early-April afternoon sunshine.

Petite was in her proper parking place under one of the shady trees. She was dusty, but otherwise none the worse for the wear. I ran across the parking lot, only belatedly noticing I was barefoot, and flung myself on her dusty hood. It was still just a little warm from travel, gasoline fumes rising up and clogging my throat. At least, I blamed the fumes for the clogging. After a couple of dusty sniffles, I patted the hood and whispered, "Okay, baby. No more cross-country trips without me, okay? We're gonna go do the salt flats in Utah. Just you and me, babe. Well. Morrison can come, too, if he wants, huh? Except I'm not sure he really gets the need for speed.

Which reminds me. You didn't tell him about the drag racing, did you? Because that's gonna go over like a lead balloon...."

"You really think I don't know about that, Walker?"

I levitated two feet into the air and twisted around guiltily before landing on Petite's hood again. Morrison examined me solemnly. "You're filthy, Walker."

I looked down at myself. I was, indeed, filthy. Hugging unwashed cars would do that to a girl. I started to try to explain how she, or possibly I, had needed a hug, but gave up immediately. Morrison already knew the depths of my relationship with my car. He didn't need any more reason to roll his eyes or look amused at me. Besides, there was something more important to pursue. "Um. You know about that?"

"How many purple classic Mustangs do you think there are in this city, Walker?"

That was three times in a row he'd pulled out my last name. We were really going to have to learn to call each other by our given names. "I, um. Well. She looks black enough under the amber streetlights...."

"Yes, and you cover her license plates, which gets into a level of illegal I don't even want to discuss."

I bristled. "So does everybody else!"

Something that narrowly avoided being a twinkle sparkled in Morrison's eyes. "And do you really think I don't know who they are, either? There are traffic cameras everywhere. We have a database of you people, Walker. A top ten list of the most regular racers in the city."

My bristles faded into a squint. "I shouldn't be on that list, then. I only race a couple times a year."

It was definitely a twinkle this time. "That's true, but if I said you were on the top ten list of the best drivers in the city it would be too much like a compliment."

My eyebrows shot up. "I better be number *one* on that list!"

Morrison gave up any attempt at being stern and let out a shout of laughter. "Your priorities need some work, Walker, but I love you anyway. Oh, no, you don't, you're covered in—" I hugged him anyway. He grunted, then put an arm around my waist and gave me a kiss. "You now owe me a shower."

"It's a date." I sat back on Petite's hood, pulling Morrison with me. He sat more gingerly, though his two-hundred-pound frame wasn't going to do any damage to her solid steel body. I considered his now-dusty hip. "Maybe I owe you a car wash first."

"Only," he said straight-faced, "if you're wearing a bikini. And singing 'Shaman's Blues.'"

I laughed. "Singing what? Ba-da-da—*DA-dum!*" I did my best blues riff, then laughed again. "Is that a real song? I don't even know it, so your bikini-and-serenade scenario seems unlikely to me."

"You asked my favorite song. That's it."

"…seriously? Your favorite song is called 'Shaman's Blues'? Since when? Seriously?"

"Since I was about seventeen, Walker. It's got nothing to do with you. Or it didn't. It's a Doors song." Morrison looked faintly abashed when I laughed again. "I know, but it was either learn their music or change my name completely. I'll play it for you sometime."

"Don't tell me. You've got it on vinyl? Or wait, do you play the guitar?"

"I do, but I meant the record. Which is, yes, on vinyl. How did you know?"

A grin split my face. "Lucky guess, but you never get to tease me about my car again."

"Fair enough." Morrison put his arm around my shoulders and I leaned in, glad to just sit there in the sunshine with him awhile.

Not that long, though, because there was something I hadn't brought myself up to asking yet, and it needed doing. "What about Coyote?"

A line of tension I hadn't even realized was there slipped out of Morrison, like he'd been waiting for the question and couldn't really relax until it had been asked. "I called his family. It was just him and his grandfather, I gather, and his grandfather flew in last night. He's supposed to bring him home this evening, but he'd like to meet you first."

"Yeah. Yeah, of course. I want to meet him, too. I wish..."

"I know, Jo. I do, too."

"Yeah. Yeah, okay. I guess I should get ready to do that. Where's he staying?"

"In my guest room."

"I thought my da—" No, Morrison had said Dad was in the spare room. "You have a guest room and a spare room? How many bedrooms does your place have?"

"Three. Is that enough?"

There were all sorts of blush-inducing implications to that question. "It'll do for now. I need to go see Suzy, too." Two points to me for awkward conversational direction changes.

"You have a lot to do," Morrison agreed. "Maybe you should go put some clean clothes on."

"Maybe I should wash Petite first."

Morrison looked like he wanted to object to my priorities, but gave it up before he even got started. "I'll get a bucket."

"You're an angel among men, Captain Michael Morrison."

"I wouldn't go that far." But he did go get a bucket, and didn't say anything when halfway through washing Petite it all hit me again and I slid down against her front wheel to hide my face in soapy hands and cry again. He just came and sat beside me, an arm around my shoulders, and after a while said, "Over here," to someone I couldn't see.

I looked up into a tear-blurred world to find Gary and Annie coming toward us. A snotty smile broke through my sniffles and I got up to fling my slightly dirty, very soapy self into Gary's arms. These emotional ups and downs were already exhausting, even though I'd only been up an hour. I was going to need to go back to bed by five o'clock.

Gary kissed the top of my head. "You're wet, doll."

"Petite needed a bath." I hadn't done a good job of it, either, but she was sparklier than she'd been. Maybe I'd go over her with a Q-tip on the weekend. Although I didn't have a job anymore, so I didn't really have to wait for the weekend. For a moment that, too, was overwhelming. I heaved some gasps into Gary's chest, trying to keep myself from crying again, and he tightened his arms around me. When I was in less danger of sobbing, he let go, smiled and said, "You okay, sweetheart?"

I nodded, then shook my head. "I mean, you know. I'm a horrible mess, but I'm okay. I'll be okay."

"Good." Gary's eyes shone. "So I'd like to introduce you to my wife, Annie Muldoon."

I blurted wet laughter and turned to Annie, offering a hand and the straightest face I could. "Pleasure to meet you, Mrs. Muldoon."

Annie took my hand and, with considerably more strength than I might have expected, pulled me into a hug. "Thank you, Miss Walker."

I sniffled over the top of her head. "Call me Jo."

"Call me Annie." She didn't exactly let go, but she put a little distance between us and looked up at me with soft eyes. "Thank you, Jo. For everything. Gary's been catching me up a little, the past day. You're an extraordinary young woman."

"There's a quote about that. About people having extraordinary things thrust upon them. That's me, not the other way around."

General derision met my comment, but nobody actually argued with me. I leaned against Petite, not caring that my butt got wet. Annie looked wonderful. She barely topped five feet in height, but she glowed with presence. In fact, when that word ran through my mind I stopped to check her with the Sight, wondering if she was actually glowing.

Not quite. Cernunnos's green made faint sparks around her edges, maybe, but that could have been the blur of new leaves in the distance, too. Mostly she was just copper and flame, healthy and gaining strength like a young horse.

Or a young stag. Her spirit animals appeared at the thought, a stag who stretched forth one leg and bowed, and the cheetah, whose black spots had stars in them, and who wound around Annie's legs like any oversized housecat might do. Like the stag, it met my eyes, then wound back into Annie, followed by the stag's more delicate steps.

"What do you See?" she asked curiously. I startled and she waved her hands at her eyes. "Your eyes are gold. What do you See?"

I'd forgotten that I had a tell-tale sign of using magic. Morrison's cell phone rang and we all blinked at him a moment. He stepped away to answer it and I looked back at Annie. "I see your spirit animals. You. Just in general. You look good. And Gary looks like he's full of helium and about to float off." Honestly, the two of them looked like a walking advertisement for healthy living over seventy. Or sixty-five. I wasn't sure how old Annie was, technically, what with having taken most of five years out of the usual time line. Either way, they really did look like an ad, with Annie in a nip-waisted print dress and Gary in a flannel shirt and jeans that looked suspiciously like they'd been ironed recently. They were both completely silver-headed, and Gary's white-winged raven sat on his shoulder, eyeing all that silver hair covetously. "You look good," I said again, smiling.

The Muldoons beamed back at me. "How are you feeling? Both of you, just...how are you doing?"

"We're all right, doll. Got a lot to figure out, but we're gonna be okay. Don't you worry about us, arright? How're *you?*"

"Like I could not worry about my best friend."

Annie smiled. "Perhaps you should put off worrying about us for a few days. I'm not sure any of this has really sunk in for us yet. It's hard to understand that most of five years have passed while you were sleeping. It probably won't all really come home to us for a little while yet. You can worry about us then. How *are* you, Joanne? You look peaked."

"I am peaked. And..." And I felt like I should probably grill them and take them apart psychologically to investigate their state of okayness, but since I lacked the doctoral credentials, I thought maybe I'd let them have their way. Whatever scarring they would have to deal with could wait a few days. I pushed away from Petite and brushed at my wet hiney to no avail. "I have to go talk to Suzy. And Coyote's grandpa. And..." My eyes welled up again, but I was too tired to cry. I wiped the tears away with a sigh. "And Billy and Melinda and Dad and probably a hundred million other people, too. Maybe we could all just get together in my apartment and have a group hug." I was only half kidding. A group hug sounded like the best possible therapy available.

"Walker." Morrison headed off any vocalization of that idea with the seriousness of his tone. I straightened up, gut clenched against the worst. He looked me straight in the eye, like a cop ought to when delivering bad news, and said, "Your friend in the motor pool. Thor. I'm sorry, Jo. He's in the hospital. It's serious."

CHAPTER THIRTY-ONE

In the end, I was smart enough not to drive. Morrison did, while I stared out the window at a city I could barely see. Whole miles of the streets were dirt, concrete having been swallowed up by Cernunnos's passage. There seemed to be an incongruous number of trees, plenty of which had been chain-sawed to pieces and dragged to the sidewalks, but an awful lot of which were new and young and strong-looking. I noticed those things because the road was bumpy and enormous fallen trees were hard to miss, but the details were all a blur.

Morrison, who couldn't bring himself to double-park even in an emergency, left me at the hospital's front doors. I went in and identified myself as family to the receptionist who told me where Ed Johnson was. In the critical-care burn unit, which had spilled out over half a floor. There was an air of palpable tension in the whole hospital, of crisis waiting to turn to chaos. I made my way upstairs to the burn unit, half relieved my eyes were constantly blurred with tears. I didn't want to see the pain and injury done to so many people, and I particularly didn't want to see what had happened to Thor. He was so damned beautiful.

Somebody said, "You can't be in here," as I drifted by, but I didn't listen. I could disappear right out from under their noses if I had to. I probably should have on the way in, since they were right: burn units were not places for casual observers.

Gasoline burns, Morrison had said. During the chaos, a fire had caught in the station's motor pool. Almost everybody had gotten out. Not Nick, though. Not my onetime boss who had been unable to look me in the eye after my magic had awakened, and who would never be able to again. He'd fallen, and Thor had been hurt, badly hurt, trying to get him out.

I found Thor mostly with the Sight, rather than sight. His aura was still lightning and storms, but tamped down and foggy under so much pain medication I was surprised his automatic nervous system remembered how to breathe. I knelt beside him, and I thought very, very carefully about bubbling paint and scored metal on his massive monster truck—The Truck—instead of letting myself think about bubbled flesh and burned bone.

I'd never met a paint job that needed this much work, but I clung to the metaphor. Rusted-out body beneath the paint. Rusted-out frame. So much to rebuild, and even if I could nominally See it correctly and lay that right down over the damage, fixing it instantaneously—and Thor wasn't in any position to disbelieve that I could—I was still basically taking universe juice and turning it into human flesh. It was not an especially fast process.

More, there was no way I was going to heal Thor and leave everybody else here to suffer. At some point I became aware of Morrison standing over me with a badge and a solid presence that silenced, if didn't reassure, the doctors and nurses who were supposed to be here. I stayed where I was, letting threads of healing magic spread past Thor and throughout the unit.

Throughout the hospital, eventually, because again, I wasn't going to patch a few people up and leave the rest. I did stick to critical or otherwise desperate damage, because it was much, much harder than it had been the day before. I was too tired, and I didn't have Cernunnos boosting me. There was a lot of raw energy in the hospital, prayers and grief and hope, that I was able to draw on, but it had been, to put it mildly, a rough few weeks. I'd left the bottom of the barrel behind some time ago. But I stuck it out, long past when I knew Thor's injuries were healed, long past when good sense would have sent me home to sleep for another week.

And it was worth it, because after a terribly long time, my ex-boyfriend opened his eyes, smiled faintly when he saw me and whispered, "I knew you'd have my back," before sinking into a soft painless sleep.

The breath rushed out of me as my chin dropped to my chest. I'd known he was okay, but knowing and *knowing* were two different things. Seeing his smile, however briefly, helped a little bit with having failed Coyote. It didn't make up for it. Nothing ever would. But it helped a little, and it allowed me to let the magic go.

It turned out that without the magic, I couldn't even sit up on my own anymore. Morrison caught me as I tipped over, then put an arm around my waist and helped me from the burn unit. I was faintly aware that people stared at me, hushed with awe, horror, confusion or a combination thereof. I hoped I'd had the presence of mind to not give my name at reception on the way in. I didn't want to spend the rest of my life as the prize display in a faith healer's tent.

Not until we were out of the hospital, back in Petite and on our way off the grounds did Morrison say, "You okay, Walker?" I nodded, which was apparently insufficient, because he said, "You look like hell. I'm bringing you to my place. You need another shaman to look after you."

I swung my head around to look at him bleakly. "Coyote is dead."

"Your dad and Coyote's grandfather are at my place, Walker."

Oh. Right. I'd forgotten that. I'd forgotten that I knew any other shamans, or knew of them. Thank goodness Morrison was on hand to think for me, because I clearly wasn't doing a good job of it myself. I closed my eyes and didn't open them again until he said, "Wake up, Jo. We're home," and opened Petite's door for me. He helped me out of the car, too, and half carried me inside.

I didn't think of him as a vain man, but for the first time I noticed a mirror in his front hall. I'd have been just as happy not to notice, because I looked hollow, like I hadn't eaten or drunk anything in at least a week. My hair was dull and unhealthy and my skin was an awful color under a tan that had no business being there. I stared at it for a few seconds, then remembered the blazing sun of Big Coyote's desert. It had tanned me once before, too. But even that color didn't help make me look even slightly healthy. I said, "Wow," out loud to the glimpsed reflection, and Morrison's gaze met mine in the mirror.

He winced. "I told you."

"I know, I just didn't…" I stopped the explanation halfway through, because it was too much effort to say the obvious: I just hadn't thought I looked *that* bad. Morrison winced again and pretty much carried me into the living room, where my father and an older man I'd never met both came to their feet in obvious concern.

Dad looked tired, although not nearly as bad as me. His long hair was tied back, temples showing the first threads of white, which I was pretty sure hadn't been there when I'd left the Qualla just a few days earlier.

The other man's long hair was iron-gray and fell loose

around his shoulders. Other than that, and the lines of age and sorrow marking his face, he was clearly the die from which Coyote had been cast. I could see his youthful beauty in aging features, and though his aura was dark with loss, it even had the same desert dune and sky tones to it. My eyes welled up and I put a hand out toward Coyote's grandfather.

He took it, and the world fell away.

I opened my eyes in the Lower World. How I knew it was the Lower World was anybody's guess, because I lay not under a yellow sky or red sun, but under a wattle-and-daub dome so dark I couldn't tell its color. The air inside was thick and wet with heat, clogging my chest when I drew breath. I coughed, but even that was difficult. I wondered about the feasibility of not breathing at all while in the Lower World.

The heat came from a fire pit not all that far from my face. Not all that far from any of me: I was curled in front of it like a dog, head pillowed on my arms. I thought about rolling away, but I was pretty sure the dome wasn't big enough for me to escape the fire's intensity no matter where I went in it. For such heat, it didn't put off very much light. Burning embers, probably. Now that I thought about it, there was a heavy scent of cedar in the air. It was used to cleanse away bad spirits and maybe in transportative magics, I wasn't sure.

Oh, yeah. Of course. I was in a sweat lodge. That had taken an embarrassingly long time to conclude.

As soon as I realized it, the shadows moved. For a couple of wild heartbeats I went cold with panic, which turned my skin nastily cold and clammy in the heat. But before I could even unlock my muscles and try to run, Grandfather Coyote appeared in my line of vision. A moment later, so did my father.

They were both painted with demon faces, terrible black-and-white streaks, huge blackened eyes, wide angry mouths. Red cut across their cheeks and dribbled down like blood, and their hair was stiff and wild with white woad. They both wore what I thought of as traditional garb, leather and feathers and bare feet, and my father had my drum in hand.

The first bang of that drum made my teeth vibrate and my skin hurt. I'd had enough pain lately, and wasn't one bit brave about it. I whimpered and folded my arms over my head.

Amazingly, that made the thick wet air even hotter. I couldn't breathe at all, and Lower World or not, I wasn't comfortable not breathing. I unfolded my arms and sent a truly pathetic look at my father. "Please don't do that."

He paused, obviously surprised, and glanced at Grandpa Coyote. The old man was less of a soft touch, glowering in return. Dad's expression turned guilty and he banged the drum again. A billion jillion needles pricked my skin all at once. "Stop. Stop. Stop it!"

Grandfather Coyote sounded surprised. "She resists it even now?"

"Oh, fuck that shit, brother." The words popped out before I even thought about them. "I'm not going oh-my-god-no, not-shamanism! anymore. I'm just tired and in pain and the drum hurts my skin. So give me a break."

It was not the most respectful speech I could have given an elder, particularly an elder whose grandson had just died and who was presumably trying to help me. Dad stopped banging the drum, though, as he and Grandpa Coyote's eyes met in a long and silent exchange. Eventually Dad said, "I did tell you she wasn't traditional," in an apologetic tone.

"How can we help her if she refuses the very foundations of our magic?"

"We're in a *sweat lodge*," I said, and if I'd dared hide my face again, I'd have said it into the safety and comfort of my arms. "I'm sure we don't also need a drum, do we? Really? Because I'm going to get hallucinogenic from the heat any minute now. Or

puke. And I ate a lot of breakfast. You don't want me to puke."
This was not going well. Even I could tell it wasn't going well.
Much more quietly, I said, "Please just stop," and, heat or not,
put my arms over my head again. I was too tired. Too tired to
argue, too tired to deal with pain, too tired for much of anything. And the fact that I was in a Lower World sweat lodge
heavily implied that there was a boatload of something coming
down the line at me, which meant I was going to have to deal.

But Dad didn't start pounding the drum again, and after
a moment I heard the two men murmuring to each other.
When they stopped speaking, a moment's silence filled the
lodge, then was broken by song.

A lot of the native music I knew was high-pitched and tonal,
and right then would probably take the skin right off me.
Grandpa Coyote brought it down a few octaves, which sanded
the edges off, and Dad started a countermelody that sounded
a lot like gospel. I was so grateful I sagged into the dirt, which
took some doing. Without the drumbeat piercing my skin I
was able to listen to, absorb, embrace, inhabit, yeah, inhabit,
the music and the heat. Or it was able to inhabit me. I couldn't
tell which way it was worming its way inside me, the music on
the heat or the heat in the music, but they both worked inside
my skin, into muscle and bone and into my marrow, where
together they began to break up the leaden exhaustion within
me like it was dirt in a fuel line.

I chuckled at the ground, wondering if my car analogies
would infect Dad and Grandfather Coyote, or if they had
their own imagery that they were overlaying onto my healing. It didn't matter. Mostly it was just nice to feel the clogs
and lumps loosening. The music definitely lifted all that muck
out, uplifting the way the best music does, and leaving heat
penetrating my bones until they felt like melting butter. Even
if I was lying on a dirt bed, I was more comfortable than I

could remember being in weeks. I drifted into that fugue state of dreaming without quite being asleep: I could hear Dad and Grandfather Coyote's song, and feel the heat and mugginess, but it was all wonderfully distant and slightly surreal. Sometimes it all faded out before snapping back into focus, though even those snaps didn't bring me close to waking.

Gradually a visual component added itself to my half sleep. First the sun, taking up a mantle as the source of heat. That was another thing I liked about this stage of wakefulness: the dream state seemed slightly more logical, as if there was just enough waking mind to feel things needed an explanation. The sun's gently pounding heat didn't explain the wet air, though, so I wasn't entirely surprised when I started to hear water gurgling, like a waterfall had grown up nearby. Bit by bit so did other things that didn't make quite so much sense, although the undulating wind was obviously representative of the voices singing in the background. Artistic, I complimented my brain, and in response it finished building my garden.

At least, I thought it was my garden. Lush growth spread from just beyond the top of my nose as far as my heavy-lidded eyes could see. Aidan and I had torn the garden's containing walls down just a few days ago, but I hadn't expected *this* from my next visit. The air smelled good, fresh and rich and clean. So did the dirt, which I discovered by trying to take a really deep appreciative breath with my face half buried in it. I coughed and rolled over, unwilling and possibly unable to get to my feet.

Thunderbird Falls poured down a cliff face just a few feet away from me. Or maybe Thunderbird Falls' older, larger and highly metaphysical brother, because even from the view at ground level, it was clear there was no lake just a few yards below us. Through the warm misty air, it looked fairly possible that I was lying at the very edge of the world.

That inspired me to scooch forward on my belly so I could

peer over the cliff's edge. There was world down there, quite a ways down, but definitely there. A lake pooled at the falls' foot, and a river cut away into land that became foggy with distance long before logic dictated it should. That implied I had a lot of personal exploring to do. That seemed fair enough. I scooted back from the cliff's edge and rolled over again, contemplating whether sitting up was worth the effort.

Big Coyote trotted across the rich green landscape. Water droplets beaded on his metallic fur, scattering rainbow fragments across gold and silver and copper as he dipped his head to touch a cold black nose against mine.

For a heartbeat I wanted to scream at him. I wanted to rail and hit and lash out, wanted to demand why he hadn't saved Coyote, why he hadn't made him *hold on* until I could get back to save him. Then a surprisingly warm and wet pink tongue dragged across my face and all I could do was grab the beast's glittering fur, drag him down and sob into it.

He wasn't a dog. He wasn't even a coyote. He was an idea, an enormously large idea, but he was an idea put into familiar shape and form, and in that form, he behaved as a mourning dog might. Soft yips and whines met my tears, and Big Coyote, archetype trickster, twisted around in my desperate grip until he could lick my face again and butt his head against my shoulder, my ribs, whatever part he could reach. Ideas couldn't love things, but in our shared sorrow, I thought Big Coyote had loved my Coyote anyway, and was as distraught over his death as I was. I slept for a while, when the tears were done, slept with my head pillowed in Big Coyote's ribs. I dreamed of deserts, and when I woke up, it was to meet the depthless stars in Big Coyote's eyes.

They told me a necessary truth. I hadn't had the strength to reshape the Master without the grief and anger of Coyote's death driving me. I had sown a monster's new shape in love and rage, in despair and punishment and hope, and nobody, not even me, went that deep or that far without paying for it. I would never have let Coyote pay for it, even if I'd known to the core of my being that it was necessary. I wasn't that ruthless.

In the end, it seemed that Coyote had been.

I put my forehead against Big Coyote's and my arms around his skinny coyote shoulders, wrung out but no longer devastated. Accepting, maybe.

When I sat back again, a coyote still sat beside me, but it wasn't Big Coyote anymore. This one was more like my Coyote, with golden eyes and normal, if gray-grizzled, fur. He did his best to look as alien and remote as Big Coyote, and I laughed at his complete inability to do so. "Grandfather?"

"Is it so easy to tell?" Even if I'd had any doubts, that put them to rest. Big Coyote never talked. He typically just smashed me in the head with his own and then went along on his business. I smiled and nodded, and Grandfather Coyote heaved a sigh very like the ones I'd seen his grandson offer. "Are you ready to come back now?"

"No."

Grandfather Coyote flicked an ear and looked at me sideways, but I was—for a rarity—absolutely certain of myself. "No, there's something I need to do first." I drew a circle around me in the dirt as I spoke, leaning awkwardly to include the coyote in it. "Renee?" Less hopefully, I also said, "Rattler? Raven?" but the only one I expected was Renee.

She was the only one I got, too, her quiet presence awakening not in my mind, but in front of me, manifesting as her physical form here in the Lower World. We stared at each other a long time, Renee waiting with the calm patience of one of her species, me trying to keep myself from reaching out and breaking her long thin legs and spine into pieces. Maybe that wasn't fair, but it wasn't fair that the spirit guide who had survived was the one I liked the least, either.

I finally started talking, because somebody had to, and it wasn't going to be the walking stick. "This wasn't what I wanted. You weren't what I wanted. I mean, in the beginning, none of this was, but things have changed. Raven, Rattler…" I crushed my eyes shut, pretending I could see them: Raven's feathers gleamed blue and red with blackness, and Rattler glowed gold and brown in my mind's eye.

"I needed their gifts in my everyday magic. Crossing the barrier into the Dead Zone, healing, maybe even the fighting speed, I need those. But time travel, that's not something anybody should be messing with. I get that my life, the last year and whatever has been, um. Unusual. I get that we've been trying to set things right that went wrong so long ago that maybe, yeah, maybe actually having to go back and fix things was necessary. But that fight is *done* now. I know there are going to be ramifications right, left and center, but they're going to be ramifications that go forward, not backward. I only want to travel one way through time anymore. Forward, day by day, just like everybody else."

I wet my lips and looked down, then met her gaze to add the rest of the truth. "And I'm angry at you. Unforgivably angry. Maybe Rattler and Raven taking the thunderbird from me and dying in that fight was necessary. Maybe you three had a little powwow without me and they agreed it was the right course of action. I don't. I can't. So I'm left not trusting you, and a shaman should trust her spirit guides. So I thank you, and I honor you for your gifts, but…it's time for you to go now."

Renee looked at me impassively. Birds and snakes didn't have much in the way of ability to present physically different expressions, but compared to the walking stick, they were paragons of emotive capability. I couldn't read anything in her heart-shaped face, and her presence was as calm and reserved as it had always been.

Then she spoke, and maybe I imagined the faintest hint of pride and approval. "Your very name ties us together, Joanne Walker, but you are not obliged to use the gifts I offer. I will not—I cannot—leave you, but neither must I stay waking in your mind. Call me, and I will answer. Until then, unchanging sleep will be welcome." She bowed, a little dip of her forearms and head. I bowed much more deeply in return, eyes closed, and when I opened them again, she was gone.

I immediately couldn't help myself, and poked around inside my mind to see if she was still there. Kind of to my shock, she was gone. Really gone, no sense of her at all. No sense of any of my spirit animals, just an empty quietness that felt totally unfamiliar after over a year of presences in my mind. My throat seized and a miserable shudder ran through me. I leaned forward until my forehead touched the ground, trying not to cry. "I guess that's over."

"It isn't quite that simple," Grandfather Coyote said. "Your father and your son still carry the walking sticks with them."

I nodded into the earth. "That's their decision and their path to travel, though. I know it's part of my heritage, and part of theirs, and I guess they'll do what they need to with it." I sat up again, barely fighting tears away. "Me, I'm done with that. I hope I'm done with it. I think I'm done with it."

"Good. A shaman should know not to speak in absolutes. I hope..." The coyote hesitated very like a man would have done. "I hope you might someday come to study with me, for a little while."

My eyes spilled over, after all. "I would be honored."

He offered a coyote grin, old and sweet and solemn instead of my Coyote's rakish teasing. "Then maybe we are done here, my student."

"Maybe we are." Smiling, I opened my eyes.

CHAPTER THIRTY-TWO

Morrison's living room floor was not drafty. That was really the first thing I thought when I woke up. *My* living room floor was drafty as hell, but Morrison's was comfortably warm.

So was his lap, which my head and shoulders were resting in. I opened my eyes to smile at him, and saw the shimmer of magic beyond him. A power circle, or, really, a power dome. The sweat lodge I'd seen, inside. Somehow that surprised me. I hadn't expected it to have a real-world physicality at all, even if Dad and Grandfather Coyote had both been there.

They were both here, too, kneeling on either side of me and Morrison. I looked at their three faces, then grinned. Morrison, with his blue eyes, fair skin and prematurely silver hair, looked very white-bread between the two Native American men. I could only imagine that if I could see all four of us, me with my dark gold tan playing up my Cherokee heritage, he would look even more white-bread. He saw me smile and returned it, upside down from my angle. "What's so funny? We're not doing anything."

"What do you mean 'we,' white man? Nothing." I slid a hand upward and pulled him down for a kiss.

He grunted and, when I let him go, muttered, "I'm going to have to start practicing yoga if you're going to do that kind of thing a lot."

The idea of Morrison practicing yoga made me grin again. "If I'm going to kiss you often? Better break out the yoga mat, boss."

"If you're going to wrench me around upside down for kisses," he said loftily, but the loftiness faded almost instantly into relieved concern. "You look better."

"I feel better." Morrison helped me sit up and I did what I had done when I'd entered: reached for Grandfather Coyote's hands. This time I succeeded, clasping fingers with him and feeling the fragility in thinning flesh and old bones. "Thank you. Thank you. I'm so sorry."

The old man drew me into a hug, his iron-colored hair falling past my face and hiding me from the world. "I am less sorry now that I understand you a little, and why my grandson chose as he did. Do not forget, granddaughter, that he chose, too. For good, for bad, he chose, too."

I nodded against his shoulder, and didn't object when he held on for a long time. When we finally broke apart, I lurched toward Dad and hugged him, too. "Thank you. We gotta talk about the condition you left Petite's clutch in, though."

"We—you—what?" Dad spluttered in real enough offense that I laughed, and laughed again when he managed to get out, "I taught you to drive on a stick shift! Her clutch is in perfect shape!" through general incoherence.

"I know. I know. She's fine." I sat back smiling, and Dad's offense faded into chagrin.

"You did that on purpose."

"Yeah. I thought we could use a little grounding. How are you doing, after all of this?"

His face turned solemn. "Your mother would be proud of you, Joanne. I'm proud of you. I'm also… I'm glad it wasn't me," he confessed in something just shy of embarrassment. "Not that I'd have wished any of this on you, but…I don't know if I could have handled it."

"You would've if you'd had to, but I guess I'd been lined up to bat since before I was born. That's enough of destiny-with-a-capital-*D*," I added firmly. "I have had enough of that crap, and I think I've by god earned my lifetime of free will."

"Your free will had better want you to get over and visit the Hollidays," Morrison said. "Melinda called three times while you were out. Nothing's wrong," he added hastily, as I turned to him in alarm. "They just want to see you and make sure you're all right. And find out what's happened the past… week." He said the word like he couldn't believe it had been so little time.

I fully sympathized with that, though I got hung up on something else. "Three times while I was out? How long were we in there?" As if in response, my stomach rumbled. I glanced out the living room window, noticing the sky was dusky. "Please tell me that's sunset and not tomorrow's sunrise."

"It is, but it's still been a long day."

"I can no longer remember a day that wasn't. I'll call them, but I'm not going over there tonight. At this point they can wait until tomorrow. Oh, crap. Suzanne. Has anybody talked to her?"

"She's still at her friend's house. Most of the roads are impassable, not just in Seattle but statewide. Up into Vancouver and down into Oregon, really. Her aunt can't get up here. She said she's all right." Morrison sounded cautiously accepting of that, which was good enough for the moment. I would have to go see her soon and not only thank her for her part in saving the world, but give her a thorough psychic checkup to make sure the burden she'd taken on wasn't poisoning her. That, I suspected, was going to become a lifelong habit. I couldn't imagine just leaving her to cope, even if she was the granddaughter of a god.

It could probably wait until the weekend, though. I nodded, trying to catalog all the things I needed to do, and my stomach growled again.

"Food," I said aloud, like it would put everything into perspective. "Food and sleep and…would it be all right if we had a memorial for Coyote tomorrow, Grandfather? At Thunderbird Falls, I think. I know you meant to leave tonight, but…"

"A memorial," he agreed. "I will not leave his body here, though."

"No. No, he'd want to be back in his desert." The desert which he had never intended to leave, and where I had never been willing to join him. I nodded again, and accepted Morrison's help in getting to my feet. We ordered an awful lot of pizza for only four people, and when it was demolished, I slept in Morrison's arms all night without waking.

Tuesday, April 4, 10:39 a.m.

Police tape still marked off the murder site at the falls, but it looked like no one had been there to pursue the investigation in several days. Given the shambles Seattle was in, I thought it might be weeks before anybody was able to come back down here. I paced the outer rim of the circle, trying not to look at Morrison as I did so.

Apparently I needed to work on my subterfuge, because

after I'd made a full circuit, he said, "What are you think-ing, Walker?"

"That there's no answer to this that anyone is going to like, and that maybe it's a terrible shame the scene was disturbed during all the chaos."

My boss—my former boss—looked pained. "I was afraid you would say something like that. What do you want to do?"

"Cleanse it. I managed to clear up the falls once—" and I didn't look at them, either, all too aware of what that partic-ular job had cost us "—but this area here is still stained with the murders. I'd like to wipe up the mess, like Melinda did at their house after the serpent attack."

Morrison took a few steps back, like he could see over the top of the cliff and watch the Hollidays pull up in the park-ing lot. They weren't here yet. Nobody was except me and Morrison. The memorial was going to be held at noon, one of the quarter points of the day, but I'd wanted to come over early. The falls had featured heavily in my redesigned personal garden, so I thought spending some time with the real thing would be a smart choice. We'd driven Petite, leaving Mor-rison's Avalon for my dad and Grandfather Coyote to drive over. Dad's expression at the idea of driving a modern, top-safety-rated vehicle had apparently been so similar to my own that Morrison was still inclined to grin when he thought of it. In fact, he did smile as I watched him, then chuckled, clearly thinking about it again. But then he drew himself back to the matter at hand, nodding at the police tape. "Are you going to do it yourself?"

"I thought I'd ask Melinda to lead it. She has more expe-rience, and if we all come together to do it… I think Coy-ote would have liked that. It's the best memorial I can think of for him."

"You know not all of us can do magic, Walker."

I came over to slide my arms around his waist. "We don't all have to. Being here, sharing that energy—God, I can't believe the things that come out of my mouth these days—"

"I'm going to buy you some hippie skirts and hoop earrings to go with the vibe you're feeling," Morrison said, straight-faced.

I was too close to kick him, so I knocked my hip into his and tried not to laugh. "*Anyway,* you know that it's being here that counts."

Morrison, deadpan, nodded. "Sharing the energy."

"Oh, for heaven's sake." I threw my hands in the air and stomped away, although I had nowhere to go and no actual pique to burn off. When I looked back, he still had the most neutral expression possible, making me laugh. "Stop that."

His solemnity cracked. "Sorry."

"You shouldn't lie to a woman who can read your aura."

"Your eyes are green. You're not using the Sight."

Damn. I was gonna have to do something about that. Not right now, though. Right now I went back to him to steal a kiss, then began working on a power circle. It wasn't just for Coyote: it was for me, kind of marking this as my territory. I was responsible for the falls' creation. I wasn't going to leave it vulnerable to attack again. Besides, leaving a long-running circle here would link me to the falls and to Seattle in a way I was beginning to think was important, particularly in light of all the rebuilding we were going to have to do. I wondered if shamanic magic could convince the state legislature and politicians that rebuilding Seattle as America's first totally green-energy city was an awesome idea. It was worth a try.

I was reasonably certain that that, and a lot of other random thoughts, went into the circle itself. I was also fairly certain it *would* influence the politics and decisions made over the next years and months, and since I'd already been riding the Acts of God horse pretty hard lately, I couldn't find any dismay in myself over the idea. By the time I'd walked the circle a dozen times, imbuing it with a lot of *be kind to each other* and *save the humans* suggestions, the sun had climbed nearly to its zenith, and people were starting to show up.

Billy and Melinda were among the first, and came to envelope me in a hug I never wanted to escape from. All of their kids glommed into it, too, to the utter delight of Caroline, who was in a chest-strapped baby carrier and squealed happily as she left big slobbery baby kisses across all our faces. Through hugs and squishing and family, I whispered, "Thank you. Thank you guys for being there yesterday. Whatever. For being there when I needed you."

"Always," Melinda promised. "Always, Joanne." Then pure wicked teasing splashed across her face. "Congratulations, by the way. It certainly took you two long enough."

I looked for Morrison, who was greeting my father and Grandfather Coyote, and didn't even manage to blush. "I guess there's no point in that betting pool at work, then, huh?"

"You work with detectives," Billy said dryly. "You really thought they wouldn't put it together when five days after you take off, the boss takes his first vacation since he's started, and says it's emergency family leave?"

I wrinkled my nose. "Yeah, yeah, when you put it like that…"

Billy tugged me against him again. "It's good to see you, Jo. It's good to see you in one piece. I'm sorry about Coyote."

"It's good to be in one piece. Thank you. Oooh, *Robert*…"

The oldest Holliday boy cringed so guiltily that I nearly laughed. "We'll talk about it later."

"Talk about *what* later?" his mother demanded.

Robert sent me a look of terrorized pleading and I caved. "Oh, somebody told me Robert had a girlfriend. An older woman, even."

"It's *Kiseko,* Mom," Robert said frantically. "We play chess together, that's all."

Melinda's eyebrows rose and she looked between us, but more or less let it go with, "Kiseko seems like a nice girl. She *is* a little old for you, Robert."

He wailed, "She's not my girlfriend!" with such embarrassed outrage that I figured that he either really liked her, or was desperate enough to play into it so his parents wouldn't find out he'd been working summoning magic without their supervision. Either way, I *would* talk to him about it later, but the horror of being teased by his family about a girlfriend was probably entirely sufficient in terms of punishment. More people had shown up while we were talking. An awful lot of them were people I never expected to see: guys from work, headed by Thor, who probably shouldn't have been out of bed, never mind the hospital, yet, but there he was. I went over to hug him, and the embrace lasted a long time, even if we didn't exchange any words. Jennifer Gonzalez from Missing Persons was there, which wasn't much of a surprise even if she hadn't known Coyote, and Ray, looking ruined and terrible in black, was there with a photo of Laurie Corvallis. Her cameraman, Paul, was with him, looking like the only thing holding him together was helping Ray hold it together.

Heather Fagan *and* her niece the coroner's assistant were both there. Heather didn't quite meet my eyes, but Cindy did, forthrightly, and flicked a salute like we belonged to some kind of secret brotherhood. In a way I guessed we did. Suzy and a cute girl who had to be Kiseko showed up. Kiseko made a beeline for Robert, but Suzy edged her way through the growing crowd to find me.

She looked older than she had when I'd last seen her, only three days earlier. Less ethereal, somehow, though that could have just been weariness dragging her down. Still, I drew her in and hugged her before asking, "You okay?"

"Kind of. The blackness is gone." She didn't sound as happy about that as she should. I put her back a few inches, eyebrows beetled in question. "I still can't see the paths anymore, Ms. Walker. I don't know if I'll ever be able to again. I'm afraid... *he*...is stopping me somehow."

"I don't think he's separate anymore. So don't try to split that part of you out, okay? It'll just get confusing. Besides, your visions will come back."

She lifted a dubious eyebrow at my confidence. I smiled crookedly. "You've been through a really rough patch here, kiddo. Even the best of us shut down what we can't handle, sometimes. Hell, I shut it down for more than a decade, when it came to magic. I seriously doubt you're going to bottle yourself up that badly, but give it a little time, hon. You're going to be okay."

"But I feel..." She put a hand over her heart. "Empty, somehow. Like there's a part of me waiting to get filled up again and...and I'm not sure what's going to fill it. I'm afraid—" She broke off again and eyed me. "He. What else do I call him?"

"Can you feel him? Separately from you?"

She shook her head and I put my arm around her shoulder for a hug. "Then all that's going to fill you up again is you, honey. What we did there was as close to making the Master human as we could, and humans heal. You're going to be fine. And I," I said firmly, setting her back from me with my hands on her shoulders, so I could meet her gaze, "*I* am going to keep a close eye on you to make sure nothing at all goes wrong."

Gratitude filled Suzy's green eyes. "Okay." She hugged me again before slipping away, back to Kiseko and Robert, whose parents were watching them with interested amusement. I thought Robert might never stop blushing. Smiling, I looked to see who else had arrived while I'd been speaking with Suzy.

Sonata Smith had, along with a number of people I half recognized from the murder scene a few mornings ago. They were the people I'd charged with going home and keeping the city safe, and there were pools of relative calm and order where they'd done their work. It was as they arrived that I began to realize the memorial wasn't just about or for Coyote, but for Seattle and for everything the city and its people had been through recently.

Somebody said, "Hey," behind me, and I turned to find my fencing instructor, Phoebe, standing there uncomfortably. I'd freaked her out with my magic and we hadn't parted on the very best of terms, so I was completely taken aback to see her, and swooped in for a hug before I thought better of it.

She made a surprised sound and returned both the hug and the status quo, smiling in shy embarrassment as she backed away again. Things were going to be all right there. I could feel it.

I wasn't looking at a clock or the sun, but I heard my voice lift unexpectedly, drawing attention to myself. "Thank you for coming." As I spoke, church bells from somewhere nearby rang out the hour, which backed up my call for attention. Dozens—maybe even hundreds—of people turned my way, and I realized slightly too late that I really had no idea what to say. There I was, wearing my ridiculous white leather coat, bright enough in the noontime sun to be absolutely certain no one would mistake at whom they should be looking, and I hadn't prepared a speech.

"A lot's changed recently." Hah. Mistress of understatement, I. "A lot of us have lost friends and family in the past few days, and Seattle's a mess. There's a god wandering the earth now, you might have seen him."

A ripple went through the crowd, one part uncomfortable and one part thrilled. Some of them—the Sight came on, telling me this—some of them were true believers. Others were reluctant believers, and others still wanted to believe but couldn't. Plenty just flat-out didn't, of course, any more than people believed in other kinds of magic, but that was okay. "We're here to say goodbye to the ones who have died, and maybe to greet the things that are rising in their wake. I'm not… I don't have a big plan here. I'd just like everybody to hold hands, maybe, and make a circle and…fill it up with what we've been through. Put some thought and hope into the shape of things to come, because I really believe—now—that we get out of the world what we put into it. A friend taught me that—"

That was when I realized I hadn't seen the Muldoons. My hands froze and my heart turned lumpy as I looked around for Gary's shock of pure white hair.

"Right here, doll." He came up on my left side and put his hand in mine, squeezing. A relieved breath rushed out of me and I gave him a suddenly watery smile that turned to slow astonishment.

He looked different without the tortoise. A little less…solid, in spiritual terms. No more armored shell offering protection against the world, no more slow steady strength shoring up a long life. Instead, the white raven sat on one shoulder, preening and proud of itself. It was all warrior spirit somehow, confident and strong.

On his other shoulder sat a walking stick. As long as my whole arm, its front legs folded in his hair, it met my gaping gaze with perfect equanimity. I squeezed Gary's hand back in a kind of involuntary reaction, but my heart was stuttering with disbelief.

I mean, one walking stick spirit looked pretty much like another. But I knew, right down to my bones, I *knew* that it was Renee. That my spirit guide hadn't bowed out of my life entirely, but had found a better place to reside. Somewhere she could do some good, because never mind the time traveling, walking sticks were symbols of eternity. She'd taken something away from Gary when we had fought in the Upper World, and now she was returning it. She would be the link to strength and long life that she'd helped destroy.

Turned out I had it in me to forgive her, after all.

I'd stopped breathing when I saw her. I started again in a gasp of tears, lifting my hand, fingers entwined with Gary's, to dash them away. The white raven hopped over to my knuckles and peered at them, then tipped his head to examine me with one bright black eye. I gave him a watery smile and he stepped even closer, tasting one of the tears right off my cheek before spitting it out. Quoth the raven, "Nevermore," and for a silly, heartening instant I thought he meant I'd never have to cry again. Then he stuck his head against my chin and pushed, making me turn my head.

The world faded out as I did, waterfalls and lakeshore bleeding into nearly infinite blackness. Nearly: it had the faintest curve to it, just enough to give me a sense of perspective and feel incomprehensibly small. It felt like it had been a long time since I'd been here, in the silence of the Dead Zone, though in a lot of ways my adventures had started in this place. I'd met Seattle's dead shamans here, and lost Coyote for the first time here, and…and too many other things to count, really.

Seeing it made me realize that somewhere, subconsciously, I'd never expected to come back here again. Raven was my guide in this territory, and he was gone. Intellectually I guessed that didn't make sense, because traversing the Dead Zone was part of my job description, but still. I hadn't expected to come back. I exhaled and turned my face away, finding Gary's raven still there, perched on my lifted hand. I started to say, *Let's go,* but his attention was a million miles away, intent on the nearly invisible horizon.

Well, I hadn't come this far down this road to ignore a spirit animal, even if it wasn't mine. I sighed and looked where he was looking, wondering if maybe Seattle's long-dead shamans were going to put in a final appearance. A benediction, maybe. I hoped. It'd be disappointing to get my hands slapped now. After a minute or two, I had to admit I was even kind of grateful for the silence. There was a lot going on out there in the Middle World, but it would be waiting for me when I came back, and the truth was, I hadn't had a lot of really quiet personal time in the past several weeks.

It was probably a bad sign when hanging out in the no-man's-land between life and death counted as quality personal time, but I would take what I was given. I stood and I waited and I wondered, and finally, after what felt like the short end of forever, I saw movement.

It was *so* far away, and so feeble, that it could have been my eyelashes fluttering. The only reason I knew it wasn't was that Gary's raven became even more alert, sticking his head out and rustling his wings like he'd take flight. When I didn't move, he gave me a sharp look, then a sharper peck to the temple, like he was saying, *Get on with it already.* I flinched, then twitched into motion, muttering an apology. He was right. Of course he was right. No matter who or what was out here, if it was on the edge of the Dead Zone and trying to come back, then I had to go help it.

If I'd been asked, I'd have said it wasn't possible to reach the edge of the Dead Zone. Not for me, anyway. Not for somebody still corporeal. But we ran and after a while we leaped and then we flew, great distances eaten up under my strides and the raven's wings, and suddenly we were there: an abrupt cessation of one place and the equally abrupt start of another.

It reminded me of the Upper World, only not: there it was all spirits and guides. Here it was the difference between a hope of life and death itself.

And there was a raven on the wrong side, battering at that wall.

He was a creature of light and lines and laughter, and of great determination. I couldn't hear his raven calls, not from the wrong side of that horrible wall, but I could imagine the impatient *klok*s and warbling *quarks,* and found myself trying to echo those sounds from a throat too tight to make noise. Gary's raven bit my cheek, then jumped forward to strike the wall with white claws. I put my hand out, pressed it against an inestimable coldness, then had to strike away the tears that ran freely down my face. The second time I touched the wall, that warm salt water fizzled against it, softening the barrier. I laugh-sobbed again, my heart breaking with hope. I felt on fire, healing magic turning my tears to something more. Despite every part of me knowing it was probably stupid, I leaned face-first into the coldness, letting tears scald its surface and praying.

It shouldn't have opened. I knew it shouldn't have, but I was trying *so* hard, and Raven was trying *so* hard, and maybe once, just once, the universe was willing to cut me a break, because suddenly there was a hole, and my raven fell through it into my arms.

He was so ragged, so light and thin, like he was made up of nothing more than a wish. I collapsed to my knees, cradling his delicate weight. I was numb all over, not from grief, but from relief and gratitude so overwhelming I couldn't feel anything else, not even my body. After a long time I realized I was whispering. "It's okay, baby. It's okay now, Raven. It's going to be okay. You're safe. You're with me. We'll be okay now, sweetheart. It's okay."

I didn't really notice when Gary's raven carefully swept us

up, got me on my feet and started me walking home again. I didn't notice much of anything except Raven's eyes fixed on mine, and his awful fragility reminded me of my own state as I'd knelt by Coyote's bier after the battle. There had been nothing left of me, and there was even less than that of Raven. All I wanted to do was make him better.

The Middle World, when I emerged into it, was dreadfully bright and loud. I still held Gary's hand, but my arms were tucked against my torso now, Raven's insubstantial form nestled against my chest. I was at an absolute loss for what was happening, whatever thoughts I'd had completely undone. I could hardly bear to take my eyes from Raven, afraid if I stopped looking at him he would disappear.

Morrison stepped up on my right, concern creasing his brow. I whispered, "See?" helplessly, and to my astonishment, his eyes flooded gold and he *Saw*. Saw Raven in my arms, and understood.

He didn't try unfolding my hold on the frail bird. Instead, he folded his left hand into my right and smiled. "We're here, Walker. All of us. It's going to be okay."

Just beyond him, just beyond Gary, through the film of my tears, I watched the Hollidays take up on either side of us, Billy holding Annie's hand just to Gary's left, Melinda and the kids on my right. All of my friends, my father, Grandfather Coyote, they joined hands as close to me as they could, offering solidarity and love as they stepped into place, and I remembered what I'd been going to say.

I squeezed Gary's hand again, giving him one brief adoring look even as tears ran down my face. "This friend. This man taught me to believe, and I know I wouldn't have made it this far without him."

I looked back at my exhausted Raven, making sure he was still with me, and spoke, uncertain if anybody would even hear me. "So whatever you're bringing here today, I'm just asking you to share it. With words, with song, with silence, if that's what works for you. Just hold hands for a few minutes and offer what you've got toward making this world a better place. We've had a hell of a time of it, and we could all use a little of that kind of positive thought."

All over the place, people *were* taking one another's hands, which kind of surprised me. I'd have thought it was a kind of hokey request, and maybe it was. But maybe I was right, too, and it was something we all needed.

As the last hands joined, energy crashed into the circle—the meandering, looping, lopsided circle—that they formed, and a pulse of magic swept me. Went right through me and sluiced into Raven, though I tamped it down, afraid that too much at once would blow him away. The lines of him strengthened just a little and I caught my breath on another sob, gathering him close to nuzzle his soft feathers. He pressed his head against my chin and made the softest sound I'd ever heard from him, a *quark* that was mostly my imagination, it was so quiet. But it was real, and it was him, and the tears that spilled over my cheeks were exhausted and joyful and so, so thankful.

It was only as I snuffled into Raven's feathers that I realized I'd forgotten to ask Mel to take the lead with the circle. Oh, well. There was so much strength here, so much good-will and hope and sorrow, tinged with faint embarrassment at participating in this, or delight at participating in this, that I would have to be really trying to screw it up. And at this particular moment in time, for the first time ever, I was absolutely certain I wasn't going to screw anything up, because I'd gotten Raven back, and I wouldn't do anything to risk him.

There were stains in the earth, blood-brown and black from the murder that had been done here. I Saw them running deep, like they were trying to escape the gathering magic here, and I smiled. *Change.* It was so simple and so hard, all at once. *Just change.*

The stains never stood a chance. White magic poured through them, sizzling, burning them away, and in less than a blink the land surrounding the falls was clean. I sent pure white magic deeper still, offering it to the strained earth, and felt its sigh of thanks. I sent it back into the people gathered here, healing touch to lessen their strain, and felt that ease, too. With each pulse of power, Raven got stronger, returning to form, until he finally gave a happy, familiar *klok!* and hopped from my arms to my shoulder, where he pushed his face into my hair and bit my ear as if to prove he was really there.

That was my future. Not the chaos of the past year, not the dreadful, exhausting knowledge that I was going to have to face something way out of my weight class, not all the predestiny and tangled time that had driven me forward whether I liked it or not. Healing people, healing places, making the world a better place: *that* was what I wanted to do now. I wanted Raven to help me, as if there was any chance he wouldn't. I wanted to do it with Morrison at my side, and with Gary and Annie guiding me. I wanted to improve my relationship with my father, and get to know my son. I wanted to watch Billy and Melinda's kids grow up, and see what kind of person Suzanne Quinley was going to become, and where her choices would lead her. I wanted all of that and more, and for the first time, all those dreams seemed within reach. Gary really had taught me the thing that mattered the most. All I had to do was…

…*believe.*

★ ★ ★ ★ ★

ACKNOWLEDGMENTS

My grandfather, for making writing seem a natural occupation.

Mom and Dad, for telling me I could do anything.

Ted, for looking out the window in the first place.

Trip, for illuminating the world-structure error in the early drafts of *Urban Shaman*.

Trent, for being the first reader for every. single. manuscript.

Bev and Gary, for being forgiving when I wrote during family vacations.

The War Room en masse and Laura Anne, Mikaela, Michelle and Chrysoula in particular, for being there at all sorts of stupid hours when I needed a kick in the pants.

Jennifer, for ten great years.

Matrice, for taking a chance.

My readers, for carrying this story through all the way to the end.

Thank you all so, so much.